Blue Sabine

Also by Gerald Duff

Fiction

Fire Ants and Other Stories

Coasters

Snake Song

Memphis Ribs

That's All Right, Mama: The Unauthorized Life of Elvis's Twin

Graveyard Working

Indian Giver

Poetry

Calling Collect

A Ceremony of Light

Nonfiction

Home Truths: A Deep East Texas Memory

Letters of William Cobbett

William Cobbett and the Politics of Earth

BLUE SABINE

A NOVEL BY
Gerald Duff

moon city press
springfield missouri
2011

www.mooncitypress.com

Moon City Press
Department of English
Missouri State University
901 S. National Avenue
Springfield, MO 65897

Text editing by Donald Holliday
Text design byAngelia Northrip-Rivera
Cover design by Jesse Nickles
Cover photograph: "Shadowy Sabine." Photograph by Kerry Casey

Portions of this book have appeared in different form in the *Kenyon Review*, *Southwest Review*, and *Fire Ants*, to whose editors grateful acknowledgment is made.

Library of Congress Cataloging-in-Publication Data

Duff, Gerald.
Blue sabine : a novel / by Gerald Duff.
p. cm.
ISBN 978-0-913785-34-8
1. Families--Texas--Fiction. 2. Texas, East--Fiction. I. Title.
PS3554.U3177B57 2011
813'.54--dc22

2011023255

For Duff Grace, Sadie Rae, and Connie Mack Overstreet
with love for you in the story and for the story in you

In early 19th century Texas, the valley of the Sabine River, first inhabited by the Adais Indian Nation, then the Spanish, French, English, and Americans, was claimed and disputed by all. Its neutral ground was haven for outlaws, desperadoes, and filibusters. By the time it was finally occupied after the Civil War by settlers from the Old South, it was known as No Man's Land.

—James Ward Lee

If it form the one landscape that we, the inconstant ones,
Are consistently homesick for, this is chiefly
Because it dissolves in water.

—W.H. Auden, "In Praise of Limestone"

Sabine River, so dark and deep and wide,
I'm crossing over to Texas, Lord, to the other side.

—Alger "Texas" Alexander, "Sabine River Blues"

1867

★

Sabine Crossing

Carolina

I am named for a place where I never lived, a state so far away I cannot think it. It lies behind, beyond the mountains and the forests and the rivers, and the widest one of all those waters is the Mississippi and that one I have seen, though I have not in my knowing had to cross it.

When I came to myself as a child and could hear my name called and know the sound *Carolina* meant me, I was already on the Louisiana side of that big water and did not have to fear going over it. That had been done, the coming through it, and one of my brothers or sisters must have held me in their arms when whatever boat or raft we were all on had floated us over.

And when something happens and you in your mind do not know it is happening, that is the same as if it were not. There is a comfort in that, and I have always felt it, and it has made parts of living easier to bear. What comes from a thing's happening which you do not know can later cause you pain. I learned that, and I know it in my heart. But you have missed some of it by not knowing where the start was, and I have made it my custom to think of that instead, that blank spot in my head. The stillness of it, the quiet, the nothing that's there for you to see and hold to, when you need.

The faces of my people, the Camerons and the Holts, have always been turned to the west, and what is behind us, the little clearings of land in the forests with the marks of the plow and the house places and the wagon ruts and the springs that are muddy, some of them, and the ones that are clear, and the dug wells for water are all things of the east. And our backs are toward them, and we never go back there, though we may remember them for a time, a time, a time.

When land is played out and a river is crossed and people moved away from and left behind, the thing is finished and the sun is low in the sky and my people journey toward it.

The stream before us now is called the Sabine, and where we are standing with the mules hitched to the two wagons full of our goods and the children is still Louisiana. But across the water which is dark and so slow it makes not a sound, not a whisper, not a splash, is another state. It is where we are going. It is waiting, and it does not notice us from its side of the water. We look at it, but it is studying nothing of us. It is Texas.

"This here is the ford all right," Amos says, pointing to the wagon track which leads into the water and goes underneath it as though it were a road people would take to go live in a land under the river. How would they breathe, I ask myself. How would they build their houses? Would they wash away?

"See yonder you can tell."

He is talking because he has come to a thing he is afraid to start grappling with. He is not ready just yet, and until my husband has given himself enough time to talk to himself and to whoever is there with him, he will not begin the thing he knows he has to do, want to or not. He is always that way, and must allow the words he speaks aloud space enough in his own hearing to make him know he will take the path there before and go on. Go on because he has to, toward the one thing before him with the nothing behind him to turn back to.

Before I allowed him to speak to me of marriage back in Livingston Parish when I lived as a girl in my father's house and was a Cameron, Amos first talked to me in his way. Throwing his words out into the air before me like a scarf so light it floated in the sun open for all its colors to be seen, the weaving of them together light and dark, bright and muted and dim.

And when I let Amos say enough to satisfy himself, I let him speak of our marrying and then we did that before the preacher and our families gathered beneath the brush arbor in that hot day, and we made our own house and the first two children came, Abigail and Maude. And they lived, and the next did not, and I do not say his name or let others, though he was in this world for almost one year and knew his name when I called it then.

When Amos had to speak aloud at length the next time to me and himself about what he must do about a thing before him was when the war came in the east, and the states fought with each other in Virginia and Tennessee and Maryland and Pennsylvania, a place so far away I could not dream it.

"Louisiana," Amos said to me and to himself, and "the South" and "my country" and these were the words and the ones around them he used to make himself be able to leave me and the two girls in Livingston

Parish and to go back in the direction from which we had come, the Camerons and the Holts and the Ellises and the Dowdens and all the other families living in that parish, and make himself stay away those years living in that fight.

And when he came back after Clytie and Mose and the Broussard boys and I had made the plantings and the three harvests, walking from Virginia with no shoes, his feet were so ruined he could not stand on them to work in the fields. I lanced them finally with the point of a heated knife, the deep carbuncle and knots and boils, to make my husband whole again.

He did not speak the name of the state where we lived again, nor the words *country* nor *South*, and after the next planting and the harvest, Amos talked only of one place aloud as he made himself ready to be able to do what he believed he must. That was to move us and the girls, but not Clytie or Mose who were gone in their own direction by then forever, belonging to nobody but themselves anymore. The word now was *Texas*, another state, and the location in it was to be Bandera County where the land would be cheap and unplowed and rich.

We are standing for the last time in Louisiana, watching the ruts which wagons have made as they vanish beneath the waters of the Sabine River, and Amos is wearing the same coat he had on when he walked back from Virginia two years ago. He has torn off a marking it had, and I can barely tell where it had been on the sleeve.

"Look, Carolina," he is saying, laying the words out in the air again for me to look at and admire, "there on the other side. See where the road comes out of the water in Texas? All we must do is aim ourselves in that direction, and when we are yonder, we will be in a new place."

The baby is moving strong now within me, as though it had heard its father's voice and wishes to see across the dark slow water to the other side, too, and I give Amos the nod he is waiting for, and he begins to move toward the head of the lead mule of the first wagon. I put my hand on my belly and feel a knot rise up and shift, but I will not let myself think of the other, the one who is gone and whose name I cannot say.

"I figure," Amos calls back to me, "to lead both wagons over while you and the girls wait. Then I'll carry you over one at the time."

"We'll stand here and wait in Louisiana," I say, "for you to go to Texas and come back for us."

"What did you say, Carolina?" he says, pulling at Dex's head to get him moving forward. The mule does not trust the water and looks away from it. "I couldn't tell what you said."

"Nothing," I say. "Go on to Texas, Amos, and then come fetch us. We'll wait here on this side of the river."

Amos hears what I'm saying, and he knows what the words are I said, but something in him is uneasy. He knows I am saying more than I seem to be, and he never likes for me to talk in two ways at once. It is my way, though, and I like to do it.

"It's just a little old muddy river," he says. "You can't even tell it's moving. One bank of it is the same as the other, whichever side of it you're looking at or standing on."

"No, Amos," I say back to him. "Over yonder is Texas, and Louisiana is where I'm standing with the girls."

"Where will Papa be when he's in the water?" Abigail says, "After he steps off the bank and ain't in Louisiana?"

"He'll be nowhere, Abby," I say to her as she hangs to the skirt of my dress and leans her head back to look up at me. "Your Papa will be between two places, and he won't be anywhere then."

"Don't tell her such things as that," Amos is saying as the mule finally begins to move forward slowly, blowing its breath out through its nose as though something has got up inside its head and won't get out. A fly, maybe, or a wasp or a piece of trash the wind has lifted up into its face. "You'll scare the child, telling her that."

"It's the truth," I say to him. "A little bit of it she needs to hear. Abby must get used to it, to the truth, by drips and drabs."

"Oh," my husband says, "Carolina," and then his feet are wet, and he's knee-deep in the Sabine River, out of Louisiana into a moving stream, and Texas is over there waiting on the bank as solid as a green tree stump just after it's been cut.

What would it feel like to the inside of a tree for the air to get to it for the first time, I am wondering, as Abigail watches her father lead the mule drawing the wagon deeper into the black water and Maude whimpers in my arms. Would the tree stump know it was dead yet, or would it like feeling the air move over it for the first time while it sees light and open space which it never could have imagined touching it inside where it's always been dark and safe before?

It would be good, I decide, to the tree stump, as I watch my husband reach to the middle of the river deep enough now that the water is halfway up his chest. It would appreciate the experience, even if it took the time to realize it was coming at such a great expense.

"But it wouldn't be thinking about that part," I say aloud to the top of Abigail's head as she observes her father moving away from us. "No, sugar. It would be enjoying the view too much to let such thoughts as that bother it."

My daughter nods and says yes, mama, still looking toward that wet place between us and Texas, always agreeable as she is, wanting to please whoever takes enough notice of her to say words in her direction. "I know I would," I tell her. "I'd want to feel that air and see that light and know there's something else outside me besides me. Wouldn't you?"

Yes, she says again, and now Amos is at the deepest part of the river and the water is touching his throat and trying to float him off his feet, and Flony, our best mule, is snorting so loud we can hear it back here in Louisiana, and I expect Texas does, too, but it's not making a sign it does or not or that anything is happening. Just some more folks coming to me, coming west, headed for here, that's all that state is thinking, probably, but I'm not going to show any interest or surprise. I'm Texas.

She comes up out of the dark into the light of the cook fire and stands there so I can see her, swaying back and forth a little from side to side as though she's tired and wants to lie down but can't find a place to do it. She is old, and her hair is all white, hanging down in two thin braids worked with beads and string, and I can tell by that she is not some white man's wife who has gone to settle in Texas but something else altogether different. She is an Indian, and she is carrying a bag that looks like it has come from the inside of some animal. There is no hair on it, so maybe it is just cured hide, I'm thinking, but something about the way it looks in the firelight tells me it did not come from cattle or deer or any creature I know.

Both our wagons came across the Sabine River without losing wheels or breaking loose from the harnesses holding them to the mules, and the water that rose inside them did nothing but wet our goods. Nothing was washed away downstream, and the flour and cornmeal sat high enough in the wagon bed not to be ruined. Amos is proud of that, the way he brought his family and our belongings safe from the river's bank in Louisiana through the flood to Texas, and the fire he built, his first one in Texas, is bigger than it has to be because he wants to show how bright and warm all prospects are for us in the new country.

The mules are eating leaves off the lower limbs of the hardwoods at the edge of the circle of light, making blowing and chewing sounds, and the girls are asleep in the little wagon after the supper of corn dodgers and smoked pork I cooked for my family. My husband is looking into the heart of the fire as though he can see something, maybe a map of the way we must travel south and west to Bandera County where the land will be new and unbroken, and he is making the little groaning noise he utters when he is content and rested in himself and where he is.

He does not hear these sounds he makes and will not believe me when I tell him he does, so I no longer note them to him. I learned soon after we were married, even before he left for the war in the east and the part he thought he had in it, not to make him know that I saw how he felt about what happened around him. Amos does not want to know he has a state of mind that changes and that allows others to see when it does. He wants always to think he is the same, no matter what he is facing, or thinking of facing, or getting over having faced. I allow him that. It comforts him, and it is a small thing.

Because he is looking into the flames, lost already in tomorrow, and making his small grunting sounds, not that different from the noises the mules are making as they graze, he does not notice the Indian woman standing at the edge of our circle of firelight, her animal-hide bag held before her.

"Do you reckon she just now walked out of the woods," I say to him, "or has she been watching us all the time we were crossing the water and setting up for the night?"

"What, Carolina?" he says without looking away from the story the fire must be telling him, "Who?"

"The old woman yonder," I say and look back at her. She has not come any closer, but she lifts her head now in my direction as she sees me turn toward her. "I think she's by herself. I don't see no other Indians with her."

"Indians," Amos says, beginning now to look up at me and then, when he sees where my head is turned, in the direction I am looking. "There ain't no Indians left in this part of Texas. They all been drove out of this country."

"One at least," I say, "is still here." This causes Amos to hop up from his squatting place and spin around to look toward the darkness at the edge of the firelight. He has stopped making his little groaning sound now, I notice, but the mules have not quit pulling and chewing at the leaves they can reach. It has been a long haul so far and farther to go and they are hungry. They eat when they're not hungry, though, I know. They're like we get when we're around something to put in our mouths, ready always to do it.

"What?" Amos is saying. "What do you want?" He says this toward the old woman with white braids and the animal-hide bag, and then to me he directs the next words, the scared ones. "The rifle's in the little wagon with Abby and Maude. I didn't think to get it out. I ought to know better than that."

"You don't need to," I say and nod my head toward the old woman. "She's not fixing to hurt us. She just wants to sit down, I reckon."

"Mother," I say in a louder voice to her, "are you cold? Do you want to get closer to our fire?"

I do not expect she will understand what I am saying, but she seems to, all right, because when she hears me say that she begins to come toward where we are standing by the fire, Amos and me. She takes small steps and keeps holding the animal-hide bag before her as though she is about to offer it to somebody who has been waiting to receive it. Her face is plainer to see now as it picks up the light from the fire, but she has no expression on it, neither that which a body might have when she is meeting people for the first time nor the one to show she is uncertain about how she will be greeted by those she is coming toward.

As she comes our direction, taking those small steps like somebody weary after a long journey but knowing she is nowhere near the end of it, Amos moves to the side and cranes his neck to try to see behind the old woman, way back into the darkness from where she has come. His beard is shining in the firelight, and his eyes are popped wide open to let all come in that might be out there where he can't see. There is nothing. I know that, but Amos is afraid there might be and is now trying to catch up with seeing what's around him, as though that could be done to satisfaction.

Once a thing is over and behind, you can't reach back into that time before now and pull it up before you again. I have learned that and written it on my heart, because I have had to live in this world each and every day it comes to me, sliding away steady as it does. Amos looks before and behind, as though *now* was a stile built up to a fence between two fields, a place to stand where you can get the advantage to look in both directions. At the field behind you, and the one you're coming to. Where you're going and where you've been. The advantage to stop the world and hold it still.

There is no such stile. There is no stopping point of advantage between the two parts of your life, the before and that which is coming. All that is is *now*, a little word and a narrow place where you must stand and one which crumbles off beneath your feet on both sides, of what was and what will be. You cannot reach either place from here.

"I don't see nobody," Amos is saying to me in a voice higher and quicker than his usual one. This shows me where his mind is now.

"They could be hiding back in them woods, though. In the dark out yonder somewhere. I got to get the rifle."

"Leave it where it is," I say. "Say howdy to the lady coming to visit with us. She's all the Indians there is out there."

"You don't know that, Carolina," he says. "You can't tell that."

"I can," I say and put my hand on his arm. It is tight and jerking a little as he moves forward and then back, not knowing what to do next. "It's all right," I tell my husband, there on the bank of the river where we are, in Texas for the first time. "It's all right, Amos."

The old woman is close to us now and stops taking her small steps, but she is looking deep into the fire, not at our faces. I wonder what things she is seeing in it, how different they are from the map of our journey I imagine Amos had been dreaming before I made him look away from it.

Her animal-hide bag is before her, and she shifts it a little to one side and says something out loud, a word I do not know, because it is in her language, not ours. She says it again, and then she speaks a word I do know.

"Hot," she says and looks toward us for the first time since she has been standing inside the circle of our firelight. "Hot."

"She knows how to talk," Amos tells me. "That old woman has been around people."

"Yes," I say to her and draw my arms in across my chest and above my belly where I am so big with the child inside me. "But it's cold, the wind," I say. "It's cold tonight."

The old woman nods, her white braids swinging so they brush against the bag she is holding. I can see that what I thought were strings are really strips of rawhide woven into her hair along with colored beads and small pieces of carved wood.

"Baby," she says and points toward my belly upon which I am resting my arms.

"Yes," I say. "It's coming two months from now."

"No," she says and then she speaks another word in her own way of talking. Reaching out her hand toward me, she touches just the tips of her fingers to the cloth of my dress and then slow, slow draws the hand back to help support the animal-hide bag.

"Now," she says and looks back into the fire. "This night."

The first pain comes.

Amos

I like to think I don't scare easy.

When a thing threatens to happen that will throw me or mine in the way of destruction, I do not turn tail or show the white feather at calamity's first notice. I try to stand up and put my face toward it, let it know it has a man to deal with, that it can't just go on its path and not show no mind of what might be opposing it. It's got to move something first, whatever it is and however strong it might be in its furtherance. Somebody is in its way.

Saying all that, though, I will admit that there have been times when I have run. It has been things before which I have quailed, I have faltered, I have give ground.

Sometimes it's happened in front of other men who could see me beginning to back up, needing to tend to that feeling that has come all down in my liver and lights, like the voice of a small thing whispering a message only I could hear, telling me to lift foot and turn tail and seek a place somewhere other than here.

Those men that could have seen me give way and remarked upon it were generally in a situation too close to my own to notice what was happening to me, though. They didn't have no advantage, such fellows, because they were getting the light-foot and the shake-leg themselves.

I'm talking about being in battle, and I'm thinking back to all them scrapes we were in up there in Virginia and Maryland and Pennsylvania during the years we gave up to rebellion on the part of our country.

We didn't know then we didn't really have a country, though we thought we did. They showed us that and taught us a lesson. And in a way I'm grateful for learning it. Once you understand you don't have something you thought you did, why you are set free to go on and do something else. You don't have to think about things near as hard as you did before you learned that lesson and got it by heart.

You can watch what you considered to be your property walk off the place, never looking back, and it does not bother you near as much as you thought it would. In fact it makes you easier in your mind than you have ever been before. You can leave the homeplace yourself. Head on out, and every step you take you feel lighter. You can float right on off, like one of them observation balloons they used against us up yonder back then.

Hell, you can pack it all up and go to Texas.

I don't talk about such things to Carolina any more. I don't mean about the times I showed the white feather. That subject I never brought up to her because a woman does not need to hear about the occasions on which the man she is married to broke and ran. Talk of that subject will unsettle a wife.

No, what I mean that I do not bring up to her any more is such confidences I used to try to speak of when I told her how easy I found it to move on. To turn my back on where I lived and had been living for a while and to do it without feeling the need to look back once.

I remember the last night in particular when I spoke to Carolina of such a subject, back in Louisiana in Livingston Parish on our place twelve miles from Denham Springs. It was a cold night, up in December, way after sundown and the children all in bed asleep. I remember that Thomas, the littlest one, had been gone for several months already by then and wasn't the littlest one no more, and she wouldn't let me talk about him. She would just hold up one hand when I would say his name or mention something about the ways he had already got about him before he sickened and died. She would hold up that hand, Carolina would, like she was trying to knock down something I had just flung at her face. A little stone, say, or a piece of rotted fruit.

I would never do anything like that, of course, throw something at her, but the way she would raise that one hand toward me puts that kind of thing in my mind.

I had already got in bed that night on her side to warm up the bedclothes for her before she would come to lie down beside me to sleep. She had taken all the pins out of her hair and let it fall down her shoulders and back so she could brush it.

I was watching her hair as the brush moved through it, how the fire reflected from the hearth was picking up spots in it that looked lighter than the rest, though I knew that was a trick of the shadows. Carolina's hair is an auburn color, as people call it, not a speck of gray in it even today and her a woman with two living children and other ones likely to come.

"Carolina," I called to her from where I had moved over to my side of the mattress. It is a good one, combed cotton with not a seed in it and covered with a smooth ticking. I have never wanted my wife to have to lie on a bed made of corn shucks. "What are thinking about, combing your hair so long over yonder in this cold room? You better come over here and get warm."

"I'm thinking about how I might plant me some more flowers by the door come springtime, Amos," she said after running her brush through her hair a few more strokes. "Dig some up from off the side of the hill at the back of the place and put them there by the front stoop."

"You ought not to spend much time studying that, Carolina," I said. "We might likely not be here by the time September comes. Flowers'd just be wasted work."

She stopped brushing her hair, I remember, and sat there for the longest spell, not moving or saying a word, her back turned toward me and the only sound in the room a noise a chunk of firewood made when it burned through and fell in on itself with the rest of the embers.

"Why do you say that?" she said finally and made one more lick at her hair with the brush. I had bought that brush for her off a drummer up from New Orleans. It was a good one. I had paid top dollar for the best one he had in his valise. "What are you meaning when you say that?"

"Well," I said. "I figure if we make one more good crop out of this gumbo clay, we might ought to be thinking of moving on."

"Moving on?" she said and turned slow to look at me, lying there in the bed. I couldn't see her eyes in the dark with her back turned toward the fireplace the way she was sitting, but then a little flare-up happened in the embers and a glint of reddish light come over her face for about as long as it takes to tell about it and say it happened.

"Yes," I said. "Moving on, you know. West to Texas. This here Louisiana is about all used up for us, sugar girl." That's one of the things I like to call Carolina when we're by ourselves just talking.

"Texas," she said. "That's a long ways off, Amos, and it's not anything there we hadn't already got here in Louisiana."

"It's got possibility," I told her. "Texas has. There's land in Bandera County that's never been broke by a plow. It'll grow crops as high as your head. All you got to do is just throw seed at it, they say."

"They say," she said and laid her brush down. Then she said that same thing again. "They say."

"I seen a flyer there at Turner's store in Denham Springs. They begging folks to come settle out there in Bandera County. They'll give a man a quit-claim deed for just a little bit of money on enough land to put this little old Louisiana farm down on it eight or ten times and have space left over to spare."

"No," she said, but it didn't seem like she was saying it to me. She was just saying it. "No." Again, and then she let her head drop down like she was noticing something on the floor she had never seen before and now had to figure out.

"No, what?" I said. "I tell you I seen it. There on the flyer in Turner's nailed up there. Everything you'd need to know about it to be able to decide to move to Texas. It'd convince anybody."

"Convince anybody," Carolina said. "You mean convince you, Amos. You, that's who you're talking about."

"Why, yeah," I said back to her. "I'm talking about myself as being the one who read the thing. I'm a man open to persuasion."

She didn't talk any more about it that night, nor the rest of the winter or during the planting time in the spring. But after the crop was made and the time come to load up the wagons with the goods I didn't sell and the consumables we'd need for the journey, Carolina pitched on in and helped and got the children and the household fixtures ready to move.

But it wasn't on that night when I first told her about Bandera County in Texas that we got the next baby started for us. Then she just laid down on her side of the bed in the warm spot I had made for her, and she kept her back turned toward me and wouldn't face my direction until we both fell on off to sleep, no matter that I had put my hand on her hip which had always told her what I wanted. She could always tell that.

Up to then.

We are across the river now in Texas, and naturally the Sabine is nothing up beside the Mississippi. It takes a big raft and men pulling on ropes close up to the bank and praying all the time in the big open water of that stream, the one you cross to get to Louisiana. It is muddy, and you can't see into it, and it has waves on it like you was on an ocean instead of fresh water, and you lose sight of where you've been and where you're going because all you can do is look right at where you are and nowhere else and hope for the best.

But that Mississippi crossing was way back yonder and years before in the time when the Holts were coming to Louisiana, and now I am in Texas with my wife and my children and my goods.

And the Sabine was not wide, and the mule pulled hard and nothing much got wet, and I can look back now in the direction I want to without worrying about some force of water washing me away.

That old Indian woman who walked up on us out of the dark was by herself, just like Carolina said she was as soon as she saw her, and what they say is likely true. The bad Indians, the Comanche, have all been driven out of this part of the country and killed off and are out there somewhere in the Staked Plains, a part of Texas I am not headed for. And it's fewer of them all the time, and that is a blessing to the people who are trying to make a decent living out of plowing and planting the land and harvesting the increase.

If the old woman herself is any sign of what the Indians still left in this part of Texas are like, they are not much and nothing to worry about. All they'll want from a white man is just something to eat and some whiskey, if you'd give it to them. I for one will not give them that. Not because I will not share what I own with the next fellow, though. I like to consider myself an open and a generous man. If somebody is hungry, he is welcome to eat some of what little I have and to take a sup of my whiskey, if I've got some and he has a medical need.

But not the noble red man. Not Lo, the Poor Indian. Him I will not give whiskey to, because it is no telling what he will do when it hits his belly. He is not built the same as a white man is, and the whiskey turns to a fume as soon as it hits the back of his throat and it rises up into his head, the fume I'm speaking of now, and it paralyzes any sense of right and wrong he may have had before he supped it.

I learned this account of how whiskey works on an Indian from a man who come through Denham Springs several years back. He had lived among the tribes in the west, and now he makes a living telling folks what they are like and how it is to be around them in their natural setting. That is what he called it, their natural setting, and I felt like the ten cent piece I paid to get in the hall to hear his lecture was one of the best I ever spent. Natural setting, a good way to put it. A man that does not want to learn and that keeps his mind closed is little more than a beast of the field. I believe and know that to be true. I like to study a thing out.

So when I see a creature like the old Indian woman with her medicine bag all hugged up to her chest, I understand her in ways Carolina cannot. I do not fault my wife for her lack of understanding of matters like this. I simply state a fact.

Carolina sees an old woman who appears to be tired and hungry and needing to get close to the fire, and it is the softness of her heart that will not allow her to judge the truth as it stands before her. She sees only the particular thing and not the meaning behind it, like I am able to do. Like I try to do and must do.

The old woman with her hair all twisted into knots with little pieces of trash worked into it represents to me her race. A tribe of beings like us in shape only, as the lecturer explained they was back there in Denham Springs, a people who have never produced nothing of value and whose idea of worship is to dance around in circles and mumble prayers to a bunch of rocks or a tree or a cloud or a wild animal.

The Christian thing to do is to convert the ones who are worth saving and to get the ones that's not out of the way of us folks that are trying to make something out of this country. I explain this notion and its truth to Carolina in bits and pieces that are not beyond her comprehension. I try to, anyway, and she does attend to what I am saying most of the time, as she is able to understand.

When the old woman talks the words that she has heard some white man use, Carolina looks into her face as though she is conversing with anybody else. Sleetie Woodson, say, back in Louisiana, or Carolina's own sister before she died, Myrtle Cameron.

I look away from this, back toward the wagons like I am being sure there is nobody else sneaking up out of the woods to try to pilfer something of ours, but what I am really doing is wondering how little a woman pays attention to what her husband tells her about different things. Such as what I explained to Carolina over a good long period of time about the nature of the Indian and his prospects. I think it is that her mind will not rise to general principles. That is not her blame, though, and I do not fault her for it. She is made that way and could not choose it.

The old Indian woman, close up to the fire now, says another word to Carolina and puts out a hand to touch it to the swell of my wife's belly. When she does, Carolina looks up at her in the face, sudden, and an expression comes in her eyes like she is hearing some noise far off that she has to attend to so as to be able to understand. It is faint, this sound, whatever it is, that has spoken to Carolina, but it is one she needs to hear, and I can see her listening to it for all it might be saying.

"What is it, sugar girl?" I say and move to put myself between her and the Indian woman. "Is it something bothering you?"

"Amos," she says, speaking my name slow and careful like she is telling somebody who has just asked her what her husband is called and she wants to be sure the person hears the word right the first time she gives it voice. She does not want to have to say it again.

"My baby," she says and turns partway from my direction to face toward the old woman warming herself by our fire. "Its time is coming now."

"I'm not sure about that," I say, making my voice a little louder than need be so my wife can tell I know what I'm talking about. I notice that the wind had picked up some and is cutting me a little on the side of my face away from the fire. "It's way too early for that, ain't it? You just ate too much of them corn dodgers, I expect. That's all you're feeling."

But the women, the two of them, my wife Carolina and the old Indian woman with that white hair all twisted up into knots, appear to have quit listening to me and are moving closer together there before the fire I have built up.

"It can't be that time," I tell her. "We left Louisiana in plenty of time to get to Bandera County, Texas, before you have to do any lying in."

They are moving off together now toward the wagon Carolina has pointed to with the hand the old woman is not holding, and my wife is stepping like she has just all of a sudden got many years older. Now she leans against the old woman hard, putting a good bit of her weight on the woman's shoulder, acting like she has gotten not only older but a good amount heavier in her body in the last little time that has passed.

"I thought ahead to that," I call after them, "I planned in enough time to allow for us to get where we're going first before any birthing has to come. I have made sure of that. I am telling you now."

They don't give any sign they have heard me, neither one of them women, and they are now far enough from the light of the fire so that you can't tell which one is the white woman and which the Indian.

"I'll build up the fire," I am saying to them. "I'll build up the fire real big."

Carolina

Here is what the pain tells me. I do not speak of the discomfort or pressure or the little hurts that come once and then go, say when I am holding myself wrong or when a small change is taking place inside me. No, not those. I mean the first real pain that comes, the sharp one that lets a woman know it is but the first of many that are to follow, the one that foretells a separation to come.

It says you know me when I come. It says I am here. It says get ready, it says I am final.

At that time any woman knows what it speaks to her, and I would not place myself apart from all the others of my kind, but I know that pain carries another message, too. Maybe it is true all women hear it, this thing the pain speaks in private to the one who contains it, but I do not know that. I can see only what is within me.

And I would not be proud. But no one who has borne a child has ever told me she has heard the thing the pain tells me. Maybe it is a secret each woman has for herself and can see it only on her own alone, but if she were to say it aloud all other women would agree. They forget it later or they believe it vouchsafed to them alone, and they hug it to their bosom in the dark like a jewel given them by a man not their husband in the eyes of God and all others.

It says this. Another came into you, into your body, and that is where you live, but it is not your home. A hope for pleasure caused this thing, whether pleasure was found in the doing of it or not, and that portion is the joy which feeds the growing of another life within you.

That is the side which profits, that part which leads on to something of you still being alive after you are gone, after you are nothing in the earth. But there is a loss to be reckoned, too.

That is what the pain is reminder of, the letting into yourself of another, the entrance of a self into yourself where you dwell alone and secret and satisfied with the person you are. To let another inside the body in which you live for the mere pleasure of a moment, a thing that does not last, is to betray that part of you which lives alone and above all change and shift and dislocation. That is to be Eve, and that is to suffer the pain which announces the separation to come.

If you had not been joined, you would not now be left behind. You would not have ever to bear loneliness. That pain says greeting and farewell together in one.

She is old, but she is strong, the Indian woman, and as I lean against her she gives no sign she feels the burden of my weight. I think she is like a walking cane, a crutch such as the one Drewie Watkins used to get around on back in Livingston Parish. As we walk toward the wagons, I imagine her gray hair to be the cushion Drewie had placed on her crutch to soften where it came up underneath her arm, and I lean my head against the top of the woman's head for support. The Indian woman does not pull away or seem even to notice my doing it.

The pain comes again, harder this time, and I let out a groan before I can stop myself, and the old woman says something to me as we hobble along together. I wonder how a walking cane can talk, and I know that is foolishness, but I let myself think it again because doing that seems to help me walk. What if every tool or support we use could talk to us, I ask myself. Would a crutch or a cook pot or a broom say I have reached my limit now and you must ease up before I break?

I laugh at my thinking that, and the old woman laughs, too, and I tell myself that the things which help us, which hold us up and let us work, those implements can be happy, too. They can take pleasure in getting a job done, just as a woman can do, and if that is true that they can be satisfied, they can also sorrow over something not accomplished or a thing lost and broken.

Thinking this makes me cry a little, only a sob or two, and the old woman says something, whether in her own language or mine I cannot tell, and we are at the wagon now, and she is turning me around so that my back is against the tail of the wagon, and she lifts me up so that I am sitting on the edge of the wagon bed. She does this with no strain and gives no sign of what it costs her but for one deep breath.

"Mother," I say, "you will hurt yourself. Call Amos to help."

"No," she says in English, "he must do what a man does when he tends a fire. I do my own work."

I am lying on my back now with my feet planted on the wagon bed, and the pain has come to me like a house moving down a road on its own. It is too big to fit between the trunks of two oak trees on each side of the road just ahead of it, but the house does not falter in its progress, and I open my mouth to scream, thinking that will cause whatever is moving the house to notice and stop before it is too late. The old woman is beside me in the narrow wagon bed putting something in my mouth under my tongue. It tastes like dirt, but I suck at it as though it were as sweet as a piece of honeycomb, and the house keeps moving toward the place where the trees are standing so near to each other.

I cannot scream through the sweet dirt in my mouth it is so dry, so I close my eyes to shut out the sight of the house and the oak trees coming together. For a space I can still see them on the inside of my eyelids, dark as it inside the wagon, but then they are fading, and the last thing I know is the sound of the Indian woman saying something close to my ear in her language, which I can now understand though all I have known before in my life is my own tongue. I wonder at that, at how it can be, as I leave my body, and now I am not worried about the moving house and the trees anymore.

Abigail

It's not crying.

Maudie when she came, now she did cry. I heard her hollering as soon as Mama hushed. So loud she was, Maudie, that I opened my eyes when I hadn't wanted to, wanting them to think I was asleep so nobody would take me out of the place where it was all happening. But I couldn't keep them closed when I heard that first holler from Maudie, like the little possum that time Papa had let me keep it, the sound it made when it was mad or hungry and wanted something to eat.

It didn't live long. It got out of the house once, and the dogs got it. One of them did, I don't know which dog, I think it was Belle.

It's not crying, not making a sound, and that makes me want to open my eyes even more than I did the time when Maudie was born. That was in Louisiana, and this is Texas, everything on this side of the river is. That's what Papa says. Texas wherever you look.

I picked up a rock just before dark and showed it to Maudie when we were lying down in the wagon.

"You know what this is?" I said to her, her with her fingers in her mouth so she couldn't have answered me even if she knew how to do it. "You know what it is?" I said. "Texas," I told her, and she didn't say anything. "Texas all over the place," I said. "This rock, them woods, the dirt the wagon's standing on, that water Papa put in the bucket. All Texas. Everything Texas."

"I ain't Texas," Maudie finally said, after she had pulled a couple of fingers out of her mouth. "I ain't."

"Now you are," I told my sister, "and don't you forget it. You used to be Louisiana, and now you're Texas, little girl, like it or not."

"Nuh uh," she said and started into crying. "I'm not. I'm not Texas."

"Are, too," I said, "and don't go bothering Mama about it, neither. Go on to sleep." We was in the sleeping wagon where the bed stuff is, and Mama and Papa were outside by the fire. "Might as well get used to it. You're just Texas, that's all. Like this rock, like everything. Texas wherever you look."

Maudie didn't say nothing else, just kept on crying, wanting to still be Louisiana, until finally she went on off to sleep, worrying about being part of Texas, I reckon.

It doesn't bother me none. I like it all right. Like Papa says about things that happen to us, I have to live with it.

But it's not crying. I know. I'm listening for it, and it ain't made a peep yet. Maybe it's because it's being born in Texas and hasn't got to worry about getting used to it. It already is part of everywhere you look. I'm holding my breath to listen and hear it when it does. I'm just waiting to hear.

It's not crying.

Carolina

It is a comfort now that I cannot hear water purring in that river that marks off Texas from the other state, Louisiana, our last place to be. As soon as I came to myself in the night with the light not yet breaking, and could feel who I was again, I knew I had to get away from the water, the way it laps and purrs and pulls at what all it touches.

That is what I cannot stand to think of now, the steady tugging it makes at all that bounds it. Come, it sings, come, let loose of all that holds and keeps you. Be in this flow, slide away, slide away, be with me forever.

So the thought in my head, in the very center of my brain, as I came to myself, was not to wonder about the child, if it was there, if it was all right, if it was warm in the cold of the night, if someone was holding it, if it slept.

I knew where it was. I knew. It was nowhere, and I would not let my thought touch that. The cursed thing that saved me was the river, hearing a sound of flowing coming from it, and knowing that if I could direct all that was in me at that flow, at wanting to get away from the sound it was making before it brought my mind back around to a place where it could not live, I could keep myself. I could be Carolina Holt still, the wife of Amos and the mother of Abigail and Maude, together across the dark water in Texas.

So I took the thought of flowing water up to my bosom and hugged it to me, to the wet spots on the gown where the milk was gathering and soaking through, and I screamed at Amos to get me away from the river. And he tried to say something back to me, but I would not hear it, and all the world became getting away from the sound of moving water, and that held the broken parts of me together.

It does so now, and I must suck at that like a bad tooth to make it boil up in my head and keep me whole.

The sweet dirt the old woman put in my mouth when the big pains first came is gone now, but I lick my lips at the inside of my mouth wherever my tongue can reach to find if any bit remains. I would savor it again, for it took me away from what hurt me, and I could stand at a distance from myself and watch.

I saw myself turn and struggle and strive against what was moving through me, but I was not there to suffer it because of the sweet dirt she had given me. And I would have that not-feeling true again, as I stand beside the hole Amos has cut out of the earth at the center of the clearing in a stand of pines and hardwoods.

It is too small, this hole he's made with mattock and shovel, too small to hold a thing large enough to make me feel myself this hollowed out and empty. There must be more of the earth and this world removed to match up with what has gone. I will call him to enlarge the emptiness, to get it big enough to satisfy what it has to do, to hold a space broad and deep and sufficient to the task. But first I must stay quiet and listen, my mouth open a bit to let me hear better and my eyes closed against any sight that might hinder the hearing to which I must give my attention. Is there the sound of the river? Is there hint of water moving and pulling and tugging at what touches it? Can I hear such?

That is the question, and the answer must not be yes.

The old Indian woman is quiet beside me, knowing what I must not hear, though I have not spoken word of that to her. Abigail and Maude grumble to each other on their pallet in the wagon, Amos speaks to himself under his breath, thinking no one will notice, a breeze moves across the treetops with a sigh of someone crying far off, one of the mules stamps a foot to shake off a buzzing fly, rattling the chains of the harness as it moves.

All those things are sound, but it does not matter, since there is no water flow in it, and I keep my ear open for only that, the purr and trickle which alone can speak of the reason for the hole in the earth of this thicket, this wilderness, this place in Texas where I have never been and now will never leave.

Amos

I have learned a lesson from a stillborn child, my own, and it is this. When a man sees the light of reason in his wife begin to flicker like a dying candle, he will allow himself knowingly to take actions that are without sense or true direction.

The child came too early by a long draw of the bow, and who is to understand the cause or question the purpose of the Lord in that? Maybe Carolina strained herself in some manner when she lifted some weight beyond her, one of the children maybe, or it could have been undue exposure to a cold wind or a scare give to her by the old Indian woman with her hair all twisted with bits of trash off the ground and rawhide strings, wild-looking as she was when she come up on us just when we thought we could rest and be easeful in our minds, across the Sabine safe in Texas. Maybe Carolina had just let her guard down too soon.

But when the old savage called me over to the wagon bed to look and I could see that the child had not and would not draw breath, my first thought was to comfort my wife, as any man worth his salt would want to do, to explain to her satisfaction the cause for the sorrow come upon her and me, to relieve her worry and ease her mind by setting facts straight.

"Carolina," I said to her as she strained to raise her head and look at what the Indian woman held wrapped in a piece of cloth with heathen designs on it that she had got from somewhere, "honey girl, let me tell you what I expect has happened, what the Lord's plan has done."

She hollered at me then, my wife did, in a way she never had before, and I can call up the sound of that now, if I want to let myself hear it again, and then she commenced to command me to get her away from the river.

"Not the water, Lord Jesus," Carolina said. "Not the water. Move me and my child out of the sound of the water, Amos. Take us away from the water."

I could see there was no reason in her and that she would not hold still for argument, so I did what she asked me. Or the old woman and me did, I got to give her credit for that. We gathered up my wife and carried her between us, the signs of what had happened still plain upon Carolina and her garments, and we headed for the dark woods away from the firelight and the bank of the river. And to give the truth its due, I let the Indian woman guide our way, for I had no notion of where to step or what direction to take.

She knew a path into the woods, dark as they was away from the big fire I had built up, since that is the way of them kind of people and a habit of knowing the wild they have. It is a compensation God has given them for being heathen, I reckon, the way they are at home in thickets and woods and unmarked prairies where no white man can find his way without first making a decent clearing through it.

As we were toting Carolina through the trees and brush and brambles in the dark, steady away from the wagons and Abigail and Maude all hugged up together in one of them, it came to me that I could smell the scent of the old Indian woman and the rags and hides she was wearing, and it was not what prediction would have foretold. I mean to say by that that I would have thought the smell of some creature like her would be rank, much like that of a varmint caught in the woods.

It was not, it was most bearable, even to the sense of a white man such as myself, and I calculated that as an advantage, that smell mainly of wood smoke and pine rosin. She was cleanly, the old Indian woman, and that was a comfort, since I did not have to worry about standing clear of her, and could think about tending to Carolina with all of my mind.

I have always wanted to put one thing at a time before me, to do that thing before going on to the next, and then to follow that straight line way of working in all my doings. That is not Carolina's way. At times when I watch her, I believe to my soul she never accomplishes a single thing while looking only at what is required by it alone.

If she is preparing a meal for her family to eat, I can tell by the look in her eyes that she is thinking of something else altogether different from the peas she is shelling, say, or the corn fritters she is shaping to cook. What that other thing may be, I do not know, and I have learned not to ask her what is on her mind or where her thoughts might be tending.

It is not that she holds back from telling me the answer to my question to her, though. Rather, it is the other thing. She is too ready to describe all that she is considering and the ways the parts of it come together, twist around each other, and depart different directions down roads no man would guess or suppose.

That swarming way of thinking is not for me, that kind where all is mixed together in a snarl with no end and no beginning in sight and no manner of puzzling out the connections in between.

The way she fears the sound of water now is a swarm of thought, as I try to understand it, here in these woods in the Sabine River bottom. It is the very way of considering which Carolina entertains and suffers from, everything all clotted together in her head, one thing making another one rise up to plague her.

I want to make plain that I do not fault her for it, though such a habit of letting her mind take her over I do take to be a weakness, though I do not call it that name to her.

How is it that the sound of water moving in a river can have anything to do with a woman's baby being dead? I ask you that, and anyone who takes time to study on it will say there is nothing to draw two such unlike things together. I don't know how to put it but to say that one is one thing, and the other is another thing separate by itself. One sets here. The other sets over yonder.

Yet here in these woods as the light gets better every minute to show that the sun is coming on, I can see her straining to listen if she can hear any noise of water moving from behind us from where we come to get to here in this clearing in the middle of the thicket.

I start to say something to my wife, a little thing that doesn't mean much, like "Caroline, how are you feeling by now," but I don't get the first word out before she hushes me by putting her hand up toward my mouth, as though she could reach from where she is lying on a pallet on the cold ground all the way to where I'm standing a good ways off and put her hand on my lips to stop me talking.

I hush, and she listens, listens, listens with her eyes moving back and forth in little jerks like they will do when a person is trying to hear a small sound that they suspicion is there.

"Do you hear it, Amos?" she says, and then twisting to the side where the old Indian woman is standing, asks her the same thing, "Do you hear the water, mother? Do you hear it?"

The old woman puts out a hand to touch Carolina on her forehead, like she is testing for fever, but I am just supposing that. I do not know if an Indian even recognizes fever, or how to judge the signs of it. This wandering around in the night in a river bottom has got me guessing at things and making ideas up in a way that is not usual for me, nor is it helpful to any endeavor.

Trying to figure out whether an old Indian woman dressed in hides and rags and trash knows anything about fever in a white woman. How would I know I was right about such a thing if I was right about it? How is a man to say the truth in such a matter?

One thing I do know, though. And that thing is that there is no sound of water moving. No river, no stream, no water. Not one drop.

And yet them two women are looking at each other here in these woods and listening to hear something not there, with the light coming up steady around us.

Abigail

Maudie doesn't want to hear it, but I'm telling her what has happened. She has her fingers stuck inside her ears, and she has her eyes closed so she can't see me, but I know if I get my mouth right up beside her head and keep on talking she's bound to hear what I'm telling her. Enough of it to know what I'm saying, anyway, whether she wants to or not, and that's what will satisfy me.

"He was real little, like a doll," I say to the side of my sister's head. "He wasn't no bigger than a skinned squirrel, and that's what he looked like, too. A squirrel after Papa has taken his knife to it and cut its hide off of it."

"Not a squirrel," Maudie says real loud, and takes her hands away from her ears to slap at me. "A baby, not a squirrel."

When she does that, I feel a little sick feeling come up inside my stomach, like the time I ate too much honey from the jug Mama keeps on the high shelf and it made me want to lie down and run outside to let the air get to my face and to drink a whole dipperful of water, all at the same time.

I couldn't keep on doing what I was doing then because I didn't feel like it any more even though there was honey left in the jug, and I can't do it now, either. So I don't slap back at Maudie even though she hit me first, and I didn't tell her nothing more about the way the baby looked when none of them could see my eyes open and I saw the Indian lady holding it in that piece of rag.

It was too like a squirrel, though, and it wasn't crying nor moving its mouth to cry like Maudie did when she came to Louisiana. That's what Papa called it when he would tell folks about Maudie being born. She came to Louisiana, he would say, and he'd wait for the one he was talking to to laugh, keeping his mouth fixed like he does when he wants to laugh himself but has to wait for a while until somebody else starts it up first.

I think maybe the new baby has come to Texas, not Louisiana, but maybe it don't count when it's not crying or moving its mouth. It hasn't come nowhere. It's still waiting to get to some place where it can be with me and Maudie and Mama and Papa, but it has a long time to wait, a long, long, time to wait.

"Maudie," I say to my sister, her hands back up to her head to poke her fingers into her ears again, "you know what the monkey says when you give him a banana?"

She pulls her hands away from her head to say "eat, eat," and then she puts them back and closes her eyes.

"That's right," I tell her, "eat, eat," and then I reach out to hold her up against me like I always do with the cornshuck doll Mama made for me. She lays quiet against me, and I say it again. "Eat, eat."

I'm looking at the woods now where Papa and the Indian lady carried Mama, and it's daylight outside the wagon. They'll come back with Mama directly, I know they will, but the baby won't be with them no more. It has come to Texas, as far as it can.

1912

★

Double Pen Creek

Abigail

Lucille is the last born of my children, and she is the only one who ever wanted to sit down and listen to me talk. I say last born because I thank the Lord that business is over and done with. When I learned she was coming, it was a surprise to me, and a disappointment, something I didn't say out loud to anybody then and for certain not to her when she got old enough to understand people talking to her.

But it was that, a disappointment, and a disappointment sorely felt. The one before her, Jacob, I had calculated was the last child I would bear, and I was counting on that to be the truth. I am not like Mama was, now, and I would not be misunderstood when I say that. I do not talk against her.

I have my fair share of children, five of them living and only two that came to term and did not survive. I do not let myself think of the ones I lost early in the carrying of them, since to my mind they were not intended by the Lord to live and should not be a continuing occasion for sorrow.

I have taught myself to think that way and to know the truth behind what some women waste their attention on their whole lives long. Think on the ones that are here to be tended to, I tell myself, and just put away what can't be helped. Do not let your mind weaken.

But with the coming of Jacob, I believed that would be the last and final one for me to raise up into a good hardworking Christian man, and thinking that let me take a long breath and let down for a spell, ease the burden a little as I kept moving along through my life with him and his older brother and his two sisters. And Ferguson, my husband and the father of my children. I don't forget him when I talk of my family. But easing up was where I put my foot wrong, I figure now. Ease up, and things happen you had not foretold.

I was lucky not to have to put up with what Mama did. I mean being with child almost every year from the time she was married until she died. And, I won't die the way she did, in childbirth, with eleven living children and her looking like an old woman at thirty-nine years of age and as used up as one. I will not have to do that.

She is there in that big picture I have on the wall over the mantel piece, the one the photographer took of all of us standing out in the yard in front of the old place in Sabine County where the Holts first lived in Texas. Every child is there, all eleven of us, and Mama and Papa, every one of us looking straight ahead at the man with his head stuck up underneath that black cloth fixed somehow to his camera, looking like we're all holding our breaths.

I say all of us are looking straight ahead, standing real still with our eyes wide open, like the picture man said for us to do to make it come out right, but I'm wrong when I say that. Lewis wasn't.

He has his face all drawn up into a frown, and he is looking off to the side like he is seeing something nobody else has noticed and it is important for him to regard it since nobody else is smart enough to do it.

He always claimed afterwards, Lewis did, that he was looking off to see if anything was wrong with one of the dogs, Grip, I believe it was, but that couldn't have been true because I remember Papa had tied them all up behind the house with pieces of rope, Grip, too, in particular to keep any of them from wandering in front of the camera and messing up the picture.

You know how a dog will do, much less a bunch of them together snapping and playing with each other. The fact of the matter is Lewis has never done exactly what anybody has ever told him to do. He might do close to it, but he will not do the thing itself. And not doing it, that would be on principle, if he was the kind of person to know what is meant by the word principle, I'm saying.

I expect Lewis Holt was looking off to the side like that rather than directly at the camera as the photograph fellow had told all of us to do exactly for that reason. Because it was the thing he was told not to do. So he did it.

Lewis was born third from the last of the bunch, and when that picture was taken at the old place in Sabine County, all of us were in it. Mama is holding Louselle who is close to two years old, right there in the middle of the picture, and she is sitting in a cane-bottomed chair just in front of where Papa is standing behind her. Louselle has on that white tatted dress most of us spent some time in, boys and girls alike, when we were little enough to wear it but not so big we'd be in danger of getting out of which one's lap we were in, toddling off the porch into the yard or somewhere and tearing it all up or getting it muddy.

It's too short on her is how I can tell that Louselle is getting on toward two years of age. You can see her feet and on past them halfway up the calves of her legs. So Mama when that likeness of her was taken was close on to being six months or so along in her term, the last one she'd ever have, and she has one hand on the hem of that tatted white dress pulling it as far down the legs of her baby girl as she can. Looking at Mama's face, you can't see any sign she's thinking about anything but looking straight ahead at that big old camera box, but I know what I'm talking about. Her hand is clenched to that dress hem, pulling it down as far as she can without letting it look a strain or cause anybody who would later on see the picture to know she was trying to cover up how that fine tatted dress, white as it was, doesn't fit anymore.

She was always thinking all the time, whatever it was she was doing, and most generally she was not studying what was right at hand, the way most people will do. As in that picture took there in Sabine County in the 'eighties of all of the Amos Holt family together, the first bunch of them I am meaning now, what my sister Maude has always called the top crop. Papa and Mama, his first wife and their children, together.

When I look close at Mama in the photograph that came of that pose, I can see her skull beneath the skin of her face, and I do not mean by that her cheekbones nor the point of her chin. It is deeper than that, what I see, and it is the pure bone that lies beneath the flesh I mean, not as a feature of beauty like people intend when they comment favorably on the shape of a woman's face or the outline of her profile being like a silhouette cut out of black paper or a shell from the sea.

My mother would be lying a corpse in less than three months after that photograph was made in the front yard of the old place, and nobody knew it then, certainly not Papa standing behind her where she is sitting in that cane-bottomed chair. I say nobody knew it, of all of us standing around her, but one thing did, and that was the camera that photographer used. Like I said, the picture it took shows the skull behind my mother's face and it shows death coming on her. And a camera sees truly what's in front of it. It doesn't care one way or the other what it records. No hand draws its pictures.

There Carolina Holt sits, looking straight into the glass eye of that camera, her littlest child in her lap wearing a tatted white dress too small for her, and behind Mama stands her husband, one hand on her shoulder and the other one held up close to his side like he is about to reach for something in his watch pocket, but will wait to do so until the camera has recorded his likeness.

What he is really doing is favoring that hand, or more exactly, the arm that left hand is partner to, the arm that Font Nowlen had cut clean to the bone with his Bowie knife not more than three weeks before the Holts all stood up together in front of that photographer to get our picture made that hot day.

I saw that thing happen and what came after, and I saw what caused the whole affair to begin.

It started in Blue Water Chapel, there in the southwest corner of Sabine County, close to where all those baygalls and marshes set a limit to farming. The church building at Blue Water is not standing any more, having burned down over twenty years ago, but the graveyard there is where a lot of the Holts are buried, Papa and Mama among them. We don't bury there now, naturally, since almost everybody has moved out of that part of the country. All those clearings they put so much effort into to grow cotton have grown up now into a regular jungle of yaupon and saw-briars and slash pine. It appears to me like man has not trod there when I go back now to visit the graveyard.

But that Sunday morning in Blue Water Chapel found Papa preaching in the pulpit on the theme of redemption, and people had come from all over those little communities around in that part of Sabine County to hear him do it. There were folks from Cold Spring, Standard, Rock Hill, Horse Pen, and all up and around Ellis Landing, back there on the river. I do not know all that part of the story on my own, why there were so many attending worship that day, since I was just a yearling girl at the time, but when people have talked about it over the years I have learned more of the names of places and the families that lived around them and who was there to see it start up.

Papa had built himself up a real reputation for preaching the gospel by that time, though he hadn't really started good at it until after we came to Texas in 1867. Something happened in his mind and in his soul crossing that river and leaving that life back in Louisiana, and he just started in reading the Bible every day in earnest, though he had read it plenty before, naturally. Something just took him over in Texas, though, once he got to living and farming there with Mama and the children that kept coming, and he felt the need to tell people about it, that new thing that had him. I reckon it was the grace of God, I don't know. It was one of those things preachers talk about, I imagine. Grace, salvation, eternal life, conviction, whatever they call those ideas that plague them when they get to worrying about something other than wringing a living from the sweat of their brows and that of everybody else around them.

Papa found out he could preach the time when the old fellow that used to lead worship back then in people's houses on a Sunday, traveling around to one and the other house place in Sabine County, a Brother Ahi Moye, didn't show up one Sunday like he was supposed to do. It was being held at our old place that Sunday, the worship was.

"Brother Holt," somebody there asked him, "would you lead us in prayer at least so we won't a wasted the whole journey over here?"

So he did, and the praying he did went on for a long time, I remember, and as Papa said afterwards to Mama, it seemed to get good to him, the praying did, so he turned it into a sermon. The only thing was he never said amen before it turned sermon on him, so everybody there in the house had to sit with their heads bowed until Papa finished an hour later.

What he said, though, was put well enough that nobody had call to complain, crick in their neck or not, and that day marked the time when Amos Holt came to know he could preach the gospel. So he did, from then on until he died. That and farmed, and taught school.

Redemption was the main theme of all his preaching, he always said, no matter what in particular he talked about in one sermon or the other, but it was not always the subject matter of what his talk treated on. He saw a difference, and he declared it, and when he would explain that difference in one of his messages to the congregation that was when he was at his best as a preacher. Everybody who saw him preach more than two or three times always said that about Papa, and they felt the holy ghost moving when he would get into explaining to the congregation why he was preaching what he was preaching and doing it in the way he was.

Young folks, and I call myself among that bunch, didn't care much for that kind of sermon, but the older ones did. I was always proud he was my father at times like that, though, since everybody was so taken up with listening to him and watching him struggle to explain so all could understand and get spiritual benefit from the message he was trying to bring. But I couldn't listen close to his argument, I admit, liking instead to watch how his facial expressions changed in the course of his talk and the way at times he seemed to work so hard to get the right word said. It was like he was hungry, starving, famished to speak. He was dying for the word and longing for it to come into his mouth.

That Sunday morning in Blue Water Chapel the singing had gone on for longer than usually it did, I don't know why, but all those folks there had sung on for a long time as one and then another among them lined out the verses for them, enjoying it, I reckon, or feeling the spirit beginning to move as they thought ahead to the sermon on redemption that Amos Holt was going to preach. I figure lingering over the hymns was like the way you will put off doing a thing you know you want to do for longer than you need to, because thinking about it and knowing it is there for you to take whenever you decide to do it makes it sweeter. Contemplation is a relish.

Waiting for a thing you know you'll get is sometimes better even than actually getting it. Say a helping from a blackberry cobbler you have picked the berries for yourself and baked, and you know it's there to eat, and a bunch of children are clamoring for it. But you wait, and make everybody else wait, too.

That was the kind of mind folks at the Blue Water Chapel worship service were on that morning, at least most of them, while they sang hymns and listened to another offer up prayers. Putting it off to make the having of it better.

I was sitting about halfway back from the front of the chapel building near the end of one of those old split-log benches country churches used back then, and during all the singing and praying that went on, I could tell Font Nowlen right in front of me was not in accord with the way the congregation was feeling—satisfied, looking forward to what was coming, joining in together with each other in the worship, all manner of that.

His people came from down in there close to the Romayor settlement, river bottom land that flooded out pretty bad every now and then, but they were the kind of folks that just put up with that happening and never had enough gumption to move when conditions didn't suit. It was good land, rich enough for cotton to grow quick and make big in a season, I'll grant them that, but it was a gamble every year, even more than is ordinarily true for anybody bound and determined to try to make a living off cotton.

The old man, Alton Nowlen, was always talking about how their bunch was from Georgia before coming to Texas, not Louisiana or Alabama like were behind most families who moved to that country after the war, and he meant by that Georgia business to set a premium on him and his somehow. I never could figure out why he believed that or why he broadcast it around, nor could anybody else in Sabine County. As far as I'm concerned, Georgia is not any place but Alabama put further off. It is certainly not a distinction worth making to a Texan.

Font Nowlen kept craning his neck around to look behind him while everybody was singing hymns, which part he did not join in, and a couple of times during the offerings of prayers by one and then another, he looked up from bowing his head like a buzzard trying to see where something dead might be lying. How I could tell he was wobbling his head around doing that was that I have always had the ability to keep my head down but roll my eyes up really far, far enough to see what's happening around me and not give a sign of my doing that. No one's ever complained about that regarding me, because I assume they can't tell it.

One reason Font Nowlen, as old as he was to be acting that way in a worship service in Blue Water Chapel, was doing so much to call attention to himself I figured out as soon as I saw him in front of where I was sitting that morning. He had on a new made shirt with an extra big collar that stuck up from the neck of the dress coat he was wearing, and it was not white in color but a shade of blue. And that on a grown man with a full set of whiskers. Font was as proud of that piece of apparel as a jaybird stretching its wings out to fly from one limb of a sweet gum tree to another. Both Font and that bluejay constitutionally wanted to be seen, and they would make enough ruckus to assure that notice took place. I figured some girl had made that shirt for him, not his mother, the way he was acting, but I don't know that to be true.

Just at the end of a prayer that old man Adolphus Collins had offered up, all quavery and high pitched and as mixed up as a jar full of stray buttons, Font Nowlen twisted his head around to look behind him and then he said something to me. I remember when he did I could see his bottom teeth and they were an ugly shape and color.

"Abby Holt," he said, "here to see her old daddy rear up and holler." He had cast his voice low to keep people sitting to each side of him from understanding what he was saying, but people around could tell he was talking in the middle of worship, no matter what he was saying.

I didn't say a word back to him, but something must have showed in my face because I could see that Papa, standing up there in front of the congregation to preside during all that would go on before he started his sermon, was looking straight at me. Usually, he would not look at any one of his children or Mama during a service, because it was not the proper thing to do, I suppose, though he had never expressed that in my hearing. I just figured out on my own that a preacher during a worship service in a church is not really part of his own earthly family while it's going on, the service, I mean. He belongs to the party of the Lord during that spell of time and is no more a member of his own family than he is of any other family of people in the congregation. He is of everybody and above everybody at the same time.

That thought is satisfying to me, and it has been since I first came up with it. I like to put things where they belong and keep them there. It makes sense of things. That's what I try always to do, make sense of things and see how all fits into a pattern.

Papa's eyes were on me, when I looked up toward the front where the preacher stands in a church, and I had not answered Font Nowlen when he made that low-minded statement to me, but I was fearful that people, and most especially Papa, might have thought I did. I was in a predicament. I wanted to stand up then and there and announce to everybody in Blue Water Chapel something to this effect: "I did not invite this piece of trash to speak to me during worship, and I most assuredly would not and did not exchange remarks with him."

That's what I wanted to say, or something approximate to it, but all I could do, naturally, was just turn red as fire in my face and throat like a sign board declaring my guilt for a misdeed I did not commit. Thinking that made my coloring become even more of an intense shade, and I sat there with my own father looking at me, convinced probably that one of his daughters was talking in church to a jaybird-looking excuse of a man while he was fixing his mind and soul to preach a sermon on redemption which people had come miles to hear.

And with another part of my mind, I was envying my sister Maude once again for having that dark hue of skin she got from Mama while I was blighted with the pale skin of Papa which showed every emotion that went through me, no matter how trifling, and magnified it for all to see.

Like I said, this rude and ignorant action of Font Nowlen's took place at the end of Mr. Collins's prayer and before Papa had begun to say anything toward commencing his sermon, so it had grown perfectly quiet in Blue Water Chapel, while Papa fixed his eyes on me. They were snapping like blue fire.

And then the fool sitting in front of me did it again. Twisted around, showed the bottom inside of his mouth to me—but he wasn't thinking about that, it goes without saying - and said something else.

"Did you bring a dinner bucket with you, Abby Holt?" he said, the sound of his voice louder this time in that quiet after his prayer ended. "I'm going to be hungry when all this hooting and hollering is over."

I began to entertain two thoughts at the same time, both of them amounting to the same thing, though a little different, these being "Has Font Nowlen gone crazy?" and "Is this fool in front of me drunk on a Sunday morning in Blue Water Chapel?" But by the time I was coming to the conclusion that whichever was the case it made not a hair's distinction between them anyway, Papa began to speak directly from the pulpit right in our direction, mine and Font's. Not that he and I were in any way, shape or fashion part of any kind of a combination, naturally. I would not be mistaken in that matter.

"Mr. Fontaine Nowlen," Papa said in the voice he used when preaching before a gathering, one with a kind of ringing note to it, "I would request your full and undivided attention."

I remember the church got quieter than it had ever been in my memory, at that moment. You could hear a dirt dauber buzzing somewhere up close to the shingles of the roof, working on building its mud nest, though I did not look up to verify the truth of what I knew the insect to be. I knew it was not a wasp, though, because the sound of the wasp buzzing is different, being a higher pitch and more energetic sounding than a dirt dauber.

"You want what?" Font Nowlen said back in a kind of a drawling tone, lengthening the words so they didn't carry their true meanings, the ones they would have if you read them off a page of print. The way he said those words was nasty sounding and insolent, apart from and in addition to their substance and content. Then he added this statement: "I know what this girl of yours wants."

"I had meant to inquire if you wished to speak to this congregation," Papa said, "but let me amend that. I would state now that I do not know the name of the man you would have second you. But I assume you will be able to find someone willing to perform that office. I request that you have him consult with my second, Mr. Wayland Austin of the Cane Creek community, as to date, location and choice of weapons. I will be at your service at the time appointed by them."

Font Nowlen rose up from his seat on the split-log bench, and he did so slowly, shrugging his shoulders a little to make his coat set better, I suppose, though to an interested observer it might have appeared he was fixing himself in a pose. I thought that, sitting there behind him as close as I was, though what was happening right then kept getting mixed up in my head with the sound of my heart pounding and of the dirt dauber buzzing away at its work above us. I can still hear that exact insect drone today or any day, if I want to call it up in my head to listen. I reckon I always will.

"Reverend Amos Holt," Font Nowlen said in that same drawling tone, "I will attend to your wishes, and I will do so with pleasure."

And then he walked down that space between the benches, reached the aisle, put his hat on his head before he got to the door, and left Blue Water Chapel in a strut.

Everybody in the building just sat there, not saying a word, and we all could hear Font Nowlen outside getting up on his horse, the saddle creaking as he did, like leather will do and the horse groaning. But before we began to hear the first hoofbeats as Font commenced to ride off, Papa had begun his sermon on redemption, the one everybody had come to hear him preach at Blue Water. And it was what folks called a stemwinder, then when he delivered it and all the years since when people have talked about it. They still do, the ones left, that few of them.

I do not hold with dueling, now and back then when so much of it went on, being a Christian and a civilized person and most particularly a woman, of course. But I knew, sitting there in Blue Water Chapel listening to Amos Holt quoting scripture directly from the Bible without having to refer to the book and then explaining to the congregation what it meant as regards redemption, that I was going to find the way and the means to observe my father meet Fontaine Nowlen in mortal combat.

I knew where it would take place, naturally. Every soul in Blue Water Chapel did, and that was Honeysuckle Island, in the middle of the Sabine River, about three miles downstream from Sabinetown. So while I sat there, listening to Papa line out the necessary and inevitable steps toward redemption, I was calculating how to find out the time the seconds of the involved parties would set for the duel to happen.

It came to me fairly quick who to ask, as I sat there beneath the buzzing of that dirt dauber still at work and the sounds of Papa's comments on the scriptures from Matthew and Luke and John. Maude could find out, from Drusilla Austin who was bound to hear her father Wayland talking about arrangements for the duel with her mother. Wayland Austin couldn't keep anything private from his wife Myrlie who could and would prize information out of anybody as neat as she could get the meat out of a black walnut shell.

It would be no real project for me to get over to Honeysuckle Island, whatever day the seconds picked for the event to take place, since like all the young folks around Sabinetown, I had been there to picnic many a time. I could find some boy to paddle me over to the island in a skiff or canoe or on the off-chance I could not, I would do it myself. Through the course of my life to that point, I had found that boys generally liked to do favors for me. That has not changed yet, though it has slowed considerably.

The time of day for the meeting would be just after daylight, just like when most every settlement of an affair of honor was held back then, so all I needed to find out was the date itself. And from the offense Papa had taken from Font Nowlen's act and the way he had called him out there in Blue Water Chapel, I felt in my bones it would not be many days off from that particular Sunday.

The way it worked in those days in Sabine County, Texas in such matters was that if honor could be satisfied by just a show, why then the seconds would go through a lot of palaver and arranging and arguing for a long spell and set the date several weeks off. Everything could kind of die down by the time had come for the parties to meet on Honeysuckle Island, and satisfaction could be gained by one of the parties not showing up because he was taken sick or his wife was in a sinking condition of some sort or another, or one of the children, maybe, was at death's door. And the opponent would forgive that, as a gentleman.

And, if both parties ended up facing each other finally at the appointed time, there in that clearing on Honeysuckle Island, back in behind those stands of water oaks with the Spanish moss hanging down from their limbs, the weapons of choice would have been settled on as pistols. Then, nine times out of ten, with one of these agreed-upon dates set by the seconds long after the triggering offense itself, the first man would miss his shot and the other one would shoot up into the air or into the ground after that miss, and everybody would be satisfied with the outcome.

Then they all could go separately home and eat breakfast and listen to their folks go on about how honor had been fulfilled and bravery demonstrated and a lesson learned by the other fellow. And the combatants would avoid seeing each other from then on, or sometimes they might even shake hands as time went by and even get to be friendly toward one another. I have seen that happen, as have other people in those days when the name of Honeysuckle Island would send shivers down people's spines, men as well as women, not even to mention children.

The settlement of the affair of honor between Amos Holt and Fontaine Nowlen would not fit into that category, I knew, though. What had begun in Blue Water Chapel that Sunday morning right after the praying stopped and before the sermon began would not lend itself to a lot of talk between seconds arguing and speechifying about arrangements and choice of weapons. It would be settled in one sitting, as soon as Font Nowlen named his man as second and as soon as that man met with Mr. Wayland Austin of the Cane Creek community.

I knew that by two things, and as I think about it today, I remember saying those two things to myself as Papa coolly worked his way through his sermon on redemption before the congregation and that dirt dauber above buzzed away at molding its mud nest together in the rafters of the church. Not Papa's words, I kept hearing my voice in my mind say over and over to me, not Papa's words to Font Nowlen, not his words but the way he said them. The cold in the words, the cold in the words, and the heat in the eyes, the fire blazing up in the eyes.

That afternoon, after dinner around the table with Mama setting the vessels of food out to feed all of us and her completely silent and the rest of us the same way, the only sounds that of the knock of the bowls as she set them on the table and of the utensils clicking on the plates, I put my sister Maude to work on learning the day of the week the duel would occur. Told her who to talk to, Drusilla Austin, swore her to silence, which I knew she would observe, and readied my mind to allow me to watch my father meet a man in combat some morning soon on Honeysuckle Island with the air still cool, the light steadily growing, and fog coming up from the ground like tendrils from a fern or tatters from a woman's veil.

It would be Wednesday, only three days after the offense made and taken, and the settlement of honor would be accomplished with Bowie knives.

When Maude told me that, she did so on Monday at the schoolhouse after Professor Runnels had let us out to eat our noon meal. Since I was one of the older girls and Professor Runnels had early on learned how much sense I had, I had been sitting with some of the little ones in one corner of the room helping them recite their words, as was my habit and duty. He depended on a couple of us to help him out when we could, given that it was a large school with over a couple of dozen scholars to teach.

So when Professor Runnels hit the little bell on his desk at the front of the room to signal all of us to line up to leave the building and go outside to eat what we had brought with us to school that morning, I looked up to see that Maude was trying to catch my eye. I nodded at her real quick, just one little bob of my head, so as not to call attention to the fact that two of us Holts were communicating with each other in school, and I went to my place, at the front of the line.

As I walked toward the door of the building to let the rest of the scholars get in behind me, I felt a little something kick up low in my stomach, not like I was about to get sick, but more like a message my body was sending me, telling me to get ready to hear a thing I wanted to know but dreaded to receive.

Outside, by the bole of the sycamore under whose shade the older ones liked to sit while we ate our dinner on those days nice enough to be out in the open air, Maude looked at me with a piercing gaze.

"Well," I said, "did you talk to Drusilla?"

"I did," she said. "Is it some more of those crowder peas?"

"What else?" I said. "That and some corn pone. Here." I handed her the tin vessel we carried back and forth between the old place and the Double Pen schoolhouse every day lessons were in session. "What did Drusilla say?"

Maude began to look into the crowders as though she was likely to find something new and surprising to eat, but I refused to ask her again about what I wanted to know, not being willing to let her make me do that. I was usually able to outwait her in these matters, being older and more possessed of myself than she was then, and to tell the truth, have been all my life. Maude may dispute that, but it is a fact.

"Drusilla heard her Mama and Papa talking last night after supper," Maude said and lifted up a spoonful of peas toward her mouth, hoping I'd break down and ask her to get to the point. I did not. So she put the peas in her mouth, chewed them more than needful, and swallowed them down.

"Mr. Austin met with Fontaine Nowlen's second on Sunday afternoon. It's John Milton Redd who's the second. That's who Font Nowlen picked to speak for him."

"I don't like to hear that," I said. I didn't have to explain to my sister why. Everybody in all the settlements in Sabine County knew the reputation of John Milton Redd for hotheadedness and a rowdy nature. He would rather argue than eat, and he was way too young to be acting as a second to a party involved in an affair of honor with a man of our father's substance.

"He is disputatious," Maude said, showing off a word she had learned, which she has always been bad to do, though I do give her credit for always being a girl eager to increase her vocabulary. I don't question that urge, but I do have an opinion about the manner in which a woman chooses to offer up the accomplishments of her mind.

"John Milton, I am speaking of," Maude went on. "He is ever eager to fight."

"I know what that word means," I told her, "and he is not eager to fight himself, but to talk about fighting and to encourage others to do so as he watches the battle."

"That is what I meant, of course," Maude said and took another bite of crowder peas, adding a portion of corn pone to her mouthful.

"All right," I said, breaking down, finally, in my desire to know what my sister had learned about the matter at hand. "When will it happen? What are the conditions?"

That was all Maude needed to hear from me, a sign of surrender, and she ceased parceling out her information in dribs and drabs, and told me the rest of it in one burst of speech. Wednesday morning on Honeysuckle Island at dawn, Bowie knives because as Mr. Wayland Austin reported John Milton Redd's statement to him, "Font Nowlen wants either to kill that damned Amos Holt or cut him up so bad he won't never preach another lick."

"Damned, indeed," I said to Maude, the words bursting out of my mouth, "Papa will show Fontaine Nowlen what damned means. That jaybird will rue the day he crossed Amos Holt at Blue Water Chapel in the middle of a worship service."

With that, I immediately felt hungry and took the tin of crowder peas and corn pone out of Maude's hand and pitched in. She was through eating, anyway, and she was beginning to cry, not loud, but enough so you could see the tears starting to streak down her cheeks.

"I'm going to be there to see him do it, too," I said. "Want to come with me?"

Maude didn't answer, but I knew she wouldn't be on Honeysuckle Island that morning in any shape, form, or fashion. She has never had stomach for such matters as duels. Sitting under the sycamore, my sister weeping beside me, I ate with relish every last pea and swabbed the bottom of the tin container with the last bite of cornbread until the metal shone clean. And then I ate the bread.

It is a strange thing to admit, but I must report that I don't remember how I got to Honeysuckle Island that Wednesday morning before daylight, nor how I returned across the water of the Sabine River after the events that took place that day were over. But it's true. When I cast my mind back to then, what I recall first is how wet the leaves of the undergrowth on the island were as I kneeled at the edge of the clearing where I knew the meeting between the opposing parties would take place.

That I remember clearly as my first impression of that day, that, and the dress I was wearing, a light-colored one which showed every drop of water from the leaves which spotted it as they dripped. The morning was cool, and the sky was beginning to brighten in the east and the outline of the limbs and foliage was becoming more visible. Birds were tuning up their songs, and from somewhere in the shallows of the river flowing about the island came the croaking of a couple of bullfrogs looking for each other, there in no-man's land between Texas and Louisiana, a location nobody claimed and a place subject to no law.

As Mama had said to me back on the very day the Holts first came to Texas, the place where I now knelt in concealment on an island between two states was nowhere. By nature, it was between places.

Papa and his second arrived in the clearing first, and I could have predicted that. He was always a man prompt to get where he was appointed to go and determined not to keep others or any business waiting.

He and Mr. Wayland Austin walked out together well into the open space at the heart of the stand of water oaks, not talking and making little sound as they pushed through the low grass and weeds of the clearing. Mr. Austin was smoking a small black cheroot, the plume of smoke from it disturbed a bit by a light breeze that was coming from the east and stirring the fronds of Spanish moss on the limbs of the water oaks. Papa was not smoking, since he seldom used tobacco, and when he did, not in a smoking form. He would chew a small amount now and then of bright leaf, but only as a tonic. He had, in fact, ceased doing even that many years before he died in 1906.

He was wearing dark pants and a dress coat, over a white shirt fastened at the neck with a black string tie. He was carrying nothing in his hands, but Mr. Austin had a black leather valise, the sight of which made my throat constrict when I saw it, enough to cause me to begin swallowing over and over with difficulty as though I had bitten off a mouthful of something too dry for me to get down.

I put my hand over my mouth to help me swallow with no sound, and I was instantly glad I had done so, because at that moment Papa took off his hat—he was wearing his black dress one—and shook his head a little, causing his hair to move in the breeze. The gray I could see in it, even at that distance, in the growing light of the morning was what affected me, and I believe I would have made a sound if my mouth had not been fortunately covered already by my hand.

Wayland Austin said something to Papa, which I could not make out, and Papa nodded and answered him, and I could hear and understand what he said back, "Oh, he will be here, all right," and it was just then that Fontaine Nowlen and John Milton Redd stepped from the stand of water oaks and yaupon bushes opposite, making their way into the clearing where what had begun in a worship service in Blue Water Chapel would meet its termination that cool morning on Honeysuckle Island.

"Gentlemen," Mr. Wayland Austin said in greeting and nodded his head in their direction, but John Milton Redd didn't answer, choosing instead to turn to look directly into the face of Font Nowlen beside him, as though checking to see if his companion had heard the same noise he just had.

Fontaine Nowlen didn't look back at his second, but instead continued swiveling his head around from side to side as he appeared to be inspecting the complete circle of the clearing he had just stepped into. I remember wondering at the time as I peered between the boles of two water oaks and just over the top fronds of a palmetto bush if Fontaine Nowlen was afraid he was walking into an ambush. No chance of that existed in an affair of honor involving Amos Holt, I knew, but a man will always fear the possibility of what he knows he himself is capable of.

So Font Nowlen was revealing his character in every particular of his behavior that morning, just as he had in his violation on the Sunday before in Blue Water Chapel. That's what was making him suspect the underhand on Honeysuckle Island that morning.

"Reverend Holt," Font Nowlen said in a pert voice, "I see you have chosen to show up."

"I have," Papa said, but he didn't bob his head as Mr. Austin had done earlier, and he kept his gaze fixed on Font Nowlen, not choosing to survey the scene from side to side and in all dimensions as the man he faced continued to do.

Neither of the principals spoke again, but waited in silence as Mr. Austin and John Milton Redd walked up to each other in the middle of the clearing and began to converse in their roles as seconds. As they talked in murmurs low and indistinct, I watched the morning breeze lift and move my father's hair, and I kept my hand pressed to my mouth. It was not that I felt any longer that I might make an untoward outcry or groan, but I remember thinking that if I kept the pressure of my hand applied to my face I would be able to forestall any shaking or tremors which might move the leaves behind which I shielded myself. That does not make sense now, but it did then and was a comfort to me.

After Mr. Austin and John Milton Redd had said a few words, each of them opened the valise he was carrying to show its contents to the other, and both looked intently within. I knew what they were examining, though I myself was in no position to see. It was the Bowie knives.

I thank the Lord the Bowie knife has largely passed from the scene in Texas these days, but back then it was of great moment in situations of dispute and reputation in the state.

The Bowie was a knife in name only, in a realistic sense. It was actually a long, heavy blade, more like a hatchet with a razor sharp edge, attached to a handle which allowed its wielder to employ it to chop as well as to thrust and slice. It was serious, it was deadly, it was Hell held in the hand.

Thinking of what those two men in the middle of the clearing filled with birdsong were considering as they peered at the contents of their valises, their heads together as though they were a team studying a water moccasin's fangs, I knew I had to look away from them or collapse into the saw-briars and underbrush around me.

Naturally, I fixed my gaze first on Papa, but I could not maintain it there, with the breeze continuing to ruffle his head of hair, revealing the silver mixed with black. So I focused instead on Fontaine Nowlen, now standing with his head back and his eyes fixed on something higher up, the tree line maybe, or the sunlight touching the leaves, or the empty sky itself.

He was wearing that same new made, light blue shirt with the oversized collar, the garment which I took to be at the bottom of all this before me, the reason that Font took it into his foolish head to strut and flare and forget where he was in a given location and how to behave in that place. I believed to my soul that was the truth of the matter there on Honeysuckle Island that morning, I believe it today, and I will go to my grave with that conviction.

Around the neck of that oversized collar, Font Nowlen was sporting a canary yellow tie, which in a situation other than the present one, would have made a nice contrast. Say at an all-night gathering in a house full of young people dancing on a floor cleared of all breakable furniture, or at a church singing outdoors with dinner on the ground to follow.

Here on Honeysuckle Island with seconds approving weapons of choice at daybreak and Amos Holt standing across the clearing, prepared to rectify an insult to himself and to the honor of his family, the yellow tie and blue shirt Font Nowlen wore did not fit the circumstance.

But seeing the yellow tie and being able to consider the thoughts it brought to my mind eased and calmed me enough to allow me to bear and endure the situation I had got myself into, I would not faint, I would not cry out and reveal my presence, I would not shame Papa in the performance of the duty he had no choice but to owe himself and accept.

The seconds finished their conference, looked each other in the eye, shook hands, turned and walked back to their principals. Every bird on the island was in full song, the sun rose steadily above the tree line to the east, and its beams lit the clearing like a stage.

A duel fought with the Bowie knife, for those who have not seen one, is in its progress slow at first and then lightning quick. I watched that entire struggle between my father Amos Holt and the provoker of the affair of honor, Fontaine Nowlen, and I choose not to describe it in detail.

I will say this much, however. At the end of the encounter, Papa was cut to the bone on his left arm, high up toward the shoulder, enough so that arm was not the same in its strength and use to him ever again, from that point until the day of his death. He favors it in the photograph taken those years ago, three months before Mama's death, and he continued to do so, learning to use his back muscles and his right arm more from then on in discharging the duties of farming and all other physical labor. I am convinced his rheumatism, severe in his last years, came as a result of that morning's struggle, as well.

His shortage in that arm, as he always termed it, began that day on Honeysuckle Island. Fontaine Nowlen's yellow tie at the end of combat was yellow no more, nor was it intact about his throat, and his new made light blue shirt was cut into ribbons of red. Amos Holt walked to the small boat he had used to cross from the Texas bank of the Sabine River to Honeysuckle Island, but Fontaine Nowlen was carried by John Milton Redd, assisted by Mr. Wayland Austin, to the skiff he had rowed to Honeysuckle Island that morning in a state of perfect health and strength. He departed his life on earth before he arrived at his home near noon in the Romayor settlement and before he had opportunity to say farewell to his mother. His last words, uttered in the skiff to his second in the affair, John Milton Redd, I do confess, included my name.

Maude

I could tell as a child that there is a balance in all things, a give and take in the world that works behind each dealing a man or a woman has with another human or with any other part of their lives or the things in them. Furniture, food, the weather, the ones they marry, how they come to die.

At the time I happened on this truth, I had not sat down to study on such a notion. Neither did it come to my mind all of a piece, like some connections between things you had never realized will of a sudden leap before you in the way a bolt of lightning will let you see for a flash of time what was all in darkness before. And after, return to itself and its darkness.

This balance I came to realize, this connection of gain and loss, loss and gain, at large in the world did not give me ease when I knew that I knew it.

Understanding why an event happened, being able to trace back its beginning and to look along the lines of its furtherance to come, and then to nod in acknowledgment as the expected becomes the accomplished—this knowledge is no comfort to a body, young or old, man or woman, rich or poor.

Today, I live in the middle of my family, my husband and children and the others of my blood around and near me, sometimes more than I want them to be and I can recite my location and the date and time of the parts of my existence. And anyone hearing me do so would agree and confirm the facts as I name them.

I am a woman in her later years, now Maude Holt Winston, who was Maude Holt Blackstock once, situated in the Double Pen Creek community of Coushatta County, Texas, in the year 1912.

That person confirming these facts about me and all other facts attendant would see them as they are and believe them set to be such from the foundations of time, ordained and fated and comfortable.

I learned different as a child of three years barely across the Sabine River from Louisiana into Texas. And my conviction, grown so strong over the years up until this day, as to the balance in all things, had its birth in the stillborn death of a brother, who never had a name.

That brother I never saw had a grave, however, and a natural stone, unworked, put to the head of it, and I heard my mother Carolina Cameron Holt say those words which allowed me to begin to know about balance in the world.

"Amos," I heard her say to my father as I lay with my eyes closed beside my sister Abigail, "I will not leave my child alone in this wilderness."

And my father said over and over the word *Bandera,* and I knew he wanted to go there and take us with him, but I heard my mother speak her words and they were never different and did not vary with the times of her saying them. And as a child, I came to know, lying by my sister Abigail in that wagon bed, that my father could not have Bandera and what that word meant to him and my mother, too, though of course at the time I could not have said those words.

A child can know, with no language available to express its knowing. And so a child who was never alive and forever nameless and who had nothing ever in this world but a grave would shape all my days to come and make my life what it has been and is.

And that is one of the balances of which I speak, and one I know in my bones.

Of my brothers and sisters, Abigail is the one who accompanies me those times I must journey back to the old place in Sabine County. It is not yearly we go, though in one six-month space we traveled the fifty-two miles between the Double Pen Creek community and Blue Water Chapel three times. And once there were four years between visits, and little of Blue Water Chapel and the graveyard came to touch my mind in all that spell. What did was fleeting and on the surface of thought and did not reach deeper into my thinking than a gourd dipper might when used to fetch water for one drink from the deepest hole in Double Pen Creek. Lifted, consumed, unnoted and forgotten.

They are not regular, those visits from Abigail and me, but they are needful when they happen, and I know when the time for one comes. Abigail is the one of us who talks most about what each journey means, though, and she explains to me as we travel, sitting together in the wagon driven most times by her husband, Ferguson, the reason for that return, particular and singled out.

"This year marks the thirty-fifth anniversary of the Holts coming to Texas," she may say, and I nod and speak in agreement, listening to my sister remember and recount the lineaments of the story as she wants to tell it, never quarreling about the bits she wants to bring forth to admire and polish and taste.

It is not worth the struggle to me to be judged right in small things, though often I detect lapses and omissions and additions not proven in some of what Abigail may say. I allow her precedence and defer to her memory in such matters, so important it always is to her to be accorded the right when she sifts through what is her past and thinks is mine, too.

I give her the words she needs as we travel, the "yes" and "I didn't remember that" and "is that the way it happened," and doing so as we move along in the wagon on the bench behind Ferguson or whichever son of one of us sisters is holding the reins of the mules allows me room to savor my own story and the journey I am making.

The only time I challenge my sister's version of the days behind us which have led to this one do not concern the exact words of the conversations she remembers between our people among themselves and with others, or the color of someone's hair or eyes or apparel at some given moment, or the weather which held some happening or the season of year it took place. These accidents and surfaces of history I grant Abigail, and I do so with ease and calm.

It is when she does not recognize how one part of the past links to another or when she breaks the drift of connection, the interlocking of event and feeling in the whole of one life or many, that I must contest her accuracy in the dreams she creates.

Then I will look up from wherever my gaze has been fastened as I have been moving toward Blue Water Chapel by an agency not my own at the center of a stream of words from an older sister whose every thought is always spoken aloud, and I will deliver my glimpse of the truth lying behind whatever it is she has misread.

Abigail is seldom bothered at such a moment, though she cuts off with reluctance the stream of her language at the sound of my correction, her mouth always still open a bit as she waits for me to finish and the air to clear so that she may reinstitute the course and direction of her narrative, thinking all the while as she delays just how to mark her place correctly and allow no seam to show in the resumption of her tale.

"Papa," she is saying as we ride in the wagon between stands of dogwood to the left and right of our way, not two miles from the Sabine County line, the dogwood in full blossom, its flowers seeming to float unattached in the fading light of day, "Papa always had in his mind something other than and more than just raising cotton in Bandera County, Texas, if he had ever got there, after crossing the river from Louisiana."

"Did he?" I say. "What?"

"I'm talking about why he wanted to come to Texas, leave a perfectly good house place in Livingston Parish, Louisiana, and a parcel of land rich enough to've produced a bale of cotton an acre not two years before he left."

I realize I've spoken too early in the midst of Abigail's explanation of Amos Holt's reason for uprooting his family and coming to Texas after the war, but I excuse myself because it's a new story I sense coming from my sister, one she's not laid out before for appreciation and marvel. If I offer a comment or question before she wants one, Abigail will often slow down a story, add some more decoration to it, go back over parts she's already covered, postpone a point she had been near delivering—all this designed to punish her listener for getting in the path she's been treading. So I hush, and look off to the side just ahead at a stand of dogwood whose blossoms are pink, not white. I will think of them, and then look at our driver, I say to myself, as Abigail mends the tear I've made in her sewing.

The driver for us of the wagon this journey is my son, the oldest, Richard, one of the two I have by Valery Blackstock, my lost love too sweet and kind to live long in this world. I did not bury Valery at Blue Water Chapel since his people are not from there, and I've always been glad over the years of that accident to time and place. If he were in a grave in Blue Water, I would not be able to visit the place where Mama and Papa are buried. I will not go where the earth holds Valery, not after I have seen it close over him and felt what that means.

I look at what I can see of the back of Richard's head as he sits bolt upright on the bench ahead of ours, the mules' reins precise in his hands, and by squinting my eyes a little in the dimming light, I can make his hair look near enough like his father's in color to cause a small pain to come into my chest, just in the middle, and fleeting.

Abigail has paused in what she's been saying, giving me a signal that she is ready for a question to prompt her revelation of another reason for Amos Holt's move to Texas. It's not taken her long to repair the part of her account that I damaged by speaking too soon, so I repeat my comment, filling the eddy I'd made in the flow of her talking.

"What?" I say. "What other reason could he have had to leave such a good situation back in Louisiana?"

"I have thought about it," Abigail says in a lowered tone, her voice richer now in quality as she nears the announcement she's been doing all this work to get to, the way you might slow down in eating a slice of fruit cake when you feel with your tongue and teeth a sweet bit of dried citrus ripe for the chewing, "and I've talked to old people that came to Texas around the same time we did. You know old man Tump Barlow, don't you, on that place out the Zion Road?"

"I thought he was dead," I say.

"Well, he is," Abigail answers, ready to come to her revelation and a little cross at what I've said, now causing her to have to respond unnecessarily but duty bound to do so, to set me straight, "That doesn't make any difference. I talked to him many a time, and I did that before he died. I haven't been communing with the dead, Maude."

"No, I understand," I say, making my answer soft and dutiful, "I wasn't thinking that."

"Anyway," my sister says, mollified, "some of the things Mr. Tump Barlow said to me right before he joined the Great Majority just fit right in with what I had been figuring out about the real reason Papa was ready to walk away from that nice little cotton holding in Louisiana and come to Texas, headed for Bandera County."

"What?" I say again, careful to hit the same soft note with my voice, "What, Abigail?"

"For gold," she says simply, looking straight into my eyes, and then turns her head with a snap and repeats the words in the direction of Richard ahead of us, committed so truly and well to his control of our progress toward Blue Water Chapel. "For gold. Amos Holt was coming to Texas to look for gold."

"Gold," I say, "Gold. Abigail, please don't say that to anybody else. People will think the Holts are crazier than they believe we are now."

"Huh," she says, gone instantly sullen, "I know what I think, and I know what I've figured out. What are you talking about, crazy?"

"I can't let you go around Double Pen Creek peddling this stuff about Papa," I tell her. "And I'll tell you exactly why you're wrong about this gold business in a minute, but first I want to know why you want to make your own father into a fool."

"A fool? I loved Papa," Abigail says, "You know I did. A lot more than you ever did. I'd never say anything that would go against him or his memory. I'm just trying to show what a forward-thinking man he always was, right back to the beginning."

Now she's getting tearful, and that's what I want her to be, since when she breaks down, then is when once in a great while I've been able to talk some sense into her, make her see how she'll get so caught up in wanting the world to be a certain way that she'll make things up about it to match the dreams living only in her head, and then proclaim them to one and all.

What I'm doing, as always, is trying to show my sister that balance I've realized in the world, that gain and its loss, what's taken away for everything that's given, commensurate and equal.

I don't explain this notion to her directly, knowing she will not understand what I'm trying to convey, much less agree to it. Instead, I have adopted a policy to instruct her by examples, as Jesus did with his parables to his questioners. I would not be misunderstood when I say that. I know how little I can know, and that the little I know can blind me. But I would not give up the small understandings I have struggled so to gain, nor betray the meager triumphs my mind has granted me. So I speak as I must.

"Your love for Papa was always clear, Abigail," I say, watching Richard sitting before us begin to fiddle with the mule's reins and fidget in his seat. Like his father, he cannot bear quarrels or contention, and he is feeling the words between me and his Aunt Abigail pressing against his back as though they were the cut of a chilly wind. "And it was true, and Papa knew that, and we all did."

"Well," Abigail says in a tone just this side of a sob, "I never raised my voice against him, and you know it, too, little sister."

"I do know it," I say, "and I admit that I did question him, and I did that many times."

"And you raised your voice," Abigail says, gaining strength from my admission, "on more than one occasion. And I loved him too much to do any such thing."

"I did raise my voice against him, and I don't apologize for ever doing that, not a single time. When I opposed Papa, I did so on the basis of the right as I saw it."

By saying that, I've given Abigail the wherewithal to gather herself again, and now I judge her ready to listen, as much as she can, to my explanation of why her saying Papa came from Louisiana to Texas in search of gold in 1867 borders so closely on pure foolishness and falsehood unadulterated.

So I do that, not addressing her words about measuring amounts of love, and she listens as best she can, as we ride along in the gathering darkness where we will spend the night just over the Sabine County line with the Fate Waldrup family on their place. They don't know we're coming, Fate and Velda, but they'll be glad to see us, glad to see anybody different from them and their gaggle of children, living where they do as one of the last bunch still in that part of the country almost everybody else has left. Almost everybody except for the dead in the graveyards of Sabine County, at Menard and Ruby and Blue Water and the plots too small to be named, and that's who we're coming to visit. They'll be waiting. They'll be there, and they won't be taking measure of love.

Richard knows the way to Blue Water as well as I do, better probably, but he always defers to Abigail and asks her directions each time we approach the places where the roads fork, the first one just past the old Murphy holding near Little Duck Creek and the one after that, the one splitting off past Big Burn-off. I expect Richard doesn't know why that section is called that, though he never asks about it those times he drives Abigail and me on our visits.

It's all grown up in pine and underbrush now and has been for years, with no sign of the fire that took out all the forest for miles around those years ago. It's green now, and healed, and nobody lives there anymore, nor tries to farm that part of the country.

We had a fine breakfast at the Waldrup's, Velda sets a good table always, but the hour to start seemed early, especially after we had to sit up so late the night before talking, letting Fate and Velda and their children know what was happening outside of Sabine County forty miles away on Double Pen Creek. So I am tired this morning, but not Abigail who's sitting forward on her seat explaining to Richard what he must look for to be able to tell which fork to take. Her mood is good, recovered from the lesson I delivered yesterday, and I expect in no time she'll be telling again her story about Amos Holt hot from Louisiana in search of Texas gold, but I don't think she'll try it with me again. I'll settle for that.

I can see the deep green of the cedars among the oaks and gum trees ahead, there in the clearing of the Blue Water Chapel graveyard, and the cedars are not so tall as the other trees coming toward us, but they are more serious. A deeper green, thicker in leafage, more gathered into themselves, silent in a way oaks and gum and sycamores can never be. They are restless, those trees not cedar, moving and sighing in whatever wind blows, their leaves turning and dying and falling by season, putting forth new growth, tender and delicate and pale in the spring. They are never finished, never settled into themselves the way a cedar is in its beginning, its growth, its flourishing and its death when its time comes, the same always. The other trees move, the cedar is.

I would like to think people plant cedars in graveyards because they recognize statement and meaning in them, and they may do so partially, but I am not content to believe they see more than one word of the language a cedar speaks. And that one word they translate into human language is *evergreen*, and that satisfies them, in the way an infant is first satisfied and clings so long to the first connection it makes between sound and what it conjures, whenever it learns to say that word *mama*.

What the cedar says in a graveyard is more and is part of the balance, too, I have come to know and believe, and the psalmist understood that when he sang of two meanings that tree has, each true and each opposed one gain and one loss. The psalmist declares his hope when he says that the righteous shall flourish like a palm tree, he shall grow like the cedars in Lebanon.

And there in that song is celebration and the knowledge of the deep green of the cedar, and there is the comfort a cedar announces in the silence of its place in the graveyard, and in the intent of its planting there by the living.

But the psalmist sees the balance, the loss attendant upon the gain, the emptiness that accompanies the full, when he sings the other notes of his song, the remainder of the language beneath language. That is what he proclaims when he says the voice of the Lord breaketh the cedars, he breaketh the cedars of Lebanon.

And this song makes up the rest of the balance I see in the world as testified by the cedars, and in the people who spend their lives in it, the end that comes to each beginning, the coins that must be spent to empty every purse.

Abigail is speaking to Richard, pointing ahead over his shoulder as she leans forward on the bench to hurry the wagon toward the destination she craves. "Look," she says, "there's where the old church building stood before it burned, there's Blue Water, there's the cedars. See how green they are."

Papa's stone draws her first, as it always does, and we walk directly to it, past the clump of Moye and Johnson and Snodgrass markers, Abigail leading the way with Richard close behind and me trailing, the mules still hitched to the wagon and snorting as they crop the weeds and grass outside the graveyard. I let my fingertips graze the top edges of each stone I come to, rough and heated by the sun, and I don't allow myself to look yet to the left side of the way we go, toward the smaller blue granite one set off to itself, some distance from the spot we are headed.

That belongs to Carolina Cameron Holt, my mother, and Abigail's mother and Lewis's mother and Estelle's mother, and the mother of all the rest of us, alive and dead, and I will wait on that one and view it last, since by then I will need the balance it represents.

Abigail is saying again what she always does when we come to Blue Water, telling whoever is with her, whether they listen or not, about the way Papa's stone has been moved. It's now by Nelda's marker, and of course it's not the original one put at the head of his grave only a few months after he died and paid for by what his and Mama's children got together among us to make sure anybody who chose to look would know Amos Holt was resting by the wife he brought to Texas, Carolina Cameron Holt.

That stone is gone now, and no one knows who took it nor how they disposed of it, as small as it was and as light, light enough for a strong man to carry unaided. We thought at first, it would be in the woods around Blue Water Chapel graveyard, thrown there somewhere in the underbrush, in a location in the vines and creepers and palmetto and saw-briars, close naturally to the graveyard itself, where a person of that character who would commit such a deed would toss it aside, too lazy and sorry to spend the effort to transport it further away from the site from which it was stolen.

But it is not there, where we suspected, buried somewhere beneath the green thorns of summer and the dead leaves which fall and rot each year in the fall and winter. We have not found it, though each of us has looked every visit that's made to Blue Water. Abigail will do it again this time, I know, poking about with a stick and kicking at this year's accumulation of decay and damp, hoping to turn up that flat stone with Papa's name and dates cut into it.

I stopped doing that years ago. Whoever took the marker away we underestimated, and I am satisfied to accept that fact and to recalculate the depth of his intent. But my mind has eased about it, and what came to comfort me began in a dream granted me about Papa's stone and where it was hidden.

I had looked that day in the woods around the graveyard, with Abigail and Calvin from midday until the dimming light of the sun's going down made it impossible to see what might be at my feet. I forget where my sister and brother and I spent that night, somebody's house in Sabine County, I know, but somewhere in the course of my sleep I found myself watching a figure dressed all in gray, carrying the marker from my father's grave clutched tight against its breast and moving steadily away from me.

The stone was smaller than in reality, little more than the size of a book, but it was exceedingly heavy and the man who carried it, his face hidden from my view, struggled to hold the marker as he moved ahead of me in a stumbling walk. Yet he persisted to move away and seemed to know where he intended to go. I followed him, as you will in a dream, my legs heavy and reluctant to move and every action of my body slower than I wanted it to be, and my feet seemed barely to touch the ground enough to give me purchase to carry on. But I did, at great cost, feeling tears course down my cheeks from the strain and effort it took.

Then, of a sudden, the man before me reached the edge of a pond circled with high grass and bending willows, and I was surprised enough in the dream to wonder at where we were, knowing there was no pond of any description near Blue Water Chapel, and I was aware that I was thinking too much, and I became afraid I would awaken from the dream before I saw what the man in gray would do with the book-sized marker from Papa's grave. I don't know how to explain the next part of what I dreamed except to say that to my mind all the world began falling into layers, and I could see everything about me and before me repeated over and over, one level on top of the other and each changed in small detail from the one beneath yet still part and parcel of what had gone before and was to follow one step above it.

And the figure held the stone cut with the name of my father and his dates of coming into and leaving this world out before it over the water of the pond, and then he let it drop. It entered the water without a splash and sank from sight, and though I couldn't see beneath the surface of the pond to verify what I knew to be true, yet I did know that the stone reached the bottom of the pond upright, fixing itself in a position to last all time and forever, and I was as relieved by that knowledge as though a cool breath of air had come up to move across my face on a hot, close day in Texas.

In the dream I closed my eyes to relish the full benefit of the cooling breeze, and when I opened them again the figure in gray was gone, vanished like a fog burned off by sunlight, and the surface of the pond glistened before me like pearl.

And the memory of that dream has sustained and satisfied me from that night to this day, and that comfort allows me to accept what Abigail cannot.

When my sister looks at the slab of gray granite reared up beside its twin, the stone engraved with the name of our stepmother Nelda Faye Holt and her dates and the words *Beloved Wife of Amos* beneath the other letters, she sees repudiation and bald announcement. She reads a claim made that Papa never loved our mother in the way he loved Nelda, that his true wife and soulmate lies beside the gravestone put there by the children he had with her, that the words carved beneath his name and dates are truth and deed and monument to that love. "In Paradise Together," the words run as a bottom line across the gray granite of Papa's marker larger than Nelda's beside it.

These words are gall and ashes to Abigail, each time she sees or recalls them, and they draw down her lips into a look of disgust and dry up her mouth like cotton.

They're nothing to me but chisel marks on a stone slab shaped by a machine operated by a man, I imagine, somewhere in a state far off, a man who has never set foot in Texas, much less Sabine County, and who never will. There is no heart in that rock, nor in the inscriptions upon it.

I know where Papa lies, and where he will for all time, and it is next to Carolina Cameron Holt, no matter what statement on what surface in what location at what amount of expense of dollars spent to achieve it. I am satisfied.

"I wish you would look at this," Abigail is saying to Richard, speaking to him because she knows from experience there is little chance to gain satisfaction from addressing me. I cannot give her what she wants and needs, to hear about Papa's stone, though she thinks it is a matter of will not rather than cannot where I am concerned. "I believe to my soul somebody has tried to plant a rose bush between these two gravestones and get it to grow."

Richard murmurs something to her I can't hear and turns to look back at me where I am standing by the blank spot Papa's first grave marker occupied, the place by Mama's small blue one. From a small boy, Richard has always been tender about the feelings of others, and he wants to be sure now he is not leaving me out while talking to his Aunt Abigail. I nod at him and smile, and he turns back to say something to her.

"By the way the ground's been dug up, that's how," Abigail says, making sure she's talking loud enough for me to hear every word. "And see that little broke-off root there? That's a cutting from a rose bush, and I bet it's a Victoria Pink."

Giving in, I walk on toward where my son and my sister are standing by Papa's stone and Nelda's grave, and I can tell that Abigail is glad to see me coming.

"Look," she says, pointing straight down at the spot between the stones where she is convinced she's discovered evidence of a rose bush planting, her finger held at a stiff angle as though she's telling somebody where not to step in order to avoid getting something nasty on clean footwear, "they are trying to force a rose bush to grow up between these gravestones."

"They are?" I say, neutral as I can make it, "who is?"

"Oh, some of that bottom bunch," Abigail says, "who can tell which one? Lurleen, maybe, or Frances Marie. It'd be just like that two to come up with the idea to coax a Victoria Pink rose bush to pop up between Nelda's and Papa's stones and twine all over them. Can you imagine how it would look? Pink roses just all over everywhere, just growing and blooming and smothering away."

Abigail sounds as though she's about to cry by now, so I say not a word back to her, neither to comfort nor conspire with her mood. Instead, I stand quiet near Richard and watch her pull at the rose cutting that speaks so contrary to her opinion of Papa and Nelda together, muttering beneath her breath and so eager to remove the offending Victoria Pink she has cut her hand on its thorns.

"Haven't you got a pocketknife?" Abigail says to Richard, not cross but rushed in her voice's delivery, "Can't you see I need a hand with this cursed flower bush?"

Richard says yes ma'am and bends to help Abigail prevent any chance of pink rose blossoms popping up between the gravestones of husband and wife dead together for the ages, and I lift my face toward a little breeze just sprung up, relieving to me in the bald sunlight of that part of Blue Water graveyard, out of the shade as we all are.

Papa's true gravestone is cool, too, I tell myself, where my dream tells me it stands in the bottom of its pond, fixed in position upright for all time and touched on each surface always by the hush of water. Quiet, dimmed, unseen.

"I've got it all pulled up," Abigail is saying, clutching a dirt-covered root before her in both hands, as though to prevent any possible movement by it toward escape, "There won't be any roses growing around here now."

"Good," I say to my sister. "Good for you."

Richard

They always talk to each other just like they're doing now, every time they come to Blue Water Chapel to look at the graveyard, Mama and Aunt Abigail do. When they get to going at each other this way, it puts me in mind of the time in school when Mr. Chambliss gets out one of his old books he tells us he studied in the academy and starts reading out loud to us. It's Latin, he tells us, and what I get from listening to him read it in his high little voice never makes any real sense. He could be reading anything to us, and saying it wrong on purpose, or leaving things out or putting wrong words in. How am I to be able to know? It's Latin.

But some of it sounds enough like words I do know and have heard and have read in books to make me think that what he's saying is actually true words that mean. There is something about what's coming out of his mouth to make me think that sensible matters are being treated of, people and places and things are being talked about, something took place sometime that somebody took notice of and wrote down.

Sometimes I imagine if I listen hard enough and take in what is being said out loud quick enough, why then I'd understand what he was issuing forth in a foreign language to me. It's foreign all right, I say to myself, but it's real close to making sense. If I could strain hard enough to get it in my head and my understanding, that is. Or if I could make myself want to strain that hard, maybe I could get my mind around enough of it to pick up some meaning, understand what's behind the sound.

So it is with Mama and Aunt Abigail, here in the middle of the Blue Water graveyard, standing next to my grandpa's headstone and the one by it, Aunt Nelda's. That is the spot, the very location where on each visit they start talking like a teacher reading Latin out loud in a schoolhouse to a bunch of half-grown boys and girls in East Texas.

Let me say it straight. Aunt Abigail and Mama are talking in English, all right, but the words they're saying, if you saw them written down on a piece of paper in print or in longhand, wouldn't be carrying near the meaning they have on them as they're going back and forth in the air between the two women right now in this place where all these dead people are under the ground.

Roses, Aunt Abigail is going on about, roses, pulling so hard on a root full of thorns that she cuts a gash in her hand deep enough to make blood run clear down to her wrist. Yet she is so glad to get the thing pulled up out of the ground between the gravestones that she's smiling like somebody's just handed her a Christmas gift. I'm glad she didn't give me time to get my pocketknife out to let her use when she asked for it. She probably would have cut a finger off, the way she was going at that rose bush, and not even noticed she'd done it, happy as she was to be finished with the job.

But she did put a stop to Aunt Nelda getting a flower bush started up by her head stone, Aunt Abigail did, and it was done all on her own, too. The reason that is such a satisfaction to her I don't understand completely, but I do know it comes from the same source that caused Aunt Abigail and Mama and the rest of my aunts and uncles to teach me and my brothers and sisters and all my cousins to call Grandpa Holt's wife Aunt Nelda instead of Grandma.

They let all of us know as soon as we could understand what they were saying, one by one as we got old enough to listen, that Grandpa's wife was not our grandma, but just a woman he lived with we were all supposed to call Aunt Nelda. Our real grandma was dead and buried in Blue Water Chapel graveyard, but that didn't matter. She was still truly our grandma and the mother of our mothers and fathers and the real wife of Grandpa Amos Holt, not that lady in his house, the one who managed somehow to have had half-children.

That notion of half-children, or half brothers and sisters, spooked me for a while when I was a chap, and I remember looking real hard at the uncles and aunts I was told were only half ones, whenever I happened to be around them, seldom though that was. Until I got old enough to have better sense, I believed that if I kept close watch on one of these half-uncles or half-aunts—Felder, say, or Effie or Nokomis or any one of them—that they might forget I was studying them and let me glimpse where the part was missing that would have made them a whole and not just a half uncle or aunt to me. But none of them ever slipped up and showed me that lack during those years I was young enough to believe they might. They always looked and seemed the same, up one side and down the other.

Aunt Abigail is still knocking that rose bush root against the top of Aunt Nelda's headstone to get the dirt off it, careful not to let any trash fly across the space between it and Grandpa Holt's and maybe land on his stone, even though I know she doesn't like the one cut for him or approve of it since it's not real somehow in her mind, and in a minute or so she's got the root cleaned up enough to allow her to sling it away to one side with a big grunt. You would think the root weighed as much as a cotton sack picked full-up.

I let my eyes follow it to where it comes down three or four graves away, over among some other family's stones, the Moye's I guess them to be, and that's when I first see the woman standing close to the bole of one of the big cedars, almost all hidden in the shadow of its branches, darker green than any of the hardwoods around it and not so easy to see into.

What my gaze first settles on are the shoes she's wearing, picked out of the cedar shadow by a beam of sunlight—hightops they are, a man's workshoes, worn and busted out with the toes curled up as they will come to be from getting wet and drying out over and over. There's no strings in the grommets, and it comes to my mind that you'd have to be thinking all the time if you were wearing them how you would have to step so as not to come out of your shoes whenever you put a foot down.

The legs going into the workshoes are thin and black, like straight lines drawn in ink on paper, and the woman is wearing a mingled-colored flour sack dress that comes down past her knees to just above the tops of the shoes. She has her arms crossed over her breast with one hand on top of the other one, so if she was in the same position lying down she would look like a woman laid out to be buried. But then, of course, she'd have her eyes closed, and that she sure doesn't. She's looking straight at me out of them, and they're not covered by a cedar branch in front of her which is hiding most of her face, and her eyes are opened wide, looking whiter and bigger than they really are, the way eyes always do on a person whose skin is black.

"Mama," I say, nodding toward the woman looking straight at me with her eyes fixed and unblinking, so big and white in the shadow, "Aunt Abigail, there's a colored lady over yonder standing inside that cedar tree."

Abigail

The root of that Victoria Pink has finally come loose after all my pulling on it, my nephew just standing there watching me work away at cleaning things up, when he says what he does about a woman inside of a cedar tree and her colored. My first thought is not even to listen to what he is saying. All his life back to the time when he was first beginning to learn to talk and right on up to the present day, Richard has been a boy who imagines things and makes up stories, stories not to fool whoever he's telling them to, really, but because he's made himself believe them and just has to give somebody an account of what he's come to think is true.

I remember Maude telling about how he would come in the house at the end of day at supper time, back before he was even big enough to be a help around the place, and she would find all manner of trash in his pockets when she was putting him and the rest of the bunch to bed. It'd be little rocks, or pieces of string, or leaves or maybe a bent nail somebody had thrown away, all manner of stuff, that Richard had found, and when his mother would chastise him for filling his clothes up with such truck, he'd start explaining how whatever it was she'd pulled out of his pocket was a thing he felt obliged to pick up.

Why? Because it was lost off from the rest of the things like it, he'd say, and it was lonely and afraid, and he felt like he had to bring it home to save it from the situation it was in. I'm talking about rocks now. And nails. And twigs and sticks. Just plain junk.

And then he'd cry and carry on, and Maude, would let him keep whatever was the current item of attention, and she'd indulge him in the story he told about it and listen to him like he was making sense and was onto something worth worrying about.

That behavior from a mother will ruin a child, naturally, and no one would ever find me making that mistake. But that was Maude, and her child, and none of mine, thank the Lord.

So when he says that thing there to us in Blue Water Chapel graveyard about a colored woman, I just think to myself, well, Richard's a little old to be seeing people growing out of trees or being part of one or whatever it is he means by that statement out of nowhere. I guess he's entertaining himself again, trying to pump a little interest into what's probably a boresome space of the day for him. So I take my time in looking up or giving any indication to my nephew that he's fooling me or diverting my attention away from what we're there in the Blue Water graveyard for, to honor Papa, and Mama, too, and to undo any foolishness of public display that bunch of Nelda's might be up to.

Maude, being all ears all the time to whatever Richard might volunteer to say, has shifted her position where she's standing, which I can tell by hearing her shoes crunch in that sandy Sabine County soil in the graveyard, and is looking just as hard as she can in the direction her boy has indicated. Sometimes I think if Richard was to tell her he'd spotted a whale in Double Pen Creek, she'd throw down whatever she was holding at the time, no matter what it was, and run down to the water's edge to see if she could harpoon it.

But then Maude speaks, and I know I'm obliged to look up from where I'm focused on getting Papa's headstone properly redded up, if I want to know what's going on.

"Why, hello," Maude says, "are you trying to stay out of this hot sun?"

I look up toward the cedar tree Richard has been facing, and still is, knowing that Maude will be looking at the exact same thing he is, and I'm thinking two things at once. One is that if you could draw two lines on a piece of paper to show how Maude's line of sight and Richard's would look side by side that you'd have to use a ruler to do it, they'd be that parallel. The other thing in my mind along with that notion is that by the way Maude is speaking, the tone in her voice and how she has cast her words, you wouldn't be able to tell if she was conversing with an imaginary colored woman in a cedar tree or Governor Branch Colquitt at a tea party in his mansion in the state capital. It is all the same to her, no matter who she's talking to.

But the colored woman is not imaginary, I see as soon as I straighten up to look where Maude and Richard are facing. My nephew didn't make her up for entertainment while his elders worked, after all, and she is stepping out from the shadow of a big cedar I hadn't even noticed the whole time we've been in the Blue Water Chapel graveyard, and she's fixing to say something back to the white lady that's just greeted her.

"Yes, ma'am," she says. "It is cooler in the shade, but I guess I wasn't thinking about that none."

The woman makes a good appearance, not mumbling her words and looking down at the ground so you can't understand her, as so many darkies will do when talking to a white person, and the dress she's wearing looks clean and fits her pretty well. Her gaze is toward Maude, as it ought to be, since that's the white lady who's spoken to her, but the woman's not looking directly at my sister, just a little off to one side, showing she's got manners and knows how to act.

That's a nice thing in a colored woman, or in a man, too, when they know how to do and let you see evidence of that fact, as soon as you start dealing with one of them. It doesn't take much of a sign to do that, to let you know the one before you is going to behave in a dutiful and civilized manner and that you don't have to be worrying the whole time that some kind of event between a white and a colored is fixing to take place.

What a colored man or woman giving such a signal to you does is simple enough, to run the risk of belaboring the point, and it's important, too. It greases the way to a clear communication. That's the way I see it. And, I swear, fully half the trouble that comes up between us as white folks and them as colored has got more to do with them not taking the time or effort to let the white person understand there's no reason for concern, nor harm is intended. But to do that, of course, requires the colored to think ahead and be mindful of appearances and the possibility of misunderstanding.

That is not the black man's long suit, thinking ahead. Nor the black woman's neither, though being a woman helps in all cases of understanding what somebody other than yourself might be thinking or meaning, no matter what color you are. Men are the ones who fly off the handle, not women, nine times out of ten, and men are the ones who go off half-cocked about situations.

But this woman now before me, talking politely to Maude like she's doing, and showing she knows how to address a white lady, I do feel good about right off, though I don't know who she is or what she's doing in Blue Water Chapel graveyard. She's dressed presentable, in addition to the way she's carrying herself in front of the white people she's faced with, she has got a nice head cloth tied close and flat around the front of her hair and hanging down loose in the back, showing she wants to control the way kinky hair can lump up on a colored person's head if they're not careful, and she's holding one hand in the other in a composed way, which testifies she's ready to pay due attention to what's going on and her part in it.

I can tell she is not fully calm, though. She is nervous, but holding it in. Her lips, which are not real thick ones, are tight pressed together, and there's a little tremor in her hands, clasped together so close as they appear to be. Some of that condition is understandable, and I would expect her to be on edge about what's going on, her being in a white graveyard by herself having to talk to white folks who belong where they're standing.

So when she says what she does to Maude about the difference between being in the shade and standing in the sun, I figure I ought to speak up, too, say something or other, not just let my sister set the tone of the conversation with this strange colored woman who's popped up in Blue Water graveyard unannounced, notwithstanding that she seems to know how to act when dealing with a white lady who's just spoken to her.

"And what might that be?" I say in a clear voice, careful not to hurry my words, "This matter you're thinking about other than how it is today?"

"This is my sister," Maude says to the woman, as if she's just asked my name and Maude is compelled to answer, "Mrs. Abigail Mott, and I'm Maude Winston."

"She's married, too," I say to the colored woman who is still looking at Maude, despite the fact I'm the one speaking, "just like me. Winston is her husband's name, not her maiden name. We're Holts. Me and my sister, Mrs. Winston, both of us are. Holts."

"Yes, ma'am," the colored woman says, turning her attention finally to the woman who's been talking to her, me, I mean. "I done already know that, Miss Abigail."

"Mott," I hear myself say back at her quick, twice, "Mrs. Mott." I don't even have to think to do it; the words just come out when I hear her call me by my first name like that. The woman has moved further away from the cedar tree where she's been standing, a good deal closer to us and Richard a little way behind still, and Maude actually reaches out a hand toward her when she hears my first name come out of the woman's mouth, as if my sister is about to touch her on the arm.

"I know you," Maude says, "You're Joleen, Joleen Bobo."

"Yes, ma'am, Miss Maude," the colored woman says, now a step even closer to my sister, who's smiling at her like the sun coming up in the morning, "but I'm like y'all are now. Married, too. I'm Joleen Broussard now."

"Broussard," Maude says and then does reach out to grab hold of the colored woman's shoulders, using both hands to do it and moving to face her head on, "what a pretty name that is. It's French, isn't it, Joleen?"

"Yes, ma'am, Miss Maude," the woman says, "redbone French." She's smiling too now, not so much as Maude is—nobody's ever smiled as big as she does when she feels like it—but the two of them together, white and black in Blue Water Chapel graveyard, are fairly beaming at each other. But as soon as I can notice that to even remark on it to myself, the colored woman's smile turns down, and she just of a sudden bursts into tears, as the saying goes, just sobbing and moaning with her hands all drawn up to her cheeks as though she is trying to keep her face from splitting in two. Maude is embracing her, as if the woman is a child grieving over something lost and gone, and my sister is cooing like a turtle dove and saying the woman's name over and over.

"Joleen," Maude says, "Joleen, what's the matter, honey? What's wrong?"

"Maybe she's just overjoyed to see you again, Maude," I say, "All broke up over it." Neither one of them pays me or what I've said any mind, though, and I am not surprised one bit by that. They're just having a high old time, standing there hugging and crying over each other not over twenty feet from the graves of mine and Maude's mother and father, and I note to myself for future consideration that at least Maude is proving she's still capable of shedding a tear in Blue Water graveyard. By now she's proving that by joining Joleen in her weeping, and that's the first time I've seen my sister cry in the vicinity of Papa's grave in years. That breaks a drought.

I remember Joleen Bobo by now, and I did as soon as Maude said her name before all their waterworks got started up. Not having thought in years about her or any of the rest of that family of colored folks who sharecropped down in the Sabine River bottom close to our family's old place all that time ago, I couldn't have been expected to recognize Joleen all grown up at the age she is now, backed up into the shade of a cedar tree in Blue Water graveyard. Why should I have?

"I guess your mama and daddy are dead by now," I say to her, trying to get a little attention directed away from all the crying that's going on and toward some sensible communication between grown women. "I know our's are gone now, these many years, mine and my sister's, Mrs. Winston's." I point over toward Papa's real grave, the empty spot next to Mama's little old blue stone, but neither one of the two of them there, still locked up in an embrace, make a sign of looking where I'm directing them, still too wrapped up in commiseration.

"Papa's buried yonder, but you can't tell it if you don't know how to find his resting place. We could tell you a story about that, Joleen, that would make a stone cry, if we had time to do it, me and my sister. Couldn't we, Maude?"

My saying that seems to make some difference in the situation before me, and both women break their holds on each other and step back a little, though Maude keeps a hand on Joleen's shoulder, patting away at it as if she has been assigned the task of soothing the woman down and is determined to make her best effort at it. I look over at my nephew, and Richard is studying the ground at his feet as though he has found something fascinating to consider about sandy soil in East Texas. I feel like saying something reassuring to him, something like "Just hold on for a while longer, son, and your mama will be calmed down here directly enough to rejoin the human race," but I don't say that, of course.

"Yes, ma'am," Joleen says, "Miss Abigail. I know where your papa and mama are buried. I seen both of them put into the ground here at Blue Water them years ago."

"You did?" I say, not believing a word of it, but figuring she meant well by the statement. They will say whatever they think a white person would like to hear from them, about any matter. I have never held that against colored people, though, like some people will do when they're arguing that you can't believe a word a darky says to you. Black folks do mean well, most of the time, when they're telling you stuff like Joleen is saying, and they're like children that way. As long as you understand that and can separate out the truth from the fiction they give you, you can know how much to depend on their stories and statements. It just takes patience and experience, and a whole lot of forebearance.

"How did you happen to do that?" I say, pushing Joleen just a little to see how much truth I could get out of what she had just said, conscious or not. "I didn't see you here, and I do believe I would've noticed you. I saw everybody that came to Papa's and Mama's funerals both."

"No, ma'am, Miss Abigail, you wouldn't have seen us, over where we was standing in the woods yonder."

Joleen points across the graveyard toward a stand of pine and youpon and palmetto where the ground slopes down toward the spring that bubbles up at the base of the hill. I never spent any time over there even when I was a young'un at the graveyard workings. It's too snaky for me and for anybody else who's got sense enough to be careful where they put their feet in the woods.

"We?" I say to Joleen, who at least by now has stopped all that crying and carrying on and is speaking clear enough to be well understood. "You said we. Was somebody else with you?"

"My sister," she says, "she and me always liked your mama and the way she treated us when we used to play with Miss Maude back in behind y'all's place them years ago."

"I think many times about those days," Maude speaks up to say, and I'm afraid if she gets started into recalling childhood memories with this colored woman we might be in for another session of crying and carrying on, so I rush on to ask another question, which I already know the answer to.

"What is her name, your sister? Isn't she a twin to you?"

"Yes, ma'am. She was. Boleen her name was, and she's been gone now for over two years."

Oh, Lord, I think to myself, this will get her all fired up again, her twin being dead, and we'll never get to the bottom of why they were sneaking around Blue Water graveyard, watching white folks bury their kin. What's going to be next?

"Boleen's with Jesus, now," she says, teetering on breaking down, but she doesn't as she keeps on talking, thank the Lord for small favors. "That keeps my mind satisfied, knowing that Boleen's done in Gloryland before us and that I'll see her up yonder again and we'll be together for eternity."

"So y'all watched Mrs. Amos Holt's burial," I hurry on to say, keeping things moving as well as I can manage it, "and Reverend Holt's, too."

"We did," Joleen says. "Yes, ma'am."

"I'm so glad to hear that," my sister pipes up. "That was so good of you and Boleen to do that. I wish I had known that before."

"Reverend Holt did many a good deed for my daddy and mama," says Joleen, " and I done told you ladies I thought the world of your mama, Mrs. Holt. So did Boleen. We just wanted to come see their funerals at Blue Water Chapel and think about their souls going on to be with the Lord."

"Thank you, Joleen, thank you," Maude says, her voice all low and choked up, so I see I've got to plunge in again to provide some direction to things so I'll be able to find out why in the world this colored woman has showed up from the past here at Blue Water on the very day Maude and Richard and I arrive from fifty-two miles and a county away.

So I ask her in the form of a direct and pointed question, and after just a little hemming and hawing she gets some explanation out for us to consider. She says she knew we were coming, though I don't see how that's possible, and when I press her to prove the truth of what she's claiming, she relates that some colored man got word to her about the progress we were making in the wagon from Double Pen Creek, and the way he knew came from another colored man that had connections with Mr. Fate Waldrup on whose place we had spent the night before.

She doesn't say how all that communication got to her and how she got to Blue Water Chapel before we did, Joleen doesn't, and I think to myself it must have been by African tom tom, but I don't say that out loud, though I do think it's a funny thought, one Joleen wouldn't understand and Maude for sure wouldn't appreciate or ever forget I'd said, if I said it out loud.

Colored folks have ways of getting news around, that's all I know, and it doesn't depend on government mail service or telegraph wires or telephones, even if there happened to be that kind of machinery in Sabine County that they could get at and use. When they need to know something or want to know it, they will and do find it out and then spread the news everywhere.

All this about how Joleen happened to be standing in the shade of that big cedar tree waiting on us when we got to Blue Water Chapel takes me a while to learn, what with Maude's interruptions of Joleen's discourse and her encouraging words to the woman as she parcels out the story. I shouldn't leave out how its progress also has to wait for Maude to remember out loud the happy times together as girls running through the woods she and Joleen and Boleen had enjoyed, catching turtles, picking blackberries, tying June bugs on strings, and getting into I don't know what all.

I know one thing that comes to my mind during Maude's reminiscences. If my sister and those colored twins had done half of what she claims and had Mama found out about it, Maude would've been a child well-acquainted with a limber switch across her legs.

I don't quarrel with anything she says, not wanting to prolong the performance, but I am well satisfied with the amount of childhood memories Maude trots out long before she runs out of her supply of them.

So when she slows down at the conclusion of one of her anecdotes, something about her and Joleen and Boleen finding a baby squirrel in the woods and trying to raise it on cow's milk—an event I have no recollection of, and I am a woman known by all for remembering—I see a chance to jump into the conversation.

"Did you just want to say how-do-you-do to me and Mrs. Winston then?" I say to Joleen. "That's why you came to Blue Water when whoever this man was told you we were on our way up here?"

"I am glad to see you, Miss Abigail, you and Miss Maude, I certainly am, but that's not why I come out here to wait for y'all to get here in your wagon. No'm, it's not just that."

Maude is giving me one of her looks, her head turned a little to one side and her eyes cut over at an angle, like she is just daring me to say something that she knows is coming and despises to hear. As always, I can't predict just what that terrible thing is that she dreads so to hear me say, and I don't know any method of figuring it out. So I just speak up.

"If you're looking to borrow some money, Joleen, I can't help you, and I don't calculate that Mrs. Winston can, neither."

In answer to that, my sister says my name to me like it is something that hurts her mouth to spit out, her voice almost like a growl, and then she adds on to that a curse word, not even under her breath, but loud enough for Joleen to hear perfectly plain and her standing there a colored woman.

"The Lord's name in vain," I snap right back at Maude, and I'm proud to say that I'm not even feeling like I'm in danger to cry yet, "you just took His name in vain right in the presence of Papa's grave, right here at Blue Water Chapel."

"I can say *Jesus* all I want to," Maude says back to me in that same tone of voice, "Jesus, Jesus, Abigail, Jesus, Jesus, Jesus."

I am speechless, of course, on hearing that kind of use of the name of our Lord and Savior coming from my sister in such a location, but Joleen begins to talk, answering the question I had posed to her, acting and sounding like she has not even heard the exchange between me and Maude. Maybe she's not understanding what just took place, I think, and believes that there's only one way to say the name of *Jesus* and that it can't be misused so as to sound like a curse word. Such a simple faith and a simple mind must be a blessing and a consolation to those so constructed, but that's not me. No, I know better, and I understand what's going on between people, almost all the time, and that's the burden I have been given and have to endure. But I wouldn't trade that talent for anything, nor hide it under a bushel.

"No, ma'am, Miss Abigail," Joleen is saying while I look deliberately directly at her as she speaks, though I can feel, like a heavy presence, a pressure, on the side of my face, Maude aiming that look and the expression of her eyes at me. The skin of my left cheek feels hot and drawn from the weight of that gaze.

"That's not why I decided to come here to Blue Water just as soon as I found out from Sully Boatwright that y'all was on your way in the wagon. I hadn't planned to ask nobody for no money. I don't need that. I need y'all to help me."

"Help you?" I say. "How in the world can we help you, Joleen?"

"I need y'all to help me save him. You the only ones I could think of, and when Sully told me you was coming to Blue Water, I knowed the Lord was figuring a way to answer my prayers. He's sending Miss Maude. And you, too, Miss Abigail."

"Save who?" Maude says, "Who are you meaning, Joleen?"

Maude's voice when she says that is different as night from day from the way it sounded when she was speaking to me not a minute before, and I literally can feel the pressure ease on the side of my face where my sister has been laying her look of utter meanness on me. Thank goodness she's aiming her attention in some other direction, I am thinking, even if her doing that is evidence she cares more about a colored woman's feelings than her own sister's, and that colored woman somebody she hasn't seen since they were girls running through the woods together like wild Comanches.

"Eldridge," Joleen says, and I can tell she's on the verge of another spell of tears, "my husband Eldridge Broussard, that who and that's all."

"Save your husband?" I say. "Is it drink or gambling? Won't he work, Joleen, to earn y'all a living? Maybe the one to help you is your preacher, if you believe your husband needs saving from some weakness of character."

"No, ma'am. It ain't nothing like that. Eldridge done gave his heart to the Lord a long time ago. He's a churchgoing Christian man and been that way long as I known him."

"What's wrong, then?" Maude says in that same soft voice she seems to use with most everybody in the world but you know who. "What is your trouble, Joleen, you and your husband?"

"The worst kind it is, Miss Maude," Joleen says, "the very worst kind a colored man can have."

I start listing in my mind what kinds of trouble that a colored man might think was the worst that could happen to him, or at least what a colored woman would think was the worst predicament a colored man could get himself into, and I haven't got past wondering if there was a possible way Saturday night could be outlawed, just removed from the calendar somehow, when Joleen goes on to tell us what the cause of her being in Blue Water Chapel graveyard today is.

"They claiming Eldridge did something to a white lady, but it ain't true what they saying, and if they catch him they going to hang my husband to a tree."

A loud buzz comes into my ears and head, so strong I can't hear anything of what Maude is saying to Joleen, though I can see her lips moving and know that she's talking to the woman who has by now collapsed onto her knees next to somebody's grave, mounded up to show that the family of the dead person buried there still takes good care of what's left of them in this world. Maude drops down beside Joleen and is holding her again all clutched up to her breast, and Joleen's mouth is twisted and her eyes shut tight as though she is a woman who's been in a dark cave and has been snatched out all of a sudden into bright sunshine and cannot bear the burning light.

Somebody is not there, somebody who was, and I look around to see who it might be, like a person will do trying to see something they actually know is not present but can't stop themselves from looking for. I see my nephew Richard who's moved off to do something with the mules still hitched to the wagon, and when I glimpse him I feel a relief that maybe he is the one I've missed, and that feeling lets me start to hear something again other than the deep buzzing sound in my head.

I can tell Maude is talking to Joleen now by hearing her, though I can't make out what she's saying yet, her words just a murmur on a level beneath the rise and fall of the whirring inside me.

"Richard," I call out loud, thinking if he hears me and looks my direction that will mean he is the one I thought was missing and things will begin to come together again in the graveyard and we'll all be back where we were before Joleen said what she did.

But he doesn't look up from whatever he's doing to the mule harness, and that tells me he's not the one I thought gone missing. Richard is there, I can count him and Maude and me and Joleen on four fingers. But there's still one not there that I cannot find to number, no matter where I look.

Maude

Somewhere in the thicket of pines and palmetto and yaupon that comes all the way up to the last row of graves at Blue Water a mockingbird is calling like a mourning dove and is doing a good job of it, the sequence and number of notes it copies convincing enough to persuade anybody listening. But the tone is not right, too deep for a bird the size of a mocker to reproduce, and not resonant in the way a dove makes it when its song carries that dark sound of loss and solitude.

Thinking of that distinction between a good performance by the mockingbird with no living investment of feeling and that dark song of the mourning dove which can call forth a true absence in the listener's heart helps me as I kneel there in the graveyard, my arms around Joleen. I keep my mind on that difference, even after the mockingbird has hushed its attempt to deliver the dove's song, and has gone on to a bird's song easier to copy.

In a little while, Joleen will tell us more and maybe we'll be able to understand then what she means and think of a way to comfort if not aid her, but in the meantime she has to weep and mourn and there's nothing to be done to lengthen or hurry that. What she expresses she must express, and that is no copy trotted out for display.

I look up at Abigail who's standing with both arms extended as though she is balancing on a log thrown across a stream for a bridge and is afraid to move forward or back. Wobbling a little from side to side, she moves her head in a semi-circle as she appears to be looking for something and then she calls out my son's name.

"Richard," she says, twice, her voice gathering strength the second time she speaks. "Richard."

He pretends not to hear, fixing his attention even more firmly on whatever he's found to do at the wagon. My son doesn't want to be where he is, as he has not for most of his life. The thing he dreads most are people disagreeing and yelling at each other, particularly the women folk in his family, and especially his Aunt Abigail seeking to enlist him in some exchange between her and me.

Abigail seems to have found some better purchase on the sandy ground of Blue Water graveyard and has let her arms drop to her side, having crossed that treacherous log to the other side of the stream, I figure, and now she is touching her forefinger on one hand to the tips of the ones on the other, over and over.

"Abby," I say, "Abby, are you feeling all right? Are you faint?"

Joleen is withdrawing to herself now, beginning to wipe her eyes with the sleeve of her dress, and I expect we'll begin to learn more from her soon. Richard has unhitched the mules, and they are cropping at weeds and grass, and I sit back and begin dusting away at the sand on the front of my dress.

"Who is it, Maude?" Abigail asks me. "Who is it? I can't get them counted up right, no matter how many times I go over it. See, look at this. One, two, three, four."

"We'll figure it out later, Abby," I say. "Go over to the wagon, please, and bring me that jug of water. Joleen is completely parched, and so am I."

As Abigail trots toward the wagon at a good clip, looking relieved to be told what to do, I think back to the first time I met Joleen and remember we were both thirsty then and looking for a drink of water.

Behind our first dwelling place in Sabine County was a little spring at the foot of a hill at least a quarter of a mile from the log house Papa had built for us. We used it for our supply of water for the first couple of years we lived there, but carrying buckets that far was a burden to all of us, especially during the daylight hours when Papa was clearing land and planting and chopping cotton and bringing in crops and all the rest of the work that goes into farming. So as he could find time and get other folks to help him, he got the property close to the house witched by Mr. Jesse McNeill who had the diviner's gift, and he dug a well where the willow fork indicated the sweet vein of water underground would be.

It was a good well, and the water was clear and always abundant, but it bothered me always that it was quiet and dead and unmoving. When the sun was at the right angle in the sky, I could look over the edge of the plank enclosure built around the well and see the surface below as blank and fixed as a mirror, showing my face staring back at me smaller than it really was, of course, and so dark I couldn't make out my features.

I never liked what looking into that still water said to me about the existence beneath the surface of the earth—the silent, the fixed, the unchanging, the inexhaustible nature below what we all walked around on. It said to me that all our movement to and fro, the freedom we assumed was ours to go where we wanted, the way we talked and made plans and laughed and ate and drank—all that was a lie. Nothing ever really moved. And we were fooled by thinking so.

To save myself from dwelling on the truth revealed to me in the still water of our well, I made it my habit back then to drink only from the old spring, our first source for water for our life in Texas. The water in the spring bubbled up in constant supply, it moved and rushed and sang and flowed, and it was alive. When I dropped pebbles or leaves or flower blossoms into the bowl it had scooped out for itself, the spring pushed these things aside, tumbled them over and over, carried them away in the stream it made as it worked away day and night, in light and shade and darkness.

But when I dropped a pebble into the well near the house where we Holts all lived, it made a plunking sound and a ring of ripples disturbed the image of my face in the water, but that movement slowed always to a stop, and the mirror of water was still and fixed and dead again.

The day I met Joleen I had gone down to the spring to drink and watch the water bubble and flow in the manner I had come to count on, and I remember I had gotten hot on the way, coming across the field of cotton, almost waist high to me that time of year. It was cooler by the spring, as always, and I was kneeling beside it, my face wet from plunging my head into the water over and over, to cool off and to drink from it. I always kept my eyes open when I did that, thinking that someday I'd be able to see the exact spot from which the water came from the darkness of the earth into the light of day in the life above ground. I never could see the exact source, naturally, that hole into the earth beneath, but I always sought it.

I had just lifted my face from the surface again for a breath of air, my eyes too full of water to see anything but a blur when someone spoke.

"I always look for little fish when I do that," the voice said. "But I never did see one, not nary a time I have looked."

That was Joleen speaking, a colored girl I had seen only at a distance before then, with her sisters and brothers and now and then a grown person or two in the yardplace of the little cabin across Hickory Creek which marked the boundary of our property. I didn't know her name, nor that she had a twin or anything about her or her people, except that they were colored and lived on a place we could see from where we lived.

I don't remember what I said back to her then at the spring or anything else about the time we met on that hot day, but it proved to be the beginning of a phase where we saw each other almost every day for what must have lasted for over two years.

Then that phase stopped on a single day, one I didn't mark at the time and never thought about since, and Joleen left my consciousness of her as though a door closed to a room I had been in once and was never to enter again. Why that time ended, I don't know, except to think that grownups were a part of it. That, and Valery Blackstock, who was to become my husband. When I think of that time now, what comes to mind is the spring where I first met Joleen.

The water bubbling then in that spring pushed on as steady as ever, and what it touched moved with it, and it still does, it still does, it still does.

"See what my sister has brought us," I say to Joleen, calmer now beside me in the graveyard, "a jug of water that's been sitting in the shade. Don't you want a drink from it? It's still a little cool."

Joleen

I do not feel sorry for myself, never a time, no matter what is happening to me or my own. I was taught that from when I was a child, and my daddy was the one who brought it home to me, that way of doing and looking at life in this world and getting through it the best way you can.

It took him a while to do that, with me and my twin sister and the other sisters and my brothers, too. It's a lesson you have to get in your mind over and over, he would say to me, and you have to learn it by heart. You don't get that lesson by hearing me tell you to get it, neither, he would say, the way you understand what a bird's name is when somebody tells you and you remember you supposed to call that name each time you see that same bird or hear it holler in the woods.

That is a connection that can be told you, and it is a easy thing to get right the first time you hear it and then carry with you the rest of your days without having to worry about whether you got it right. You ain't got to check it for the truth every time you see a blue jay. That bird is always a blue jay, and if you got normal human understanding, you got that right and you got it learned the first time through.

But there's another way of getting a thing set in your head and in your heart, and it is never just a simple connection another person can tell you once and be done with it.

"It goes like and is like this, but it comes to your understanding a little at the time, bit by bit, and it is engraved upon your heart, the mind behind your mind, in the same way I can take a pocketknife and carve you a doll out of a piece of soft pine that wasn't nothing but a lump of wood before I got to work on it. You understand what I'm telling you, child?"

"No," I said, "I don't, Daddy."

"Child," he said, "Joleen, pay attention, you and your sister."

He's telling us this while we're sitting by the fireplace. It's cold outside, but the fire is built up and the whole house is warm, and I can see the shadows of the flames on the hard clay wall of the chimney behind where the fire's burning. They're making all that they touch move up and down, not the same way each time, but it's still the same fire burning and the same fireplace and the same house and my daddy the same man talking to us. I like that, and I can tell Boleen does, too, though she never talks as much as I do or asks as many questions.

It's good when it's cold outside, but warm inside, and I shiver a little bit because I want to, not because something's making me do it. Shivering makes it better.

"Yes, Daddy," I say. "Tell us some more, but not about the blue jay, the other thing. I understand already about the blue jay's name and the way I know how to call it."

"When you're hungry," Daddy says, talking to us, but looking at the fire burning and the shadows it makes on the clay wall of the fireplace, "when you're hungry, how do you know that? Does somebody have to tell you? Does your mama have to say she believes you want something or another to eat?"

"No sir," says Boleen, the first thing she has said that night. "I just know it all by myself."

"That's right," Daddy says and looks at her and nods his head. "And the way you know it is because you tell yourself what it is your feeling means. It's inside you, the thing you know and have learned, and it don't depend on nobody else letting you know what it means."

"How did you learn it in the first place, then?" I say, "if nobody told you what it was and the right word to call it?"

"Bit by bit," my daddy says, "Bit by bit, from the inside out. You learned it as you went along, and it all come to you that way because you was made to know it, and that's the way you got that lesson. It becomes your own because you got it by heart, from all the things you go through in your life, day by day, staying in the world and making it through by noticing and bearing down by yourself, just like you got to do."

He stopped talking for a minute and looked back at the fire and the shadows moving up and down, never the same but coming from the same place always, no matter how the shapes it's making might change from one thing to the other.

"Depend," my daddy says to me and Boleen, "on yourself. Get it by heart."

So I did learn that by heart, and I never do feel sorry for myself, no matter what troubles come to me in this world. And I still keep what I learned by heart inside me, without worrying about it any more than the flames of a fire care anything about the shape of the shadows they cast, and how the shapes can change, big and little, clear and cloudy. They got no choice and are not able to find their own way, and neither am I or anybody else that's got knowledge locked inside them, learned by heart.

I take my troubles and sorrows one by one as they come to me, and I think about the shadows on the wall and where they come from, and I get through the living I got to do in this world, by putting my mind in that location.

So did my twin sister Boleen, I know and feel in my heart, and so could anyone else of my brothers and sisters that paid mind to what our daddy said about lessons and the way they're learned. Not everybody can give full attention to what is offered them, though, and even if you do, there come shaky times when nothing is solid and you forget the true names of what makes up the world and this life in it.

What difference does it make, I have done asked myself when times have come hard on me, what word is stuck to what? What does bird mean, or cotton, or water, or work, or living itself, when nothing seems to have any weight you can appreciate or lay hand to?

But when I have found myself thinking that way, when I have tried to put too much faith in what somebody else has told me is true and real and matters most, I think of that firelight rising and falling as it casts its shadows, not caring what the shapes might mean or if they even do mean. Then there comes what comforts and soothes me, and that's the things I have got by heart.

Boleen, my twin, is dead now, and that's all right. And Eldridge Broussard, my husband, is hiding in a canebrake by the white folks' graveyard at Blue Water Chapel, no more home left for him and me together than if he was the last bear in Sabine County, Texas, one jump ahead of a pack of baying dogs.

But I'm thinking of the shadows thrown by fire on a clay wall, and I am depending on what I got by heart and on myself.

I am through crying about it now for a while, and looking at Maude Holt, I can tell by her eyes that she is about through just remembering me and her as children playing together them long years ago and is beginning to study on my predicament. She is coming to terms with what's real now here on this hot day in a graveyard, not just what used to be, and that makes my heart lift.

I can feel it in my breast, beginning to rise up, as I see Maude turn her mind in the direction of where we be now, with everything dislocated and shook apart.

"You want some more water, Joleen?" she says. "Where is he right now?"

"He's just yonder," I say. "In the middle of the canebrake just the other side of the spring where we used to go, you and me."

Maude's big sister hears me tell that location, and she begins to sway back and forth again like she was before Maude sent her for the water jug. She's not knocking her fingers together over and over this time, though, like she was before. But she's bad restless.

"Lord," Abigail says, sounding like she's fixing to start moaning, "Lord, what did your husband do to that poor white woman, Joleen? What did he do?"

"Abigail," Maude says before I can begin to think what to say back, her voice as hard as I ever heard it, "he didn't do anything. You heard what Joleen said. Mr. Broussard didn't do anything to anybody."

"Mr. Broussard? " Abigail says. "Mr. Broussard? Who?"

"His name is Eldridge," I say. "That's his given name."

"All right, then," Maude says, "Eldridge. Eldridge Broussard is the name of Joleen's husband, Abigail, and we'll be meeting him here in a little while, I expect. Until then, I want you to go talk to Richard about the mules and the shape they're in this morning after that fifty miles they pulled the wagon from Double Pen Creek in the last couple of days."

"Fifty-two miles," Abigail says, sounding a little like a schoolteacher. "It's a good fifty-two miles."

"You're right, Abby," Maude says. "I never have had your head for figures."

She stops talking and looks off toward the treeline and the shadows the sun is casting, and so do I. It's a little before one o'clock.

"By about two this afternoon," Maude says, "we ought to be able to start back toward home, don't y'all think?"

"I thought we were going to see if we could find some crepe myrtle somewhere for cuttings," Abigail says, "and bring some back here and plant them by Papa's grave, his real one. Now you're telling me we can't?"

"We can do all that, too," Maude says. "I expect Joleen knows right where to go to get some crepe myrtle. Don't you, Joleen?"

"Y'all want pink, or y'all want purple, I know exactly where we can get the prettiest in Sabine County. Drova Jessup has got a yard full of both kinds at her house. Even got some crossbred, pink and purple on the same bush."

"You don't mean it," Maude says. "I never saw that done before."

"I have read about it," Abigail says. She's looking like she's standing more flatfooted on the ground now, and she's swigging away at the water jug like she is full thirsty. "It was in a book Ferguson got from somewhere. I already knew about that subject, how that will happen in nature."

Abigail looks over at me now to let me know something. "Ferguson is my husband. Ferguson Mott, that's who I'm referring to when I say that name."

"Yes, ma'am," I say.

"My sister keeps up with current developments," Maude says. "She always has, since the time we were children together here in this part of the country on the old place."

"Well," Abigail says, "I have always liked to read up on things and keep current."

"You always had a book in your hand, Miss Abigail," I say, "I remember that like it was yesterday."

"Let's go get us something to eat," Maude says, reaching out to touch Abigail on the arm and get her started up to moving. "Mrs. Waldrup packed us some biscuits and ham slices, wasn't it, Abigail?"

"Pork shoulder," Abigail says, "some call that ham. I don't, because shoulder's not ham."

It seems like the air in the graveyard has lightened up somehow, like it will after a rain has finally come after threatening for a long time, and I can feel myself being able to get my breath better. We all go to where the young man they been calling Richard has got the wagon and the mules under the shade of a sycamore, and Abigail pulls some food out of a clean sack in the wagon bed, pokes it at me, and then starts eating away like she is plumb hungry.

I can't stand to look at what she's eating, but I drink me some more water and ask Maude if I can put aside a little of what they got for Eldridge to eat when I go back to where he's lying down hid in among all that cane. She has already thought about that, naturally, as she would, and shows me what she has put together for me to give him.

"Am I allowed to ask Joleen now what's been going on with her husband and that white lady, Maude?" Abigail says, then she tells Richard to go down to the spring and fill up the water jug. "I don't want him listening to what Joleen may have to say," she explains to me and Maude, but neither one of us says anything right back to her.

"Joleen may tell us whatever else she sees fit to," Maude says, as we all watch the young man follow the path out of the graveyard down the hill toward the spring. You can't see him for the underbrush after he takes the first two steps out of the clearing. "If she wants to speak about her and her husband's trouble, we'll listen. But if she doesn't, that won't influence what we do."

So I start telling them what has happened, and as I begin to do it, I feel like I did a minute ago when the air seemed to lighten up and let me breathe better. It seems to help the way I feel when I start to talk and to let go a little bit of what I been holding back inside me.

We are standing in the shade of one of the big sycamores at Blue Water, the mules and Abigail making eating sounds as I begin to talk, and here is what I start to tell the Holt sisters. As I talk and lay things out, it begins to help me in my own mind to get what happened set out straight.

"Eldridge and me been cropping twelve acres of cottonland for Mr. Lee Lester for a long time. I don't know how many years it's been now, but it goes back a good long while it seems like."

"I know Lee and that whole bunch of Lesters," Abigail says as she's finishing up her last bit of that pork shoulder and biscuit. "Him and the Sexton girl he married, Edith her name is."

"Not no more," I say, "Mrs. Edith Lester done dead, and that's part of the story, but that comes later." When I say that, Maude holds up her hand to Abigail like she is stopping a child from busting into the grown people's conversation, and Abigail hushes up, looking a little pouty again, but I'm glad Maude does that. Abigail won't be putting in her share, like she always has liked to do, so I'm going to be able to keep things straight and move along the way I need to do to get what I'm remembering told right.

"I say Eldridge and me been sharing that crop, but I mean we done it along with our children, too. Of course, a boy or girl bound to leave home when they get old enough, and so everything changes bit by bit, but me and Eldridge stay the same.

"Everything go along all right for a long time with Mr. Lee Lester, it go along, go along, go along. Sometime the cotton come in good, sometime it don't, sometime it rain when you need it, sometime it don't. Y'all know all about farming. I don't need to tell you the ups and downs, and the droughts and the floods and the boll weevils."

"Not hardly," Abigail says, but that's all she feel she have to add, and I ask for it when I say y'all. I remind myself not to do that again. We got things to do here, and Maude has got to have time to figure out what they going to be, so I get back quick into putting people and what they done into the right way for making sense of a situation.

"When the trouble started up between Mr. Lee Lester and my husband, it come after Mrs. Edith Lester died and Mr. Lee Lester married him a new wife.

"It was some kind of a sickness in her breast killed Miss Edith," I say fast to cut Abigail off from asking about that and getting me all sidetracked again. "It come up quick, and it killed her quick. She was walking around one day, pert as could be, and they was burying her less than two months later, right here in this graveyard. I could show y'all her marker if we had the time, but we don't."

"In her breathing, or in the heart itself?" Abigail says, but I act like I don't hear her because I'm thinking what to say next. I go on talking.

"Mr. Lee Lester didn't stay single long after his wife died, but he went after getting married again quick, like a man will do lots of times. They are used to having a wife, even if they don't know it during the time they got one. So he married a widow lady from up around Teneha, and showed up one day on his place with her and her child, the only one she ever had, from her husband that died. The lady's name is Corinne, and her little girl was Alice Jeanne.

"She was the one that caused it all, that little girl Alice Jeanne, but it wasn't no fault of her's. What happened to Eldridge and me come out of her being in the world, that poor child, like things will. When one rock starts sliding down a hill, it make another one start moving, too. But it didn't mean nothing to begin with, that one rock when it slipped loose, nothing you could see coming.

"She was the same age as our granddaughter, the one who live with me and Eldridge because her mama can't take care of her no more. I say can't, not won't. My grand and Alice Jeanne remind me of how me and Miss Maude used to play together all the time back when we was little here in Sabine County, them years ago."

"What's her name?" Maude says. "Your granddaughter?"

"Opal," I tell her. "Opal and Alice Jeanne just two little girls together, playing all around the place whenever they could, and that was most days, since Mrs. Lee Lester, the new wife to him, she liked for her girl to have the company. She told me that, Miss Corinne did, many a time.

"That went on for over a year, and them little girls was never cross with each other, and they knew how to act, and they purely enjoyed themselves. And Mr. Lee Lester, he never took no notice, nor exception, and neither did anybody else.

"And then, oh Lord, it happened, and sometime it seem like it was a long time ago and sometime it feel to me like it was just yesterday on that morning when my grandbaby come running up from the creek bottom screaming and covered with mud and her eyes just wild."

"What was it?" somebody says, and this time it's not Abigail, but Richard who's speaking, standing at the far side of the wagon from where I am, holding a jug of water, back from the spring.

"That baby had got snakebit," I say, "not Opal, it was Alice Jeanne, and I had always told them girls not to play down there where it's water moccasins all over the place."

"We always used to," Maude says, "you and me."

"Yes, ma'am, we did," I say, "and it's times these few days when I wished it had been me bit by a water moccasin back then when I was a girl. And then none of this misery would've ever come on us all."

"Don't question the working out of providence," says Abigail, looking not at me but at her sister. "That's the business of the Lord."

"I question it night and day," Maude says. "Let Joleen talk, Abigail."

"The poor little girl ended up dying from that snakebite," I say. "Eldridge run on down there where Opal told him she was, and he toted her back up to Mr. Lee Lester's place. And her mama was there, of course, and they tried to bleed her where the snake had bit. But it had got her twice, and the place where the fangs had hit was on Alice Jeanne's throat. You can't cut into that spot and have nobody live after you done it.

"That poison worked fast, and she was gone before they could get to nary a doctor, even if a doctor could have helped her."

"Lord in heaven," Abigail say, "just the one child was all the one that woman had."

"Yes, ma'am," I say.

"How did that lead to any trouble between Lee Lester and your husband?" Maude says. "Surely Lee nor his wife didn't blame any of y'all for what a snakebite did, did they?"

"No, Miss Maude," I say. "That wasn't what made all this trouble come on us. It wasn't no blame ever laid on us by nobody for what caused Alice Jeanne to die. Not by Lee Lester, and sure not by Miss Corinne. Everybody seem to understand that to be a terrible thing that wasn't nobody's fault but little girls being where they shouldn't a been, after they been warned off from doing it.

"The next thing that happened didn't come directly from Mr. Lee Lester. It was Miss Corinne. Her mind got wrong. She couldn't get over thinking about it, and mourning and grieving about her girl being gone. She just roamed through Mr. Lee Lester's house all night, from what I could tell, not able to sleep nor rest, and she walked over the farm everyday, every part of it, wandering down through the creek bottom where that moccasin fang put the poison in her little girl, and talking, talking, talking to everybody she see on the place.

"And the main one she wanted to talk to was Eldridge because she had it in her head he was the last one to be with Alice Jeanne when she was still able to speak and know who she was and who people was around her.

"She would come up to him at all hours of the day whenever she saw him, out in the field plowing or grubbing at weeds with a hoe, or carrying water up from the spring, or tending to the vegetable garden, anything he might be doing. And she would make him tell the whole story of what he saw when he got down to the place where Alice Jeanne was after the snake bit her, and what she looked like, and did she say anything, and could he remember this time something he had forgot the last time she talked to him. All like of that, over and over, again and again.

"She was what you could call crazed with grief," Abigail says, looking around at all three of us to be sure we appreciate what she's figured out. "That poor woman was."

"Yes, ma'am," I say. "And that was the way my husband understood it and what it was that was making Miss Corinne the way she was, and that was the way he treated it. He would put down whatever he was doing every time that lady would come up to him, asking him to tell her what she needed to hear, and he would do just that. Talk about it each time, as full as he could, trying his best to call up all he could about that morning and put it in words for the mother of that little girl again."

"How did that affect Eldridge?" Maude says, "I know it must have been a strain on him."

"It was that, but he never showed that to Mr. Lee Lester's wife. Never made a sign, and he never cut nothing short in going over every bit of what he could remember. Just as patient the twentieth time as he was the first.

"I asked him about that, said to him maybe he could kind of keep an eye out for her and when he was able to do it without her noticing, just kind of get out of her way, you understand. Plan what he was going to work on so as to let him stay out of her sight whenever he could manage it."

"Did he start to sneaking off, then, after you told him how to do?" says Abigail.

"No, ma'am," I say. "Eldridge ain't that kind of a man. Told me he figured it was a comfort to Miss Corinne to hear him tell all he could about the last little while of that child's life in this world. Said he wouldn't try to hide from her in no way and that she would finally wear out listening to what he had to say, and little by little get over it and not need to hear it told to her again, again, again."

"Did your husband ever make things up to tell that lady?" Richard asks. "I think I would have been tempted to, myself."

"Richard," Abigail says. "What an opinion to express."

"I told Eldridge that very thing, Mr. Richard," I say. "I said to him that after I had told the same thing so many times I would've tried to put stuff in to try to satisfy whatever it was Miss Corinne needed to hear, and then maybe after she heard that she would leave me alone about it."

"I would have put in new parts to the story just to entertain myself," Maude says, "for the sake of variety."

"But no, Eldridge wouldn't do that, and he just looked at me funny when I said what I might want to do in the situation he was in. So I never mentioned it to him again.

"But Eldridge was wrong about thinking Miss Corinne would get her fill and slack off. It seemed the more patient he was in talking to her and answering every little new question she had thought up to ask since the last time he had told her about what caused her to lose her only child, the more she wanted to look for him to talk to. And that's what it was finally led to it, finally caused what got Mr. Lee Lester to get bad in his mind toward my husband."

"Was it one thing in particular?" says Richard, "That made it get worse, I mean."

"It was, yes oh Lord, and it happened just two nights ago, but it seem to me like it's been two years done passed since then," I say back to him. He had done left off fooling with the water jug on the other side of the wagon and has walked around to stand by his mama. Maude acts like she hasn't noticed Richard doing that, but I can tell she has. She moves a little to give him room to stand.

"It was way past sundown, full dark, and I had done put supper on the table for Eldridge and Opal and me, and I was just putting away the last of the dishes and the cook pot I'd just finished cleaning up. Opal, she had gone on off to bed but wasn't asleep yet, I don't think. Eldridge was sitting at the table close to the kerosene lamp trying to put something together that was broke. I never noticed what it was, nor paid no attention to what he was messing with there, thinking about something else and turning it over in my mind, I reckon.

"Since then, though, these last two days I have wished time and time again I had looked at what Eldridge was trying to fix that night, sitting there in the lamp light, and everything quiet in the house, and the same as it always was at the end of a day before we'd lie down to rest before the next sunup come to get the next day started. Because that then was the last usual and expected time we ever going to have together, me and my husband, where life is going on like it's supposed to be. The same, you know what's coming, and it's waiting there ordinary as that dishpan I had before me, full of water and soap to make a dirty thing clean.

"In these last couple of days it seem to me if I could just know what it was Eldridge was working on before that knock come on our door that it'd be a comfort to me somehow. It'd be a thing I could hold in my mind and know what it was for sure and for true, and it would be a marker I could call up whenever I needed it and behold it as the final end of something."

"What knock on your door?" Abigail says. "Was it that crazy woman Corinne Lester?"

"No, ma'am," I say. "It was the girl been working for her, one of the Jefferson bunch, her name LaVelle, and she was sent to fetch Eldridge. You got to come up to Mr. Lee Lester's house, she start saying, almost yelling at us, as soon as Eldridge he opens that door to see who's banging on it. Oh, you got to come up to the house. Miss Corinne say come get you, come get you now."

"I would not have gone up there," Abigail says, shaking her head back and forth like a mule or horse will do when it's refusing the bit. "I would have kept on sitting in that chair, working on whatever I was working on, like my feet was nailed to the floor."

"Oh, yes, you would," Maude say. "Anybody would have gone, with things being the way they were. Being the way they still are."

"My husband didn't hesitate," I say. "Eldridge just turned back to look at me and said he would be back home as soon as he could, and he followed that Jefferson girl on out of the house, and that was the last time I seen him his normal self and things the way they ought to be. Me, I felt the same way you would have, Miss Abigail. I felt like I was paralyzed, like I couldn't move my legs or arms, like the strength just all give out of me. I knowed something bad was going to happen. I knowed it in my bones, and they had done turned to water."

"Was Mr. Lee Lester up there at the house, too, with his wife?" Richard says.

"No," I say. "No, no. Not at the first. And that's what make everything come to grief. It was just Miss Corinne waiting when Eldridge and LaVelle Jefferson got up there, and she had done got into one of them bottles of whiskey Mr. Lee Lester keeps to sip toddies out of, and she had done started that, started drinking it, because she was feeling so bad about that little girl being dead and gone, and she was crying and hollering and carrying on and calling for Eldridge to talk some more to her about that day down in the creek bottom when that poison from the snake first got set.

"That little Jefferson girl, LaVelle, as soon as she see Eldridge go in the backdoor to the house where Miss Corinne told her to bring him, she just run on off back to the cabin where her folks stay."

"And mighty glad to do it, she was, I expect," Abigail says. "She was quit from the whole thing then."

"Yes, ma'am," I say, "I expect that's what LaVelle was thinking, if she was thinking anything at all. With her done and gone, that just left Eldridge there with Mr. Lee Lester's wife in the house, and she start in like always wanting him to tell what all he seen happen when he run down to the creek bottom to do what he could about Alice Jeanne snakebit. He never complained, but he start in again saying all he could, remembering every little bit he have in his mind about it trying to answer every question Miss Corinne come up with to ask him, all like of that, on and on."

"Was she asking anything new that time?" Abigail says, her hand held up to her forehead like she is trying to imagine what else Miss Corinne might be able to come up with and want to know. Abigail is looking way off with her eyes half-closed like a person will, concentrating hard on something. "Had she already asked your husband if he actually saw the water moccasin that bit her little girl, or had it already crawled off and hid somewhere, maybe back in the creek of under some bushes or something?"

"For God's sake," Maude says, "Abigail, will you let Joleen talk?" That hushes Maude's sister up, and Abigail stands up real straight now and folds her arms across her breast with the look on her face of a person not much interested any longer in what is going on around her. I expect she's not likely to ask me nothing else here for a while, so I pick up where I left off.

"I don't know what all Mrs. Lee Lester ask him, Miss Abigail," I say, to give her something, which I can tell she appreciates me doing, "Eldridge never told me. But he do what he can to satisfy the questions she did ask him, and then Miss Corinne she offer my husband some of that whiskey she been drinking as he stand there in the kitchen of her house. Hold out a water glass toward him and fix to pour from the bottle into it.

"He say thank you, ma'am, but no, I don't want none of that. See, besides him not having a drink of liquor nor beer nor nothing else like that since he take Jesus Christ as his personal savior years ago, Eldridge knew it wouldn't be proper for him to be drinking no whiskey in the company of a white lady. Miss Corinne pour some anyway into that water glass and hold it to him and say something like come on and take a sip of whiskey with me, Eldridge, just for social sake. That probably wasn't the actual words she use, but that's the meaning, and Eldridge say no again, as polite and nice as he could make it. He take the glass out of her hand where she has put it right up in his face close enough to where he could smell the fume rising up, and then he put it down as soon as he touch it, right there on the table in the kitchen.

"That's when he heard somebody stepping up behind him, and he look around, and it's Lee Lester coming through the doorway from the room at the front of the house. He never even heard the man come into the building until then, and neither had Miss Corinne, Eldridge said, because she looked real surprised and said well look who's here for a change.

"My husband greeted the man, said something like howdy, Mr. Lester, how you this evening, and then Lee Lester start in hollering at Eldridge. What you doing in my kitchen, nigger, he said, drinking my whiskey, making my wife get drunk with you? What you fixing to do to her, look like I got here just in time to stop you from doing something else, too, don't it? Have you put your damn black hand on her yet? He turn so red in his face, Eldridge say, until he thought Lee Lester was going to fall out on the floor in a full fit.

"Eldridge start in to say no sir, I ain't done nothing of that kind, I'm just here up at your house 'cause Miss Corinne send somebody to my place to get me to come talk to her again about y'all's little girl being killed by the snakebite.

"Miss Corinne start to say something to her husband, but he tell her to keep her damn drunk mouth shut, he knows what's going on, and he will be found in Hell with his back broke before he will let a nigger molest his wife in his own kitchen. And Eldridge try to say something again about why he's there in the house talking to Miss Corinne, and Lee Lester said goddamn you, don't call my wife by her first name. And then he hit Eldridge full in the face with his fist all balled up, and Eldridge turned to leave out the backdoor, and Lee Lester picks up that glass of whiskey from where Eldridge had set it down on the table after Miss Corinne push it up at him. He throw that glass to hit Eldridge, I expect, but it miss my husband and hit Miss Corinne on her forehead and broke.

"By then, Eldridge is going out the back door to run through the dark toward where we stay, and he can hear Mr. Lee Lester cussing and screaming at Miss Corinne and her crying and hollering, and that sound follow him like the Devil himself is stepping in every footprint Eldridge makes on his way home.

"And now look where we be. Me standing here in the graveyard, my grandchild Opal yonder staying with Claudine Ramey and her bunch, and my husband hiding in that canebrake with white folks wanting to put a rope around his neck and hang up to a tree."

"Maude and me will just talk to Lee Lester," Abigail says, "and see if we can't straighten this whole thing out. We'll take care of it, Joleen. Don't you worry."

"I appreciate you saying that, Miss Abigail," I tell her, "but things've done gone too far for y'all to make no headway talking to nobody. That road done been took."

"Joleen is right," Maude says, "but bless you, Abby, for helping us think. You put your finger on it, though, the problem we've got to deal with now. Everything has gone beyond reason, I'm afraid, and we can't afford to put any faith in trying to deal with Lee Lester."

Maude gets quiet for a spell, then, all of us do, not speaking, and we stand there in the shade of the sycamore, while Maude looks way off like she is trying to see into the woods beyond the graveyard to find out if she can tell where a noise she has heard is coming from. I notice she is patting her son on the shoulder. Richard has moved up a little closer to her, and he looks in his face as though some pain has kicked up somewhere in his stomach and he is waiting to see which direction it will take. Will it pass on off in a minute, or will it just get worse?

"What is going on back in Sabinetown, Joleen?" Maude says. "What have you heard?"

"We didn't wait around none after Eldridge come busting into the house and told me what happened at Mr. Lee Lester's place," I say. "He started throwing some things into a tow sack, some cold biscuits left from supper, and his other shirt and what all, and I rousted Opal up from bed and walked her over to Claudine Ramey's to leave her there. Time I got back to the house, Eldridge was done outside waiting in that little pine thicket behind the hog pen. I didn't know where he was until he whistled low to call my attention."

"What did Lee Lester do after Eldridge ran out of his house? Could you figure that out?"

"I don't know exactly what he done, Miss Maude, there in his house with his wife, but by sun-up, I'd done had two people from the quarters come to tell me what Mr. Lee Lester did after he left his place in the middle of the night."

"He spread his story, did he?"

"He did that. Told all that bunch of white folks around Sabinetown that Eldridge tried to molest Miss Corinne and he had caught my husband in the act of trying it. Said he chased him out of the house, but not before Eldridge had fought real bad with him and put scratch marks and bruises all on his face and neck."

"At least she did that to him," Richard says. "Give her credit for that."

"Didn't Corinne say anything to people to tell what really happened?" Maude says, then answers her own question. "No, she didn't. Nothing they'd listen to."

"Miss Corinne, they say she's out of her head," I say. "Supposed not to be making any sense in anything she says, after what Eldridge tried to do to her there in the kitchen of her house."

"I wish Papa could get ahold of Lee Lester," Abigail says, pointing over real direct toward a graveplace, holding her arm straight out and steady as she talks. "He'd teach that booster a lesson."

"We're on our own, sister," Maude says, "Papa's gone, but that's nice to imagine, I do grant you."

"Joleen," she says, looking at me with her eyes all settled like she has come to where she wants to in her thinking, "how long have they been looking for Eldridge? And are they using dogs?"

"Since about the middle of the morning yesterday, and they wasn't using no dogs at first, but they got them now. Sent over to Hemphill to get old man Buck Tolliver and that pack of redbone hounds he runs.

"First thing they did was to come to our place, a bunch of men together to ask me stuff and look under and in everything they could put their hands on. Turned the house upside down like they might find my husband hiding under the floorboards or up in the rafters. They even looked in the hog pen, like they might find him hid somewhere in there."

"I expect Lee Lester is right there now with old Buck Tolliver and his pack of hounds," Abigail says, "looking to cause as much mischief and confusion as he can."

"Far as I know," I tell her, "Mr. Lee Lester ain't able to leave Miss Corinne there by herself in his house yet. Claim he got to stay there to tend to her, keep her kindly quieted down, he say, till her nerves get better and she stop having all them troubles in her head."

"That lady keeps saying things her husband doesn't want to hear," Richard says. "I bet that's the trouble with her."

"I expect we've talked as much as we need to," Maude says, "here today in the graveyard. We have to start doing something practical other than trying to figure out Lee Lester and the everlasting trouble he's made for himself."

"That man has got plenty to worry about, all right," I say. "Here in this world where he's been stirring up misery for everybody, and in the next one, too, where Jesus be waiting, just restless to get at him."

"We need," Maude says, looking sharp around her, toward first Richard, then Abigail and me, "we need to get those crepe myrtle cuttings first. Who did you say had all those bushes growing in her yard, Joleen? And how far is her place from here?"

"Drova Jessup, she the lady with the crepe myrtle. Pink and purple both, and like I said, even got some bushes with pink and purple blossoms side by side."

"Crossbred," Abigail says, "Y'all remember I said that before."

"Yes, you did," Maude says, "Now where is her place, Joleen?"

"Not over a mile, mile and half down the Damascus Road," I say, and point in the general direction I know it to be. "This end of the quarter is where Drova got all that crepe myrtle growing."

"Now, Maude," Abigail says. "I know I said we had decided before we left Double Pen Creek to come up here to Blue Water Chapel that we needed to get some crepe myrtle cuttings to plant by Papa's grave, his real one. But do you think we have time to be driving the wagon all over the country hunting for flowering bushes when we got Joleen's husband to worry about? I mean, Lord, sister, we got a pack of hounds trailing in these woods. Do you think Buck Tolliver's going to wait around for us to get crepe myrtle cut and put in the bed of that wagon before he shows up here with his dogs?"

"No, I don't think that," Maude says, "but we have to have the crepe myrtle cut and loaded before we put Mr. Broussard in the wagon, down under it, covered up."

"Down under it?" Abigail says, looking at Maude as though her sister has just remarked that cows can fly, if they just put their minds to it.

"If it was dark," Maude says, "we could take the chance of having him lie down in the bottom of the wagonbed and probably nobody would see him while we were going to Drova Jessup's to cut and load the crepe myrtle. But we can't take the gamble, middle of the day like this, and bright and clear as it is."

"Oh," Abigail says, "I guess I'd thought of that myself in a little while." Her face dropped when she was saying that, but then it brightens up a little when another idea hits her. "But what if the dogs track him down while we're gone?"

"Did Eldridge come straight to that canebrake from your place, Joleen?" Maude asks me.

Eldridge hadn't, and I tell them how Eldridge had walked in the creek north first, then got out on one side, and got back into the water again, and come downstream and then turned back again, and finally down creek until he reached the mud flats where the bottom gets wide, circling around until he ended up in the canebrake in behind Blue Water Chapel graveyard.

"That'll work for a good little while, to confuse the dogs," Maude says. "Go tell your husband what we're doing and for him to be ready by about four o'clock for us to come fetch him to come up to the wagon."

"Is Joleen going with us?" Abigail says. "Won't it look funny to anybody seeing her?"

"Yes," Maude says, "you're right. Give her your bonnet, Abby, and you have to ride in the bed of the wagon going over there to Drova Jessup's, while Joleen sits by me."

"Coming back, too?"

"It'll be easier on the way back here," Maude says. "You'll be sitting on all that crepe myrtle."

After I took Eldridge the biscuits and pork shoulder meat and told him what Maude done had us doing to get him out of Sabine County and away from all the lies Mr. Lee Lester been spreading to get him killed, we all four of us get in the wagon and Richard hums up the mules to get us going to Drova Jessup's place. I'm wearing Abigail's bonnet, a big one with a long top and sides and extra material cut into it to hang down over the back of the neck.

Abigail tells me three times she made it herself, big like it is to keep the sun off her face and neck as much as could be since her pale skin burns always in the sun like it does. Her bonnet gets the job done all right, it shades, I got to allow Abigail that, and when we pass the one wagon we come to on our way to Drova Jessup's, can't nobody see nary sign of my face or who I am. I keep my head dropped like I am dozing off as I ride, like people will do. I keep my hands stuck up under the material of my dress front, and with the long sleeves of Abigail's dress I'm wearing, can't nobody even tell what color I am, much less who I am.

Maude made Abigail and me switch dresses, too, after she gets a look at me with Abigail's big old bonnet on. "It needs more," she says to me and Abigail, "y'all step off into the woods and swap garments."

I think about how my husband looked, backed up into that stand of cane in the mud, as we get close to Drova Jessup's house in the wagon.

Eldridge is a cleanly man, always careful to dress himself particular and neatened, and there he sat on the ground covered with that old black creek bottom mud, clothes all nasty and torn and scratches on his face and arms from running through briars in the woods and along the streambed. Nowhere of his own to lay his head no more.

I'm not going to dwell on that sight of him now, though, and let myself get to crying again about what all's happened. I'll look at all the pink and purple crepe myrtle, instead, coming toward us as we come into view of Drova Jessup's yard, and I'll make myself find some of the different color ones mixed up together on the same branches of a single bush. There is one, standing out, just at the corner of the yard where the road goes right by it, some bigger in size and fuller than the rest, and I point it out to Abigail, speaking low to her as I do.

"It's one of them crossbreed crepe myrtles, Miss Abigail," I say, "looky yonder at it, all by itself."

"Well," she says, leaning forward from where she's riding in the bed of the wagon, feeling the bumps from every rock and every hole in the road we're traveling. "I have read about this freak of nature, and now I've seen it." Abigail sounds satisfied, nodding her head up and down hard while she looks.

Drova is home with some of her children, and they help us cut the limbs off the crepe myrtle bushes and stack them in the wagonbed, not stopping until the pile reaches plumb over the level of the sideboards. By the time we get enough cut and stacked to the standard Maude has set in her mind and has put us to work to get to, the bushes in Drova Jessup's yard look like a small storm has come through, snapping off limbs right and left.

"Naw, naw," Drova says when Maude start saying she's sorry we took so much off her crepe myrtle bushes, "them things grow back like a weed will do. It tickle me anyhow to watch how Miss Abigail go after them mixed color bushes with her knife. She act like she got plumb mad at them boosters. Just stacking them up."

Everybody laughs, and I join in to be social with people, but inside I'm feeling like I want to jump back in the wagon and whip up the mules into a gallop and get gone from here. Maude speaks up to say the very thing I'm thinking, when she declares it's getting on in the afternoon and we got to get on the road with our crepe myrtle cuttings.

I'm leaning forward in the seat as we start back down the Damascus Road, as though I could hurry us on by straining myself toward the front of the wagon. All my muscles feel hard in my legs, and my neck is stiff from leaning ahead.

"Hum up, Jack," Richard says to the mules, "hum up, Shirley," and then he pops them a smart lick with the reins, and we get going back toward Blue Water Chapel graveyard, back where my husband is laying down in the mud hiding from dogs.

Abigail

I have never in my life seen purple and pink blossoms on the same crepe myrtle bush, and here I am riding in a wagon bed just full up with them. Talk about your freaks of nature.

Maude

Every nerve, every fiber, every ligament in her body is stretched to its limit. I try not to look directly at her while we ride along together side by side on the wagon bench, since I know she always feels obliged to acknowledge every glance, every notice, every sign of attention directed toward her. She has lived all her life, at least the part of it around white people, on a hair-trigger, constantly on edge and ready to respond to any acknowledgment of her existence, knowing she can't ever afford to appear unprepared to furnish whatever one of us may be wanting from her. A bowl to be handed to us, say, or an outcry from one of our children to be dealt with and solved, a needle to be threaded, a nod, a smile, a reassurance to be served up to us on demand.

Riding along beside her now, though I keep my gaze fastened straight ahead for the most part, looking at the back of Richard's head as he drives the wagon or glancing off to the roadside as though I'm interested in whatever presents itself, I can tell from the corner of my vision that Joleen's mind and body and soul are bound together as tightly as hard knots in a strand of yarn. The ligaments and arteries in her throat stand out like wires running just beneath the skin, her eyes opened as widely as a blind woman hungry for a flash of light, her lips parted in anticipation as though she was starving for water in a desert and she believes she hears a trickle somewhere ahead and unseen.

Why isn't she mad? Why isn't any last mustard seed of her reason scattered and vanished and lost? Why doesn't she tear at her own flesh, throw back her head and howl at the empty sky like an animal with its foot half-chewed off by a steel trap?

When we were young girls together in Sabine County, there in that brief phase when Joleen was the first thought in my mind each morning and the one I sought out to see every day as soon as Mama would release me from chores and the house and her and my sisters and brothers to run down the path which led to the spring and the colored quarters beyond it, Joleen was the same as she is now. Heart-set and ready in mind to meet whatever the new day might bring.

That morning when for the first time I knew I was not simply my mother's daughter, not just one of the girl children of Carolina Cameron Holt's, I came to that knowledge because of Joleen Bobo. It was nothing Joleen said nor did that led me there, put my mind up against the knowledge no child desires ever, but cannot push aside nor forget when it comes. But it will come, and the child who struggles with success not to receive it will always remain a child, no matter how many days and years march across the calendar to disappear into the dust.

And that day is a sad day and a long one not to be measured by the sun's rise and its setting and the moon's coming up. The prophet's truth is written then in the mind and blood and spirit of each person alone, not in the words put into God's book, saying that knowledge is sorrow.

I had risen that morning earlier than usual, up even before my mother and father, to sit quietly in the dark and wait for the light of the new day to come. A clear cut-glass vase, the only beautiful thing my mother ever had and the only thing brought by her from Louisiana into Texas that had lasted, she kept always high on the top of a sideboard, out of the reach of me and my brothers and sisters. I was in the habit, when alone, of standing on a chair, taking the vase down to touch and press against my face to feel its coolness and pattern on my skin, and then returning it to its resting place, undetected.

That day it came to me that if I were to put the vase in the middle of the table where we took our meals, setting it there in the dark before I could even tell by sight what I had in my hands, that I could keep my gaze fastened on it as sunlight came to announce the day, and thus be able to appreciate the ending of the darkness of one day and the growing of the light of another.

I didn't put thought to myself in those words, child as I was at the time, but I acted on the impulse and was able to observe the vase coming into itself and defining its existence against the smooth wood of the table as the light grew around, in, and through the cut glass. First I could see a difference develop between the vase and all that was around it, then the shape begin to announce itself more and more clearly as the light opened up the world of the cabin in which I lived, and the county of Sabine, and the state of Texas, and finally as fuller day came, the vase stood alone and separate and not anything but itself.

I beheld the vase, I watched its light, and I saw it become itself.

At the sound of movement from someone other than me in the house, I replaced the vase on the top of the sideboard, and no one could know what I had been able to see come into the place where I lived with the people who thought I was simply part of them, a girl child named Maude Holt, awake and needing to eat and drink and breathe early one morning.

As my mother tended to what she had to do, and my father worked outside with the animals before he would come back inside to breakfast on what his wife prepared for him and his children, I carried out the duties of helping my mother as she directed. But I held in a secret part of myself the experience of the vase growing into itself in the light, and I planned what I would say to Joleen about what I had done and what I had seen take place. Something had happened, and only I had seen it. It was mine.

Breakfast eaten by my brothers and sisters and me, the table cleared and food put away in the safe, my father gone outside to his work—I then asked my mother for permission to leave our place and find Joleen.

"Why do you want to do that so early this morning?" she said, not looking at me as she spoke, busy with something I can't remember. "You played with those twins yesterday, and the day before, too. I think you ought to help Abby red up the house this morning."

"All right, Mama," I said. "I'll help Abby right now, and then after we're done, can I go see Joleen? And it's just her I want to see, not her twin sister."

"Is there a real difference between those two little colored girls, Maude?" my mother said. "They look just alike to me, Joleen and Boleen Bobo, no difference between them at all."

"They aren't the same at all, Mama," I said, "and they don't really look just like each other, either, if you know them. I like Boleen, too, just fine. But I love Joleen."

I remember it was then that my mother first really looked at me that morning, turning from whatever it was she was doing, and putting that thing aside. Her eyes as they fixed on mine had a look in them I had never seen before, one that made me think my mother had forgotten who she was talking to, that she had thought she was speaking to one person and had discovered a stranger before her, instead.

"Mama," I said to reassure her, convinced by the way she was looking at me that she had made a mistake in her thinking as she sometimes did when her mind was burdened with one thing and someone asked her about a completely different one. "I'm Maude,

Mama," I said, that being what seemed logical for me to say at the moment.

"What did you say?" she said.

"I'm Maude."

"No, not that. Before you said that, you said something else. That's what I want to be sure I heard you say."

"I said that Boleen and Joleen don't really look just alike," I said, looking away from my mother's eyes and searching about the room for something else to fasten on, something that might appear to me the same it always had been. That was the cut-glass vase, and I stared at it, but the light I had seen it take into itself earlier in the morning was now gone, and the vase seemed flat against the wall behind it, like a picture of a vase, not the thing itself at all.

"If you know them," I said, " and who they are, they aren't the same at all."

"What else did you say?"

"I said that I liked Boleen," I answered. "I said I liked her, and I said that I love Joleen."

"You like them both, Maude," my mother said. "You like the little colored Bobo twins, Boleen and Joleen. You like to play with them."

"Yes, I do," I said. "I do like them both, but I like Joleen more. I love Joleen."

"You do not love Joleen," she said, coming closer to me and lifting her voice to cause me to look at her again, and I did. There was no comfort to be had now in the cut-glass vase, flat against the wall and empty of light, no different in that from the cups on the table. "You do not love Joleen. You cannot love a colored girl from the quarters. And you may never say that again, you must never say that again, to me or to anybody else, particularly."

"All right, Mama," I said and put my eyes on hers and tried to look into them deep enough to get behind the knowledge that I was not really seeing my mother's eyes, but an eye that might belong to anybody, a sister or a brother or a stranger I had never met before. But I could not believe it was her eyes, stare though I did. The eye that looked back and fixed me in its stare was as flat and indifferent to me as the cut-glass vase brought from Louisiana to Texas across the Sabine River by Carolina Holt had become. It was not my mother, the way she always had appeared to me, looking at me now.

"I won't say that to anybody ever again," I said. "I won't tell people that I love Joleen."

That promise I kept, and it was on that day I learned I was not truly a part of anything or anybody but myself, and I never lifted my mother's cut-glass vase again from its due and proper location on the top of a sideboard where it was kept, not subject to direct light from the sun, ever.

We are moving at a good pace, the mules leaning into the harness and Abigail rustling around behind me and Joleen in the wagonbed full of crepe myrtle branches as she tries to find a way to sit that will crush as few blossoms as possible, paying particular attention to the limbs covered with the mixture of pink and purple flowers, the ones she's so taken with. The angle at which Richard is sitting as he handles the reins matches almost exactly the way Joleen is leaning forward to strain at the distance between her and her husband.

Her position reminds me of the way I always felt when I was apart from Valery Blackstock in the years when I was with him and he with me in this world—at attention, poised to move at an instant toward him as soon as I caught sight of him waiting somewhere for me. And he always was, each time we were away from each other, no matter if it was a half-day with him at work in the field or it was overnight for some reason or someone from my family or his with a matter to be attended that had drawn us apart. He waited to see me, and I waited to see him, and that was always.

Thinking of those times, I reach over to pat Joleen on her arm and she turns her head to look at me out of the stovepipe bonnet borrowed from my sister, her eyes dark and deep as I have always known them. She tries to offer me a smile, and that smile is now different, remindful though it is of something familiar and almost known to me, in the way a passing thought will be when it barely touches your mind and vanishes not to be had again no matter how you strain to recover it. You know what came before and what came after, but there's nothing but a blankness in between. And you are not satisfied.

"We're on our way, Joleen," I say, "and we've made a good start. You'll have him with you again in just a little while now. You just wait and see."

"Yes, Miss Maude," she answers, "please, Jesus." And she lifts her hands from beneath the material of the dress where she's been holding them, and she shows me her fingers crossed one over the other, all four on each hand.

"Double," I say.

"Double doubled," she says back to me, and we laugh together again, the first time in forty years we've done that and traded those words between us.

When we arrive back at Blue Water Chapel graveyard, meeting no one on the way this time, Richard drives the wagon around the margin of the cleared ground all the way back to the far line of trees where the woods begin, without being told to do so. We all climb down to the ground, Richard walking around to the front to the mules and Abigail the last to alight, fighting her way out of the wagonload of crepe myrtle and groaning a little with the effort.

"It's a bit after four o'clock," I say, looking at the length of the shadows of the headstones the sun is casting. "We need to leave here as soon as we can to get to Jasper County before dark."

"You want me to go fetch Eldridge, Miss Maude?" Joleen says. "Bring him up here from out of the canebrake?"

"Yes, but don't y'all step out into the clearing just yet, when you get back. We need to take a good look around first and see what we're doing."

"No," Joleen says, "we won't," and she heads for the yaupon and pine thicket at a fast clip, out of view in no time.

"What am I supposed to be doing?" Abigail says to nobody in particular, sweeping her gaze from one side of the graveyard to the other as though checking to make certain no one has slipped in and rearranged something in our absence.

"What would look nice," I say, "I think, would be some cuttings of those mixed pink and purple crepe myrtle planted in between Papa's and Mama's graves. Don't you believe that would suit all right, Abby?"

"Yes," she says, lengthening out the word so it sounds like she's planning a campaign as she speaks it. "I'm going to need some water waiting on me after I get the hole dug. Where's my shovel I brought with me from home?"

"Here it is, Aunt Abigail," Richard says. "I'll go down to the spring and bring back a bucket of water."

"Help me start getting all this crepe myrtle moved around, Maude," Abigail says. "We got to do that anyway to fix a place for Joleen's husband."

"Yes, sister," I say and move toward the wagon, glad to speak up and give her that acknowledgment of family rank. Abigail appreciates it.

It is not until we've crossed the Jasper County line and gone maybe a mile beyond it that we see them up ahead. There are several silhouettes, and it's not easy to get them all counted in the fading light of day, particularly since a good number of them are moving around, busying themselves with one thing and another. They've built a fire, of course, like a bunch of men waiting together somewhere always will do, summer or winter, needing to cook or not, and some of them are throwing chunks of fallen timber onto a pile to make ready for the night to come.

I can see an ax go up and come down, and it's on the way up again before I hear the sound of the completed blow from the first lick. The sound is dull, as though it's coming through a thick curtain. Six, maybe, or five visible to me, I count, men at the end of a day of deer hunting you might think, if you didn't know better. They'll all be acting the same way deer or bear hunters do, anyway, finding something to eat, looking into the fire which is built up well beyond what's needful, telling stories of famous hunts they claim to have been part of, and passing around whiskey somebody's brought in good supply. They'll talk, and they'll laugh, and they'll do that as long as anyone will listen to them do it.

"Oh, Lord," Joleen says, sitting beside me, her voice which had calmed considerably back at Blue Water Chapel as soon as Eldridge was in the wagonbed, now crawling higher in her throat. "Sweet Jesus, hold my hand."

"It'll be all right," I say. "Just sit where you are and don't make a sign. We'll say all that needs to be said, Abigail and I will."

Before we left Blue Water, when Joleen came up from the creek bottom and the canebrake with her husband beside her, she had already begun to settle in her person and behavior, even though all three of us had stopped whatever we were doing to watch them take each step of the way from the edge of the thicket across the graveyard toward the mules and wagon. None of us could resist doing that, even Abigail as she put the last touches to the two-colored crepe myrtle she was planting between Papa's and Mama's graves. She set the bucket of water down, not yet painstakingly emptied at the new location for her flower bush for Papa, and turned to watch, her muddy hands held out in front of her so as not to soil her dress.

The first thought that came to me was that Eldridge Broussard was much older than Joleen, his hair gray and age lining his face, and I wondered at that until I looked at Joleen beside him. Taken together and viewed as husband and wife, they were indeed of an age, and it struck me that I had been seeing all day not really the woman but only what was left of the girl in Joleen, my companion from that time in childhood when we saw ourselves in the other's face and time was of no consequence to us.

"This is my husband," Joleen told us in a strong voice, "Eldridge Broussard." He stood beside her covered in mud, but his stance erect and his gaze directed toward us.

"We are pleased to meet you," Abigail said, taking the lead as I stood there speechless, "Get into the wagonbed, Eldridge, if you will, and start covering yourself up with all this crepe myrtle."

"They see us coming, Mama," Richard is saying to me, pulling back on the mules' reins, "What am I to do?"

"Tip your hat to the gentlemen, son," I say, "as you're supposed to do, and stop the wagon when we get there so we can see what they may want to say to us."

Well before we near the spot where they're gathered, one of the men lifts a hand to hail us and begins walking up the road toward our wagon. His hat, a light colored one, is squared up on his head in contrast to those of most of the other ones, I notice, and I figure from that that he's in charge of the bunch and is ready for business. He is dressed neatly, as well, his boots appearing to be brand new, and he is carrying something in his left hand, gloves I think, which he is tapping against his pants leg as he walks our direction.

I start to tell Richard to slow the mules as we approach, but he's already doing that, and our progress stops with the man still several yards away. All four of us watch him near us in silence, the only sound that of the mules groaning and blowing their breaths now that they've stopped and the rhythmic flick of the gloves against the man's pants leg.

"Good evening," he says, "ladies," and then nodding toward Richard, "young man."

We greet him, Abigail's voice some louder than mine and Richard's, Joleen saying nothing.

"You've got a nice brace of mules to pull you, I see," he says and puts out his hand to make a patting motion at the head of the mule nearest him, but he doesn't actually touch the animal.

"My husband's proud of them," I say. "Thank you."

"And who is your husband, Ma'am, if I may inquire?"

"Ezra Winston," I say, "of the Double Pen Creek community in Coushatta County. We farm a few acres there."

"I know what you mean by saying a few," the man answers, "it never seems to be enough, does it, to grow enough cotton to get ahead these days, no matter how much you put in."

"Yes, indeed," Abigail says, her voice falling into the lighter tone she habitually uses with men, particularly those she doesn't know. "But my sister's husband does tolerably well. We all do, so far in Coushatta County, the ones willing to work hard at it. My husband is Ferguson Mott, and he's pursuing the same livelihood as my sister's."

"Well, yes," the man answers, no longer flicking his gloves as he stands near the head of the team of mules, but bouncing them up and down in his hand as he looks from one to the other of us there in the stopped wagon. "I've heard there's some productive land in Coushatta County, all right. But me, I'm a Sabine County man, and I guess I'll never leave these old gumbo bottoms, no matter how hard they are to work."

"We're from Sabine County ourselves," Abigail says, "to start with. Raised over there close to Blue Water Chapel. Our father's buried there. Amos Holt. Maybe you know the name."

"My goodness, yes," the man says. "Now I'm too young myself to be able to claim it, but I remember my daddy saying he had heard Amos Holt preach. Even went to school to him for a while."

"What is your family name?" Abigail says.

"Slater, I'm J. T. Slater, and my daddy was Truman Slater."

"Y'all's place was north of Bear Creek," Abigail says. "Your daddy's brother was Jesse Neal Slater, and I can't call up the name of a sister in the Slater family, but there were several ladies, as I remember."

"That's the way this part of Texas is," the man who identified himself as J.T. Slater says, "if you talk long enough to people, you're bound to find out you know somebody in their family. Might even be kin to them, if you're unlucky."

We all laugh at that, of course, in obligation, Abigail louder than Richard and I, and I can tell my sister is warming to the occasion and would be prepared to converse with J.T. Slater until full dark, given the opportunity. I take a deep breath, and the sleeve of Joleen's dress is touching my arm now, so that I can feel a steady tremor transferring through it.

"Yes, yes," J.T. Slater says, smiling as he looks around at all of us again, his gaze on Joleen's face a beat longer than it is on the rest of us.

"But let me tell you folks why we're all here this time of day on the road, these other men and me, rather than home eating supper and getting ready to go to bed and get some rest before tomorrow gets here. I expect you're wondering."

With that, he turns his head a little to one side as though he's about to look over his shoulder toward the clot of men a good distance behind him, but he doesn't. Instead he flicks his gloves in their direction and takes a couple of steps closer to the wagon.

"It's not a thing I like to talk directly to ladies about, but I must let you know what's happened. I'm obliged to, you understand. Maybe you've already heard about it if you've been up in Sabine County, but it bears repeating, just to be on the safe side."

"My goodness," Abigail says. "What is it?"

I figure it's time for me to speak up, so I chime in. I can't just sit here mute. "What do you mean by mentioning the word *safe*, Mr. Slater?" I ask, casting my voice a tone lower than Abigail's. "Has someone seen a panther or a bear somewhere in the county? I remember when they used to sometimes take pigs right out of the pens at night when we were children in Sabine County."

"No, ma'am," J.T. Slater says. "I wish it was that, to tell you the truth, but it's a whole lot worse than a bear or a stray panther looking to make a meal out of somebody's livestock. That'd be easy to handle compared to what we're facing."

J.T. Slater is pushing up his hat brim now as he looks in my direction and twisting his body a little to one side as though he's about to deliver news to us that may physically knock us as a group off the wagon benches where we're sitting. The tremor coming from the sleeve of Joleen's dress ceases suddenly as though she has willed every muscle not to move, and I tell myself to keep the expression on my face what it now is until the man before us reveals all he thinks we can stand to hear. He has shifted his eyes a little to look directly at Joleen now.

"We've got the worst thing you can have happen, right here in Sabine County, ladies, and I would not unduly alarm you. But it's my bounden duty as county constable and as a Christian man to give you warning."

"My Lord," Abigail says. "What could it be?"

"We've had a nigger man go crazy and molest a white lady, and we're looking for him everywhere we can think to."

"Did he kill her?" Abigail says, her voice crawling higher in her throat as she speaks, that letting me know she's almost convinced herself she's learning a truth for the first time, brand new to her, and horrible. "Is she dead?"

"No, ma'am," J.T. Slater says in a tone calculated to be reassuring to this wagonload of white ladies and their colored woman and their boy. "He didn't get to do that. Her husband fought him off, thank the Lord, but he's loose now still, and we're after him fulltilt and foursquare."

"Was he able to," Abigail says, still caught up in her conviction she's hearing an account of a disaster and a violation for the first time, completely unknown to her. "You know, finish what he was trying to do, the nigger man?"

For once, I am gratified by my sister's ability to work her imagination so fully into an expression of complete shock and belief. It serves well now in the current circumstance, if it never has before. I could hug her.

"No, praise God," J.T. Slater says, slapping his gloves briskly into the palm of his hand. "She's unstained, though marked up pretty bad."

"Who is the man?" I ask, knowing it's time for me to add something to the conversation if I want to appear to be a normal woman in East Texas hearing news of such abomination. "Do y'all know?"

"We do, Mrs. Winston," he says, "and it's a puzzling thing, but it really shouldn't be any surprise, if you know the race and the breed. He's a cropper name of Broussard, never been in no trouble before that anybody knows of, a middle-aged nigger man, a hard worker, but you know how it will happen with any one of them. He just went crazy, like they are liable to do at any time. And it's not predictable, and it's always the case after something like this happens. You know how people will say they never would've expected it of him."

"You are right, Mr. Slater," Abigail says, "I've heard it said just in that way time and time again when one of them goes out of his mind. 'Well, I never,' people will say, 'never would have predicted that of Tom or John or Ben or whoever the nigger happened to be.' Everybody is just flabbergasted by it."

"Yes, ma'am, but they will go plumb African on you, and you've always got to keep watching close and tight."

"Broussard," Richard says, speaking for the first time, and I feel something inside my body give way as though I'm about to be sick when I hear my son's voice. "That was the name you said, sir?"

"Broussard," repeats J.T. Slater, "Eldridge Broussard, that's the man we're looking for. I should say that's the man we're going to find. Rest assured of that, folks."

"I wonder which direction he's running?" Abigail says, "This Broussard? I hope and pray it's not south toward Coushatta County where we're headed."

J.T. Slater begins to answer Abigail's question, but he's looking at Richard as he speaks. "Well, ma'am," he say, "we can't tell where he's headed just yet, but we know where he's doing his best to get away from, and that's Sabine County. That's why we're covering the roads leading out of here."

"That's a comfort," Abigail says, "But wouldn't this Broussard fellow run through the woods and stay off the roads where people travel? Wouldn't he know he'd be easy to spot out in the open where wagons and the odd automobile go back and forth all the time?"

"We sure hope he'll think that way," J.T. Slater says in a pleased tone, "If he sticks to the woods he won't last long. We've got the best pack of tracking hounds in this part of the country on his trail right now. They may take a while to pick up his track, but once they do it'll be all over before he knows it. They may be a little slow at first, but this pack of dogs is sure as death."

"Praise the Lord," Abigail says, "I sure hope so. That'll ease my mind and everybody else's, too, once y'all catch him."

"Son," Slater says, tapping his gloves against his leg again and addressing his words toward Richard, "You asked about this nigger's name a little while ago. You don't happen to know him, do you, by any chance?"

"No, sir," Richard says, his voice and tone as polite and reserved as it always is, an aspect of his behavior I've always treasured in my son, but the sound of which now causes me to want to scream at him to keep his mouth shut and to sit quiet as he usually does. Why is he volunteering to speak to this man before us as we sit stopped here in the road?

"I don't know the man at all, but the family name is one I've heard before. It belongs to a family of colored folks up in Shelby County that my Papa trades seed with. You remember, Mama," Richard says, looking at me in his guileless, earnest way, "that fellow Papa gets the cotton seed from, that seed for the higher-growing variety?"

"Oh, yes," I say, fixing my eyes on a spot on Richard's forehead just below the brim of his hat, "I do know who you're talking about. Certainly. Broussard."

"Shelby County?" Slater says, "all that way away from Coushatta County where you folks are from, huh? A higher cotton plant, you say?"

"Papa claims it's easier to pick from," Richard says, "and the yield's as good as what the lower-down plant will give you. I reckon that's why he's traded with this Shelby County man name of Broussard."

"Well, thank you, young man," J.T. Slater says, "I'll mention that to my people, that there's a family of Broussard niggers north of here in Shelby County. Might not be no connection to the man we're fixing to round up and catch, but maybe it's a direction to look. Who knows? One thing I do understand about a man on the run, white or colored, he will run to cover where he's known. He will go to ground where it's others kin to him located. Seems almost like a natural instinct."

"I don't know a thing about chasing men who've committed a criminal act," Abigail announces, "but I have learned something about niggers in my time. And one thing I learned is when they get in trouble they'll run to their kinfolks looking for help."

"That is the truth, Mrs. Mott," J.T. Slater says with energy, "with both hands stuck out in front of them waiting to be filled up."

The wagon creaks as the mules lean against the harness and the reins, trying to stretch their necks to reach a patch of weeds beside the road, and J.T. Slater steps back to avoid being touched by anything outside himself.

"You ladies have sure got yourselves a nice load of flower bushes," he says, turning his head a little to look at the crepe myrtle in the wagonbed, pointing with his chin in that direction as though his hands are too occupied to lift them.

"I would say that it appears y'all are going into gardening in a big way," he goes on, looking at the wagonload of branches as though he's trying to guess their volume and weight, "but I see all those limbs have been cut off. They're all going to turn brown and die, ain't they?"

Through the sleeve touching my arm, I can tell that Joleen has begun to tremble again, and I want to touch her hand, but I can't do that. I lift my gaze from J.T. Slater's face, and I can see over the top of his hat that the men behind him have built their fire even higher, its flames dancing orange and red and great clouds of sparks flying up as someone of its tenders tosses another chunk of wood on the pile. Abigail is answering Slater's question about the dying crepe myrtle, and I make myself listen to what she's saying.

"If we intended to plant any of these cuttings, you'd be right," she says. "They wouldn't do us any good at all by the time we get back to Double Pen Creek. It'd be exactly like sticking a walking cane in the ground and expecting it to take root and put out blossoms. What we're doing, though, is getting these crepe myrtle cuttings together to decorate the church building down at the Double Pen Creek community. See, our graveyard working is this coming Sunday, and that's what me and my sister and her boy have volunteered to do. Get the decorations up, and make it pretty for folks that're coming."

"I know you ladies always like your flowers," J.T. Slater says. "You mean to tell me there is no crepe myrtle in Coushatta County? Had to come all the way to Sabine County to find something growing pretty enough to use, did you?"

Abigail laughs at that, throwing her head back to let a real chortle escape her throat. I feel a chill come over me, as though a north wind had come up out of nowhere to cut across the wagon bench where I'm sitting. It's summer, I tell myself, don't shiver like you're dying to get near a fire.

"Sabine County does have the prettiest flowers in this part of Texas, as far as I'm concerned, all right," Abigail says in a tone that sounds like she's experiencing genuine enjoyment, "but we have combined reasons for coming back to Sabine County, like we always do. You know our

Papa's buried at Blue Water Chapel, don't you, Mr. Slater? And Mama, too, and so we get a chance to visit their graves and fetch back crepe myrtles all in one trip. This here's a big expedition for us."

"I reckon it must be," Slater says, "and that's why you brought your colored woman with you, I guess, all the way up here."

He's looking again at Joleen, as he speaks, and I force myself to turn toward her, as well, reaching over to pat her on the hand. It feels as cool as marble. Joleen is suffering from the chill of that north wind out of nowhere, just like me.

"We don't go anywhere without her if the trip involves work," I say. "I must confess and own up to that. Isn't that right, Annie?"

"Yes, ma'am," Joleen says in a voice I've never heard her use before, her words blurred and mumbled like those of an eighty-year-old mammy who speaks to white folks only when she visits a commissary store to buy a little sugar or a can of snuff.

"We depend on Annie," Abigail chimes in, "that's the truth my sister's speaking. We don't know what we'd do without her."

"You know, ladies," J.T. Slater says, stepping back from his position near the front of the wagon, "that's the way it's supposed to be, and I appreciate what you're saying about our colored friends. When things're going like they ought to, that's the way it is between us and the colored population. All of us just helping each other and trying to get through this world together and make do as we go along."

"That's what we all count on," Abigail says, "don't we, sister? Don't we, Annie?"

Joleen and I speak together in one voice, "That's right, that's right," nodding our heads like twin dolls lined up on the wagon bench.

"Now, son," J.T. Slater says to Richard, fixing him with a gaze that communicates the relationship of one man to another seeking to address a shared problem facing men together, "you just drive your mules and wagon straight on. Don't stop until you get to where y'all are staying the night, and you'll be all right. Just tend to your business, take care of these ladies, and things will be fine."

"Yes sir," Richard says, beginning to fiddle with the reins. "I will, thank you."

J.T. Slater reaches up, pats Richard on the knee, and turns to address me and Abigail. His hat is on straight again, in perfect alignment with his eyebrows, and he points toward us with the gloves in his left hand, shaking them in a deliberate rhythm as he speaks.

"Ladies," he says, "put your minds at ease. That nigger will not be anywhere around y'all as you journey your way home. And if there's a length of rope left in this part of Texas, come morning, he won't be around to interfere with another white woman ever again."

"Praise Jesus," Abigail says, and the mules lean into the harness, the wagon groaning in sympathy as its load begins to move forward. "I thank God for you men of Texas who protect us women so well."

J.T. Slater lifts his right hand slowly, extending his arm at full length as he watches us move by, holding that stance much longer than a farewell ordinarily will require. As we reach the place where the fire is burning beside the road, the men who've built it nod at us sternly, a couple of them tipping their hats as we pass by. I look in their direction, but I don't focus my gaze on anyone in particular, concentrating instead on my sense that the cold north wind from nowhere that has been cutting me into a shiver seems to have abated.

Up ahead the road bends to the right to avoid some obstacle long vanished that it was laid out at its beginning to bypass, and I feel like urging Richard to whip up the mules to get around that bend as soon as we can. But I don't say anything of the sort, and I strain my body forward a little on the wagon bench in place of speaking, instead. Move, I am thinking, move, move.

Beside me, Joleen says something which I don't hear well enough to understand, and I ask her to repeat it.

"Annie," Joleen says, "all I said was Annie. The name Annie. My, my."

I turn back to look over my shoulder at Abigail, sitting a little sideways near the front of the load of crepe myrtle branches, under which Eldridge Broussard rides more than two feet beneath, near the rear of the wagonbed. Abigail is holding a branch of crepe myrtle, the two color variety, pink and purple, frowning intently at a cluster of blossoms. I can't see her feet for the flowers.

"They sure are fading fast," she says, "and I wish we did have the chance to decorate the Double Pen Creek church building with them all fresh and pretty for the graveyard working."

"Someday we will," I tell her. "We'll plan for that to happen some graveyard working, and we'll do it. We'll carry out that idea that you came up with. It's a perfect one."

"We won't have the ones with pink and purple together on the same branch, though, when we do. Never again."

"No," I agree. "We won't. We'll just have to make do, like always."

We've rounded the bend in the road now, and there's no sign behind us of the roaring fire and the men who built it. Richard asks a little more out of the mules, and we're moving more quickly now away from Sabine County. Joleen has twisted back to look toward the rear of the wagonload of crepe myrtle hiding her husband, and she calls Eldridge's name.

"All right," comes his voice from beneath the flowers, low and distinct, "I'm all right. Just rolling on, thank you."

Joleen's hand is warmer now when I touch it, telling me that north wind from out of nowhere has died down for her, too.

"Abigail," I say, "big sister, you did so well for us back there. I'm so proud of you for that."

"Maybe that cutting I planted by Papa's grave was fresh enough to take root," she says. "If Sabine County gets some rain in the next couple of days, it just might take hold and make it."

"I predict it will. We'll be able to see it the next time we visit Blue Water graveyard. Just you wait and see."

"That's right," Abigail says. "We will. Now let's get on back home and get Mr. and Mrs. Broussard situated right."

And so we do.

1941

★

Holly Springs

Dicia

She is dying, and it is taking a long time for her to do it.

Like everything else she does, she is taking on this job seriously, working at it to do it right as though it's a lesson to the rest of us, and if we pay good attention and learn from it, we can do it like it's supposed to be done when our turns come.

When I think in this way to myself about my grandmother, I don't mean to find fault with her conduct or the way she presents it to the people around her, the ones left of her sisters and brothers, all the nephews and nieces and cousins, and the grandchildren and the great-grandchildren, and the other folks who live around Holly Springs.

She doesn't lecture. She doesn't tell us anything about what we all know is going on, but don't speak of to each other. I wonder sometimes if many of us admit it to ourselves those times when we're truly alone and not being bothered by somebody wanting something from us. Talking, or being talked to, or being asked to pay attention to something one of us thinks is important enough to expect other people to take an interest in.

I know I do. I let myself admit it, especially at night when I'm lying in bed not yet asleep and wanting sleep to come now, now, now, and her face comes up before me not to be escaped. I think of it then, what the long slow dying my grandmother is doing across the hall in another room is like to experience and what it might mean, or if it does mean at all.

Do all of us with our different names—the Blackstocks and Winstons and Motts—lie there alone at night before sleep comes to release us for a while with the picture in our minds of her going a little at the time, but all the time, steadily moving away from where being alive is located?

Maybe some of us do. Maybe one of my cousins or aunts or uncles is the same as I am inside, and neither one of us is able to reveal that to the other, afraid to show they think such things and so hug them to their breasts, alone.

I know one who does not brood on such, though, and it's easy for me to say that, of course, since to know a thing is not is always more certain than to know a thing is. Nola Mae does not lie in her bed at night with her eyes shut because she is making them stay that way, hoping to trick sleep into coming to blot out what's in her head and give her relief from it.

Sleep knows you better than you know yourself, and it is not to be had for the asking and never on demand. If sleep comes to know you're noticing it, if it detects your attention put upon it, it slinks away like a cat you're trying to call to you to pet. Fasten your mind elsewhere, put it on a matter far off or so close up you are part of the matter itself, and sleep may come creeping near to purr and rub against your ankles. But if you offer to bend to pet it, it slides away again to its own distance to nap alone curled in a knot.

Nola Mae is younger than me by half a year, but Great-Aunt Abigail always says her granddaughter is older than any of her sister's grandchildren and that means me. I'm the one she's singling out. Like most of us, Nola Mae's name is something other than Holt, but Great-Aunt Abigail says that makes no difference in who we truly are.

We are Holts by blood, and that blood is stronger than that of any of the men who have married Holt women. It is stronger in some of us grandchildren, the females, than in others of us, too, Great-Aunt Abigail says. And it is strongest of all in Nola Mae, she declares. And she declares that over and over again, as though to give it voice makes it truer.

"Nola Mae," she said at the last graveyard working, "is a Holt." And then she pointed at her where Nola Mae sat at the middle of one of the long tables beneath the sycamores in the graveyard, and said it again and added to what she had announced first.

"My granddaughter sitting there," Great-Aunt Abigail said, aiming the tines of her fork in Nola Mae's direction, "is eating her share of this dinner on the ground like there's no tomorrow. Look at how much is on her plate, and look at the dent she's putting in it. That's how a Holt eats."

Some of the sweet potato casserole caught in Great-Aunt Abigail's fork flew off as she shook it at Nola Mae's location, and I looked to see where it landed. Glued to the side of my cousin Wilma's waterglass some distance down the table, I noted, and that pleased me, particularly when Wilma gave a little shudder as she saw it hit and stick. Her eyes met mine, and she looked away quickly, so as not to have to acknowledge to me that her grandmother had just carelessly launched food at her which adhered. I tried to take enough satisfaction in that event to avoid hearing Nola Mae's response to her grandmother's praise, but I wasn't successful.

"Well, grandmother," Nola Mae said around the bite of food in her mouth still under chew, "if what a Holt does when she eats is to enjoy good cooking and a whole lot of it, I'm proud to call myself that, a Holt, no matter what my daddy's last name happens to be."

Nola Mae couldn't have come up with a response more pleasing to her grandmother Abigail than that if she had spent a week thinking up alternatives, and Great-Aunt Abigail showed that by throwing back her head to guffaw, her mouth open wide enough to display any and all things in it, if anyone was interested in what they might be. I was not, so I looked down into my plate at the crowder peas some lady had brought as her offering to the graveyard working as though one of the peas had just called my name.

"Dicia," Great-Aunt Abigail called down the table, and I looked in her direction. She was still beaming from the effects of Nola Mae's remark, looking up and down the row of eaters at the table to measure their admiration for her granddaughter's declaration of membership in the Holt family, her expression that of a person encouraging others to stand up and give a cheer for someone it would be a sin not to love.

"Yes, ma'am," I said and gave my crowder peas a little stir, careful not to let them wet the piece of fried chicken breast in my plate. It was nicely done, crisp and not too brown, and I was saving it to eat last.

"Have you found something you can bear to eat, sugar?" Great-Aunt Abigail said, and then addressed the table at large more directly even than she had in that question. "Dicia just picks at her food. She won't eat half of that little bit she's put on her plate."

"If she doesn't like what all these ladies have brought to Holly Springs graveyard working," a white-haired old man, Doll Collins, a couple of people away from me, said, "she never will find anything worth eating the rest of her days."

They all enjoyed that, every one of them in earshot, the McNeills and Overstreets and Garners and Braziles and the rest of them, even the ones who couldn't hear what Mr. Collins had said and had to ask their neighbors and seatmates so they could join in the hilarity. I listened to their chuckles and snorts, and sat there staring at a pea, wishing to myself in words I had heard my Grandfather use so often in reference to fools that these people were all in Hell with their backs broke.

"Unlike me," Nola Mae said after the snickers and guffaws had died down some, "my cousin Dicia has the good sense not to eat until she founders. That's the reason she's so slim and why her dresses always looks so good on her."

"Sweet girl," Great-Aunt Abigail said among all the sounds of appreciation from the feeders for the comment Nola Mae had made. "Sweet girl, that's the way she is, all the time."

Old man Doll Collins put out a hand to pat at Nola Mae's, the one that wasn't carrying a forkful of potato salad or squash or some mushy dish an off-yellow color toward her mouth, and Nola Mae gave him a smile before accepting what her hand offered her. Rather than saying something to her and her admirers, I did what I usually do to avoid having to talk when I'm not in the mood for speech. I smiled in her direction so broadly I could feel my ears move. Sometimes I can make my lips sting when I go all out with one of those expressions of delight and good will.

"I will say one thing that nobody can successfully dispute," Doll Collins announced, shaking his old head up and down until his hair moved, his hand still imprisoning Nola Mae's, "when you look at Dicia Blackstock and Nola Mae Ferguson or at any of the rest of these girls with Holt blood in their veins, you are beholding the prettiest bunch of women in Coushatta County."

I widened my smile even more, concentrating on seeing if I could coax a lip sting out of this one, but I couldn't quite get there. The attempt did earn me a little relief, though, and I felt some distance open up between me and where I was sitting at a long table at the Holly Springs graveyard working with all these people around me, however small the distance was. I was grateful enough for it to allow myself to watch Nola Mae make a perfect little red bow of her lips as she cocked her head to one side to acknowledge the compliment, turning slightly to assure that more of the audience could benefit from seeing her.

My cousin is sound asleep now, though, lying in the bed beside me nearest the wall. Her deep breaths are as regular as the ticks of the clock in the hall outside the room, and she doesn't hear the moan that comes from my grandmother in the room directly across from the one we occupy. It is a moan louder than usual, and it begins with a low tone and reaches up higher, breaking off at a zenith and not coming back down again to where it began.

It sounds unfinished, incomplete, and that causes me to put my hands over my ears to guard against the possibility of hearing another moan begin and rise to a critical point and not descend to the place where it started.

If it would do that, complete a pattern, flow from one point away and up and then return to its foundation, I would be able to see a plan in my grandmother's suffering, a start and a building up and away from that start and an ebbing back to it, and a finish that had a shape. Then I could say to myself, while I waited for sleep to take me, that her expression of pain is a statement, that it is full and orderly and has meaning.

That would say that when you are leaving life you are departing from an end point that had existence in the beginning of the life and was waiting there as part of the pattern asserting itself. Then when it begins in a low tone and rises to a higher level, where the sound is sharp and clear and full, there will come surely the return to the beginning where sound is not. Where it has not begun yet, but it will and that is expected, and set.

My hands over my ears make no difference because you always hear better in the dark, with nothing to distract, and when a person beside you sleeps with regular breaths coming in and going out, you hear even better, and I hear the moans from my grandmother across the hall start and rise and falter incomplete and remain unfixed, and no pattern is ever there. And in the dark where I am lying with my hands pressed to my ears against that sound, meaning is not.

Her eyes are closed, though it is near daylight and I cannot remember a morning when I was awake before she was. I was often up before she was, coming into her room as soon as I left my bed, armed with a question to ask her or the remnant of a dream to relate or something to tell her that I'd forgotten the day before, but I never entered her room to discover my grandmother still asleep.

She always knew I was coming in, no matter how slowly and quietly I opened the door, and her eyes were on me the instant I could see her.

This morning they are closed, though, and I tell myself that's because it's still so early. The clock in the hall has not yet struck five, not all the roosters have finished crowing, and I can hear only one other person moving around in the house—Uncle Lewis, probably, finding his way to the kitchen with his hands stretched out to touch the walls and the gaps for doors in them that have guided him in his blindness for all these years—and I know that Nola Mae is still asleep in the room across the hall, her breathing as regular and untroubled as the light steadily growing in the windows on the east side of the house.

My grandmother's eyes are still closed, but I know she's awake behind her eyelids, and I make a noise deliberately by pushing the straightback chair beside the bed until it scrapes the floor with a rasping sound. That way we can both pretend I've waked her by being careless, and she can open her eyes to look at me and I can say I'm sorry for making the noise, and everything at the break of day can be supposed to be expected and matter of course and normal.

If someone who did not know her had come into the room and seen my grandmother lying in the bed in the position she's in, that person would assume she is awake already, of course. That observation would be mistaken, but understandable.

My grandmother is lying on her back, her head on the pillow neatly in position against the bedstead, she is covered with a quilt with a fold of sheet showing beneath it, and her legs are drawn up so that her feet are flat against the bed itself, as though she has folded herself to lie down while maintaining the ability to rise and stand upright instantly, if the pull of gravity would allow that.

As a child, seeing the way she positioned her legs in that manner as she slept, I imagined she was creating a warm triangle of space beneath the covers where one of her succession of cats might doze in comfort on cold nights, protected from the chill. Midnight, or Lustre or Coolidge. And I tried to teach myself to sleep in that position, neat and controlled and defiant of collapse, but I would always each morning be disappointed to awake and find myself in a sprawl to one side or the other, my legs disorderly and patternless and never a sleeping cat in sight.

How do you do that, I would ask my grandmother, and why, and she always told me that if you had to think about it you could not do it, but that it was the most comfortable way to sleep of all positions possible.

"I'm sorry I woke you," I say, "I should look where I'm going and not run into things."

My grandmother opens her eyes, which seem bright as always, but they have a look of having been somewhere else deeper and farther away from where we are together in my grandmother's house in Holly Springs. They are like a traveler who has arrived at where he's going, but all of his body and mind don't know that yet. Everything that makes him up to be what he is is not there yet, and he is still in the motion of his journey, though he is standing still where he intended to arrive. There is a lag, and he is in it.

In my grandmother's eyes, there is a lag, as well, a space between where she has been in the nighttime dying a little each tick of the clock in the hall outside and here in the room with the steady light growing to show her again the place where she's arrived all those mornings of her life before this one. It is another day, a new one, and her eyes work to reach it.

"Dicia," she says, moving her lips to smile at me, but falling just short of getting to that place, too, the location where the two of us are when we meet together once more since before I can remember. "Did you sleep all right?"

"Yes, GrandMaude," I tell her, working to put my tried and true expression of greeting on my face, but failing to get to that point where my lips begin to sting from my smile. "Except for the times when Nola Mae kicked me in bed."

"Is Nola Mae here? I didn't know she was."

She is trying to move toward sitting up now, and that allows me to fix the pillow behind her and let my smile die while I'm out of range of her seeing me. She straightens her legs beneath the bedclothes, and that makes the triangle of her knees vanish, and I'm glad my grandmother is not able to see my face as I watch that take place. There is no cat to be disturbed in her bed by that movement, and there has not been for years. Coolidge was her last one, a big gray with white feet and an intelligent face, and when he went finally, she said he was the last one she would have, and she has held to that.

"Yes, Nola Mae is here," I'm telling my grandmother in a chirpy voice as I adjust the pillow and help her in her gesture toward sitting up in the new day. She doesn't make it all the way to where she intends before she has to sink back, but she has tried yet another time, and we're both glad about that, though neither of us acknowledges that anything has or hasn't taken place. I'm pleased with myself for being able to achieve the tone of voice I'm using, but I still am not ready to let GrandMaude look into my eyes again. I step back toward the head of the bed and turn my back as I fiddle with a glass and the water pitcher.

"She's been here since Wednesday," I say, "and we've been having a really nice visit. Do you remember talking to her yesterday?"

"Was that yesterday?" she says, and I can tell from the sound of her voice that she is turning her head to look at me. I pour some water into the glass, too much, so that I have to pour some back into the pitcher. But that's good because it gives me more time to prepare.

"I thought Nola Mae was here last week and had gone back home already."

"She was, but she came back. She left to be in a program Sunday in church. That's why."

"I suppose she sang," my grandmother says.

"Oh, yes. And everyone thought she did it beautifully."

"Did she tell you that, Dicia?"

"She did," I say, and thinking of that event, Nola Mae up on stage, singing to all those people looking at her, allows me the distraction I need to be able to turn back and face my grandmother in her bed. "Nola Mae always lets me know what she's been doing and is going to do."

"She's good about that," GrandMaude says, "Nola Mae does sing those hymns so well, and she's a pretty girl, just as pretty as you are, Dicia."

"She's much prettier than that," I tell her, allowing myself now to look directly into my grandmother's eyes. I do it without a bobble, and I'm proud of myself for that. "Nola Mae is a real beauty. She's the flower of the family."

"Flowers," my grandmother says and then pauses as though she's heard a strange sound and wants to identify it, waiting for a moment for it to come again. When it doesn't, she goes on. "Flowers come in all shapes and hues. Nola Mae is the fair beauty of us all. She has that pale complexion her grandmother has. She has Abigail's look about her. She's a Holt."

"Nola Mae's hair is like honey," I say, offering the phrase everybody uses when talking about my cousin. I wonder who was first to say it. Great-Aunt Abigail, probably, since praising Nola Mae allows her to call attention to herself, but I don't mind that. I don't.

"Your hair is like your great-grandmother's," GrandMaude says, carrying on her part in the conversation we've rehearsed and performed time and time again, in that first and most lasting play I ever beheld. But it is a good play, and I've always appreciated it, no matter how well I've gotten its lines by heart and how many times I've anticipated its progress and its turns.

"Carolina Cameron she was before she married Amos Holt," my grandmother says, moving to speak the next line she must deliver in her part, "and her hair was dark, and her skin would brown in the sun each summer until when she smiled her teeth looked as white as cotton."

Saying that about her mother cost her an effort, I can see, and she closes her eyes for a space before she goes on to the rest of what she has always believed she must tell me. "You have my mother's coloring and her hair, and more than that, too."

"What is that, GrandMaude?" I say, giving her the next line in our dialogue and placing the back of my hand against her cheek, which is like cool velvet to the touch. "What's more than that?"

"You see things the way she did, I can tell, and you say things Carolina Cameron might have said."

"Thank you, GrandMaude," I say, getting the words out without a tremor, and I'm proud of myself for that again. "Look at the window," I tell her. "Look, it's daylight."

Nola Mae

I know when she gets up and leaves the bed, quiet as a cat though she's always been, and the room still dark as midnight and not even a sound in the house outside of that big clock hammering away in the hall. When does Dicia sleep? When has she ever slept?

When we were little girls together, they always put us in the same bed at night, and I had to put up with that, having no choice in the matter any and every time we came to Great-Aunt Maude's to visit. And it was Dicia's bed and her room and all her things sitting around on dresser tops and tables and the windowsill, and everything just so in its own place, looking like somebody had thought about it first, long and hard, before leaving it there.

She never said that, Dicia didn't, never reminded me that I was just visiting and was a guest and didn't really live in Great-Aunt Maude's big old house, like she did, but I knew that, all right. I didn't have to be told. Just being treated so nicely, asked if I wanted this or preferred that and being offered every visit either side of the bed I wanted and told I could be left alone in the room anytime I wanted—all that brought it home to me.

I didn't live here then, and never did, and I don't live here still.

I have always been able to tell as soon as I enter a new place—a room or a school building or a store or a place where people have all come together for some reason or some event or the other—whether I belong there or not. Sometimes it feels like I'm in a place where I do belong, and I take a long breath then and let it out slow, and I look around me to begin listing in my mind to remember later the things that are telling me that. Maybe it's a chair made of dark wood with a deep glow to the finish, or a set of curtains in a window hanging in folds that look like they just happened to fall in lines so nicely all by themselves but really didn't. Somebody worked on them for a long time to make them look that way. It takes a hard struggle to look easy.

Once in a while when I feel that way, it's because a person in that place looks at me with an expression that says they're glad to see me and don't want anything at all from me. They're just glad I'm there. If it's a woman, she's smiling because I'm a woman, too, just arriving there, and she sees me to be company.

If it's a man, old or young, he likes the way I look, and he appreciates that for its own sake alone, as he watches me come into his view, unexpected.

But if I'm there, wherever it is, long enough to sit in the chair, say, I find being in it doesn't stay comfortable for any length of time, and I feel like I have to get up and find another better place to settle, and I haven't even finished listing yet all the parts of the space which welcomed me at first. And the woman who smiled when she saw me has now looked away, and she's done that on purpose not to have to keep looking in my direction and making comparisons and judgments. And the young man or the older man, generally the one who's older, is no longer looking at me the way he did at first, as he might view a flower in blossom or the full moon or a field of cotton fully open in September—interested and taken by the sight, but calmly so. Now what's in his mind is the need for use and satisfaction. The smell of the flower, the light from the moon, how many bales of cotton to the acre, what would I feel like to touch.

But I haven't quit looking for that one right place, the room I can enter where all the parts that make up an early welcome stay the same no matter how long I study them, nor how long I stay there.

I used to test Dicia when I was younger and would be brought to Great-Aunt Maude's house to stay by someone in the family—my mother and father or sometimes an older cousin and mainly by my grandmother. How nice can my cousin Dicia be, I remember asking myself? How long can she last? What would it take to cause her to pull away from me and look at me that way the other ones always end up doing?

Once when I was thirteen, just a day after my actual birthday, we got to Great-Aunt Maude's place at night, already so late everybody else in the house was sleeping. I forget why that happened. Maybe my grandmother Mott's Model T had broken down on the way to Holly Springs or a tire had gone flat or the car had run out of gas or water. Something had made it take a long time for us to get there, and I had had plenty of time to think about being a year older than I was two days ago. Thirteen now, I had said over and over to myself as we traveled the roads to Great-Aunt Maude's place, thirteen now, thirteen now, thirteen now.

Doing that made the time pass faster, I had found out when I got to be ten years old and able to count my age in two numbers instead of just one, and it kept me from having to pay attention to all the things Grandma Mott had to say about every house place we passed on the road and who used to live there, and how the cedars were taking over all the old cotton fields where people used to farm, and how bad the ruts were in the roads now since cars drove up and down them all the time instead of just wagons.

Thirteen now, thirteen now, I made myself listen to in my head, saying that over and over while it still sounded good to me, and older and better than where I was just a day before. It felt real. I knew that feeling wouldn't last long, because it never did each year as I got further away from the day that marked the new year in my life. It would fade out, like the music and people talking on the radio did when the battery got weaker every minute you ran it.

But that was the way everything was, I had learned, it got weaker as time went by and didn't mean now what it had a little while before, and that kept on happening, the going away of everything, and you had to live with that, feeling it get harder and harder to hear, no matter how close you listened.

So the only way to be able to stand knowing that, the realizing it was all going away even as you had it right now, was to make it as big as you could in your mind as it was happening. Thirteen now, thirteen now, thirteen now. Saying that and feeling the way it made me feel as I had it, and getting ready for it to fade out like the music coming on the radio from Beaumont or Houston when the battery is steadily sinking lower and lower—that's the only answer, short of shutting it all down.

But you can't turn the radio off and stop the battery from losing what's in it that makes the music come. It goes down anyway, the power does, just the way a block of ice in the icebox will, even if the door is kept shut all the time. You have got to open it to be able to eat the food that's in it, and if you don't it turns yellow and green and black and stinks and rots anyway. And if you don't turn on the radio and make the music loud enough to fill up your ears and your head, it's never going to be there to have ever, at any time.

It all gets weaker and slides away and the radio finally won't work, and what's inside the icebox finally gets as hot as the rest of Texas is outside the walls and doors of the box. Everything is the same all over, everywhere. It's all heading that direction.

So I was thinking about that, without wanting to, because you can't fool your mind for long, either. It's just as ready to tell you what's going to happen as it is to tell you what already did and what's going on right now. It will do what it wants, always.

So all you can do, I had learned by the time I was ten and able to count two numbers to my age is to be ready for the next good thing to come along, to look for that to get here, and to make it last as long as it will when it arrives. Open up the icebox and stick your face into the cold spot and put something cool and fresh into your mouth as quick as you can. Turn the radio on, and make the music in it coming in the air from Beaumont and Houston loud, loud, loud, and let the battery work itself to death as fast as it can.

So as soon as the car stopped in the yard of Great-Aunt Maude's that night, and whoever was driving it, one of my uncles I guess—Jesse or Felder, maybe—cut off the engine, I ran inside the front door and down the hall to the room where I knew Dicia would be sleeping, pushing open the door hard enough to make it slam against the wall with a bang, and listening to the voice in my head say "thirteen now" over and over.

When the noise woke her, Dicia sat up in her bed in an instant, starting to smile big before her eyes were even all the way open, and said my name. "Nola Mae," she said, like she was saying ice cream.

"Dicia," I said, "I'm thirteen years old now. Thirteen, thirteen."

"Happy birthday, Nola Mae," she said, her smile now in full bloom as she threw back the cover to get out of bed. "I thought about you all day yesterday when you had your birthday."

I put up my hand in a way that would have let me slap her if I had let it go, but I made it and the other one and the arms that carried them hug her instead.

"It's real late," I told her. "It's been dark for a long time, and they're going to make us go to bed right now."

"I know it," Dicia said, "but we can whisper as much as we want to. They won't hear us. They'll be too busy talking."

She offered me her side of the bed, as she always did, the warm spot where she'd been sleeping beneath the covers, and I took it, as I always did, drawing my feet up after I lay down to fit the hollow she'd already made, shorter than what fit me. I asked her if she'd been dreaming before I woke her coming into the room, and she said she had, but couldn't remember what it had been about.

"Did you like what you were dreaming?" I said. "Was it good enough that you felt sorry you had to stop when I woke you up?"

"Oh, no," Dicia said, "I'd lot rather have you here to talk to than to have a dream keep on going all to myself."

"But you're not all by yourself when you're dreaming. If it's a good one, I mean," I said. "If the people are pretty in it, and they're having a good time, it's like they're with you."

"No, it wasn't anything good in particular," Dicia said. "I think it was about me looking into water, maybe a pond or creek I was leaning over."

"Were you about to fall in? Was there a gar fish or a snake hiding under the water, waiting to get you? Were you all scared?"

"No," Dicia said after waiting a while to think about it, trying to be certain she was telling what she remembered in the right sort of way, not leaving anything out or putting in a part that hadn't really happened. "No, I don't think so. I wasn't scared of anything, or worrying if anything bad was waiting in the water. So I suppose all I was seeing in my dream was just water. Everything in it was quiet and peaceful."

"Peaceful?" I said. "That doesn't sound like much of a dream to me. I expect this side of your bed is not where you want to lie if you want to have a good dream then."

"What is a good dream?" Dicia asked, sounding like she was asking something she wanted answered and was not just being nice. She's always been able to do that. "How do you know if it's good if it's not over with yet?"

"It doesn't have to be over with to be good," I said. "Here, swap sides with me. I don't want to lie on a side of the bed where the dreams you have are not any good."

After Dicia traded places with me and I'd had to draw my feet up again to stay in the warm spot she'd made, she asked it once more.

"How do you know it's a good dream if you haven't been through all of it yet, Nola Mae? When can you decide?"

"Decide, nothing," I said. "You don't decide. If you have to decide if something's good or not, it's not good, and it's not worth thinking about, much less wasting time going back and forth over in your mind. Just put it out of your head."

"Maybe it's hard to tell," she said, accidentally touching my leg with her bare foot and then pulling it away, but not fast like I would have done if I had touched somebody I hadn't wanted to. Dicia did it like she does everything, polite somehow, so as not to offend, not jerking away but moving like she was thinking about the right way to do it and didn't want to raise an alarm or make me feel bad.

So I stuck my foot up against her leg and kept it there until she gradually moved that part of her body away from contact with my foot, too, as polite as she was the first time.

"Maybe it's good and not so good, all at the same time, mixed up together somehow," she said, "and it takes some studying about it to see which side to come down on. Maybe whether a dream is good or not is not so easy to decide."

"If it's not clear, I don't want to know about it," I said, by then talking louder than in a whisper as we had first started out doing. Somebody knocked on the other side of the wall behind Dicia's bedstead, three times loud enough to make both of us jump.

"Great-Uncle Lewis," Dicia whispered, putting her hand to her mouth and looking at me with her eyes wide. "We better turn out the lamp and not talk so loud."

"What does he care about the lamp being out or not?" I said. "Great-Uncle Lewis is as blind as a tumble-bug. He can't see a thing, even if he was right in the room with us."

"He can see shapes, he says, and the light if he looks right at it."

"He can't see our light," I said.

"No, but he hears us, and the rest of them will get up if he keeps knocking on the wall, and they'll come in the room."

"How do you know all that?" I asked Dicia, just to let her know that I didn't think everything she said was always right. I knew how to pay attention to what was going on back then, and I sure do now, even more so.

"I know how GrandMaude thinks," Dicia said, "most of the time. And I always know what Great-Aunt Abigail is liable to do."

"Who doesn't?" I said. "Here, change sides of the bed with me. I'm not used to sleeping on this side, and it's up against the wall, too. I'll hit my head against it when I turn over in my sleep."

Dicia let me crawl over her again, moving as neatly as a cat settling itself and not complaining a bit that time, either, as I got on her side of the bed. I turned down the lamp wick before I lay all the way down again, watching it fade to red and then black as the air stopped getting to it. It was all black in the room, not even a square of gray light where the window was, no moon and no stars and no sound anywhere, and not even a sound of Dicia's drawing breath. She does even that so you can't hear it.

"What about nightmares?" I whispered in the dark, thinking thirteen now, thirteen now, thirteen now to myself, "They're different from a dream."

"Yes," Dicia said in a voice even lower than mine, "they are, but I don't want to think about nightmares now." I could tell by the sound of her turning over that she was now lying on her stomach with her face pointed away from me.

"Why not?" I said, "why not talk about nightmares now when it's dark and we can't see a thing, when we're just as blind as Great-Uncle Lewis is all the time, day and night?"

"That's why," Dicia said, "that's exactly why. We can talk about nightmares tomorrow in the daylight."

I put my hand under the cover until it reached Dicia's bottom where it stuck up like little hills in the dark bed where you could know it only by touch, and I lifted my hand as if to spank her under the quilt. Dicia lay there for as long as it would take to draw a breath, and then she put her hand on mine and moved it away, patting it twice after she'd done that, as polite as ever and not saying a word.

I still couldn't hear my cousin breathe, though I lay there listening for that as close as I could. I know I stayed awake longer than she did, though, there in the dark with not a sound in my great-aunt's house just one day past the time I became thirteen.

My grandmother is going to come get me up any minute now, no matter how hard I might work to convince her I'm still asleep. Whatever she's doing she thinks everybody around her should be doing, too, and I can hear people rustling around in the hall and somewhere farther back in Great-Aunt Maude's house. Somebody's banging away with pans in the kitchen, and Great-Uncle Lewis just came by the door to Dicia's room where I've been sleeping. You can tell people by their walks, and it was him, I know, because he takes steps like a blind man does. A little scrape, then a step, and another scrape, and a step, and the sound of his hand moving along the wall and then stopping for a breath when he hits the gap a door makes. And then going on again.

I used to put hands over my ears not to hear him do that when I was little and it would scare me. No, not scare me, really, but make me feel the way I do when I see something or somebody truly ugly, like the old men on the courthouse square in Annette on Saturdays, all humped up and tottery, some of them with warts and growths on their faces, some fat and some skinny like they're sick and just waiting to die, all of them with their eyes squinched up as they look at me going by, trying to say something to me, but I always walk too fast to have to show I even hear or notice them.

Now when I hear Great-Uncle Lewis bobbling along with his blind man steps, I treat it the same way I do the words the old men on the courthouse square try to get me to listen to. I don't hear, I don't see, I don't let myself know it's happening.

Here's the way I've learned to handle things that are ugly, and it was simple once I came upon it. Put something else in your head, I came to tell myself, because you know you can't just keep things from getting in. That would be the best way, if there was a screen that everything trying to get inside you would have to go through first. Then all the ugly parts, the pieces too big to squeeze through, the stuff that doesn't belong, everything that doesn't fit—all that would be caught in the mesh the screen is made of, and you could knock it off and let it fall to the ground like they do pieces of trash in a cotton gin.

All that finally came through the screen would be white and pure and clean to the touch and to the smell.

But there is no screen, and everything gets to smelling bad if enough time passes, no matter what it is or how sweet it was at the beginning.

So it came to me, in bits and pieces, not all at once, what I could do to keep out of my head what I did not want inside it, nor could abide to allow. Take up the room that's waiting there not by trying to screen stuff out, but by filling up all the room that's there. Don't give bad stuff space to find a lodgment, nor to stay.

Dicia, my cousin, the one with the dark hair with the natural curl, does not do that, of course. She hugs it up to her, the pretty and the ugly, the good and the trashy, good-looking young men and the old tottery ones with growths on their faces and death not two years down the road, and she smiles at all of it, and says hello, so glad to see you. What a pretty day we're having, aren't we?

My grandmother is at the bedroom door now, banging away on it and calling my name and saying something about biscuits, and I've got to speak up as though she's just roused me from a deep and restful sleep, and act surprised and interrupted.

But not just yet.

Lewis

I hear them through the wall in the room that's there whispering to each other, now and then the voices getting a little louder and then falling back, and I try to keep it all down to a mumble, just sounds not words strung together to mean something. The less I understand of what they're saying to each other, Maude's granddaughter and Abigail's, the better I like it.

That's one of the worst things about going blind, having to listen to what other people are saying, hearing that and understanding it and not wanting to, but not being able to close it off. And what people say about going blind—at least part it, anyway—is true, but I always deny it when they get to yammering on and telling me what they think I ought to know about the condition of being a blind man. What I mean that's true in what they say is the notion that as you lose your eyesight you gain power in your hearing and your touch and the other ways you possess to know what's going on around you.

That is true, at least the hearing part and the touching, too. But I don't want to give them the satisfaction of feeling they're right in what they say when one of them is telling me what it's like to be blind. So I say to them, Abigail in particular, because she has always all her life harped on a thing she believes she knows over and over, out loud to anybody that's around to appreciate it, simply because she figures whatever it is she knows belongs to her alone and therefore has got to be original and deserves being recognized and admired.

Here's what she'll tell me, and what she has told me, again and again, until I feel sometimes like balling up my fist and swinging at her for saying it again, but don't, of course, since she's a woman and my sister and besides I can't see to aim right.

"Lewis," she'll say, "I know it's a terrible burden not to be able to see, to be blind, you know." She says that, repeats the word *blind*, I mean, to explain to me that's what people call it when a person can't see, as if she's talking to a man so ignorant he has to have that connection pointed out to him, to help him along in his understanding in case he's trying to figure out what to call the fact that when he looks up at the sun, which he has to tell the direction of by the way it feels warm on his face, that what he's experiencing is the state of being blind. That's supposed to be a relief to him, I guess, to have the right and proper word for it given to him by somebody out there in the world where the light is.

"Lewis," she'll say, "it is a burden, like I always say, to be blind. But there are compensations that the Lord provides for that lack, and the main one is that all your other senses just get a lot sharper. You hear better. Your touch gets a lot stronger, and lets you understand what things are just by feeling of them. I imagine that what you eat even tastes better, too, and the water you drink and the milk and coffee and all like of that are more tasty to your palate. That's one of the advantages you have over the rest of us."

Depending on the way I'm feeling at the time, I'll try to come back at my sister Abigail when she gets to lining out for me the special gifts the Lord has given to me along with plucking out my sight. I might say and have said something like this here back to her.

"Why, sure, Abigail. You know you're really on to something that's a great consolation and a benefit to me, and I'm surprised that a woman like you that's not been given the advantages I have is able to know that and has had the sense to figure it out.

"It's been plenty of times, sister, when I've felt such a gratitude to the Lord for making me able to savor my buttermilk better than poor old regular folks that I've just gotten down on my knees to thank Him. First, of course, I feel around in front of me to be sure there's nothing in the way to stop me from dropping to the floor, or to the ground if I'm outside, when that feeling comes over me. No rocks or cockleburs or standing puddles or where a dog's done his business, and if I can tell it's all clear, why I just hit my knees and start praising and glorifying His name for the gifts He's done laid on me."

One of the first times when I did say something along those lines to Abigail, she got real quiet for a minute or two to think of a way to come back at me, and then she figured she had it, had discovered the words to counter what I'd just said.

"Brother," she said, "I do guess and admit the worst thing that can happen to a person is to lose his sight, to become blind."

See, she had to explain to me even then that to lose sight is to become blind. She kindly gave me the word for that condition again, and I was duly gratified.

"No, Abigail," I said and pointed to the middle of my forehead with my index finger, "the worst thing that can happen to a person is not to be struck blind, but to be nuts."

She flounced off at that, I could tell she was going by all the bustling sounds and the shoe heels hitting the floor and the under-the-breath grumbling going on, and I felt like calling after her to ask why she was leaving and telling her I knew she was on her way out because my improved hearing carried the sounds of her departure home to me so well, praise God.

I didn't say anything, though, having got older and wiser over the years. Why waste breath or any more energy trying to get in another shot when you know your first one has hit home dead-center?

The one talking the loudest and the most on the other side of the wall is Abigail's granddaughter, Nola Rae, and that's been true for all that girl's life. She gets into something, and she's going to take it all the way beyond where it just belongs to her, and she's going to let the rest of the world know and appreciate it, too. She might start off low and quiet with the thing, whatever it is, hugged up to her like it's for her consideration alone, but she is bound to turn it loose finally like you will a frisky dog you're tired of trying to hold back from getting up in everybody's face.

It is going to announce itself and get some attention directed at it, if it kills it to do it. That girl has always been that way, seeking to turn everybody's eyes on her, from the time she hit Texas on day one right up to the present time now, where she's jabbering away at her cousin not a foot from my head with nothing but a white pine board wall between my bed and theirs. And I hear her real strong, naturally, since I don't have any eyesight to hold me back.

Dicia is talking some, too, answering what Nola Mae's saying for the most part, it sounds like, and not throwing out new subjects to be treated in conversation from her side, at least. That doesn't seem to be holding Nola Mae back much, though, given the bloodline she's come from. Probably if Dicia was to get to talking, that would be a lot more of a control on the amount and volume of the noise coming through my wall than if she kept holding back, like she's doing now and habitually does do.

Nola Mae's furtherance of herself is like the Sabine River when it gets up in the spring. It abhors a vacuum, like that old teacher back in Double Pen Creek schoolhouse would tell us about the world. Maybe it was *nature* was the word he would use. It was one of those terms teachers like to rant on about, nature or the world abhors a vacuum, he'd say. I don't know what he meant exactly, nor cared much neither, but I liked the sound of the words, particularly abhor. I'd already learned about the word *whore* by then and what whores did, so that word old Professor Duncan used, *abhor*, called all that up for me to think about, and I appreciated that and was grateful for it. That was all the good old Duncan ever did do me, now I think about it.

But what I mean by Nola Mae and her nature is if she finds an opening she is going to go through it, and if it leads into an empty spot she is going to fill that spot up. It is as normal and natural for her to do that, as it is for the river to rise in the spring when too much water comes down from the creeks and tributaries for the banks to hold it.

I saw her well and clear, I saw both of them, Nola Mae and Dicia, before the lamps went completely out on me those years ago. Of course, they were just little ones at the time, crawling around the floor, and I noticed them the way you will a litter of puppies, seeing all that squirming and some colors mixed up and noticing them not because of what they are, but for what they're not. Not still, not one hue, not quiet, not the background you're seeing them against.

Even then, though, they stood out from each other, and you had to notice the difference between them, whether you were interested in that or not. Light and dark. Plump and thin. One of them studying you close, the other one just looking you over. One moving and twisting and slamming one thing after another into her mouth to get the taste of all she could, as fast as she could, while the other one looks real close at one thing for a long time and cries when it's taken away from her, like she's not entirely finished figuring it out yet.

But back then in the days when I could see both my grandnieces as well as hear them, I paid a lot less mind to how they were different from each other in how they took in the world and tried to get along in it than I do now. Abigail is right in what she says about learning things deeper when you can only hear what's going on and not have eyesight available to take more of what's going on into your head at the same time.

I wouldn't admit that to her, satisfied enough she is with herself most of the time anyway, but like a piney-woods hog rooting around in a stand of red oaks, she is bound to turn over some of what's hiding all the acorns, given time enough. The distinction to be drawn is that the natural hog is not looking for any acorn in particular and is satisfied with whatever comes into view, and doesn't stop to reward itself with a pat on the back when it hits something nourishing.

The hog doesn't care about congratulations from itself or anybody else, either. Eating what turns up is reward enough.

But she's right, Abigail is, about the way a blind man comes to know things further down into the meat of a subject, when he's forced to get by on just hearing words said about it by folks, rather than watching them when they're giving voice to their statements.

It doesn't seem logical, that understanding doesn't, but it has come to appear to me that what I hear blind in the words people trade between each other gains something from my not being distracted by all that light playing on them, the light I can't see anymore.

It is a blessing, thought about one way, I suppose, and a curse coming from the opposite direction. I know in my blind condition more about people, and why they say what they say, and what they really are meaning beneath and behind the words they're offering each other like presents wrapped up pretty for Christmas than I ever did when the light coming in my eyes made pictures for me of the world I walked around in. I saw then what I thought was the whole truth, but now I know I didn't.

Am I glad about that? Sometimes I am, and sometimes it's a satisfaction that I hold to me like a secret to be tasted all alone. It's mine, for me only, and nobody else can ever know what I am holding. I don't have to show a one of my cards.

And then sometimes I don't give a damn. I just want my eyes back.

Dicia now is up at dawn already, stepping quiet through the door she closes behind her with the least sound needful to make, so as not to wake her cousin who's still sleeping. At least Dicia thinks Nola Mae's still asleep, but I know she's not by the way Nola Mae flops in the bed the other side of the wall between us, thinking by that she'll fool her cousin into believing she's roused a bit by Dicia raising the covers and letting cold air in.

That's all calculated, though, I can tell by the quality of the flop to a new location Nola Mae takes in her bed, and it's designed to make Dicia feel a little guilty about halfway waking her cousin up from a nice deep and restful sleep. Nola Mae knows Dicia cares about such things, never wanting to offend when she can avoid it, and so Nola Mae doesn't want to miss the chance to pick at her kin a little.

What Dicia's most worried about is her grandmother, my sister Maude, lying in her room across the hall, dying by degrees, but if Nola Mae can add a little bit to the load on her cousin's mind, why she feels obliged to do it. And she does, since it doesn't take that much effort.

I know all this, what's going on behind that wall between me and those grandnieces, blind as old Bartemus though I be. But should a man have to know that much, or want to? Hell, no, is the answer to that question. It ain't no real satisfaction in a trainload of knowing that stuff. You don't have to study on it.

I've got to get up here in a minute, feel my way to the kitchen, hoping some fool has not moved pots and pans and cold biscuits from last night's supper around on me, and find me something to eat and some coffee to drink. Then I ought to go see how sister Maude is faring this morning.

I say see, but saying that doesn't make any sense, of course. It's just another way you're liable to talk when you're using words. I don't see. I don't see a thing at all.

Maude

She comes into the room the way Richard always would when he thought he might be in danger of surprising or alarming somebody. Making a little noise at the door at first, more than needful to effect an entrance, but not so loud he ruins what he was trying to accomplish by it.

I try to open my eyes to let her know she's successful, but they're the way my fingers used to feel when a little syrup had leaked out of a biscuit on the way to my mouth, not stuck together but tacky to the touch. I like that stickiness, and I move my fingers back and forth, up and down, playing with the feel of it until it's gone. Abigail doesn't like that, and she grabs at my hand when she sees me do that. It's messy, Maudie, she says, you'll get it on your dress and then who'll have to wash it? Me, I tell her, me, I'll wash it. Let me do it. I don't mind.

"Are you dreaming, GrandMaude?" Dicia asks and puts her hand on my forehead as though she's seeing if I've got fever, but I know she's trying to find a way to help me open my eyes. Richard is not with her, I know that, though they come into the room the same way. I won't mention her father to her, though.

"Dicia," I say, "it's the syrup. A little dab squeezed out and got on my fingers." That's not right, I know that as soon as I say it, but those are the words that came out when I spoke. I don't intend to say anything like that, in one part of me, the part of me that decides what I'll let people see and know, the part that parcels out how much I'll allow to show and how much I'll keep to myself.

It's harder to make that part work exactly when I want it to now, though, and I find myself waiting to see what I'm going to say time and time again. I'm my own audience, then, when that happens, and something is opening wider and wider inside me in the place where I am.

That was altogether once in one location, and if it were sketched out on a map you could unfold and display for viewing, I could have pointed to a placename and put the tip of my finger on it and said this is me here, Maude Holt Blackstock Winston, here am I taking up my part of Texas. And here are the roads that lead here, that a person could follow when looking for me. Wherever you came from before, no matter where you started nor what settlement you left on your journey to Maude, here is where you fetch up when the traveling is done.

But the roads on that map I was able once to snap open so briskly to find that spot I thought I knew so well, those roads are all leading away from that spot now, away from Maude, headed out of town. When the eye lights on Maude, it does not settle solid and fixed any longer. It wants to wander. It finds the ways out of the settlement, ones more attractive to follow, and it is lured to go where they lead. From, not to, now. Where the roads lead.

Maude in Texas on its share of the map has become lighter on the land.

The part of me that let me pick and choose which portion of myself to reveal to travelers coming my direction is like a store steadily closing down. Almost all the timber that kept people coming to the territory has been cut now, and the lumber company commissary store does less and less trade.

When the last trees are felled and topped and cut and planed into measured board feet, no one will stay around to trade for what the store offers. Another location in Texas that once drew people will go back to volunteer cedar in the fields and fences down and at the heart of the settlement nothing but a mound of coarse wood dust left from the time the big saws did all that cutting.

I never wanted Richard to go into the logging woods, to pick up tools, to listen to the sawmill whistle, to make a living for himself that way with his back and his hands.

I thought of other ways for him, as a mother will, and I looked at his hands, his long delicate fingers and the gestures they made when he talked and the grace in his movements and the way he would look so deeply into the eyes of anyone who spoke to him, the way he listened to stories told him or books read to him, and I knew he was not suited for the shapes that men's lives take here.

And when he was taken by the army and sent to the war in France, I knew he would be killed by some other mother's son able to be hard, to deal death with a bullet or bayonet, to look on what he had done with no sorrow, no satisfaction, no feeling. God, I prayed, let this one not be lost in mud and darkness and blood and ripped flesh. Let him not be taken out of the light and air and open spaces where he has lived such a little time yet.

Let him return whole and unharmed and himself, God, I said, and I will promise you this. And I remember I looked up at the ceiling of the Double Pen Creek chapel, after I had said that, and I waited for something to come to my mind, something that God might want from me, something worth the trade of that thing for the life of my boy, my only son with Valery Blackstock, my true love, and nothing seemed good enough or big enough that I could provide that God could want from me.

Wasps were going in and out of the cells of the nests they were building above me, and the heat of the sun beating on the roof of the church was causing the pieces of tin to groan and strain against the nails holding them down. God, I said again inside my head where no one but me and Him could hear me, because a verse says somewhere in the Bible that it is better and more righteous to pray in a closet than to shout from the rooftop, God, I will promise this.

But again nothing came to me that He could want, and the buzzing of the wasps in the heat above me was loud enough to cause me to look up, and I saw them at their work, insects with no minds nor souls, possessing nothing but one thing, but that in abundance. And that was intent, and that was will.

God, I said, I will promise you in exchange for safe return, for his life to be spared and for him to be brought home to me, for him to be granted more time on this earth and in this life, a nothing. I will promise you a nothing, God, an absence of something. The things that are in me are not worthy of a gift to You, a trade for a favor so immense in Your keeping. What I can give You is not a provision in my care, but a giving up.

Return Richard, my son, to a further portion of life here, and I will kill in myself that desire, and need, and want for something other than what I am and what I have. I will shun and abjure and abdicate and quell and reject and stifle that thing in me that hurts for what I am not. I will turn my eye into myself and live all my days with no longing turned within and look no more over the walls of my fortress to the fields and the trees and the open sky beyond which always call me.

My intent will be to have no intent, my will to be unwilled, my self to be selfless.

And God made that trade with me, took me at my word, and the wasps working their way into the cells of their nest above me in the Double Pen Creek chapel continued with their striving and carried out the sealing of the walls of the compartments from which their young would spring to build their own homes and lodgment, and theirs and theirs after.

Richard Blackstock, my son, came home from the war in France with his body intact and unscarred, and to our eyes untouched by all that took the lives of so many in that faraway place.

When he came that day into the house in the Double Pen Creek community where I lived with my husband, no one expected him, and I was in bed already, not yet full asleep, drowsing with a book on my chest. I knew, that he was coming, but not when, and when he opened the door to the bedroom, I thought it was my husband Ezra back late from Saturday trading in Annette. And I admit to keeping my eyes closed so that my husband would think I was asleep and I wouldn't have to listen to his recounting his day in town and the pricings and the costs and the payments. And I owed my husband the attention, but I did not want to honor that debt just then. Tomorrow, I thought, tomorrow will do.

"Mother," he said in that tone and volume calculated not to disturb should the circumstance not be fitting. "I'm home."

I opened my eyes from what was not a dream, and looked at Richard beside the bed in an army uniform too big for him, and though the tears came in such an amount as to blind me, I saw clearly that trading with God is an exact transaction and that His accounting leaves no grain of sand unnumbered.

My son was in my house, returned to me as bargained for, and he would live further portion of a life with me and the Holts and Fergusons and all our kin, but not even God could bring all of him intact back home again as he was when he left.

"I don't care," I said to God out loud, "I don't care," pulling Richard to me so hard that the buttons on his uniform dug into my chest like barbed wire, but the rest I said to Him in private in my mind, picking each word out of those available to me for use, choosing them one by one, and looking them over in turn the way you will each egg you lift from a hen's nest to mix into a dish for serving those dependent on your cooking—coldly and with care, favoring one over the other only as to its use, not its appeal to you.

I'll keep my bargain, I said to God inside my mind where He lives and where He has set up His long tables for accounting. I'll take this in place of nothing, and I'll give you the nothing I promised in trade. I'll treasure it for what there is of it, and I accept that I couldn't have the all I would have taken if it was offered. Not even You, I said to God, could make that pure transference of what was into what is and have it be still what was.

But I'll not waver, and I'll not want, and I'll turn my eye inside myself to study the nothing at the core of all things in this world, whether the center of an egg or of the sun or of the earth itself, the point that is not, around which all that is, circles.

I will not want what is not. I will behold what is.

"You don't care?" Richard said, his lips turned into a smile as he pulled back from my arms to look at me, the smile from childhood, except now for his eyes which would never be touched again by whatever it is that leads a face to show pleasure or satisfaction or peace. I knew that spark was gone from him, then, and that it would not be coaxed back into a glow, nor a flame, nor a heat. But I would not ask for it, not desire it to leap up as itself again, and I would keep my bargain with God by strict accounting.

But I had not said I would not mourn the loss, only that I would not let others see it, and that would be mine in place of the nothing I had traded with God for Richard's life. That loss I would keep at the core of where I was located, the point of absence around which all that was Maude Holt revolved.

"Don't pay any mind to what I say," I said to my son back in Texas, wearing an army uniform too big for him, "looking at you here again with me, there's nothing in my head, and my words just tumble out with not a speck of meaning to them."

"What do you mean about syrup, GrandMaude?" Dicia is saying, her hand now leaving my forehead as she sees my eyes open to look at her, and now she's arranging the bedclothes to lie more neatly about me, patting at them.

"Would you like some syrup and biscuit this morning? I'll bring you some of that good ribboncane that Mr. Shackleford gave us. It's not heavy at all. It's sweet and light."

"No, little girl," I say to her. "I'm not hungry. But your Papa would have liked that ribboncane syrup."

"Did he have a sweet tooth?" Dicia says. "I guess that's where I got mine. I'll blame him for it."

She has the covers arranged to suit her now, and she stands back from the bed to get a better view, pursing her lips a little as she's always done when testing the quality of anything she's attempted. Satisfied enough, she says something about my needing to eat a little and leaves the room headed for the kitchen. I hope she doesn't blame Richard for the syrup. She steps lively as always.

They let me sleep, all of them, as much as I want to pretend to do with my eyes closed. People never want to wake or disturb a person who's dying. They seem to know, without having to be told it or having to talk it over with each other, that dying is hard work and requires attention and effort from the one doing it and rest from that while it's fully underway. All of my kinfolks and the ones who aren't, the neighbors who just come to see, take me at my word, if you can call keeping your eyes shut when you're really awake a message by word. If it's a word, it's an unspoken one, but of course that's the strongest word there is.

I say all of them observe the fiction and take it for truth, but I must except Abigail. Certainly, surely, and naturally, and it should go without saying, and all those phrases you use when you say a thing that needs no voicing because of the face of truth already stamped upon it, staring back at you like a shiny new silver dollar fresh from the mint with you the first one to handle it.

She comes into the room where I'm doing all I can and must do to get through and past the dying the way she always has entered the presence of any and all persons she has encountered in her life. Talking, the right words already picked out to fit the character and the disposition of the one she's meeting, right at least in her calculation at the moment and suitable to the occasion before her, as she sees it.

And she relishes that encounter just entered upon with the fullness of its experience yet to come. It's sitting there like a blackberry cobbler fresh from the oven still on the edge of being too hot to break into with a spoon, steam rising and a bubble of boil evident in the juices coming through the fork holes punched in the crust, like lava from a volcano the way it's always pictured in a geography book. Molten, hot, and to come.

Most people would hold back for a minute or two to let it cool to a temperature easier to bear for eating, but not Abigail. She wants the juice, and the sweet and the sour mixed with and against each other, and she wants to say the words her mind has prepared her to dish out to this particular hearer at this particular time.

There were times when I thought I could not bear one more demonstration by my sister of that core of her character, and I would find ways to break through the barrage of words she was leveling in order to get her to stop or at least to give me a purchase against the flood of them coming at me. I would speak sharply to her, or literally put my hands over my ears on a few occasions to let her see directly that I would not listen, and once or twice I even ran from the room or the porch or the location outdoors where she had found me in range, screaming aloud nonsense syllables to drown out her and what she was saying.

And this when I was a grown woman in my forties and fifties, not a schoolgirl or a young woman or newly wife to a man.

Some of those times I was successful in hurting Abigail enough to shut her up in midcourse of whatever she was telling me about myself or my children or our mother and father or our sisters or brothers or neighbors in the community or a flight of ducks or a broken down automobile belonging to someone I did not know or President Coolidge or oil strikes on the Gulf Coast or cotton prices falling, falling, falling in Texas.

Those little triumphs I achieved were never worth the price I paid for them afterward, though. The recriminations, the tears, the apologies, the protestations and avowals and disavowals, so I relearned what I had known as a child and forgotten for a space as I came into myself as a grown woman and came to think myself separate and above and beyond my ties to my sister.

What my mother Carolina told me as a child, the words she gave me to remember as a charm and talisman against the force of statement and opinion from my older sister, provided solace and defence then, and came to do so again. "Let your sister talk," my mother told me, "and let her words wash over and around and about you like the breeze."

"The breeze?" I said. "How does that help me when Abigail says some of the things she say to me and I can't find a way not to listen?"

"Does the breeze get inside you?" mother said. "Is the breeze like water coming into your mouth or wetting your clothes and face and hair when it comes in the shape of rain?"

"No," I said. "The breeze just touches me and musses my hair sometime. If it's cold, it makes me feel chilly, and if it's hot it cools me off."

"Do you listen to the breeze? Does it tell you things?"

"Not much, not usually."

"That's like Abigail talking then, isn't it, when she's saying things you don't want to hear? The breeze always dies down, finally, and the rain stops, and your clothes and hair dry, and you can comb your hair all back into shape again, can't you?"

"Yes," I said. "But what if it's a hurricane? Or a tornado?"

"Get out of the direct line of it, then, Maude," Mother said. "And just wait a few more minutes. Everything abates, finally."

Now when Abigail comes into my room, I'm not only not bothered, but grateful that she has always something to say. It's easier to work on the dying if the people who come to watch you do it treat you like they always have before and if they don't stand so much on ceremony as they observe you carrying out your job of work.

Abigail, not to fear, wouldn't know ceremony if it tripped her up and bit her ankles. That I am grateful for, her stomping all over ceremony.

This morning she is talking about somebody who lives in Sour Lake, down in Hardin County, she thinks it's located, but she's not sure until she manages finally to convince herself she does know for a certainty and a fact its true location.

"Hardin County," she says, "Maude, of course it is. You remember the time Papa took me and you and Mama, of course, and the rest of the children, the ones that were living then, I mean. I believe Lewis was the newest one then, just a babe in arms, still at that point, not even getting around at all yet. He was born in May, you remember, the fifth of the month, and the time Papa took all of us to Sour Lake, there in Hardin County, it was up in the summer. So Lewis would have been not even six months old yet. You remember that, don't you, Maude?"

"Yes," I say, listening to the breeze of my sister's conversation gust around and about in the east-facing room where I'm spending the rest of the time left to me. If it were a true breeze and not just the one Mama described to ease my mind as a child, the windows in my room would be beginning to rattle now. "He was born in May all right, Lewis was," I tell my sister.

"And Sour Lake is in Hardin County," Abigail is saying, "But that's not where I knew Beulahdene Dillon. She lives there now, but not when I knew her first. You've met her. You had to have met her, if you'll just think about it. Reddish hair back then, real quick in her movements, had I don't know how many children, all of them red-headed but the one, that littlest boy whose name I can't call. I will in a minute, though, if you'll just not say a name it might be, because if you do that'll affect my memory, your putting the wrong name in my head and making me keep thinking of it instead of the right one. So don't say any names yet, Maude."

"All right," I tell her, and that will be all she needs to let her return to the story about some woman I've never met at all, and if I did, I've forgotten. And what's wrong with that, forgetting an incident so unremarkable not a detail of it stays in my head?

Nothing is wrong with that, if you're considering it in connection with an ordinary person who doesn't see every momentary occurrence of life charged with meaning and portent. But that person wouldn't be Abigail, now flown full strength into the heart of the story she needs to tell me about some woman whose name she can't remember now living in Sour Lake in Hardin County, Texas, but who didn't used to, when first met by Abigail and become thereby a character in my sister's life story.

I remember Sour Lake, as anybody living in East Texas during my lifetime would have to. All that commotion when they first hit oil by drilling into the salt dome where Captain Lucas said it would be, all the men wanting to throw down the reins of their mule teams and their cotton hoes and go to work in the oil fields and get rich. Or at least buy an automobile and a new suit of clothes.

Lewis thought he would be among the lucky ones to profit, and he left home so fast he had to carry his goods in a cut-down cotton sack, shouting from the road at me that the next time I saw my brother he'd be riding in a shiny automobile belonging to nobody but him.

He did get that car, and he got another one and another one after that, and he let us all see him drive each and every one every time he came back to Coushatta County, sitting behind the wheel dressed in a suit and tie with a cigar jammed in his mouth at an angle and some poor little ugly girl hugged up to him. I say ugly not to be mean to those girls and their natural appearance but because of the way they made themselves to look with lip rouge and powder and hair permanents and dresses and skirts and hats in colors that never seemed to go together, but announced each part separate and alone.

They were nice enough, most of them, just girls from their papas' farms around and about in the country, and they never talked much or tried to show out in an offensive way, unless the times they arrived with my brother happened to catch them in a drunken state, or a crazy one, whatever the case was at the moment.

"Looky here, looky here," Lewis would say, "Maude, this little lady is Edith," or it could be almost any name, a short one generally which the girl had probably chosen for herself in place of the one her mother and father had given her. Who would want to be called Hortense or Avalene or Wilma or Maggie Lee or Mattie Lou, letting yourself be known by the label put on you by some old fool of a farmer from Colmesneil or Kountze or Hull Daisetta when you could pick out some syllables on your own that fit better your own notion of yourself? Ruby or Pearl or Jewel or Rita Jean? Some combination of sounds that matched what you had in your head that said this is what the world ought to think and ought to say when it beholds me, not some statement shouting *country*, saying *grandma*.

She was one of those girls with the snappy names who showed up with brother Lewis at our place well after dark had come one November day after the war had ended. She was half his age, if that, and the car Lewis was carrying her in was not a new one, and that was the third or fourth time that had been true of his mode of transportation. Luck had been, and was, and would be changing for the worse for Lewis Holt, trader in oil leases and Hupmobiles and dreams for big breaks just over the horizon. His automobile was proof and testimony to that, so much so by that point that Lewis's usual stunt of running his machine up close enough to the porch to almost touch it failed in execution this time.

The brakes didn't catch soon enough to stop the car's progress, and its bumper ran into a porch support hard enough for us to feel it inside the house.

"Uncle Lewis," Richard said to reassure me as I looked up startled from some book I was reading by the light of a lamp in the front room. "I expect it's all right. Nothing's really hurt."

By the time he had picked up the kerosene lamp, opened the door, and walked out onto the porch, the girl had gotten out of the automobile, but Lewis was still behind the wheel fiddling with something in front of him and stomping his foot up and down on the brake pedal, as though by so doing he could somehow reverse time and recapture that flawed moment, recreate it to allow him another chance at an exciting and fulfilling arrival at his older sister's house in the woods.

I was right behind Richard as he walked out onto the porch, lamp lifted high in hand to allow the best possible first view of what had just come slamming into the porch and into our lives, and I saw him see her for the first time. My son physically and literally staggered slightly, it appeared to me, flinched a bit momentarily, the way you will when you encounter a thing before you that you had not expected but realized when you beheld it that you were anticipating it all along and had simply not known that fact until the instant of discovery. He knew her when he saw her, though he had never seen her before.

I put out my hand to touch my son's shoulder, but he did not feel that nor acknowledge my presence behind him, and I knew at that instant that he never would do that fully again.

When I dropped my hand and looked toward the woman Richard was seeing for the first time, she was just moving into the circle of light cast by the lamp, lifting her face to see who had come outside on the porch against which the bumper of the car had just collided.

"Cut it off," she said to Lewis, not looking in his direction as she spoke, "I do believe we've got to where we're going."

Her first name, the one she had created to match the idea of the woman she wanted herself to be, was Darlene, and her last name was Simmons, an ordinary enough sounding one to be truly that of a family which had got her started in Jefferson County. Or maybe she began in

Harris, where Houston is, or Chambers, or Orange. She was later to say all those, and more. That changed, as the seasons do, and the new fact was always needful, and it always fit the time.

She was wearing a yellow hat, bright enough in the light of the lamp Richard held to be distinguished clearly from the wrongful orange of her coat and the darker print beneath it. The hue of yellow was what burned into Richard's memory, though, deeply settled enough to last from that time forward and so permanent that all he bought to give her for the rest of the life remaining to him reflected it. The little scarves, that necklace of porcelain Dicia keeps now in a small brown box as memento of her mother, the blouses he gave Darlene, the pair of earrings he sent away for to Chicago, the clutches of daisies he picked that spring for her—all were shades of yellow, little versions, Richard called them, of the sun.

In two days' time, Lewis had his car running again, and he was ready to set out for Beaumont, but Darlene by then would not leave with him, of course. He cursed her, calling her the names men give women who will not love them in return, or at least pretend to, and my brother threatened to kill my son, his nephew, and swore never to return to this part of Texas, which had always been given the back of God's hand and where no man worth the powder necessary to blow him to Hell would ever want to reside.

He could tell Richard things about Darlene Simmons that would cause him to kill her himself, Lewis said, things about Port Arthur and even Galveston, things that happened not a month before.

At that, at all the talk of killing and dark deeds in the past, I made my brother leave, calling up hurts I knew would move him, and I was glad I had done that. No, I was not glad. I was proud to have done that, proud that I had taken a stand on the part of my son, doomed though I knew he was by what I saw would come of him and Darlene Simmons.

I let no one know how much I congratulated myself for that, even though I understood that holding pride within to relish in privacy is the truest sin of all. God will allow an open declaration of self-satisfaction, but He will condemn without mercy the hoarding up of self-regard to be enjoyed in secrecy, to be eaten alone in the darkness of one's own soul. But it was all I had left, and I clutched it to me for the savor, its reminder of what it was not to have it, and to feel the life within it, if not in what surrounds it, supports it, and is its home.

That is my great flaw and has always been. The turning away from what is not me and the journeying within to the place at the core, the nothing at the middle around which I circle as me. And that is the promise of death, the reason I now work away in peace and calmness to earn that escape from a nothing.

But the selfishness of pride I hugged to myself in reward for taking Richard's part in what I saw he must have, that relishing in private, led to another act of its kind and of its family. That is always the way of a flaw in any material and in any man and woman. Allowed to be, it spreads, like a crazed line in a pane of glass. It catches the light and bends it so that clarity is lost and the eye focuses not on the whole and its smoothness and use, but on the craze itself, that which is not the perfection but its denial.

I knew as his mother that the need for a woman had to come to my son, that he would have to cleave to a wife. I would have him be allowed that fulfillment, as all mothers of all sons in all times must accept in abnegation, or else be mad.

But the secret within my secret I tried to keep hidden from myself. And now with all of them gone in their separate ways—Darlene Simmons vanished one summer night, Lewis a blind old man brought back home to live for years in his kinfolk's house that he was never able to escape, strive though he did, Richard dead before he turned thirty, me an old woman courting death and attended by my son's and Darlene's daughter—that secret is mine to study.

It is part of the duty of dying, and I attend it.

You cannot keep the secret within a secret apart from your knowing. Put it aside though you may, in however strong a box safe from pilfer, the secret within a secret will live and glow at the core of the darkness where you would hide it.

The action I took upon Richard's discovery of the woman he would have and his cleaving to her was open, transparent and subject to no question. He could not live with her, this woman named Darlene Simmons from a place the name of which kept changing to fit her own order, in my house with me. I stated that. I was firm. I was righteous. And none dared say me wrong in that.

The Holts, the Blackstocks, the Motts, all of the Double Pen Creek community upheld me in doing what I was required to do. People cited the word of God—book, chapter, and verse.

And that was the secret outside the secret. Maude Holt Blackstock Winston acts as a Christian woman in accordance with the stated will and direction of the immortal God Himself, Lord of all. This is what the others believed they saw in me. They said this to each other.

Maude would not abide the ungodliness of her brother Lewis in his anger and threats and blasphemy, his treatment of his own nephew and his sister, his judgment against a poor sinful young woman from parts unknown. And thus she sent her own brother packing, the younger one, the son himself of Amos Holt, a preacher of the gospel and a father whose own son had broken his heart by living in blatant sinfulness, as soon as he could manage it.

Maude's love for her son, Richard, the one returned broken somehow in the war in France and who had moved back into the home of his mother and stepfather though a grown man, her love prevented her from condemning her own flesh and blood for his attaching himself to the young woman Darlene Simmons, herself one of the women who ran with Lewis Holt, drunk and fornicating and unapologetic.

A Christian woman above reproach, Maude cast away her son and the woman he had chosen from her presence and her home, yet her love was such she provided money from somewhere to set the couple up in a little house in the woods near Leesburg.

Maude still holds up her head as she lives among us, and well she might. She loves her son Richard Blackstock, she forgives him, but she condemns the sin.

This opinion of the people I live with, my kin in blood and name, and the others who constitute where I find myself and where I belong in my place in the world, by choice or by chance, this opinion and expression of belief is the secret outside the secret within me. And it has the exactitude of a lie.

The other secret, the one within that secret without, is another thing altogether, held by me close to that center of nothing for all these years. But I have used the time, I have examined that thing solely my own, and pored over it from all angles and in every aspect, and I have come to know it the way you know your own face from all others, assured by feel in the blankness of night when you put your hands unseen to it.

It is this. I agreed with Lewis, my brother, when he swore and repudiated and threatened and called down death upon one he thought he loved and had to have. I joined in that, in silence, I became one in that company, I felt within me the opposite of love, and I relished it at the core of me which was nothing.

For that, for my not keeping the bargain I had struck with God to bring Richard back home safe from war to me, whatever it cost me to forego all desire and any escape from myself, for that, Richard had to be taken. And God observed his scales of justice and saw their imbalance, and He touched them with but the tip of one finger to fix the wrong I had made, and He took Richard, my son, my son, my son.

"Here's that good syrup and a warm biscuit," Dicia is saying, her hand on my forehead, "GrandMaude. I know you're not asleep. You can't fool me."

"You're right, sweetheart," I say, "as always. I'm just resting my eyes."

Abigail

Every time I go in to see her, it seems like she is always asleep, no matter the time of day, early or late, so I always make a little racket to wake her. I don't see any harm in that, no matter how hard a stare Dicia gives me when she's in the room, too, and figures out what I'm doing. It's not like I'm yelling all of a sudden or dropping something heavy on the floor or kicking a foot against that table where Maude has always kept too big a pile of books laying for it to hold without having to worry about some of them falling at the slightest push.

I'm polite the way I cause a little noise to occur. I'll clink a spoon against a cup, not hard, just enough for a person to hear if she's not dead asleep. And if there's no sign given to that, maybe I'll clear my throat and cough a little, or if there's nobody else in the room, Dicia for the most part like always or maybe somebody else, a neighbor or a cousin, say—not Lewis hardly ever, tied up like he's always been in his entire existence with thinking about himself and his own problems and concerns—I'll say a word or two to whoever it is. Not loud, now, but in an ordinary and usual tone of voice.

Dicia will answer back in a whisper, always, smiling as she does it, but looking worried while she's whispering and cutting her eyes over at Maude in the bed so she can say in not so many words but in sign language for me to hush and not wake her grandmother up.

Maude is her grandmother, all right, no doubt about that, though she raised Dicia as if she was the true mother to the child, and she was, in everything but blood fact. But Maude was my sister long before she was anything to anybody else in this part of Texas, and she still is and will always be, even after both of us are dead and gone. Blood lasts.

I'll probably be around still after Maude's gone to her reward, even though I'm three years older, the way prospects look these days for her condition. But who is to know that and be able to declare it? Stranger things have happened, and nobody can predict God's will or his timing. The only thing you can be sure of is that He is going to do what He is going to do, and the age of miracles is long past. That period was confined only to Biblical times. In these fallen days, there is no relief or exemption for anybody from the laws governing the way things happen to every creature, man, woman, or beast. Everything alive is going to be dead.

But I still feel good, generally, get around real well still, eat three meals a day with little or no indigestion, and sleep like a baby at night. Praise and thanks be to the Lord. I give Him the credit.

What Dicia doesn't realize, as tender as she's always been in her feelings toward her grandmother, is that Maude has never been above deceiving people in matters small and sometimes large, too, whenever it suits her fancy or purpose.

As a girl, when all of us children were still living as a family with Papa and Mama and after Mama was gone, with our stepmother Alice, Maude would play possum at times when she was supposed to be sleeping. She was bad to do that. Worse than that, I swear, I always suspected when on some of those occasions she would claim to have headaches so bad she couldn't even get out of bed, much less help around with the chores we had the responsibility of doing, that Maude was truly just putting on an act.

I remember the one time that Mama got so mad at me that she literally slapped me across the face that event had its origin in Maude's pretending to be suffering from one of her famous headaches. I suspected the truth of that claim on that day as soon as Maude began to complain at the schoolhouse before Professor Whitlock let us out to eat dinner.

"I can't eat, Abigail," she said to me while I was getting out what Mama had sent with us for school dinner. I think it was cold sweet potatoes and some cornbread, but I can't swear to that now. It's been over sixty years ago, and who knows the details of what they ate yesterday, not to mention a mess of cold victuals that far back in the past. It could have been field peas, for all I know now.

"Why?" I said, and I do remember my exact words even if I can't call up that day's menu outside in the yard of Double Pen Creek community schoolhouse. "Are you sick at your stomach?"

"No," Maude said. "I'm not hungry, but it's not that. The light is too bright, so much it hurts my head. I see bright lines around everything I look at."

"Uh huh," I said and went on and ate what Mama had put together for us, my portion and Maude's, too, not wanting to waste anything intended for eating. Besides, if I carried it back home, it would be there to have to eat the next day, so I tucked into it.

I didn't know what to make of Maude's comments about the light being so strong and her seeing bright lines around what she looked at, whatever that meant. That was a new symptom she was springing on me, one she hadn't thought to use before, so I didn't quarrel with her about what she meant, especially since she wouldn't say anything back to a word I said to her, sitting there under the big sycamore in the schoolyard with her eyes all squinched up.

What I do know is that she got so bad in her complaining about her misery that Professor Whitlock told me I should take my sister home right then and not stay around for the rest of the school day. I don't remember what the scholars my age were set to study that afternoon, but whatever it was I knew I could miss it and still catch up on it, and Professor Whitlock knew it, too. Like all the Holts, even the lazy ones of the bunch, I was quick in my studies, so I was not flustered to have to escort Maude back the two miles to our place, while missing the afternoon schooling.

We started out at a pretty good pace, Maude making me lead her while she kept her eyes closed against the light, even tying a piece of cloth or a rag or a scarf or something like that around her head to cover her eyes like a blindfold. That didn't last long, though, since she complained that the blindfold arrangement hurt her head too much for her to bear it, but I know good and well that was an exaggeration. I tied the cloth myself, and I did it so loose it was barely hanging on as we were walking. She pulled that cloth off before we'd gone a hundred yards.

Even having to step on the wagon ruts bothered Maude, and she kept telling me to lead her on the smooth part where her head wouldn't have to jounce up and down as she stepped, her not knowing where her feet would hit. I did what I could to accommodate all the special conditions she kept adding, and by the time we got back to the Holt homeplace, I was beginning to get a headache myself from doing it. I told her about it, too. Maude paid no attention to that, and headed directly for bed and pulled a quilt over her head as soon as she laid down.

Now I was supposed to be still in school, studying the geography of Europe or puzzling away at some ratio problem in arithmetic or some such branch of learning, but as soon as we hit the house, Mama set me to work on some chore. What it was, I forget, but I felt the unfairness of her doing that to me as keen as if I had just been stung by a bee. I believed then, and I still believe today, that what Mama should have done with our being back so early from our studies at the schoolhouse was to act just as though both Maude and I were still back there tending to our proper business of learning.

She did do exactly that, with respect to Maude. Let her lie there in the bed at one o'clock in the afternoon with a quilt pulled over her head complaining about the light hurting her eyes and her head aching so bad she couldn't bear it. That's what she said at first anyway, but I could see not ten minutes later when I had to go by the door of the room she was resting in, carrying out part of whatever chore it was that Mama had set me to, that my sister had gone completely quiet. She wasn't saying a word, wasn't moaning like she had been doing for the last couple of hours, starting at the schoolhouse and walking all the way home, me leading, with her eyes shut, and then sliding into bed as soon as she hit the house, and I had a strong suspicion that Maude had gone off to sleep, there in the dark of her quilt cocoon she had made for herself.

So I tiptoed into the room to get a better look at her, went up to the foot of her bed, one of those old metal things with curliques of iron forming the bedstead itself, and took hold of the end of it and shook it just a little bit. I was just testing to see if Maude really was asleep or possuming, as was her wont at times all through her life, and it wasn't a hard shake I gave it at all. You would have thought the way she hollered, though, that I had stuck a hot needle into her instep clean to the bone.

Mama came running, and before I could get all the way out of the room even, she had grabbed me by the front of my dress with one hand and slapped me hard across the side of my face with the other.

I say *hard*, and I know it precisely that because not only was I the one that felt the unjust force of the blow my own mother gave me, but several minutes later I could look in the mirror and still see the red marks her fingers had made.

I have never been able to forgive Mama totally for that, dead all these years though she's been, and I have always harbored a resentment against Maude for it, as well, though she wasn't the one who hit me so unfairly and so strongly all up and down one side of my face. My sister was the one who was possuming, though, and she was the one who yelled out at a little jiggle I gave her bed as though she was being killed by a maniac.

Of course, when I look at Maude now in her current condition, I feel nothing but sympathy and sorrow for the way she suffers there in the last bed she's ever likely to occupy. The worst thing to me is the way her breath comes and goes when she is truly sleeping, with that sound it makes doing it. She has not reached the point that people get to when they're closer to dying than she is now, but the way her breath makes that sound tells me she's on the way to it.

Here's the way it seems to be progressing, and in my experience around people who are working their way closer and closer to the Lord the breathing always seems to follow the pattern I mean. Maude is still taking most of the air she's breathing in through her nose mainly, so that's not where that sound is coming from. That's quiet still, her breath coming in, and if that part of her breathing was all you were to hear, you would not note it as being of any real consequence. No. What matters most is the way in her sleep she's expelling the air, and that's not back through her nostrils, but it's through her mouth. The breath of air comes into her nose quiet, then it comes out in such a way it makes her lips part with a little sound, a kind of puh noise that goes on until all the air is gone and a new intake of breath begins.

That's the part I can't stand to hear, and that's why I rattle things around and drop articles on the floor and talk out loud as soon as I come into the room and start to hear that little noise, saying what it's saying and meaning what it means. I don't care how much and how many times Dicia tries to hush me up so my sister's sleep stays uninterrupted. I want her sleep to be broken. I want it to stop that noise, and I want Maude to wake up and be herself the way she's always been, the way that lets me think about her like I've done all my life and not have to see her in any new way.

That's what life is, an interruption of sleep, a thing that's not whole and complete in and of itself. It's just a gap in something else. Once you have to look at anything as having a beginning and an end and a finished shape to it, it's all over with, as dead as Mama and Papa and all the babies that never lived to be grown, and the young ones cut off too soon. All those ones like Richard, Maude's only child with Valery Blackstock, and the one that cost her the most when he was gone so young.

I was with her when she learned it had happened, the middle of the morning that day late in August when that fellow came driving up in the Carter Lumber Company truck. It was yellow with blue lettering on it, the way all Carter's equipment used to be painted. They were the first in this part of the country to color their trucks and wagons something different from black, so you always noticed them more than you would some other vehicle driving the roads and passing by the farms and houses where people lived. That's why they painted them that way, to get attention. These big companies think like that, the ones that run them.

We were on the porch of Maude's house, her big one left her when Ezra Winston died, standing outside so as to be in good light because Maude wanted me to look into Dicia's mouth to see if I could tell if something was wrong with her gums. I was used to babies and infants from dealing with Lucille's and Mattie Lou's and the rest of the grandchildren, and Maude hadn't really been around a little one to raise for years by then.

Darlene, Dicia's mother, had been gone God knows where for a couple of months by then, and Maude was tending to Dicia for Richard when he was out in the timber woods during the day and for most of the rest of the time, too. He wasn't any good with that baby, as much as he wanted to be. Every time he'd pick her up to feed or to tend to in some way, he would just hold her and stare into her face as though he didn't know who or what she was, tears welling up and rolling down his cheeks the whole time he looked.

A baby doesn't need that, of course, to serve as a reminder of heartbreak to the one holding it, to mean so much to somebody that it paralyzes them. It wants to eat, and it needs its diaper changed and its face washed. It's a simple thing, if you look at it head on, the way I do all matters.

Maude had come to believe that Richard's baby girl was favoring her gums too much to be able to eat right, crying and twisting away from the nipples of the baby bottle stuck up to her mouth, and I was there that morning to get to the bottom of what was causing it. The main thing, though I didn't harp on it in deference to everybody's tender feelings, was that they were having to feed the child by bottle with cow's milk. Dicia should have been breastfed by her mother, like any normal child, but that's impossible to do, when the mother has left her husband and her baby and the country itself to run off on her own.

I always figured Darlene Simmons had scooted on back to Galveston or Houston or some other town she judged to be big enough to contain in one convenient spot what she was after, just as soon as she felt well enough to get up from the place where she had given birth and was able to ramble the roads again. I didn't dwell on that when I talked to Maude, knowing how she would act if I did, and I certainly said as little as I needed to in the presence of Richard, the new papa all by himself with a girl baby, about the fact that the mother of the child was gone.

He was all to pieces all the time then, and had been since the morning he woke up to a crying child and no woman to even be seen on the place much less to breastfeed a hungry infant. The only thing keeping Richard going at all was his leaving every day to work in the logging woods for Carter Lumber Company, a job about as suited for a man like he was as a top hat is for a Muscovy duck to wear.

So Maude was a mama again at her age and with her disposition, and I was having to play the part of the big sister again, as I've had to do all my life. But I have never minded that. I've always done what I've had to do, chin held up the whole time. I do what duty dictates.

"See," I was saying to Maude, pointing my finger into Dicia's mouth at what I knew were signs of thrush just at the back of her throat, "See there where that little patch of red with the white spots is? There's the problem, and what you got to do about it is get you some regular old white vinegar."

Maude was leaning over to look at where I was indicating she should, and I was about to tell her how to swab out the baby's mouth and throat with the vinegar soaked into some cotton, but I never got to finish giving directions, because that's when the man in the yellow Carter Lumber Company truck stopped beside the road in front of the house and opened his door to get out.

I looked up at the noise the truck made, and I could see that the man driving was just sitting there in his seat, hesitating to get out from behind the wheel. Maude could have heard the racket the truck made as well as I did, but she has always been a woman who gets lost in the thing she's doing at the moment and is slow to notice what else might be going on outside where she's concentrating her attention. I like to keep alert myself to everything that's going on all the time.

"Well," I said, "why doesn't that fellow just get out of his truck and let us know what his business is?"

Maude turned her head to see what I was talking about, and I will never forget the look on her face, not that it was so remarkable at first—just puzzled a little, annoyed some even, because she had to look away from the problem in the baby's mouth and throat causing it so much misery so as to learn what was diverting me away from that—but because of what my sister did as soon as she saw the truck. It was the yellow and blue color of the machine, I will always believe, her glimpsing that and knowing somehow what it meant, that caused her to do what she did next, which was to lift that baby up in both hands about headhigh toward me so that I took it from her, not even thinking to do it, but in the way you will automatically reach out your hands to take something somebody is offering you, whatever it is—a dish of something to eat, or a book turned open to a certain page to read, or a sharp knife even though its edge is turned toward you. I took Dicia, offered to me in that fashion, and as soon as I did, Maude fell to her knees there on the hard cypress planks of that porch as though somebody had cut a string holding her up to function, and she screamed as loud as I ever heard her do in her life, and I have been around for all of that, right up to this hour and minute.

The fellow in the Carter truck had come to tell the boy's mother that Richard was dead, killed in the woods that morning when he was walking around figuring the scale on standing timber, not watching close enough where he as going and what was happening around him, and getting in the way of a long leaf pine the sawyer was cutting to throw up the side of a little hill.

It was Richard's own fault, the fellow from the yellow and blue Carter truck told me later on that morning. The crew on the crosscut saw had called out well before anything could have happened to anybody around who was paying attention that the pine was going to fall where it did. That two-man crosscut team did not misthrow the long leaf, and they gave due and accurate warning of when and where it was going. I believed that then, and I still do now.

The fellow that told us what happened was actually an Indian from off the reservation in Coushatta County, the very county we're living in now. I had thought he was a Mexican when I saw him come walking up to the porch where I was holding Dicia and Maude was lying at my feet in a position that looked like she was trying to take up as little space on that cypress floor as she could. It looked to me, the way she was lying, that she was apologizing to the world for being in it, for occupying some of its territory.

But this man wasn't Mexican, dark-skinned as he was. His name was Gemar Leaping Deer, he said, and he spoke English as well as any white man in this part of Texas. He was polite and well-mannered, too, a fine man. He just had a bad job to do, and he did it the best he could, speaking in a gentle tone the whole time he was telling what he had to tell, not at all the way you might expect an Indian to talk, in one-word sentences, abrupt and harsh. You would think that he'd talk that way, I remember remarking to myself as Mr. Leaping Deer told us all he could of the circumstances of the sad event, but he bespoke himself well and fully. I suppose that was why Carter Lumber Company used him to deliver bad news to people. He did a turnkey job of it.

Maude, once she let us get her up off the floor of that porch and half-carry her into the house and put her on the bed, started saying things to me which Mr. Leaping Deer didn't have any reason to listen to, so he left, promising to be back about arrangements and all like of that later. I was still holding that crying baby, Dicia with her mouth just full of thrush, screaming with every breath as though she knew she had just lost her papa to add to the mama, the one gone from the very beginning of her existence.

I don't remember all of what Maude was saying, naturally, as busy as I was with the baby and her and not another soul in the house, what with the rest of Maude's and Ezra's children off at school and one place and another, but I do have one exchange between us stuck fast in my head from that awful morning Richard was killed those years ago.

"I am the one who got him killed," Maude kept saying. "I made it happen. I killed my own son because I was selfish and would not keep my word."

If my sister made that statement or one close to it once, she made it a hundred times while I tried to tend to her crying grandchild and to her grieving her heart out that summer morning Richard died in the logging woods.

"I would not keep my pact with God," she kept saying. "I was too selfish to let my son have what was left of his life after God brought him home alive to me. I promised Him, and I broke my promise. God does not forget. He keeps His promises, every one He makes."

"What promise?" I said. "Maude, what promise? You've got to stop thinking that way. You're just mad with grief. Just go and cry and mourn. Stop thinking whatever it is you're thinking. You just got to let it go."

"I made my boy stay here with me," she said to that. "Lewis offered to take him to Beaumont and get him a job in the oil fields. And Richard would have gone, if I'd let him. He was ready to try that. But I persuaded him to stay here with me. Oh, God, that put him into these woods to make a living. I put him into harm's reach, and these goddamned woods killed my little boy."

"Maude, Maude," I remember yelling back at her. "Richard would have got killed in the oil fields, too, if he'd gone to work on the Gulf Coast. You know he never looked out for himself, wherever he was. Rather than a long leaf pine, something else down yonder would have mashed the life out of him."

"I hate you, Abigail," my sister said to me. "I hate you, but I hate myself even more than that."

I would have left Maude's house for her saying that to me, but I couldn't do it at the time, with nobody but me to see to Dicia and to my sister, and I discounted what she said even then at the moment, as best I could. I knew Maude was out of her head, crazy with grief and suffering, but what she said about hating me did hurt me in my heart, deep down, I will admit.

To give her credit for the years since, Maude never has said that to me again, nor acted on it in any way to show that she meant what she said to me that morning of Richard's death. But it is there, that saying of the words and the way they have collected into a little dark pool all mixed up together with no order to them, and that pool has stayed in a place deep inside my mind and heart. But it is not in my soul, that collection of black words, I tell myself, and I tell the Lord that over and over when I pray to Him, and I thank Him for letting that expression of hateful feelings toward me from my sister not fester and harm me. I guess He agrees with me about it, but I don't know. How could I ever tell what value God puts on statements I offer Him in prayer? He never answers me back. That is one thing for sure.

I am going to rattle this tea cup against the saucer until Maude makes a sign she hears it and knows I am in the room with her, and I will do it long enough to make it work to my own satisfaction, no matter how hard that little dark-skinned Dicia sitting over there in the corner reading her book looks at me with her brows all knotted up and her mouth drawn down. I don't need lessons from her.

Maude is my sister.

Nola Mae

I really don't know what good it does Great-Aunt Maude for a bunch of people to sit around in her bedroom watching her sleep in the middle of the day. She can't tell we're in the room, that's for sure. But here we all are, everybody in the house gathered in this one room not built to hold more than two people at a time, at least one of which should be in bed for the other one to move around comfortably. That one, the one not in bed, could have space enough to sit at the vanity and comb her hair and put on rouge and powder and see how her face looks turned at different angles. And if the one in bed was a man, he could watch her do all that, and she would know he was watching and he would know she was thinking about him watching her, and that would make her do things in the way you do when you know you're the center of attention.

That feeling is almost like being in front of a mirror showing a mirror showing you, and that makes you conscious of the movements you make and how those movements are striking the one watching you make them. You are at least two people then, and a space opens up between yourself as the one doing what you're doing and the one watching you from a position outside yourself doing it.

I like that because it doubles me and gives me back myself in layers. I'm Nola Mae watching Nola Mae be Nola Mae, and the mirror of me picks up the me in the mirror, and strains the light through the screen until it's silver. It polishes me and makes me glow, and that all around me which is not me fades into the background and falls away, and I am at the middle while everything else is at the edge.

There's not another woman outside me who wants to hear any talk about the mirror showing a mirror showing me, not even Dicia who is supposed to be so sensitive and filled right up to the gills with imagination—reading books, and listening to music on the radio without anybody singing along with it, and writing things down in those little tablets she hides in that wooden box of hers. I looked into some of those little sayings she makes up and writes down, more than once when she was out of the house and I had the undetected opportunity, and I can testify to anyone interested that after reading one or two of Dicia's little statements you are satisfied not to have to run your eyes over any more of them. A little of the stuff she writes down goes a long way. Who but Dicia could care enough about what some old French author said to copy it out and in longhand into a notebook?

A man now, as opposed to Dicia or to another woman, on the other hand, will look deep into my eyes when and if I ever try to explain some of the feelings that come over me when I think about myself as two people, as Nola Mae watching Nola Mae be Nola Mae, I mean, but I know what all that close attention from a man to what I'm saying is really worth. I know what it's in the service of, too, and I learned that even before I was old enough to think about myself making Nola Mae be what Nola Mae is, a person worthy enough to be watched by Nola Mae.

The first time I talked to a boy about something interesting enough to me to draw my attention away a little bit from where we were at the time and what we were doing together—it was playing hide-and-go-seek at a picnic for our Sunday school class at Double Pen Creek Chapel, and we had run off and hidden together in the thicket behind the church building—he looked at me like the old folks look at the preacher when he's getting close to the end of his sermon. Eyes all popped wide open or maybe squinched up, in some cases, mouths a little open as though they're drinking from a gourd brimming over with some true thing they have just got to drink on down, eager for what they think is on its way to getting there, finally.

I forget now even what I was telling him about, but I remember why I started talking. I was bored. We had got down together behind a fallen log we could see under and watch if the one hunting us was coming into sight. We had been there probably two or three minutes, and we kept looking out from our hiding place to the clearing where the church building was, and we hadn't caught sight of anybody, probably because they were looking for people on the other side of the building. The place we were lying down in was small enough that we had to be close together, and we'd been quiet at first, not wanting to give away our location, but that got old pretty quick, so like I said, I started telling the boy something to give myself a subject to think about besides the way some of the sticks and trash on the ground was cutting into me as I lay on it face to face with him. He was Walter Slater, and Dicia liked to say his name out loud more times than normal because she liked the way it rhymed, she said. I didn't care about that, but I did like the way he had of looking out of his eyes, like he was always in a state of being halfway bothered about something he didn't understand.

Dicia, smart-mouthed as she's always been, even back then, told me when I said that about Walter Slater's eyes looking like he didn't understand something, that there was a literal mountain of things Walter didn't understand. Just pick one.

All I know is that lying there behind the trunk of that fallen tree looking into Walter's eyes and telling him about something on my mind I wanted to talk about marked the first time a boy put his hand on me like it meant something. I forgot about the way the twigs and sticks and bushes were scratching into me because of the position I was in lying down in that little thicket the minute Walter rubbed the back of his hand across my chest. My nipples had started growing bigger and tender to the touch just a few months before that Sunday school game of hide-and-go-seek, and when Walter rubbed his knuckles against one of them it made me want to close my eyes and stick the tip of my tongue out so he could touch it with his.

I don't know why that came into my head, but it did, exactly in that way, and if Betty Marie Overstreet hadn't been it and found mine and Walter Slater's hiding place when she did, I would have given that little boy a chance at touching something he hadn't expected.

But when Betty Marie hollered out we were it and started running back to tag home, we both jumped up and took off after her, with me laughing and talking as fast as I could and Walter Slater not saying a word, just hurrying to keep up.

That's the way they all are and have always been in my experience, boys and men. The closer a man comes to getting down to business with a woman the quieter he gets and the more he clams up. It's like they can't think anymore, at least not enough to come up with words and put them into a statement, at times like that, I mean. Maybe all the blood rushes out of their brain, called away to feed into another organ, that one that makes them a man. I don't know.

That's why it gets the way it does, just blood going into it, nothing else, though you would think as big and hard to the touch as it comes to be that there was some kind of muscle that moves down into it to get it into that shape.

Melba Faye Murphy said it was a bone they have, told that to a bunch of us girls there during little recess one day at Double Pen Creek school, and she said she had proof of it with her, wrapped up in a piece of cotton material down in her satchel. It came from a raccoon, she said, and unwrapped it and held it out for us to see and touch. It was a bone, all right, long and hooked at the end with a knob on it, and I picked it up in my hand to look at it better. Her brother Leonard had cut it off a big boar raccoon he had hunted and shot, she said, and boiled all the meat off to keep to show people, but we shouldn't let Leonard know she had sneaked it away from where he kept it and brought it to school with her.

"Think how big a man's is," Melba Faye said, "if a boar coon not the size of a dog has got a bone like this in the middle of its."

"Oh, my goodness," one of the other girls, Avalene Thorpe I remember it being, said, "I'm not ever going to let a boy get close to me with a thing like that to poke at me."

Avalene did just that, as soon as she could manage it, and already has three children, the last I heard, by some old boy from Sour Lake, and I knew at the time I was holding that polished bone from a raccoon's arrangement up in the light to study it better that every one of us there in the schoolyard, even the girls who turned away and ran off to avoid seeing it, would be spending our lives dealing with the human equivalent of what Leonard Murphy had shot in the woods and boiled down to its essentials.

I knew, also, by instinct and reason, that men didn't have a bone like a raccoon to slide down into an organ of flesh like an animal, to get it ready to do what it is bound to do. I had seen plenty of my boy cousins from the time they were babies, too, down there, and I knew no actual bones were involved in what they have between their legs.

Besides, when we were six years old, my cousin Jesse Monroe, let me see and touch his in trade for doing the same with mine, and even when his got hard, as little as it was, I could still squeeze it tight enough to know there wasn't anything inside it but just more of the same as was on the outside. You haven't got anything like I got, he told me, just a little crack. That's right, I said, slapped his hand away from me where he was fumbling. What I've got's inside me, and it's a secret, and you'll never know what it is.

He didn't, either, pester me to have another look at it though he did for years.

After I saw that coon bone Melba Faye Murphy showed us at little recess, I tried to talk to Dicia about it, already knowing how wrong Melba Faye was about what it meant about the true way boys were, but I still figured maybe Dicia had read something about it in one of those books she always had stuck in front of her, even back then.

"Does a boy have a bone in his peter?" I said to her, right straight out one day when I was at Great-Aunt Maude's house on a visit.

"Because Melba Faye showed us the bone from a raccoon's peter, and she claims it's the same way with a human man."

"Of course not," Dicia said, her eyes snapping at me like they always do when she doesn't want to talk about some subject I've brought up. "What an idea, and how would I know?"

"You've seen boy babies," I said, "and I have, too, and I just wondered if you have any ideas on the subject."

"A raccoon is an animal," Dicia said. "And we are not animals. We are made in the image of God, it says in the Bible. And there's no comparison of and to raccoons in any way anywhere I've read in the Bible."

"You don't think God has got a peter, do you?" I said, and that was the end of that conversation, like a lot of the ones I've tried to have with my cousin Dicia. She just marched right off, like she will do.

She won't even talk with me about boys at all anymore, like she used to be willing to do, not since the time I told her about me and Jimmy Toler when we were kissing at the play party at Suellen Popp's house and I let him put his hand on my breast through my dress and then when he put the other one up underneath my skirt I didn't stop him from going all the way inside my underwear and moving his fingers around until I couldn't bear it any more it felt so good to me and then he got scared, I guess it was, and stopped. That wasn't my idea, I told Dicia, I wouldn't have made Jimmy quit when he did, if it was left up to me. We were just thirteen years old, and he didn't have any sense at all, at the time.

But telling her that was my mistake, and that was the last time Dicia let me talk to her about anything like that, and I did miss being able to do that. She was like Jimmy Toler, I expect, Dicia was, in her own way. Scared off from keeping on going with a thing because the other person shows she likes it too much. Too much of a brand new thing is being revealed too soon, and it's about to get away from you, and you have no idea where it might get to. So you're afraid to let go of where you are, where you know the place you're standing, where it feels safe and secure right where you are. Take the next step, and you're moving into a body of water too cloudy to let you see the bottom it's covering up.

You know things are moving around down there, bumping up against your feet, and you can't tell what they are, nor how big they may be and what direction they might push you into following.

So, if you're Jimmy Toler or Dicia Blackstock, you say whoa and stop. Not me, not Nola Mae Ellis. One step makes me want to take another one, and if that dark water I can't see into gets too deep, I figure I can always swim around in it and not drown.

My grandmother is looking straight at me, and her mouth is moving at a good clip, and I know that means what it always does. Her eyes have not gotten so narrow yet that I can't see any of the white surrounding the colored part, so I've still got time to make a believable recovery if I talk fast enough.

"My mind has been just wandering, Grandma," I say. "I've been remembering some of the good times I've had in Great-Aunt Maude's and Dicia's house, especially when Dicia and I were real little, like on that one Christmas, that time Lewis tried to fool us by playing he was Santa Claus. Remember that?"

My grandmother laughs loud enough at that to cause Great-Aunt Maude to jerk in the bed the way you will when somebody calls your name while you're asleep, and I know I've succeeded in getting Grandma's attention off me and her knowing I haven't been listening to a thing she's been talking about.

"Do I remember it?" she's saying now, talking loud enough now to make Dicia cloud up even more than she has been. She looks like she'd like to kill my grandmother, and I understand and sympathize, but not for Dicia's reason to want to do that. I've got plenty of my own, thank you. "How could I ever forget the expressions on you girls' faces when Lewis came walking into the room where y'all were looking at that little old cedar tree you'd decorated?"

"It had popcorn on it that we'd threaded on a string," I say, giving Grandma more to work with that has nothing directly to do with me. "And remember Dicia had cut up some pictures out of a magazine or newspaper or something and pinned them to the branches."

"It wasn't from a newspaper," Dicia says, her voice lower than it has to be, and I know what she's intending to do by that. It's not going to work. "The pictures were colored, some of them at least, so what I cut out couldn't have been from a newspaper."

"All I know is when your great-uncle Lewis walked in there on you two and him wearing that red shirt he'd stuffed wadding in to make him look fat and with all that cotton pasted on his face for a beard, you two girls just hollered," my grandmother says, running up the volume of her voice to compensate for the whispery talk Dicia is trying to inspire in all of us. "Here's Santa Claus, here's Santa Claus, y'all said."

"I said that, all right," I say, "and Dicia believed it was really Santa, but I knew better. As soon as he grabbed hold of me, I could tell it wasn't really Santa Claus."

"You could not," my grandmother says. "Why do you want to say that, Nola Mae?"

"He smelled like whiskey," I answer her. "That's how I could tell. I knew it was just old Lewis again half-drunk."

"Don't call him Lewis," she says. "He's Great-Uncle Lewis to you and to Dicia."

"All right," I say. "I'll try to remember." I can see that Dicia's grandmother is awake now. She's opened her eyes and is listening to what's going on, and probably has been for a while, though she hasn't felt the need to announce that to everybody in hearing range like my grandmother would do.

"All right," I say again. "Great-Uncle Lewis, Great-Uncle Lewis, Great-Uncle Lewis. There."

Lewis

They're saying my name in Maude's room, but that doesn't mean I'm the topic of conversation among all the women watching my sister on her deathbed. Abigail is just using me to talk about something else that's on her mind, some kind of angle she's working to get at one or the other of that bunch in there waiting around and putting in the long hours of the job they're undertaking.

Abigail is entertaining herself by referring to me by name, the way a cat will knock a sweetgum ball or a cotton fluff or some other piece of trash around the floor with first one paw, then the other one. Just keeping in practice, working on its style with whatever's before it for a target, not really serious, about what it's doing but not wanting to pass up an opportunity to hone its skills for the time ahead when something actually worth killing and eating will show up. And it will, because something always does, and it's just a matter of time until the chance to pounce arrives.

When I feel my way in there into Maude's bedroom, everybody will look up and say howdy to me, even Maude, the one who's doing the dying and has the most serious job of all of these women waiting ahead for her. I say even Maude, but I should say particularly Maude. Particularly, because that's the way Maude is, taking time away from her dying to say howdy, and that's one of the things that's eat away at me all these years of being around her, most of all. It won't let me alone, that feeling my sister's treatment of me has built up inside me over time, and I have never been able to get it outside and shut away from me for good.

I have tried, though. I give myself credit for that. I have tried to expel it and get it out of my system the way your body will tell you to do when you've taken something into your stomach that it can't abide, can't digest, and is being poisoned by. Even when it was sweet at first and easy to swallow on down and you felt like it was doing you good, there came that time, that little uneasiness in your chest and gut that said now wait a minute, are you sure you want this, are you positive it's going to benefit you on down the road, are you counting on this to stay with you?

Why is it, I asked myself at first way back when I was a young one trying to get out from underneath Papa, the preacher and teacher and the farmer who ran everything, the man everybody everywhere respected and looked up to, why is it that I get this sick feeling inside me when Maude sides with me against him and Mama and Abigail and everybody else in the country busy taking notice of me and all the rest of the Holts?

Shouldn't I be grateful to my sister for standing up for me, for finding excuses to explain why I wasn't doing the things he wanted me to, for supplying reasons why I wasn't making myself into the man he wanted me to fit into the shoes of?

But, no, I never could explain it to myself and for sure not to anybody else why it was I never felt like thanking Maude a single time when she did something for me in all those times I didn't satisfy Papa and all those fights I had with him about every little thing he found wrong with me, every little way I wasn't being the right and true son for Amos Holt to have.

Maude would look at me when I did something that got me in trouble with the man who always had the right word for every occasion, say one of the times when I came in drunk from some play party or busted some piece of harness or forgot to feed some damn mule or another, she would look at me not like she was mad or disappointed or surprised but like she was sorry for me, like she loved me. That was what was always in her eyes when she'd come to me to try to talk to and comfort me after Papa had punished me however he'd done for whatever particular offense it was this time.

Maude loved me, she forgave me, I was her brother, and that's what I never could stand about the way she has always treated me. I couldn't do anything wrong enough ever to stop her from judging me in that way.

How, though, at the same time could I blame her? That is what I'm talking about when I say it's like taking something into yourself you believe and know is sweet and good and nourishing, and then discovering when it hits the pit of your stomach that it is poison to the system and must not be let to abide within.

That is Maude and her nature and the way it's been to me all these years to have to live with, the ones when I could see to walk around and want things, and the years I've spent where the light can't reach me to show what I still want.

Big Sister Abigail now is another proposition, and always has been, and what she provides and represents I have always been able to handle. I've even come to like her, though I'd never let her know that, in a way I've never been able to like Maude.

I don't like Maude, I never did from my childhood in Amos Holt's house all the way up to now where I'm living in her house. But I love her. And that's what makes me feel sick inside, always on the verge of throwing everything up and having to think all the time, every minute of my life, how to keep going in a way that will let me hold it all down.

I don't tell Maude I love her, and I won't. And I don't tell Abigail I like her, but I do.

I love my sister Maude in the way a man loves the air he takes in to let him live and the way he loves the light when he's allowed to see it. Just benefiting from it, and not having to think about the good it does him. And I like my sister Abigail the way a boxer in the ring likes the man he's fought who has just beat the living hell out of him. That man who's whipped him, made him know he's the lesser in the match, and let him feel down to the bone that he's not won and can never, that man is owed a debt by the man he's beat. He has taught him a lesson he needed to know.

Abigail does that for me. She keeps me whipped down and mad enough to keep going, and she always has, damn her soul.

They're looking up as I feel my way into Maude's bedroom, all of them, each one in her own location that she could point to exactly, like it was a place on the map, if somebody asked her to do that. Why, here, she could say, here is where I am, and yonder and yonder and yonder is where the rest of them are.

Now when they speak to me, and all of them do, even the one dying by slow degrees on her final bed, I can tell where they are, too, more or less, and I know they are all sitting down and in the case of Maude, lying down, and I know they're looking up at me standing in the door with my head higher than any of theirs. How do I know that, how can I figure the angle at which a man or woman's aiming words at me, and me blind, somebody might be curious enough to ask?

It's one of the blessings granted me, Abigail would say and has said many a time in my presence, a compensation God gives a blind man, a special development He allows to take place in the hearing of the one who can no longer see. What happens, understand, she will say, is that my brother's hearing has got so strong he can locate where you're sitting and how you're holding your head while you talk to him. Just watch Lewis's head while he's hearing what you say to him and you can see him turn it to face you, tracking where the sound is coming from, almost like he's trying to see the true location of the one speaking to him. You close your eyes and try to do what he's able to do, and set somebody to watch you while you're trying it. You won't even come close to matching up with him, I guarantee you. Abigail will say that and look around like a banty hen, just daring somebody to contradict her.

And explanations such as that are what I'm talking about when I say enduring a session with my big sister is like getting in the ring with that superior boxer, the one who whales the dickens out of you from far off and from close up, from way across the ring up to right inside in all the clinches.

I will say this about Abigail's explaining the way a blind man will track sound. If that's the best method God has figured out to improve the sense of hearing in a man, put out his eyes, that is, and teach him to follow vibrations in the air like a dog sniffing at a smell of rot the wind has blown up, God needs to take building lessons from somebody else better equipped. And if what's going on beneath the surface when a blind man is tracking sound in that fashion is no more than God just dishing out some more punishment for misdeeds and sorry behavior, it is my opinion that God has stepped over the line and needs to be reasoned with. If there was somebody to reason with Him, I mean, and if there was such a thing as reason.

But they are all looking up at me from their particular spots here in Maude's bedroom, and saying hello and asking how I've slept and if I've had breakfast and the other things they are supposed to be uttering in the middle of the morning of a warm day in Coushatta County, Texas, and I know where each and every one of them is sitting. Pretty much.

"Well, Lewis," Abigail is saying, "I see you've shaved this morning."

"I've made that my habit over the years," I say, not swiveling my head in her direction though I could if I wanted to. She needs to be denied the satisfaction of visiting that tried and true topic for conversation first thing this morning. That one's too easy. "I do it most every morning."

"How come you never seem to miss a patch of whiskers? " Abigail says. "Just looking real close at your face, I swear I can't spot a single place you haven't shaved all the beard off of. Now all of y'all know that an older man like Lewis is now, even if he's got good eyesight so strong he doesn't even need to wear glasses, why he will miss a patch or two of whiskers on his face when he shaves. I see that all the time on old fellows."

"I hate seeing that," Abigail's granddaughter says, getting her oar into the conversation, "on a man. It looks real ugly and like the man doesn't care enough how he looks to people to even do a good job of shaving."

Maude and her granddaughter don't add anything to this part of the discourse, as they generally don't when Abigail is just limbering up, but I know where they're located in the room anyway. Maude's bed is where it always has been, and she's not leaving that piece of furniture ever again, it looks like, and Dicia, by a process of elimination, has got to be over in the corner of the room next to the window in that straightback chair sitting up against the wall.

"The reason a man misses a patch of whiskers when he's shaving, Abigail," I say, turning my head not toward her but toward where I know Dicia's got to be, "is not because he doesn't see it, but because he doesn't care. Isn't that right, Dicia?"

"I suppose so, Great-Uncle Lewis," she says, not right off, but giving herself time as though she's according due consideration to what I've just said. "It depends on the man and the circumstance, I expect."

"That's right, girl," I say. "A man who's got good eyesight doesn't have to prove anything to anybody by the way he shaves his face. He's got seeing ability to spare, and he doesn't need to apologize to a soul for anything. All he's doing is shaving his beard in the morning. He's not having to show he can be neat and clean, even with his eyes put out, in every little thing he does. Understand what I'm saying, Dicia? I imagine you do."

"Maybe," she says. "But sometimes things we do we do just because we do them. We're not trying to prove anything."

"That's exactly right," I say. "The man with good eyesight doesn't have to prove anything with the way he shaves his face, or the way he does anything else of a domestic nature, neither. He just does it and don't have to care how anybody looks at it or if anybody looks at it. The blind man, now, has to prove things to people every minute of the day in everything he does."

"You shouldn't say *don't* when the subject of your sentence is singular," Abigail says. "The proper grammar calls for *doesn't*."

"See what I'm saying, Dicia?" I say. "A blind man has got to watch everything, even how he says his sentences, or folks will think less of him."

"You used bad grammar long before you lost your eyesight," Abigail says, "and you did it not because you didn't know better but because you did. You were taught correctly."

At that, Maude speaks up right in the middle of me gathering myself for the next shot at Abigail, and I let that one go for now.

"Lewis," she says, "will you pour me a little water into that glass on the table? I don't want to have to sit up."

I do that, and I don't spill a drop, and I put the pitcher back down where it comes from, nobody saying a word but Abigail drawing a quick breath like people do when they see a danger all of a sudden present itself. That does not rattle me. It steadies my hand.

"Do you want a chair to sit down in?" Maude says, and I hear Nola Mae get up from where she's located, seeing the chance to leave the room while kindly giving up her seat to her old blind great-uncle.

"Here," she says, "take my chair. I've got to go take care of something anyway."

"Why, thank you, Nola Mae," I tell her. "But you got to give me a big old hug first and show me where you've been sitting."

She is not going to like doing that, I know, hugging up tight to a blind man and him just old kinfolks, but she'll step on in there and do it, all right, like a little soldier, and the girl is a full-grown woman just come into her prime. Unlike Dicia who is compact and slim and no matter how close you grab her up to you for a hug, not really there at all because she doesn't want to be, Nola Mae pushes right into you, strong arms and high-set tits and a smell like perfume from a store in Houston.

Nola Mae is not really there, either, in her mind, but she lets her body be present for admiration and a touch or two, even if the man benefited in this case is just old blind Great-Uncle Lewis. My grandniece Abigail's granddaughter Nola Mae has the heart of a whore, though she'll probably never use it.

I hug her up to me.

One thing touches on another one, always, all the time and I've come to know the truth of that during these years of feeling my way along these walls between me and daylight. That was there for me to learn by sight if I'd wanted and been willing to look, back then before it happened, but I didn't, of course, care anything about wasting time doing that.

Now I've had time sufficient and plenty to learn it not by sight but by feel, and that is the surest and most solid way to comprehend any lesson. You get it by touch, and you get it by heart, and it is written in letters carved into stone which you trace in the dark with your finger. It comes into you at a point where the flesh barely covers the bone, and it moves into your system the way a dram of whiskey moves out from the belly to all parts of the body, steady and sure and not to be denied its path.

One thing touches another. It is a wad of string balled up into a knot, and there is no end to take hold of and pluck and no unraveling ever to come.

Papa knew that, and he knew that he knew it, because he had learned it on his own. What he came to understand about one thing's always touching another confirmed the teachings of the Bible, in the way that Papa saw to be true in his own life. I want to be particular and precise in thinking about this matter, and I don't want to mislead my own understanding. Papa's experience confirmed the truth of the matter as explained in the Bible, not the other way around. The prophets and teachers and apostles and Jesus Himself had their statements made true by Amos Holt's experience in his life in Louisiana and Virginia and Maryland where the War was and in Texas where he ended up living and dying.

Papa didn't have to look to the Book to support his own understanding of what means what in this life. If Jesus and the apostles and the rest of them that put those words into the Bible had had the advantage of foresight into the career of Amos Holt they could have saved themselves some trouble and a lot of effort and waste motion.

The life he lived and his measuring out of it into portions small enough to bite off, chew up, and worry down allowed him to judge which parts of the Bible to take seriously, which parts to question, and which to just glide right over. He held up the rule to himself, not himself to the rule. It didn't measure him. He measured it.

So when they brought me back to the home place in Sabine County after what happened to me in Beaumont, carrying me in a truck that passed for an ambulance, wobbling all over the roads and hitting every hole in every one of them, my head feeling like it was floating somewhere about a foot above the rest of me, like it was tied to a thin string frayed and close to snapping, I thought Papa was waiting in the room where they put me, and he had the Bible in his hand, ready to read out the scriptures that showed how Amos Holt was right on the money about how one thing always touches another.

"You are home now, Lewis," was the first thing Papa said to me where they put me on a bed in a room I couldn't see and never would, "The prodigal son has returned, and we will kill the fatted calf. Listen to the word of the Lord."

And that I did, and I did that for over a month right up to the point when one morning I woke up remembering that Papa had been dead for over twenty years. Abigail had been doing all the talking, and

I had been listening to her but hearing Papa, and I had been counting it a blessing every day he read to me the explanation and support for the truths he ladled out to me like soup from a pot never emptied. I couldn't escape the sound of his voice and the way the mind will listen to words spoken to it even though you're telling it not to, but I couldn't see his face, at least. I didn't have to reach judgment about the difference between what Amos Holt said aloud and what his countenance told of the feelings behind whatever he said.

You can't see the dark, only the light. So if and when you say a thing like, "I can see it's really dark tonight," you're speaking nonsense. What's really the truth is that there's less light than usual, not more dark. It's always dark as the pit everywhere all the time, and when you're able to see something it's not an absence of darkness coming into your eyes. It's a relief from it.

The night was dark in Beaumont when it happened, and I remember saying that to Clay Whitehead when we were walking along Crockett Street looking for the Maryland Hotel that evening. I wouldn't say it like that now, after learning what I have all these years of touching the wall and reading what it has to say through my fingertips. Maybe instead I'd say, "Clay, there's not much light available to us this evening. Be careful, lest all of it leak away."

And then I'd say to old Clay Whitehead, "One thing touches on another, Clay. Keep that thought in mind, always." But, if I'd had sense enough to know that and to have said anything like it, there'd have been no occasion to. One thing touches on another, like I've testified, and that includes every second and minute of time, but time is a snarl of string with no end showing to grab hold of. Pull at one place or another of that rat's nest of string, and there's no telling what will rise up coming toward you.

By then, Darlene was gone, stolen away from me by my own damned nephew Richard, and she had been the only one for me where things were working out between us for more than a month or six weeks in a row. I'm not talking about some permanent arrangement when I say that, naturally, not that there is such an animal as a permanent arrangement between a man and a woman not kin to each other by blood. That is a whole separate subject and one you can't get away from while you still have body and what moves it around yet hanging together.

But, Lord, I did love to touch her and look at her hair with the sun on it and the shape her face had when seen from the side.

I say Darlene Simmons was stolen from me by Richard Blackstock, Maude's only child by that first husband, but I'm using the wrong word,

I admit, when I say *stolen*. That would be an accurate description of what happened that night when she stepped into the light from that lantern Richard was holding up on the porch of Maude's house and the two of them got that first full look at each other, accurate only if the word stolen would apply to what takes place when a prize possession just walks right through the wall of your house or the fence around it built to keep things in and climbs on the truck itself to be carried off.

One thing touches on another, that's what I'm pronouncing as a truth learned by moving my fingers over the carvings on the wall between me and the light. So if that lantern held up on that porch in Coushatta County those years ago had not shown two people what it did of each other and what at least one of them thought was wantful and necessary at the time, I'd not have been on Crockett Street in Beaumont, Texas, looking for the Maryland Hotel not two years later. Maybe.

But I was, and I found it, and Clay Whitehead and I walked through that door at the bottom of the stairs and started up to the second floor where everybody and everything in my future was located and waiting.

I had been to the Maryland before, and that was why I wanted to find it again. It's not hard to find things in Beaumont, so the search I was undergoing should have been an easy one, but I was naturally drunk the first time I'd been there and was being led by somebody else. So finding the Maryland Hotel the second time was a satisfaction to me, and I was the man leading the way on this occasion, and for some reason that was a cheering notion to me. We went up the stairs at a trot, me and Clay, and I pulled the string that made the bell on the other side of the door ring hard enough to make it jangle like it was about to come unnailed from the wall.

I have made myself remember exactly the way that string looked hanging out there waiting to be tugged at, and I can see, anytime I want to, my hand reaching out to grab it. When a man is blind, he has plenty of time to call up the way light once fell for him on most any object at almost anytime. When you can see, you don't really care what the light shows exactly about most things you happen to let your eyes move over. You just waste all that light touching things in the way a man at the end of a meal, cropful of food, will throw away the last bite of steak on his plate or the crust left after eating a slice of pie. It's more coming, he thinks, if he thinks at all, and I don't need to give these leavings any scrap of my attention.

The string to the bell of the Maryland was about a foot long, what you could see of it hanging before you, it had been broken by some fool anxious to get inside with all those women, and it had been tied back together in a granny knot, it was black with dirt and sweat and grease from people's hands grabbing at it, and it was the last piece of string I ever saw.

Going into a whorehouse always made me feel two ways at once, from the first time I visited right up to the last. The first way was what might be expected—all wound up and nervous and excited and popeyed to see women ready and willing to crawl into bed with you with their clothes off. Any man working in the oilfields and shipyards around Beaumont or Orange or Port Arthur would agree with that understanding of the way you felt when the eye looked at you through the hole cut in the door where you'd just rung the bell and then the eye went away and the unlocking and opening up took place.

But I never heard anybody talk about the other feeling that door opening caused, the one opposite from being all keyed up enough to walk across broken glass in stocking feet and not notice the cost of a single cut nor one drop of blood drawn. And that feeling to me was always a sensation of relief, a relaxation, like that feeling that comes on you akin to water seeping and rising and beginning to lift you off your feet, or the way the second drink of whiskey takes hold where you start feeling it in the tops of your thighs and in the muscles of your neck.

What I felt like each time I walked into a whorehouse, apart from the sense of something good happening low and deep in my belly, was the same way I would feel when I was paying the bill at the end of a cooked meal in a café or restaurant in a town where nobody knew me. I had done a job of work, I had been paid for it, I had the money in my pocket to show it, and I had not had to see the meat and potatoes and beans and bread I had eaten planted and cultivated and raised and slaughtered and picked and cooked and brought to the table. I had had no part in any of that. It came complete.

I had just to point to the words on the menu or on the blackboard behind the counter and say I'll take that. Then they had brought it to me to eat, and I'd paid for it with dollars out of my pocket, and we were settled up. Nothing was left to consider.

The same way obtained in a place where women were selling what I wanted for straight cash on the table. I hadn't seen a one of them before, including the one I ended up following out of the big room down the hall to one of the little rooms with a bed and washstand in it, and I'd never had to talk to them before, or during, or since, if I didn't feel like it. And yet they would treat me the same, no matter how we talked or didn't or wouldn't. They'd take my two dollars, put it up somewhere, pull their clothes off, crawl into bed, and put their legs up.

Knowing that was coming was what gave me that feeling, the one opposite from being as keyed up as a stallion around a mare in heat. I was relaxed, relieved, ready to do business, and I didn't have to say a word.

So when we popped through that door of the Maryland Hotel on Crockett Street in Beaumont that February night, I was ready to see what I could, and I wasn't thinking much about Darlene Simmons for the first time in a while, and I could feel the sense of water seeping in around me and beginning to lift my feet from where they were planted on solid ground. I was about to float. I was almost tiptoeing, walking across that flowered rug in the big room to sit down on a sofa up against the far wall and wait to see the women come traipsing in with what they had to sell.

"What y'all do for a living?" the colored woman who'd let me and Clay Whitehead in the door said. "Work in a insurance office?"

"Why you think that?" Clay said. I could tell he liked what the woman had said.

"Way y'all dressed," the woman said. "Them nice duds."

"Nah," Clay said. "We just like to dress up a little when we go out for some fun. You not going to find us sitting behind a desk in a office somewhere."

"We like to work in the open air," I said, helping Clay make conversation with the woman as I looked around the room. The first thing that caught my attention was a victrola in one corner with a woman bent over it doing something to its knobs, making it ready to start playing, I guessed, since there wasn't any sound coming out of the machine.

Her dress was short, way above her knees, and split up the back, and as she bent further over to move something on the victrola, I could she wasn't wearing any underclothes. Just as I saw that, the sound of a musical instrument came out of the victrola, a trumpet, maybe, and the woman began to move her hips back and forth in rhythm to it, still bending over as she did that.

"Good God," I said, loud enough to cause Clay to stop in the middle of something he was saying to the colored woman who'd let us through the door to the Maryland Hotel. "I believe we come to the right place. Look up way underneath and deep inside yonder. That thing looks like a skinned rabbit trying to back out of a hollow stump."

I figured that would get Clay's notice, pussy hound as he always was, so I just kept my attention focused on what I saw in front of me and waited to hear what Clay would come back at me with. He would always try to outdo the other fellow, top whatever'd been said with something better of his own. Sometimes Clay could, sometimes he couldn't. He would take a stab at it, though.

But before he could get anything said back to me, somebody else spoke up. "What'd you just say to Velma?"

I had missed seeing him when we came through the door into the Maryland Hotel, paying attention as I was to the colored woman letting us in, and besides that he was sitting across the room from where the whore was messing with the victrola, and I hadn't looked anywhere but in her direction. He was dark complected enough to be colored himself, but the light was bright in the room, the better for customers to see the women by, I guess, and I could tell by his features he was a white man, though probably a Cajun.

"I didn't say nothing to nobody," I said. "I was just remarking on that wad of hair I see moving back and forth over yonder."

"You ain't been here what—two minutes?—and you already low-rated Velma twice like that."

He was sitting back in a straight chair when I first saw him, but now he leaned forward so that the chair legs hit the floor with a bang. I remember thinking it wouldn't have sounded so loud and made Clay Whitehead jump like he did if the rug in the room had been bigger and could have covered more of the wood floor. The man rubbed the back of his hand against his chin as though he was wiping something off his mouth left over from chewing a bite of something greasy and too big to get all of down in one swallow.

"I don't know her," I said, jerking my head toward the woman he'd called Velma, now standing straight up beside the victrola, her head turned to look over her shoulder. "I was just talking about what all I could see when she was bending over that music machine."

"Her name's Velma," the fellow said, moving his head from side to side like his neck was stiff, "It ain't skinned rabbit, and it ain't wad of hair." He moved his head slow, like his neck was bothering him bad.

"I was talking about her pussy," I said, "what I could see of it. I wasn't trying to call her name."

"Her pussy," he said, like it was question he was asking, "her pussy? Where you from, friend?"

"Hardin County," Clay Whitehead said, as though the man talking to me actually wanted to know the location of my home. "That's where Lewis is from. Me, I'm from Orange, Texas."

"Hardin County," the Cajun-looking man said, "That makes sense. It's coming together for me now. What do you peckerwoods use for women up in them woods? Shoats?"

"Dane," the woman by the victrola said. "We're in business here. You know that, and I want you to think about it."

"You heard what this peckerwood called you, Velma. Didn't you hear that? Have you lost your hearing, too, along with the rest of it?"

The woman turned a knob on the victrola and it made the music get louder. Somebody on the record was singing along with the music, and I could tell he was colored, but I couldn't make out what words he was saying, even though it was the same ones over and over.

"He didn't mean nothing against this lady here," Clay said. "Lewis didn't. Did you, Lewis?"

I tried to say no, but words wouldn't come out the first time, so I cleared my throat and did it again. It worked that second time, my mouth did. "No," I said. "No, I sure didn't."

"You got to give a man some leeway with what he says," the colored woman said to the man called Dane, though she was not looking at him, but at me. "A man come in that door from way up yonder in one of them counties, and he see Velma bending over, he bound to start saying things he ain't thought through yet. Ain't that right?"

"Yes, ma'am," I said, even though she wasn't a white woman. "Yes, ma'am."

"Well," Velma said, and looked at me. "You going to want to do anything about it this evening? You want to take a little walk down that hall yonder?"

I looked over at Dane, who had settled back into his chair again, far enough to let the front legs rest again on the floor, and he was not looking at anybody now, his eyes closed in fact, and his mouth drawn up as though he was whistling a tune under his breath. I remember thinking that he was probably imitating the music of the song coming from the victrola and probably knew what words the colored singer was saying, the ones he was repeating over and over, every one of them.

"I sure would," I said, looking back at Velma. "Just show me the way."

"I'll show you where that rabbit lives," she said. "Back in here behind all that underbrush. Come on now, Hardin County."

Clay Whitehead laughed at Velma saying that, giving it a lot more credit for being funny than it deserved, but I knew he thought he had a good reason for doing it. I appreciated what Clay was trying to do by giving the woman's words the acknowledgment he did, but nobody else joined in with him, and that made the room seem more quiet than if he hadn't laughed any at all or made any other sound.

I followed right behind Velma into the hall, not close enough to touch her but wanting to get as quick as I could out of the room where the man called Dane was sitting in a straightback chair with his eyes closed, rolling his head back and forth. Leaving the room, I didn't look at him, nor at anybody else, just kept my eyes fixed on the spot on Velma's back where her hairdo stopped and her skin began, dead white against the dark hand of hair bouncing on it.

I don't remember following her into one of the rooms off the hall, but I do know it was the end of the corridor because it seemed to take a long time to get there. Once we got inside, Velma did what whores always did back then and still do, I guess, told me to take my clothes off, shucked her dress in less time than it takes to tell about it, and then took a long look at my pecker, holding it up and squeezing it to see if anything suspicious came out or if I flinched like it hurt.

Then she washed it with soap and water from the jug on the stand by the bed, and I was surprised by what happened to me when she did that, which was nothing. Always before in a whorehouse when a woman handled me, I'd get hard while she was doing it without even thinking about whether I was going to or not, but this time when Velma had finished, it was showing no more interest in what had been going on than if I'd just taken a short leak through it.

She didn't say anything at first, nor look me in the face, but of course a whore never does that. Even if she has her eyes on you, you can tell she's looking through you, not at what's in front of her, the man about to climb on.

"Well," I said, "that's never happened to me before," and then I reached for one of her tits, but she put her hand up to keep me away from them, and then she looked at me.

"Not for two dollars," she said. "That's not part of the deal. You don't handle my breasts for that."

"What if I give you another dollar?" I said. "Then can I get my hands on them?"

"No," she said. "I don't care how much extra you might offer me. Nobody plays with me like that, but just the one man."

I figured I knew who she was talking about, but I didn't ask her his name. Instead, I just reached out for her belly and ran my fingers down until I found what I was paying for.

"All right," Velma said, looking at me again but this time not letting her eyes see me, "let's lie down on this bed and see what happens."

By the time we got situated, I could tell it had got over whatever was holding it back, and I was able to start in putting it to work on what I had come there for. Velma didn't say anything while it was going on, like some whores will do and like some men like to hear. All that talk about how it's feeling so good to them, and how fine you are giving them what they need, and they never had it like this before, and please come by tomorrow so they can have something to look forward to that another man can't give them and never has before.

That's all lies, and if a man can get some satisfaction from that, not even to say believe it, that's all to the good, I suppose, but I never liked hearing that from one of them. Just keep your mouth shut and let me get to where I want to go. That was my policy.

We finished up with it, and got up off the bed, and she gave me a rag to clean myself off with, and that's when it came into my head to do what I did, while I was watching her hold out that wet cloth toward me, looking at my face like she was doing, but actually staring right through me toward some spot on the wall behind my head, I figured, some place she thought was better to study than me. A crack in the paint, maybe, or a nail hole, or a blood spot where somebody had killed a roach with a shoe.

I grabbed her by one of her tits, it was her left one, I know, because I was facing her and I'm righthanded, and I squeezed it hard enough to feel my thumb opposed by my fingers through the flesh.

"I told you not to do that," the whore said and knocked at my hand with hers, "Don't touch my breast."

"What about this one, then?" I said, the idea coming into my head to say that like it was automatically given to me, something I didn't even have to think to be able to come up with, and then I reached out for the other one and squeezed it harder than I had the first one.

She hit that hand, too, my left one, but slower than she'd done the right one, and then she stepped back and looked directly into my eyes, seeing me this time, I could tell, as she settled her eyes direct and steady on mine.

"Get out of here," she said, slow and deliberate. "Don't come back here again. Not ever."

"Oh, Velma," I said, trying to make my voice playful as I looked into her eyes, "didn't I just give you the time of your life on that bed over yonder? Didn't you just fall in love with me when I did you so good?"

"Don't call me Velma," she said. "The only name you get to call me is *whore*. That's the one you paid for. Now you get the hell out of here."

By the time I had put my clothes and shoes back on and had got back down the hall to the room we first came into, Velma was already out there, standing close to where the Cajun-looking man Dane was sitting in his straightback chair, looking down at him. He had a beer bottle in his hand and had drunk about half of it, and he was holding it partway up to his mouth, as though something had interrupted his train of thought and he had forgot to finish the action of taking another drink from the bottle. Six or seven other people had come into the room since I had left to go with Velma down the hall, four of them customers, I guessed, and the other ones new women looking to make a sale.

I didn't see Clay Whitehead anywhere, and I started looking around for him, thinking as I did that if he were to suddenly appear before me I would knock hell out of him for not being there ready to leave when I got back. But, I couldn't do that, since he wasn't there, and if he had been there'd be no reason to feel like doing that to him. You want to do what you can't do when there's no reason to do it if you could.

"Where's Clay?" I said to nobody in particular, speaking out loud, almost yelling so I could be heard over all the noise of the victrola, which somebody had turned up high, and the talking going on between the whores and the men trying to get up the nerve to do some serious bargaining with them. "Where's the fellow that came in here with me? Has he done left?"

"You talking about that little fellow wearing them big red-colored boots, he gone back in the room with Dolly," the colored woman who had let us in the Maryland Hotel said. "He might be a while, too. Dolly she twice as big as he is."

"Suppose she going to have to hold him up to it?" said one of the new men in the room, looking from me to the colored woman and back again. "So he'll have a fighting chance to hang that thing in her?"

The rest of them laughed big at that, though not any of the whores did, and I joined in, too, as I began to work my way toward the door to the stairs leading down to the street. "Tell him I'll be outside waiting," I said to the spot where the colored woman had been, though she was not there now, and I turned to look back toward the corner of the room where the whore I had been with was talking with the man in the straightback chair. The chair was there, and Velma was there looking down at the seat of it as though there might have been somebody still sitting there saying something to her. But there wasn't. The man she called Dane was not in sight, and seeing that chair empty was like feeling cold air moving across my face on a hot day in August. I couldn't get my full breath.

I fumbled the lock open on the room side of the door, and I was halfway down the stairs before I heard it slam behind me. It seemed to me that somebody must have turned out the light bulb in the stairway because I remembered it being easy to see the steps when Clay Whitehead and I had climbed them on the way up, and now it was so dark I couldn't see my feet in front of me as I came in a half run down, down, down toward the square of light in the door at the bottom leading to the street.

The quiet on the stairway got so different so quick when the door to the Maryland Hotel at the top had slammed shut between me and the noise of the victrola and the whores and the customers, so different in my ears, that the absence of sound seemed loud to me. My head was roaring with a noise like a big wind blowing through cedars in a cemetery somewhere, and I couldn't get outside the building fast enough to suit me. I ran at the door at the bottom with my arms lifted to knock it open, and I stumbled on the threshold on the way out, half falling as my feet hit the concrete sidewalk.

That stumble was why when he swung the hand holding the knife at me he didn't catch me with it in the belly or chest, but in the right temple, lodging it so hard in the bone that it twisted out of his hand when I went down to the pavement. And I heard a click when that steel hit bone, though I never felt it as a pain but as the sound of a thing shutting off, the way a radio will when you twist the knob and the music and the talking stop coming out, and the light in the tubes that make it run dims down to nothing and winks out.

I couldn't see anything of where I was, anymore.

Abigail

When I see Lewis sitting there like he is now, swiveling his head back and forth from one to the other of us every time one of us says a word, just like he could see the one speaking and pick us out as truly and well as the next person, I can understand how some people still believe he's just putting on an act.

If you didn't know him and weren't around him as much as his kinfolks have to be, you could believe he is running some kind of a game of deception on you. People in the Holly Springs community have said, but not to my face, you can count on, that all Lewis Holt has done is to figure out a way not to have to work ever again. He just makes like he's blind, these jaybirds say, and lets his sisters and grandnieces and cousins and you name it do everything for him.

Of course, it's easy to figure out why some will say that, whether they really believe it or not, and the reason why they're able to make such a claim is the way Lewis's eyes look. Your ordinary blind man, or blind woman, too, naturally, has funny-looking eyes, whenever you take a good close look at them. That's why lots of them will wear dark glasses over their eyes or keep them closed so people looking in from outside can't get a good view of the way they appear.

Some blind people's eyes are white looking, like they have a skim over them, the way milk will get if you let it sit too long away from the cool. You can tell they don't work, eyes like that. Some have eyes that wobble back and forth or roll around without any sign of real control being willed over them by the people whose heads they're located in the sockets of.

They look other ways not normal sometimes, too, blind people's eyes, but you can always tell when they're not able to do the job of seeing they are intended to do.

Lewis's eyes, now, don't look any of those ways. He keeps them open all the times he's supposed to, he doesn't wear smoked glasses to hide them away, and they move around in their sockets when he's talking to somebody in a normal and well-regulated fashion. So if you didn't believe him when he says he can't see a smidgin out of them, you'd think Lewis Holt is lying through his teeth about being blind, from just the visible evidence.

I know at least two reasons, though, why I believe him when he says he can't see, and neither one of them has a thing to do with my being his sister and having been around him his total life.

The first reason comes from pure logic and common sense, and it's this. Is there anybody so lazy and so determined not to hit a lick at work on his own behalf that he'll declare he's blind at age forty and then spend the rest of his life living in his sister's house feeling his way around with his hands and bumping into every obstacle that presents itself just to prove it?

No, I say, no. A man that would do that would have to be certifiably insane or of a totally weak intellect. And whatever my brother Lewis is and has been in his life and whatever sorriness of character he's displayed at times, he is not lacking in mind or intelligence. He is the son of Amos Holt, and he's always been saddled with what that means about our family when it comes to the ability to reason. Like the Holts in general, Lewis has a quickness of comprehension and an understanding that goes well beyond that of the ordinary run of folks in East Texas.

That is both a blessing and a curse. But I will choose that burden of the Holt family over what not having to bear it would mean. Consider the Moyes and that Leonard bunch.

The other reason I know for a dead certainty that Lewis has not been faking blindness for, lo, these many years is a simple one that requires no interpretation or declaration of faith in another's veracity. It's this. I saw him in that bed in the Hotel Dieu hospital run there in Beaumont by the Catholics with that knife still sticking out of the side of his head.

The doctors were afraid to pull it out at first that morning after that man had stabbed it into Lewis's head the night before. They didn't know what to do about it, thinking it might kill him on the spot by causing some major hemorrhage if they prised it out of his temple.

I would have just jerked it out as soon as I saw it if it had been up to me to decide, but, of course, I am not trained as a physician. The main doctor there, a man named Dr. Patrick Stephens, told me it was a quandary. That was the exact word he used, *quandary*, and he thought long and hard and looked in every medical book he owned or could get his hands on before they did anything about what was sticking out of my brother's head.

I remember saying to him, "Well, Dr. Stephens, you've gone to school and got all these degrees and studied in Baltimore, so it's up to you to decide. We'll just have to depend on you." I think that encouraged him to do what he had to do, my saying that to him as the closest member of Lewis's family in attendance, and he finally went ahead and operated.

Some of the people in Hardin County, particularly the ones connected to the Holts, wanted to say that taking the knife blade out of Lewis's head was what caused him to be blind from then on. But some of these same people were among the ones later on that claimed my brother was acting like he couldn't see afterward as a way to avoid having to make his own living. So that's what their opinions are worth. Nothing.

I have always thought, though I wasn't told this by Dr. Stephens nor any other physician, that the knife as soon as it went into Lewis's head, when that hoodlum stabbed him, that it severed some connection in the cranium that lets a person see.

When that connection was cut apart, it was all over with for Lewis and any chance of eyesight from then on, no matter what the doctors did. That's why his eyes look normal to somebody that doesn't understand the matter. The damage was not to the eyes themselves, but to the ways they're hooked up to what goes on in the brain. His eyes are fine. They just can't carry what they're bringing in back on across that downed bridge in his brain. That's how I understand it, and I've not heard a better argument than that advanced by a single person, including those medically trained.

Lewis is looking right now at Dicia who's just said something to him, but he might as well be looking at the ceiling for all the good it's doing him to look in her direction.

"Lewis," I say, "don't you think Maude's voice is a lot stronger this morning? I believe the more she's able to eat the better she sounds, don't you?"

He doesn't deign to answer my question, thinking as always of something on his own rather than what's being said to him. That doesn't bother me one bit. I'm used to his ways.

Dicia

For a long time whenever I would hear Great-Uncle Lewis coming down the hall of GrandMaude's house or rocking in his chair on the front porch on nice days or see him at meals or at any of the other occasions you encounter someone who lives in the same house with you, I could not keep myself from thinking about what I know about him and my mother and father in that time before I was born or before even there was a condition to allow me to come into the world.

I don't remember my mother at all, of course, gone as she was only days after I was born, but I like to think I have a hazy memory of my father, though GrandMaude tells me I was much too young when he died to remember him at all. I have no recollection of a time when Great-Uncle Lewis was not blind and could look at me and see what there was and is of my mother in me.

I don't know who it was who first told me about the situation that existed with those three people, the two who made me and the one who introduced the happenstance that allowed the making to take place in its own time. I'm certain my learning about it came from more than one person, but there had to be a single one who was the first to tell me. An event takes place in parts and pieces, no matter how intertwined all these may come to be eventually, close up and immediate or by slow growth over a long space. There is a start.

A tree grows from one seed, but that seed has the whole tree in it at the beginning or it never exists. There is no point in the growth of a tree when you can say now it is a tree and it was not before. It was always a tree, there before it could have been visible even to a scientist peering through a microscope at the first and most elemental existence of the seed from which it came. It is itself complete from its beginning, or it never is itself no matter how long the wait for a becoming, even until the gates of eternity.

So one person first told me my great-uncle brought the woman who was to be my mother with him, as his woman, into the presence of the man who was to be my father, and that event was the seed which was me then at the beginning before any physical joining of two selves into one particle ever took place. I was there then, at that moment, as much as I am here with others in the room where my grandmother lies in her bed steadily dying.

I can never know who first showed me a part of the mystery which became me and will always be that, but as I grew into myself, others provided other parts of the story of how I came to be me, and I recall what those people said, those tellers of the true tale. The words they offered had in them the grains of truth, no matter how disguised nor the intent with which they were spoken.

One was my great-uncle himself, Lewis, the man deprived of what he thought was his alone, believed by him at least to be that, his for a while anyway, his enduring task, as he saw it, to expand that while and make it permanence. He did not understand then, at the instant the dissolution began, and he has never understood to this day what is true about the identity of a thing, what is true about the seed and the fullness within it all along entire, or else not at all, ever.

I was playing in the front yard of GrandMaude's house, arranging fallen pine needles into lines to make a pattern, first one way and then another, depending on how I chose to sweep and shape them with a small straight stick I had found and which pleased me with its smoothness and authority as a tool.

Great-Uncle Lewis was sitting in the rocking chair he always used, moving back and forth in it now and then to no certain rhythm, and I was not noticing him or the sound his chair made as he rocked, occupied as I was with the pine needles and my good stick. I had noticed that unlike GrandMaude my great-uncle seldom took much notice of me or my cousin Nola Mae when she visited and that he spoke to us even less than he gave sign he noticed us.

I had never been concerned about that or anything else about Great-Uncle Lewis, particularly on that morning when I was organizing the fallen pine needles in the front yard of GrandMaude's house, so that when he called my name I didn't even notice the first time he did so.

"Dicia," he said. "Do you hear me, girl? I know you're there. I can hear you scraping around in the dirt. What are you doing down there, besides getting yourself all dirty?"

"I'm not scraping dirt, Great-Uncle Lewis," I said, and then paused to think what I would tell him. I was making patterns out of pine straw, using a stick that seemed to me especially designed for the task, but

I didn't want to tell him that. If I did, he'd want to know, in what I had learned was the manner of grown people, what kind of patterns I was making. I wouldn't know the answer to that question, since the stick was making the patterns, and I was simply observing what it was revealing to me as it moved the pine straw in first one direction, then another, erasing as it went along, adjusting the lines according to some plan locked within the stick itself, not paying any attention to me as it worked, and allowing any people who wanted to see what it was doing to look their fill. It didn't care.

I like observing that about my good stick, and I wanted to let it do its work without having to stop to explain to me what it was discovering in the fallen pine needle arrangements it traced in GrandMaude's yard. And how would it tell me, anyway, other than in what parts I was able to read myself in the patterns working their way out? It's a stick, I remember thinking to myself, it can't say words to me.

By the time I had come to that conclusion, Great-Uncle Lewis had gotten tired of waiting for me to answer. "What're you doing, then, girl, if you're not playing in the dirt? Speak up when I ask you something. You know to speak when you're spoken to."

"Yessir," I said, still at a loss to explain to him what I was seeing my stick disclose in the patterns it made in the pine straw and noting that it had not slowed down in its work while Great-Uncle Lewis talked. The stick kept leading my hand where it wanted to go.

"What it is," I said, "that I am doing is making lines with pine needles.'

"Lines?' Great-Uncle Lewis said. "What kind of lines?"

"Lines," I said, looking up at the man leaning forward in the rocking chair on the porch, "lines that show the walls of a house. Lines that show all the walls in it and where the doors are in the house, and the hall, and the porch, and the windows."

"A house, you say? Rooms in a house. Are you making a room for a blind man to live in, too, in your house?"

"Oh, yes, Great-Uncle Lewis," I said, relieved to have a way finally to answer his questions which didn't require me to lie about my stick and pretend to know what it was up to in its work with the pine needle patterns. "I'm making a nice room just right for a blind man to live in."

"How's that? How does it suit a blind man?"

"It hasn't got any windows in it," I said, "since he doesn't need to look outside and the daylight doesn't need to have a way to get to him. And the blind man doesn't need to have a door that closes to his room, because if somebody walking by looked in his room the blind man couldn't see them doing it, so he wouldn't have to be ashamed."

"Ashamed? What's a blind man got to be ashamed about?" Great-Uncle Lewis said. "He can't do nothing to be ashamed about."

"I think he can," I said, "because he can walk around and bump into things and break them like a mirror or glass and on the table. He can make things fall. But he doesn't need a mirror, anyway."

My great-uncle didn't say anything back to me, and I looked down to see what my stick was doing, which I discovered was arranging pine needles into a circle, like a big O, with nothing inside it. "But whatever he does that a person who wasn't blind would be ashamed of, the blind man doesn't have to be. He can't see the people see him do it. Break something or spill coffee on his shirt or leave biscuit crumbs stuck to his face. And if he can't see anybody see him, they aren't there, and the blind man's not ashamed. See?"

Great-Uncle Lewis didn't say anything to me for a spell, and I looked away from him back down to the stick working with the pine needles. It had finished making the round shape, the circle, the big zero with nothing inside it but the bare dirt of the yard, and I wondered if that was all the stick would want to do that day with the dead needles off the pine trees. If the pattern it was working on was finished, I was not going to push the stick on my own. It could work in its own good time, and if I tried to force it to keep up its activity, the stick would feel dead in my hand, I figured, and there'd be no satisfaction for me in tracing lines in the yard and arranging pine needles into shapes all on my own. I wanted a partner.

"So you allow as how if a blind man can't see people watching him, the people ain't there, huh? Is that what you're saying?" Great-Uncle Lewis said, not rocking back and forth in his chair any more but leaning forward with his eyes aimed in my direction. He couldn't see me, though. GrandMaude had told me that, no matter how much it looked like he could. Don't worry, she said.

"Well," I said, "the people watching the blind man think they're there, all right. But that doesn't make a bit of difference to the blind man. He knows what he sees is there. And what he sees is nothing. So nothing's there."

The stick in my hand had begun to move again, I noticed, but this time it was not shoving pine needles around into patterns, but instead drawing little circles inside the big empty circle it had already made. Little bits of nothing inside a big nothing, that's the shape it was making.

"You know a lot, don't you, Dicia?" Great-Uncle Lewis said. "At least you think you do."

"I know what I know," I said, "and I know that I know that. Most of the time, I do, but sometimes what I know goes away, and sometimes new things I don't know yet come to me while I'm dreaming, and I know them while I'm asleep, but not when I wake up."

"Here's something you don't know yet," he said. He had turned his head more and more toward me as I talked, and now it looked like he was seeing me since his eyes were pointed right at me. So I moved a little bit to the side, not making a sound as I stepped across the pattern the stick had made in the pine needles, careful not to touch the work that was already finished and being as quiet as the dirt where I was stepping would let me. When I had done that, Great-Uncle Lewis still had his eyes set on where I had been, not where I was.

I turned my head to the side and spoke into the space where I had been but was not now. "What?" I said. His eyes didn't move.

"You don't know that you and me have been in exactly the same place, but not at the same time," Great-Uncle Lewis said.

"Where?" I said into the empty spot where I was not. "Texas?"

"We're in Texas now," he said. "But that's at the same time. I didn't mean Texas, and I don't mean inside this house where I'm sitting."

He wasn't inside the house, on the porch instead, but I didn't say that out loud. I knew it, though. I could look and tell.

"Where?" I said again to the empty place beside me, now containing nothing but air and sunlight and the motes of dust I could see everywhere all the time whenever I wanted to notice them.

"You and me have both been inside your mama, inside her belly, way up inside there."

"I don't have a mama," I said, knowing that was true, but not knowing what my great-uncle had meant by what he said. My stick knew, though, as soon as he said what he did, and it began to move in my hand, scattering the pine needle patterns, knocking them into pieces so small and unconnected that no one could have looked and told that any arrangement of any kind that meant anything to anybody had ever been there.

The stick saved the big circle, the empty O, until last, and when all of what it had worked to discover before was gone, the stick turned the circle into nothing, too. Not until it had finished doing that did the stick go dead in my hand, and I could tell by that feeling what I had had inside it until that moment was gone for good. I stuck the end of the stick into the earth of the yard and leaned on it with all the weight I could muster until it broke into two pieces, uneven in size.

I threw both pieces toward where some other sticks were lying near the trunk of one of the pine trees and looked away. When I looked back at the same spot the next second, I couldn't tell one stick from another. I don't remember what I did next, go into the house, or around it to the back yard, but I do know I left my great-uncle sitting in his rocking chair on the front porch, speaking into that empty space where I had been, but I didn't try to hear what he was saying.

"Dicia," someone is saying to me now. It's Nola Mae, come back into GrandMaude's room when I wasn't noticing. "Do you want to take a walk with me for a little while? It's nice outside."

"You go on," I say. "I think I'll sit here a little longer, in case when GrandMaude wakes up she may feel like talking a little."

Nola Mae looks away from me and down at her hands.

Nola Mae

A frigate is a boat. It's an old timey one, I guess, or Mrs. Pritchard wouldn't have tried to drill it into our heads in English class, much less picked out the poem that has *frigates* in it for us to memorize and stand up one by one and recite aloud while everybody watched us try to do it. If it wasn't old, she wasn't interested in it.

She said it would be a comfort to us in the years we lived after we left high school, if we would learn that poem with the frigate in it by heart and understand the lesson it had for us.

If Old Lady Pritchard said it once, she said it a hundred times, that if we listened to the wisdom poets who wrote all those poems put into them we would be able to count on it helping us out later on in situations we had to endure and couldn't get out of. I can't remember the exact words to the frigate poem, though Dicia could if she had been the one who had to learn it and spit it back out while people watched her. Maybe she did learn it in the Holly Springs school, maybe everybody in Texas did, but I'm not going to ask her, because if she did have to get by heart the poem with the frigate in it, she probably could still say it out loud to me today just like a human typewriter running. And would be glad to do it, too. Would enjoy it, no doubt.

What does it mean, Nola Mae, she asked me, Mrs. Pritchard did, when it says my mind is like a frigate, and is that a good way for somebody's mind to be? Answer me those two questions, she said, and then she looked around at the rest of them there in the classroom as if to say let's see what kind of a mess Nola Mae makes of this one this time, y'all.

A lot of the girls smiled at her when she said that, giving them the sign that it was fine and dandy to get ready to make light of Nola Mae, some of them even shifting in their seats as though to prepare themselves to pounce, especially the ugly ones, the ones with eyes set too close together, say, or jaws shaped like lanterns or skin rough as a

Christmas orange or a shape in the body like a croker sack full of sweet potatoes all thrown together, willy nilly.

I didn't answer Mrs. Pritchard's question, I got up and said it to all of them, that poem, not making a sign I was a bit worried or ill at ease, smiling first just like Dicia always does when she is put on the spot to do something, letting everybody know I was not one speck worried to be on display, no matter what kind of mistake I might make or words I might forget to say or however much I might put clumps of them in the wrong order.

I got a good bit of it wrong, since my idea of what to do nights is not limited to reading some old poem over and over again again until I get it all stuck in my head, and that's exactly what I'd have had to do if I wanted to get my recitation the next day at school perfect. So Mrs. Pritchard had to correct some part of what I said and remind me of some I had left out and give me a few words to get me re-started the times I got bogged down along the way.

One thing I noticed, though, and was not the least bit surprised by, is that the boys in the classroom that day paid closer attention to my recitation of that poem than they did to any other girl's, even the ones who got it dead perfect, like Merle Ann Epps who must have eaten the thing whole somehow to be able to urp it back up the way she did. She stood there in front of everybody with her eyes half-closed and her head thrown back, looking like she's just been hit with a pole-ax and was deciding whether or not to fall down onto the floor from the effects of the lick she'd just took.

When she finished, Mrs. Pritchard said Merle Ann had done it perfect, down to the last accent, whatever she meant by that, but from the way everybody was sitting at their desks looking down at the floor or the walls you'd have thought Merle Ann Epps had just announced somebody had died of diphtheria. Nobody wanted to know.

They weren't looking down when I finished up, though, repeating after Mrs. Pritchard the last two lines of the poem, still smiling as I came to the end of it. Several of the boys started clapping, Bill Avery and Tom Pennington and Donald Eugene Eustis among the ones I remember, until Mrs. Pritchard made them stop. We couldn't have any of that kind of display going on, Nola Mae being appreciated for something she'd done involving school work. Why, she had made mistakes and left things out, didn't you notice? Messed up the accents and all.

Afterward when I'd gotten back to my desk and sat down and folded my hands to look toward the front of the room to wait for the next one to get up and start reciting, knowing while I sat there that all of the boys and some of the girls had kept their eyes on me all my way back to my seat and hadn't stopped looking at me yet, Tom Pennington leaned toward me from the row of desks where he was sitting and whispered a word.

It was "frigate," of course, and just as cool as could be I said right back to him without even turning my head a single hair in his direction—nobody could have told I had noticed him much less said anything back, especially Old Lady Pritchard, the way I did it without giving a sign—I said to Tom Pennington, "Frigate yourself."

I knew what he was up to, and I was not about to let him get away with thinking he could say one thing to me and mean another, and not have me call him on it. "Frigate yourself," was what I said, and though I still didn't turn to look at him, I could tell from the way he drew in his breath and flopped back in his seat that I had put him securely in his place.

That made the day for me, and it was all over the school in no time what I had said back to Tom Pennington, and I couldn't go anywhere without every pupil in my high school looking at me for what I had said during poem recitation in English class.

That's why I remember a frigate is a boat, and I guess Mrs. Pritchard was right. What that old poet wrote about "my mind to me a frigate is" had stood me in good stead since that day I had to get up in front of the seniors in English literature class and say out loud all those lines he had written down. It has given me something to think about in boring situations which I have to endure.

I have no notion what Dicia is sitting over there in the corner dwelling on while we all sit here in my Great-Aunt Maude's bedroom where she is on her deathbed, as they all keep saying, and I'm not interested in trying to figure out what might be in my cousin's head. Whatever it is, it's something no ordinary person would come up with to ponder over, but I know what's helping me pass the time and giving me something to entertain my memory.

I'm thinking a frigate is a boat.

Maude

The sound comes most of the time, and I can hear it continually when it's going on, and I'm afraid. It wasn't that way at first, coming almost all of the time, but then when it was interrupted for a space, I would notice it more when it started again. That was worse, when it would stop, and the quiet would come, cool and distant in my ears and putting me at a remove from where I was, worse because I never knew when the sound would come again. Waiting for something you dread is worse always than being in its presence, whatever it is, when it finally is upon you and close enough to seize you in fact and truth.

The pain of being in the throes of something hurtful is lessened because it concentrates the way time feels. When you're in it, everything is now, and nothing is past or to come. It's here, and here is all, and there is a comfort in that, the way it must be to the mind of a moth flown into a candle flame. But a moth can't think, and know what it's lost or hope for cessation or change. All is immediate to such a creature, the way it is not to a woman or a man, doomed to be able to imagine what an alternative to suffering might be, and that is why it's better to me when the sound is constant and does not tantalize by granting spells of silence.

The sound is not all, even at its strongest. I can hear them behind it talking to each other, trading stories, making jokes, taking offense, explaining themselves, chuckling, even laughing aloud and full-throated at times. The sound is there always, but it is not all. It is not a blanket that covers me completely, that cuts off all evidence of others existing in the world outside me that is not me. It has not settled finally with all the air pushed out from beneath it, the way a sheet over you will do when you lift it and then let it fall until everything touching you is flat and settled and still again. How many times can you bear to lift the cover again, though, knowing in the way the moth burning in the flame cannot that no variation is possible, that all results come to the same?

I do not hear them through the sound, however, my sister and brother and granddaughter, Richard's child, and my grandniece and the others who come, in the manner you hear someone speaking to you in a quiet voice even though a thunderstorm may be raging outside the room you find yourself in. Hearing them speak to each other doesn't come by means of my successful competition with another sound working against that which they make.

I hear them not by piercing through the sound that's come to be always with me now, but by discovering ways around it. I can fool the sound at times, not by any effort to defeat it on its own terms, not by willing my understanding to prevail against it, not by main strength, but by another way altogether, a way of weakness and yielding, a way of appearing to offer up myself to it with no defense.

That sound between me and all that is not me is a wall, built high and wide and set deep in the earth, too strong and thick and massive to prevail against by main strength. So there is no hope for me in struggle, and if I attempt to move against the sound, it knows that and grows stronger, for its resources are vast, like the one of water steadily freezing in a temperature below zero, set to last.

If I scream, as I once did in my struggle, no one can hear me, only the sound can do that, and it is encouraged and fed by that admission, and it grows.

But if I am soft and quiet and patient and to all appearances yielding, I feel my understanding begin to move, like a small stream of warm water working in runnels through an ice floe, making a passage unnoticed and faint and silent.

Then, though the sound is still there with me, as proud and present as ever, yet so am I, yet me, yet Maude. And I use the power of what the sound represents to remind me of those times when I was what I was.

My husbands knew me, both of them did, I thought at first after I had met each one in turn and had come to know we would marry. We would be man and woman together, joined for all time as the Bible teaches, as people always say during worship in church and even in their lives lived outside the house where God is said to have His habitation. But He is always with us elsewhere, they say, and He listens when we cry out and He knows what we want and what we really need before we do, and He parcels out His gifts to each of us as fitting and appropriate in due and full measure.

I was taught that and believed it, and it was said that marriage here on earth between a man and a woman is a shadow of marriage in Heaven and there meet and competent and to be entered into not lightly. That I accepted and told myself I believed, and from that belief came the other and final one, the belief that would calm and reassure and support my understanding and acceptance. It would let me draw breath in ease and confidence, and it was this. My husband would know me, would fathom the depth of my self and essence, and could say to me with truth and certainty you are Maude and this is what Maude is and I can and will explain yourself to you.

I wanted that to be a true and perfect acceptance and understanding for me, and I thought it must and would be. And I wanted that condition and that settled faith, and I longed for it the way I longed for the touch of my first husband, my true love, Valery Blackstock, the father of Richard.

And one longing was solely and completely satisfied by him, and that was what happened each time he touched me, and so I learned to depend on that. I had to depend on that, because the other longing was not fulfilled, though it was the one assured by God's word and announced and proclaimed in His book.

And there were times I thought I would give up the satisfaction that came to me as Valery's wife with what happened when we touched if I could have that other, that promise made by God that the husband would know the self of the wife and the wife know the self of the husband. But that never was, even at the beginning when I said to myself wait, wait, wait and it will come, and later when I gave over waiting and convinced myself that I could by will create the condition which would allow my husband to know me and show me myself to me in satisfaction and finality. But try though I did to crush out of myself all that was separate and solitary and sensed only by me, my husband gave no satisfactory sign that he was able to know me truly and give me myself.

So when he was dying young as he was, Oh Lord, and I knew that he was, it came to me that God would give me a consolation for that loss of my true love by allowing my husband to know me at the end and present that knowledge to me. So that as I waited for Valery, my husband, to die, I kept in my mind what I would never be able to admit to another, the thought that on his leaving this world and me in it he would in his last words to me say what he had never before. Here is who you are, Maude, if you translate truly these last words I give you. Hear me speak them.

I waited for them, prepared to write them in flame on my heart, and I made everyone leave the room where he lay dying so that I would not be distracted, so that I could forget all but those words he would speak. But they did not come, beg him though I did to speak one last word to me, one syllable, one sound.

Before Valery was in his coffin, I asked Abigail once more to repeat to me the last words Papa had said on his deathbed, though I knew them, from her telling me and others time and time again what they had been.

"This time, Abigail," I said to her, "try to remember exactly what he said to Alice, his wife. I know you won't leave anything out, but please I beg you not to put a single syllable in that Papa didn't utter to his wife. Don't try to make it better than it was, the last thing he said."

"Alice wasn't his real wife," my sister said. "You know that, Maude. Carolina Cameron Holt was the real wife of Amos Holt, our Papa, and she was long dead before Papa was called home."

I didn't answer that verse from Abigail's book, not wanting to debate that tenet of her faith again, not because I thought any argument was doomed to failure, and it was, of course, and had been and would be, but because I knew once entered upon, that topic would consume all my sister's attention and energy and would not allow her to consider any subject but Abigail's eternal quarrel with the fact of Papa's marriage to another woman after the death of our mother, his taking of a new wife, or as Abigail would see it better stated, Amos Holt's yielding to the wiles of a strange woman, to use the words from God's book that my sister found fitting.

"What were the words Papa gave her, Abigail?" I said. "I know you were there and heard them, and I know what a wonderful memory you have for things that matter."

"Not just things that matter," Abigail said, and from the way she spoke I knew her attention had been shifted to a more comfortable subject for her and one more likely to yield me what I needed to hear and believe, if it was there to be found. "I could tell you the list of words I spelled correctly in that school competition in Sabine County when I was sixteen years old, if I wanted to and you wanted to hear them. I was just thinking about that event the other day, and I was recalling the last two words I had to spell to win that bee against that girl from San Augustine County. Her name was Betty Adcock."

"I know you could," I said, holding what I needed to say to Abigail balanced in my mind against the thought of my husband lying dead in a room not two doors away from where we stood. "And that's why I'm asking all you can remember of Papa's last words in this life. You can tell me. What did he say to Alice?"

"Well, Papa said what I've told you before that he said. It was that old war stuff that came to him at the end, see. It was delirium working in his mind like it will do when a person's at death's door. That's what it was, I'm as sure of that as I am that you're standing before me a widow this minute."

"Did Papa say anything before or after what you're talking about in reference to him and Alice? The words about the war, I mean," I said, the balance in my mind as finely exact as a knife edge turned up. If there's no angle to the blade, there's no cut when you touch it.

"What would he have to say in reference to him and Alice?" Abigail said. "The man was dying, Maude. He had only a little time left to think about anything, whether he could have said that or not. He knew it somehow, that it was coming. People dying know it's happening, I'm convinced, in underneath and behind that state of delirium that comes on them. No, Amos Holt would not have had any reason to be mulling over something about him and Alice. He had the dying to do, the last thing he would do in this world, and his mind was seizing upon things important to it, ramble though it might be doing. He was readying himself for Glory."

"What did he say? What were the words of Papa you can remember?"

"I can remember all of them," Abigail said, "of course. He hadn't said a thing for two days or more, lying there and drifting off in that deep sleep, like he was. Maybe his heart was slowing down, and his organs were declining. I don't know what all was going on, but I do know that medicine Dr. Peoples was giving him was a drug. It kept Papa in a perpetual doze for the last week of his life. That's how I know it was a drug. It was way yonder beyond medicine."

"What he speak, then?"

"I'm getting to that. He hadn't said a word nor known anybody for a couple of days, not a soul that spoke to him could get him to talk back or even notice."

"Not even his wife?" I said. "Not even Alice?"

"Of course not," Abigail said. "He didn't even know me."

I knew I shouldn't have said that particular thing to my sister. It slowed her, and it wasn't until I thought to put my face into my hands and look away from her that she became distracted enough from thinking about our stepmother Alice to be able to resume her account.

"Right at four o'clock in the afternoon he opened his eyes," Abigail said. "The sun was coming in the window and lit up his face, and he opened his eyes because it was bothering him, I thought, the sun was, and I went to the window to pull the shade down, Alice just sitting there doing nothing, but holding on to that Bible in her hands like she was afraid somebody was going to try to take it away from her, but just as I got there to do it, I could see Papa opening his lips to say something."

"What is it, Papa?" I said. And here's what he said, clear as a bell and in just as strong a voice as he always used. Not when he was preaching, now, I'm not saying that, but when he was carrying on an ordinary conversation.

"Chicamauga," he said. "Chicamauga. That's the place, that's the place."

"Did he say anything else?" I said. "Was he directing his words toward his wife?"

"No, Papa didn't say another word, and he sure wasn't looking at Alice when he said that. It was like he was answering somebody who'd asked him a question about the name of some place, and he couldn't remember it at first, and then he did. He was able to come up with the answer. Chicamauga, that's in Tennessee, I think. Maybe Georgia. It was like he was saying something like that."

"I see," I said. "He had no word for his wife."

"Not a one," Abigail said. "Not a single one. Not for Alice, not for me. And then Papa was dead in less than half an hour from that time he spoke that statement. He never had another word for anybody."

Neither had my husband for me, and those hours and days I waited beside his bed, as the fever rose and as it fell and his lungs filled with the matter that finally drowned him.

I would not be a fool, but I felt I had been lied to and cheated by that, not by Valery Blackstock himself who had never held back anything from me that he was able to give, but by what I had read in all those books and by the stories I had heard people tell about statements delivered on deathbeds from those going to those left behind to draw breath a while longer.

Here is what I believed, what I clung to. Those words offered as a gift make it possible for the one remaining to believe the life of the dying one had a shape. It began, and it grew, and it prospered, and then by nature it fell into decay and ended, as it must do, since nothing lasts in the world, but one thing. And that which lasts is nothing which has been able to breathe and move and feel itself to be, and neither is it stones, nor trees, nor earth itself, all of which change and erode and vanish in time.

What lasts of this world is one thing, only, and that is water. It comes, it flows, it falls, it washes away, and boils into nothing, but it always returns, and for want of it all things die.

Papa and Mama came across water to Texas, and I remember that, child though I was, and water was a consequence to them, a barrier to be reckoned with, and I knew when we stood on the Texas side of the water we had crossed that a thing of weight had been accomplished. That's when we saw the Indian woman, and that was when Mama's baby was born dead, though I didn't understand that at the time, of course.

Abigail did, and she knew too what the crossing of water meant, knew it not to speak about it, but in a way which filled her with importance and pride and threat, and she used that sense of herself as one triumphing over water on that day and all days since. If I were to ask my sister now about herself and water, she would not understand my question, but something about it would make her anxious and lead her by quick degree to anger, and she would lash out at me, even now with me here in this bed, my last one.

Abigail is not troubled with the disappointment of discovering that what had been believed is false, as I am cursed with being. I wanted Valery to say true words to me as he waited to die, words that would finish the time we had together in the way the last piece in a quilt design lets you say it is done, it is itself, there is no more that can be added and nothing to take away, it stands complete.

And so I learned there is a lie in words, a lie in the very saying of them and in the record of that saying and in the understanding of what one has said in words by another one not the person who made them to begin with, but the receiver of them. To think you understand is to lie to yourself.

What I had read in all those books, the Bible one of them, the word of God, and in what I had heard in accounts by others, words thrown out in the air to take into yourself like draughts of clear water in a time of thirst, all that was not discovered truth, but manufactured dreams intended by nature to deceive and entertain.

Since there is no shape and no meaning to give comfort to the one left behind, alone and bereft, there is nothing to do but lie. Let us invent what we think we need. And so I begged my dying husband, the first and true love of my heart, to give me words, to tell me a story which began and prospered and declined and died and meant, but he could not. I do not fault him. I fault words.

Water crossed is water gone, never to be seen as it first was in that place and in that precision, but there is water ahead still, and who can tell the difference?

Carolina Cameron Holt, my mother, died a year short of her fortieth birthday, with nine children alive and the husband whose seed called them forth yet attendant upon her. I do not count in that number those dead at birth, though I remember one well, one I never saw, the boy child whose lack of a single living breath placed us here and fastened us to this part of the world, this part of Texas, this side of the water of the Sabine.

Mama told me, and she told me alone, not Abigail, what reason prevailed and what argument determined why our journey west ended where it did. And from that came all else, for all of us. The places we lived, the houses built, the clearings we made, the wells dug, and the fields claimed by ax and saw and plow. The people around us we dealt with, the husbands and wives taken in time by the children of Amos and Carolina Holt, the children from those choices and what has happened and will happen to them and those who come from them.

All those changes and all those choices and the griefs and pains and satisfactions from them—all this came from one statement, one decision, one stand taken by my mother. It came to her what she must and would do on the morning after the child was born to her on our first night in Texas.

"The Indian woman wasn't gone," my mother said to me, "when I came to myself that morning at first light and knew that vision in my mind was true. Not a dream, not a cloud caused by the birth itself or by the dirt, the sweet dirt she had given me to hold under my tongue, after that first great pain went through me."

The day was a Sunday, and Mama and I were alone in the house. Papa had preached that morning a long sermon at somebody's house place a couple of miles away, and he was doing what he always did in the hour after eating on Sundays when the weather allowed it. Outside under the sycamore in front of the house, he was sitting in a straight chair which Abigail had set up for him in the shade, and he was reading his Bible, thinking ahead to the next preaching of the word he would deliver. Abigail stood behind him, not reading over his shoulder as someone not familiar with the truth of the scene might think if they were observing her standing near Papa in his chair, but instead watching him read and study, not reading herself, I repeat.

Now and then, my sister would reach out and touch Papa on the shoulder lightly or brush at the cloth of his shirt as though to remove something that had fallen there from the sycamore, a leaf or a bit of bark or a speck of trash, but that was not what Abigail was doing. That was simply my sister's excuse for touching our father, and he was so accustomed to her doing that he seldom acknowledged her, one way or another, either by looking up or by showing any sign he knew she was there. But Papa liked her being there in attendance, though I never heard him say so. She often claimed he did, though, and she was right in that, I do allow.

I could see the two of them through the open door, as I helped my mother with whatever it was she was doing, some small task which occupied her hands but didn't interfere with her speaking. A hum of insects was lifting and falling, I remember, and now and then the sound of voices or laughter came from others of the children, my sisters and brothers, unseen outside and farther away from the house than Abigail and Papa, playing together, running, tumbling down, getting up.

"I've tried to remember the Indian woman," I said, "and sometimes I think I can, but mostly not. I can never see her in my mind."

"You were too young," Mama said. "You were asleep in the wagon most of the time. It was night, you know, just at dark when we crossed the river."

"Yes, but I remember the mule eating the leaves off a bush," I said. "He made noise doing it, blowing air out when he was chewing, making groaning sounds."

"He was a good mule," she said. "He never got enough to eat, it seemed. Mules never do."

"I knew we were in Texas. I remember thinking that over and over."

"Abigail kept telling you we were in Texas," my mother said. "We had crossed the river, and that was large in your sister's mind."

"You said something had been in your mind. A vision you called it. What was in your mind that was true? What came to you that you knew was not a dream?"

"I knew that my baby was not alive," my mother said. "I knew that we had come from Louisiana to Texas and I had carried him all the way through the woods and across the water and now he was not with us. I saw that, dead to the world though I was."

She looked up from whatever she was doing there on a table, directly at me. Her eyes were large and hazel brown with a darker ring around the light part. Mine are brown, and Abigail always says she has Mama's eyes exactly. She got them, she claims. She didn't. Hers are blue and lack the darker ring.

"I knew your father and the Indian woman had dug a deep hole and put my baby in it and buried him," Mama said. "And I knew I would not leave him covered with dirt in that wilderness. I would not leave him there alone."

And Carolina Holt did not. That story I came to know as a child, though it was no story in the way an account told by someone to entertain others is a story. A story of that kind is subject to amendment, and it changes to fit the needs of the moment and the appetite and understanding of its hearer. Its teller keeps one eye on the way that story is being received, and is ready to throw aside parts that do not satisfy the hearer, or to add improvements and relish in the way you might throw spices into a dish bland to the palate.

If the teller detects a way to wake the taste of his hearer, he will add pepper or sugar to his tale, he will build up the parts that suit the savor, and he will boil away the thin liquid that adds nothing but bulk.

Where is truth in such a dish? It stands little chance of reaching the table as the heart of the meal if it does not surprise with a tastiness calculated to please.

When Amos Holt was asked by someone the reason for his choice of this location to make a living in Texas, this land near the Sabine and south toward the Gulf, he always took such questions as deadly serious, never recognizing a single one to be idle or intended merely to fill an empty space momentary in the air between people. His answers revealed a preparation of thought beforehand, a careful justification for the reason he found himself and his wife and children where he did in East Texas, standing in the space occupied by himself and the questioner before him.

At those times, I heard his accounts of the construction of those plans and considerations and balances of pros and cons for what he intended to do in moving from Louisiana to Texas after his return from the war in the east and what he carried out in so doing. I came by degrees not to listen to him. At first, I closed my ears to small details I did not want to hear repeated, then to parts of the account, then to sections, and finally to the whole meal itself he set out for consumption.

Papa knew what he wanted to be true about his reasons for doing what he had done and for choosing what he had chosen, and he labored to build the story which would accommodate the truth he wished to provide a habitation for. So he lopped, and he expanded, and he added the spice needful for taste and savor, and he boiled away the thin excess of bulk not servant to his intention. And the story he finished after many attempts at perfection, I chose not to endure another listening to, not to consume once again, for the story Papa made would not sate my hunger.

The story I wanted to hear, the account which provided fit home for the truth of the conditions of my existence in this state and this world, was a short one. It was undressed, it was flavored with nothing but its own essence, and it was filling and substantial. It fed my hunger.

I was here, placed here alone by my mother and father and whatever design lay behind the plans and accounts of men and women, by the will of a mother not to leave her child, dead to life though he was.

That story satisfied me then, though I did not contradict other stories beyond and beside it as I heard my father and Abigail recount them, and it satisfies me now as I lie in my last bed, waiting.

They are speaking about me now, Abigail mentioning Valery and how I came to know and love and marry and lose him, and she is fitting all that into a pattern to serve her purpose, but I will not correct or contradict what she needs to believe is true in her story. She must have that as she wants it, and what business is it of mine to deny my sister the shaping of the world which will feed her the nourishment she craves? I grant her that.

"When Valery died," she is saying, "I thought we were going to lose Maude, too. Her very mind left her for a spell, and she didn't even know who she was. Nobody in the entire Holly Springs community figured my sister would last two more weeks."

"Was she thinking about doing away with herself?" somebody asks, a young person by her voice, not Dicia, so it must be Nola Mae. "I mean, you know, killing herself? Taking poison or something?"

Abigail starts to speak, says a word or two she must believe will not be advantageous to the way she wants to answer that question from her granddaughter, even as she says them, since she stops and clears her throat to give herself time to rethink—I know that habit of hers from long experience, the way she makes a sound to announce she has the floor and needs time to set things in order in her mind before she proceeds, but wants to let all would-be speakers know it is not their turn, but hers—and now she starts her account in earnest.

I open my eyes. And I will smile, and I will speak, and Abigail will lose part of the story she intends to tell, not because she will forget it due to interruption, but because it is a story and as such subject to amendment as a new hearer appears, particularly this hearer, the one at the heart of the account she's shaping.

She does not fear contradiction in itself, since she is confident in her powers to meet disagreements and interpretations not her own, sure that her battalions are as strong as any she may meet in the field, and like any general who has survived to old age, Abigail has a history of successes and triumphs behind her, if her spirits need a boost. Her morale is always high, and forecasts are always optimistic.

No, what will cause her to amend the tale she intended to tell is not apprehension at having to meet and overcome opposition, but the nature of making stories itself. Abigail is bound by the teller's need to furnish the hearer with what the hearer wants and must have, entertainment and interest at the cost of all else, and if I as hearer display dissatisfaction or signs of disinterest in what she's offering in her story she has failed as teller. And that Abigail never wants to do.

The truth to which she testifies is provisional, in a way our mother's never was, and Abigail will sacrifice it in the beat of a hummingbird's wing to serve the demands of her story.

"Well, look who's waking up to listen," my sister says. "Maude, we were all just talking about you, of course, and must have got to carrying on so much we woke you up."

"Yes, Abigail," I say, "I've been hearing you, but it's nice to wake up and have people in the room."

"Great-Aunt Abigail was remembering grandfather for us," Dicia says. "Telling us about when you two first met and your early days together."

"It was at a dance," I say, turning my head on the pillow to look toward Dicia. I can hear the sound in my head, though well-contained and not so loud, and I believe it will not move outside me into the room, at least for a while longer, judging from its level now, and that will give some space to talk.

I can see Abigail sitting to the left side of the room, near the foot of my bed, and she's looking down at her folded hands, disappointed that her account of my behavior after I knew Valery was truly gone from me forever has been interrupted. It has been abrupt, the stop she had to make in her story in full career, and she must feel the way you do when all of a sudden the water stops flowing from the faucet into the tub because the pump has broken. A promise has not been kept.

"I forget where the dance was," I go on, to give my sister something to work with, "some family's house, the way we all used to do back then when nobody could get anywhere because of the roads and not having automobiles."

"It was at Trot Monroe's place," Abigail says, "that you met Valery at the dance. It was a Saturday night, in October of 1884. I forget the date, but Trot and Lucinda Monroe never had a problem with letting young folks come to their place to socialize with their girls, and that's where it was."

"That's right," I say. "I remember now. You're right, Abigail. The Monroe girl was named Yvonne, I believe."

"There were two of them, and the one our age was Louselle. That's where I got the name to give Louselle Marie because I liked the sound of it so much. I didn't name my child for Louselle Monroe now. I just used the name, that's all."

"You borrowed it," Nola Mae says. "You gave my mama a really pretty name like Louselle, and I wish she had given me a pretty name like that, too. Nola sounds awful. It sounds like normal."

"You don't need to worry about that," Dicia tells her. "You are far from being ordinary."

"She's normal, though, your cousin is," Abigail says. "Just like everybody else. There's nothing funny about Nola Mae."

"I don't remember Louselle Monroe, Abigail," I say, "though I don't doubt what you say. What did she look like?"

Now Abigail has the opportunity to go on at some length, and I can focus on the sound in my head again while she does, and my great-niece Nola Mae can brood about being labeled normal by her grandmother and what that might mean. It's still containable, the sound, and when I touch it a bit, it doesn't flare. I listen again to Abigail.

"Wouldn't you agree Mrs. Monroe was sweet to all us young folks, Maude?" she's saying. "Letting us bring in Lon Anthony to fiddle and us just hopping all over almost every floor in the house?"

"I don't know about old lady Monroe," Lewis says, the first words I've heard from him today, "but Trot Monroe would take a drink if you offered it to him. That's why he was always ready to let them girls of his have dances at his house. Tolar and Elvin Boles and a bunch of us would take him outside and give him drinks of busthead whiskey until the old man would get plumb loop-legged. That's all Trot Monroe was in it for."

"I don't believe that at all," Abigail says, "You're just making that story up, and these young girls here don't need to hear that kind of talk."

"I know what I did, sister," Lewis say, "and I know what went on, but you can believe whatever you want to. You always do anyhow."

"You don't need to worry about me and Dicia," Nola Mae says, "We are not interested in drinking whiskey, and it is just boring to hear about a bunch of old men doing it."

"We weren't old men," Lewis says, "at that time, Missy. We would have given your bunch of young ones today a run for your money. And let me tell you something else, too. Don't be low-rating whiskey until you feel that first drink bite you in the throat. Then you can tell me what you think."

"Hush that talk," Abigail says. "We don't need to hear that kind of expression and I am surprised you'd entertain any semblance of a high opinion of strong drink, Lewis, considering."

At that point Lewis pops up off his chair and begins to work his way out of the room, making some remark to Abigail which I blessedly don't hear. I watch the girls look at each other, Nola Mae rolling her eyes as though she won't be able to bear seeing the old folks pick at each one more minute. Abigail is satisfied with what she has told Lewis and I know that by the way she is sitting so straight as she watches our brother feel his way through the door and out of the room. She has fired a telling shot, and she congratulates herself on it.

Abigail is content enough with her work, in fact, that she says a couple of words, stops to clear her throat to give herself space to see which direction she might take the conversation, and begins to launch into her first statement of a further account of the dance at which Valery and I met.

"Maude," she is saying, "had not even wanted to go to Louselle Monroe's house that night, and so I'd had to talk her into it."

"Abigail," I break in before she gets into full stride, "I'd like to ask one of the girls to go get me a fresh glass of water. This one's been sitting here for hours, and I'd like some cooler, if you please."

"I'll do it," Nola Mae says, springing up from her chair as though she'd been waiting for a signal.

"Please go with your cousin, Dicia," I say. "Help her find me a medium sized glass in that cupboard, the big one."

Both girls leave the room, heading toward the kitchen, and Abigail has only me for audience, so she hushes what she is saying after only a minute or so. She enjoys telling about me and Valery to other people in my presence, but speaking to me alone about the topic is not much satisfaction to her and has never proved to be. She's become weary over the years of the way I respond to talk about Valery, either not believing the things I say and the way I say them, or not setting any store in a woman still affected by the memory of a husband who's been dead for all these years.

The sound has picked up in intensity in my head, and I'm afraid it might get outside into the room, though I know that's foolishness. You alone know what's in your head, no other can, even though it's so strong at times, the sound and the thoughts beneath and around it, that I can't believe others can't hear it, too. Maybe they're just being kind, not wanting to acknowledge the sound announcing something of what's inside me, hiding their knowledge out of politeness, the way you look aside when someone begins to weep and the tears come from their eyes with no sobs or any other sign of pain or sorrow. Ignore it, and it isn't there. Even Abigail does that. I know she prefers more of a show of sorrow. That's easier to discount.

Nola Mae has come back into my bedroom, and loud as the sound in my head has become, I can hear her through it, speaking to Abigail in a loud voice, asking her a question about where some place is.

Abigail is saying she doesn't know the answer to Nola Mae's question, why should she, she doesn't study geography books, she says, and that was never her long suit anyway, back when she was in school. She did arithmetic, she says, and figuring problems out and she could outspell anybody around, no matter their age nor how long they'd been in school. Spelling is like arithmetic, she says, you know when you've got it right and there's no argument anybody can launch against you about an answer you provide that's right, labor though they may to trip you up. Ask your great-aunt Maude, Abigail tells her granddaughter, she took an interest in subjects like that, unlike me, unlike me, unlike me.

Nola Mae brings me a glass of water, I don't know how the child knows I'm thirsty, sometimes she can be thoughtful, too, like Dicia always is, but Nola Mae has to work at that, poor thing, thinking about the situations of others not coming naturally to her in the way it seems to do for Dicia, but maybe there's more virtue in doing something you have to spend effort on than there is in being naturally sympathetic the way Dicia is, though I wouldn't fault Richard's daughter ever for being spontaneously sweet and good. Maybe she works at that, too, in the same way Nola Mae has to, but Dicia's better at concealing the effort it costs, and there's a merit in that, if it is the reason she appears never to have to be told what is the right thing to do in considering the needs and lacks of other people, I never have appreciated people who do a good thing in a way which announces itself and calls attention from others to their qualities and seems to expect a recognition for it and a payment in gratitude.

It must have been easier for Jesus to turn the other cheek and never require recognition and adoration than it was for Peter to have to deny Him three times in the garden before the cock crew, and I was not there and could not know, but I can imagine the sweat on Peter's face and the agony in his voice when he had to tell the Roman soldiers he did not know Jesus, when he had to deny his savior, and he did that, said no to the good because it was not in his power to be anything but a man, and men are weak and women are as well, but of course we are stronger than men ever can be, though a man who has worked in the timber woods and had to lift logs and stumps and use his muscles and back and legs can if he has to, in extremity, lift great weights and move loads in this world that no woman could even consider.

Her strengths are not of the world, and neither was that of Jesus, and that is why His task in the garden was no greater than that of Peter's, and the task of a woman weak in her body and in the things of the world which are subject to strength is greater than that of a man's. I would not say such a thing to my husbands, my first and my true love Valery, and my second, a man I married because I had my children to raise and care for and provide for, and oh I had Richard's child Dicia, too, all that was left of him to me, and I was a good wife to him, and I labored at that, and I accomplished the task before me, struggle though I did to lift the load it represented, and my responsibility in being his woman was akin to that of Peter's in the garden, and there was sweat of the brow and agony of the spirit and failure of the heart in it, and I did not let that show.

And that was my strength, and it did not partake of the natural goodness of Jesus whose task was the easier because it came pure from the heart and met no resistance of the will and was not of this world where loads are heavy and immovable and set in stone and defended with briars.

"Great-Aunt Maude," Nola Mae is saying as she holds the glass of water toward me, "Can you tell me where it is and what it is?" The water looks cool, there are not bubbles in it in the way they gather in a glass that has set too long still in the heat of a closed room, and I want to reach out and take it from her, but my hand will not do what I'm telling it that it must, and the sound is roaring again inside my head now and it's hard for me to hear her well enough to understand what her words say that she wants an answer about.

"What?" I am able to make my lips form the word though I can't tell whether I've said it or not because of the sound, and Nola Mae seems to understand because she leans closer to me, now lifting the glass toward my mouth, and I can see Dicia behind her, her eyes open so wide I can see white all around the brown center. I can't drink the water from the glass.

"Pearl Harbor," Nola Mae is saying. "Where's Pearl Harbor?" and I can see the words in my head, but I can see the sound, too, now, and that is something I've never been able to do before, see sound as well as hear it, and I can tell what my grandniece is asking me, and I can open my lips to answer, but all that comes out is a word, a single one of the many I want to say, and I say that one, and what I'm able to utter of those many is "ocean," and the sound inside is now loud, now I can see only it, not Nola Mae's face, nor Dicia's eyes, nor the glass of water, nor the question she has asked me, nor the words I would give her in return, but only the sound.

It is all I hear now and all I see, and I'm not afraid now of the sound, as I've always been before, I'm not afraid. I'm not.

1968

★

Pine Island Bayou

Dicia

I sit here looking at the television screen, watching policemen swinging their clubs against their heads and arms and legs, and pointing their pistols at them, and knocking them down in the street, and as I pray she's not one of them, I still don't know how I could have stopped her from going.

Not after all the stories I told her about GrandMaude, the ones I knew were true because I witnessed them, and the ones I took on faith from Great-Aunt Abigail, discount them though I did by reflex, as she told them over and over again right up until she died. They changed, Great-Aunt Abigail's stories about the Holts in Texas—ones about Amos himself and Carolina and GrandMaude and Lewis and brothers and sisters and cousins and the people they had dealings with over all those years, since the family first crossed the Sabine River between Louisiana and Texas where we all have lived up until now.

The stories Abigail told changed each time she told them, with added details of events and the weather attending them, the colors of people's eyes and hair, the way they held their mouths when they spoke, the clothes they wore and where they were purchased, if store-bought, and by whom sewed, if handmade, further account of minor tales supporting the main ones, histories of families of the central actors in each story—all these reworkings she did with patience and attention and in dead earnest.

But expanded and re-embroidered and rearranged in details of time and circumstance though they were, Abigail's stories never deepened, not a one I remember, in the meaning she gathered from them and the message of each she felt bound to convey to her listeners.

When she and GrandMaude saved Joleen Bobo's husband from the lynch mob, the point my great-aunt always held up for admiration and marvel in the account she provided never changed from one time to the next. The important fact, the core of the story, the theme to be pondered and studied, had always to do with the wagonload of flower bushes, the crepe myrtles, and the fact that different colored blossoms appeared on the same bush and that Abigail rode for miles sitting atop all that vegetation covering Joleen's fugitive husband.

As a child, I always used to ask, when my great-aunt launched into the telling of the story with new and improved additions to it, what happened to Joleen Bobo and the man she and my grandmother and my father saved from death by smuggling him away in a wagonload of flowers.

"Oh, girl," Abigail would say, "both of them got away, of course."

"Where did they go?" I'd ask. "What do they do? Where do they live now? Was it a happy ending?"

"Happy?" she'd say. "Happy? How should I know where they went and what happened to them? Happy, you say. I know he was happy to be all scrouched up underneath that load of crepe myrtles. I know that much. There were different colored blossoms growing on the same branch, purple and pink side by side, and I have never seen anything like that, before or since that day. I tell you, it was an amazement."

If she were still alive and sitting by me in front of the television watching blood flow in the streets of Chicago from the wounds on those young people caused by policemen swinging billyclubs, I know precisely what Great-Aunt Abigail would be saying right now.

"Chicago," she'd say, "that's in Illinois, and that's on the other side of the Mississippi River from here. The Holts came into Louisiana from across that river when they came down from Carolina all those years ago. Now I wasn't in the picture then, and to tell the truth I'm not sure if Papa and Mama had even met by then. Likely not, since they'd have been traveling with their own families, Papa with the Holt bunch and Mama with the Camerons, that was her maiden name, Cameron. Were they born even? I don't know."

"Look," I might say, "that policeman had that boy backed up against that paddy wagon I guess they call it, and the boy had his hands up to show he wasn't resisting arrest, but the policeman hit him anyway, right across the face."

"Hippie," Great-Aunt Abigail would say, "that's what people call them. That boy and the rest of them. Look at all that hair and his nasty old beard. Boys that let their mustaches and beards grow these days do not keep them neat like Papa kept his, even right up to the day he died, there in the old place, the second old place now I'm talking about, not the first one, that was in Sabine County, and where Papa died was in the Double Pen Creek community, not two miles from the chapel and the graveyard where he's lying buried today."

I know my great-grandfather's last words, and Great-Aunt Abigail if she were still alive to be sitting beside me in the den tonight watching television pictures of the riot in Chicago would have known that I knew his last words, having heard them repeated all those times when I was a child and later, but she would have told me what they were again, anyway. Anything noteworthy enough to be said once was worth saying time and time again in my family, and the great lesson GrandMaude taught me about listening was how to look interested in what was being said to me while keeping my mind completely sealed off from apprehending any meaning in the sounds washing over me.

"Put your attention elsewhere," I remember her instructing me. "Think of a thing that will entertain you and consider it from all sides. Put it in the center of your mind and move around it. Study it at leisure. No one will ever know the difference."

"In the middle of my mind," I said. "Put it there, you say."

"And you won't miss a thing," GrandMaude said. "Concentration will serve you through all your days."

Of my children, Dora is the one who lives by that principle, behaving her entire life as though she had learned it at GrandMaude's knee, though that's impossible, my grandmother dead long before Dora was born, long before I was even married to her father, gone himself now, so many years ago that if he were allowed to return to visit he wouldn't recognize me on sight. I look at pictures of him now, and he grows younger each time I do, standing alone or with other people or with me, some in front of places we lived, or beside cars we owned or holding pets up to the camera, or with one of our children in his arms.

He looks directly into the camera lens, and it shows him to be a nice young man, the sunlight falling on his face, making a shadow across his brow, an outline of the big sweep of brown hair that always needed combing back from his forehead. I see his image now, and I think he's young enough to be my own child, one I'd be proud to call my own and hold up to others in praise for his accomplishments.

The girl standing beside him in the ones of us both is me, Dicia Blackstock, and she looks into the lens with such an expression of hope and faith that I can't bear to do more than allow myself small glimpses at the way I was then.

I could be looking at Dora, when I do that, when I just snatch a quick look at the man who was my husband those years ago and the young girl standing beside him, and thinking that I am seeing Dora is sometimes a comfort to me and sometimes a pain so swift and sure and deep that I feel it pierce me like a blade.

I tell no one that, certainly not Dora. Why would I burden my daughter with such a notion, my entertaining a delusion that when I look at myself with her father I see her gazing back at me in the light from a sunbeam faded away in Texas those years ago?

I made the mistake of confiding that thought to Nola Mae once, during one of her visits back home to show off the newest of her husbands. It was the fourth one, I think, but I don't trust my memory completely in regard to my cousin's men, not keeping up as well as others of my aunts and uncles and cousins seem so able and eager to do. It's a matter of concentration, memory is, GrandMaude would have said. You remember only what seizes your imagination, what satisfies some part of you that needs to dwell upon a certain fact of life, a part that nourishes some hunger built into you.

He was one of the better ones, I do remember, though, his name was Harken, and I tried to make a joke with him and her about what that word might mean, but neither one laughed. He showed interest in what I said, though, even asking me what I meant by saying that, doing so in a genial tone and allowing that his new wife had warned him that her cousin Dicia might say funny things.

"Witty," Nola Mae said. "I said Dicia would be witty. That's what my great-aunt always called the kind of things Dicia is liable to say. Not funny, really. Witty. It's a different thing from funny."

I apologized indirectly to both of them, not saying I was sorry I thought the name Harken could mean more than the label his parents pinned on him at birth, but blaming myself aloud for being so glad to see Nola Mae that it made me babble nonsense.

Later that day, alone with Nola Mae in my bedroom going through a stack of old snapshots to find ones of her to show the new husband, I mentioned what I thought at times when I saw pictures of me and Warren together, the way it struck me that he could be my son now and my daughter Dora could be me, and Nola Mae looked up from the picture she was holding and fixed me with a stare.

"I wish you wouldn't say such things as that, Dicia," she said. "It makes me worry about you."

"Worry?" I said, staring back at her, not dropping my eyes from hers, as big and blue as always, "Why would you do that? It's just a thought that comes into my mind. It doesn't mean anything serious."

"Do you ever talk to your minister?" Nola Mae said. "When you feel that way?"

"What minister? I don't have a minister. I go to church still now and then, of course, but not enough to be guilty of having a minister."

"Maybe you ought to take some vitamin supplements," Nola Mae said. "Maybe some B-12 injections. You know, medications to calm your nerves down."

"I live a very calm life, and I'm as calm as the next person," I told her. "But I appreciate your worrying about me, Nola Mae. He seems very nice, Harken does."

"He knows people well placed in Houston," Nola Mae said. "I am completely happy now. Just all the way full up. I feel real good about this man, and I thank my stars every day I wake up beside him."

So when Dora told me she had decided to go to Chicago because the Democratic convention would be there, the expression on her face let me know there would be no profit in arguing points of reason and balance with her. She had thought the matter through beforehand, and her eyes were settled into the deep hazel hue they have always taken on when she's considering a direction to choose, from the time she was a child trying to decide between flavors of ice cream or whether to wear a red or blue dress to school right up to where she is now, marching through the streets of a city filled with guns and clubs and bayonets.

Like GrandMaude, Dora had held a vexing idea up high enough for the light to hit it, turned it from side to side to give it a good study, nodded her head a couple of times, and settled into a deep conviction.

"What do you expect to do?" I asked her the night she told me her plans, "you and a carload of college kids from Lamar? What do you think y'all can do in Chicago, Illinois, that the politicians can't? Please tell me that, Dora."

She had walked into my bedroom where I was working at my desk on a set of books for Pedigo Electric, a real rat's nest of figures and mistakes and miscalculations, which would have been a nightmare for a real accountant, not to speak of someone like me who'd learned all she knew by having to swim out of a hole or drown in it.

I was so deeply into what I was doing I had forgotten Dora was in her room, quiet as she always is when she's studying, and I jumped at some little noise she made coming up behind me.

"Are you at a stopping point, Mother?" she said, putting a hand on my shoulder as though to quiet me down from the sign of surprise I had shown. "Because if you're not, I can wait to talk until we're both ready to go to bed."

"No," I said. "There is no stopping point in Joe Pedigo's financial accounts. His money dealing is a ball of string so tangled up that if you pull at one strand of it everything moves, and it all gets more wadded. Now's as good a time as any. What's on your mind, Dora?"

"The war," she said. "Dr. King, Bobby Kennedy, the election."

"All that at once? Doesn't it tire you out, child, keeping all that going in your head at the same time?"

"It's a ball of string, all tangled up," she said, "You pull at one strand and everything moves."

"It's not fair to throw your poor old mama's words back at her."

"No," Dora said, moving away from the back of my chair to take a seat on the edge of my bed. "It's not fair at all. Nothing's fair at all, and that's what's on my mind."

"Is your homework all done?" I said. "Aren't you writing a paper for one of your English classes ? Shakespeare, right? Don't you need to get that finished?"

And then, my youngest child and the only one still home with me, made some remark in response which I knew had to be a quotation from something she'd been reading, Shakespeare, probably, since that would be most fitting for the moment, and that is what children do as they grow up and take another step in their course away from you, they know what is fitting for the moment, and you never do, and they present you with that fact.

"Is that what you came to tell me?" I said, "That everything is a mess and a puzzle, and we shouldn't try to reason what it is, or whatever it was you just said? Is that what's on your mind? Because if it is, I think you're right, and it's just a shame that life is like that."

"No, mother," Dora said, looking at me the way a teacher beholds a pupil she realizes will take a lot of effort to teach anything to. Not only is the pupil in dire need of instruction, she's also become infected with a wrong notion settled into her head so firmly that it can be removed only by a long process of chipping it away a tiny fragment at a time. Where's the chisel? Where's the hammer? Step back and give me room to work.

"I'm not concerned about the big picture," Dora went on, looking for a spot to place her chisel for the first tap on the block of granite before her. "Let the thinkers and the ameliorists worry about the nature of existence and throw up their hands in dismay at the size of the problem. That's their role, and they're welcome to it."

Lord, I thought, hearing that from her, let me not sound like Nola Mae or Great-Aunt Abigail when I try to carry on this conversation with my daughter. Not a conversation to her, of course, but what she'd call a discussion, and how do you discuss a matter with one of your children? I might as well have tried to argue with Great-Aunt Abigail that Amos Holt didn't know what he was talking about when he was preaching a sermon on the resurrection to a bunch of East Texas farmers back in those woods all those years ago. *Give* and *take* are not in the question.

"That sounds like something you must have thought about and written down to remember, Dora," I said, not able to stop myself. I was better at that when I was young. "For later use when you might need it."

"I don't apologize for thinking, Mother," she said, "and I never will."

That was designed to sting, and she knew it, and it did. But I kept my head and did nothing but smile, big enough to feel my lips tingle.

"Condescension is an easy game," Dora said, "and it costs so little. It's disappointing, and it's a little cheap."

"I know cheap," I said, again on the verge of falling into the hole my daughter was digging for me. I could feel myself teetering and beginning to slide. "Working on Joe Pedigo's account books and trying to make sense out of his dealings is cheap enough to satisfy me."

"I know you work hard," Dora said, "and that you've had to do that all your life. You're caught like the rest of us, and you've always made a good fight of it."

"I don't think about that," I said. "I can't afford that expense. I just keep my head down and do what I have to do."

"I appreciate that, Mother," Dora said. "I don't verbalize that often, and if you've needed for me to do that, I apologize for not providing it."

"All right, Dora. Other than not verbalizing and not providing and not going along with the thinkers and the other ones you mentioned—the ameliorists?—what are you saying to me?"

I had slipped now, I was sliding, the edge of the hole was slick and muddy, and the grass growing at the lip of it was providing me with no purchase at all. I was going to hit bottom, and the water at the center of the hole would splash up and cover me, and it would not be a pretty sight.

"Just tell me," I said.

"Mother," Dora said with a fine precision, "I am going to Chicago where the Democratic Party is having its convention. I'm going to be part of a thing bigger than I am. I'm going to do what I can to move this nation toward justice and the good. I am joining the future."

"How are you going to get there to join the future?" I said, smiling again as hard as I could. "When does the train leave, and who's the conductor? Have you got your ticket bought?"

Dora left the room at that, but not before favoring me with a look of deep compassion touched with pity, and I plunged all the way into that hole with mud and water and Joe Pedigo's Electric Company books filling the bottom of it. I stayed there all night, and by the time I crawled out at dawn, Joe had clean records and balanced figures, and Dora had a duffel bag crammed with books and clothes waiting by the door for a longhaired boy to throw into the back of a 1958 Ford Fairlane station wagon filled with a crew of others like him and my daughter headed north out of Texas toward Chicago and the future.

I stayed at home, and I'm watching the future on TV.

Nola Mae

I have thought about myself a lot over the years, as I guess everybody does, gone over things I've done and the ones I've passed on and not done, the people I've run into and the ones who've run into me, deciding to do this and deciding not to do that, not deciding anything at all but just letting it happen, and all in all, I've been pretty well satisfied with the way I've handled what I've had to deal with. I have never thought it's a good idea to be too hard on yourself. If you can't ease up and give yourself some slack now and again, then who else ever is going to?

So I've figured myself out for the most part, understood what I'm up to and where I'm going and how I've arrived where I am, wherever now is as I'm looking at it, and I count myself fairly well satisfied to have got to where I am from where I have come.

As an old boy said to me once when I was complaining about something that was bothering me, I forget what it was now and don't want to waste time or energy trying to remember it, something big at the time but not any more lasting really than one cough in a wind storm, "Nola Mae, girl," he said, "just let the low side drag."

And he was right, I realized as soon as he said it, about whatever that thing in particular was, and so I did in that case, let the low side drag, and it got me through it and by it and over it, whatever it was, so well I have no idea now just what it was.

The thing is, of course, you have to know when to let the low side drag, and that philosophy, as Dicia would call it, is not one a person with any sense would try to apply in all cases. I knew that, as soon as the fellow told me, and I have been judicious in choosing the times and places to put that notion into play.

He, naturally, never was judicious about that, or anything else, and he's been dead for years now, and all because he let the low side drag so much and so low that what was carrying him completely wore out and failed him at a crucial point somewhere along the way. He was named Donnie Adams, and he was a shade-tree mechanic and a rodeo-rider and a pipefitter and a welder and a drunk, and he could and did put my lights out in bed, and I let him do that for a while. But now old Donnie's lights are permanently out, and mine are still shining bright, and I am still able to afford to let the low side drag at suitable moments.

So I have learned about myself by thinking and considering what I do and why I do it, and balancing that against what I want to do and what I can afford to do now, and I don't just mean the matter of money when I say that about affording the expense.

But there is one thing I always wonder about in myself, and have wondered about, and likely will end up wondering about when checkout time finally arrives, which is a long time off, I do believe, and that's this. Why do I always end up coming back here, to Texas and to this part of Texas of all the places there are to choose from in the state, back here from wherever I've worked myself into getting to? That is the puzzle.

I have lived in wonderful locations and with men I've really liked being around, and on many an occasion I've said to myself, Nola Mae, this is it this time. You have found where you ought to be, and you're with a man you can put up with for the long haul. Girl, here you are in a heavenly situation, or at least as close as you're going to get to it in this life. Enjoy yourself.

That has happened to me at least three times, and sort of semi-happened one other. I have woken up on three separate mornings with that thought sitting in the center of my head shining like a diamond on top of one of those little velvet pedestals you see in the glass case of a good jewelry store, one of those beige or other light color holders chosen not to distract from the luster of the precious stone itself.

Here, I have heard a voice say to me, as distinct as the sound from a high dollar stereo system, here, Nola Mae, is the place. Here is the man, and here is where you know you belong and want to be. That's been in New Orleans, in Timonium, Maryland, and in Sante Fe, New Mexico, those three times.

And on every one of those three occasions, and half-heartedly on a fourth one I don't like to think about, I have said back to the voice, thank you, thank you, thank you. And especially thank me, Nola Mae myself, for making it happen.

The way I look at it, you always should blame yourself when something goes wrong because you fooled around and let that happen, and so when things work out for the best, you're only being reasonable when you take the credit that's due to you. Fair's fair. It is easier, naturally, to congratulate yourself for a job well done than it is to face up to the mistakes you made and the part you played in something that's gone wrong. I'll grant that.

And I'll say, too, but not very loud and not at all public, that figuring out what went bad on you—the scarf found where it ought not have been, the letter not thrown away when it was past time to consign it to the garbage, sweet though it was to read over and over, the wrong car parked in the wrong place for too damn long a period of time—those little failures of nerve and inabilities to let go of a thing when it's still satisfying and ticklish to the taste, figuring out just what that breakdown was is the sure sign of maturity in a woman. Or a man, either, for all I know, though I don't know how a man thinks, if he does, and I've never been one to waste time worrying about that subject.

The last time I heard that voice speak to me with such reassurance about the rightness of where I was located in terms of geography, finance, and romance was in Santa Fe one Sunday morning. It was early, and I was the only one awake in the house, a nice big adobe built all the way around a garden right in the middle of the building itself, with a fountain at the very center bubbling with clear water arranged so it ran out of an urn which a little girl made of stone held at an angle convenient for pouring. The artist had made the expression on her face completely calm.

I like to think about that exact moment, whenever I start to feel discouraged or blue about something that's going on or not going on in my life. Remembering what I had then and what I thought was fixed and permanent enough to let me play the hand dealt me all the way out has served me well over the years since.

That morning, there was a plate before me in Santa Fe colors and design, holding a peeled orange already segmented, a croissant, and a pat of butter. Beside that was a folded napkin of white linen, heavy yet soft to the touch, a setting of real silver, not just plate, and a pot of hot coffee and a cup to pour it in. Maria, the Mexican servant, had just put all that in front of me and gone back inside to get something she hadn't carried out to me yet. Sugar, maybe, brown it would have been, or a dish of strawberries or some other fruit I didn't then know the name of.

The little stone girl was pouring her water from her urn into the base of the fountain, and she would do that forever, and there was a man inside one of the rooms of the house still asleep after we had spent another night together, and it was cool enough that time of the morning for me to feel a little chill in the air where the shade was touching me.

I remember looking around me, first at the setting on the table, then at the red hibiscus and yellow climbing roses growing against and over a wall across the patio, then at the way the sun was lighting up a pot of different flowers, blue petunias, then back at the table setting, and then at the water pouring from the urn into the base of the fountain, and finally down at the turquoise in a ring on my left hand and in a pendant hanging from a silver chain at my throat.

"Nola Mae," the voice said low in my ear, coming from both inside my head, somewhere deep, and from outside, too, though from no certain direction. It was in that cool air, and in the bright beams of sunlight and in the dark shadows cast by the walls, and it came from the table spread for me alone, and the voice came particularly and especially from the fountain where the purr of water falling from the urn held in the hands of the stone girl mixed with the message the voice brought me, making them so much a part of each other they could never be separated.

"Nola Mae," the voice sang in a low tone, and that's all it had to say to let me know I was in a place prepared to hold me still and satisfied and set, and it was mine alone to have and savor.

I remember I held my breath and closed my eyes and felt the cool air touch me while the sound of water lingered. And I would have stayed in that spot unmoving forever, but finally, I had to open my eyes and take a breath, and Maria had to come back with whatever else she was bringing me, and the man inside the house had to wake up and come outside where I was.

I don't remember what happened next, just the way you can never recall the second bite you take from a dish that pleased you so much when you parted your lips for it for the first one.

It got hot that afternoon, I expect, as it always does in the summer in Santa Fe in the desert, so hot you can't sit outside in the sun without burning, and the pipe feeding water to the urn the little stone girl was holding had its faucet turned off for reasons of economy and conservation, and every flower in the garden closed in on itself with its back to the sun and dreamed about being in the shade.

The water from the fountain would have been too warm to the touch to enjoy, anyway, and after a breakfast of orange slices and croissants you want a meal with some bulk and spice to it, at least I do, and I was gone from Santa Fe headed back to East Texas in less than a month from that cool morning in the garden, drawn back home again, want to or not. Like every other time I found myself crossing one of the rivers to the east and north and west of this country, pointed in the direction of the piney woods and the Gulf Coast, a person watching me come home would have thought I'd been serving a prison sentence in a desert the way I acted when I saw all that water waiting for me.

Rivers and creeks and lakes and ponds and bayous and marshes and swamps and mudholes and hard rain showers and storms and hurricanes and fogs and mists—all that comes with where we've always lived, and all that's part of it, though I wouldn't want to have to try to explain that to my grandmother on the one side or to Dicia and Great-Aunt Maude on the other. I don't know what it means or why it means, but I need and must have water around me.

What it's come down to now at this very minute is me by myself sitting in front of a television set, watching the country come apart in Chicago and hoping to catch sight of Dicia's daughter Dora running through the streets dressed in a hippie outfit.

Dicia is scared to death that something terrible will happen to Dora, either outside to her body or inside to her head, but I can't see any real reason to worry about the girl at all. That's why Dicia is not talking to me at present and why she won't watch the Democratic convention and all the doings around it with me. It means too much to her, like everything always has to my cousin, and it means to me what everything else I've seen in my life always has, too, I have to admit.

Those flags and those placards and the long hair on the boys and girls and the peace signs they're always making with their fingers held up to the cameras and the junk clothes they wear and even the billy clubs the cops are swinging—all that Dicia sees as signs and indications, what she calls statements of belief and commitment, symbolic is another word I hear her use time and again, and of course every thing in the world that her daughter Dora runs across she thinks has got to mean something other than what it is. Otherwise, why admit it exists?

Now me, I know what all this going on and to-do is, and it's this. A big fashion statement. And it's not a bad one, I will say, and I like all the noise and colors and moving around fast from here to there a whole lot better than the stuff we had to work with, growing up back when I was as young as this bunch is today. We made do, and we got there, but it was never an easy trip.

Clement is sitting beside me on the sofa, too, his little bitty eyes as red as a possum caught in the headlights of a car at midnight in East Texas, thinking his mother has no idea he's sneaked outside not thirty minutes ago to smoke a reefer. He hates it when I call it that, not wanting to admit anything illegal ever existed before he was old enough to discover it, and particularly called something as dumb as reefer. And he'd like for me to be all concerned and torn up about it, too, like a decent mama should be.

Like always, he's not saying a word to me, but thoughts are just racing around in his spooky little head as he looks at what's happening live on television in Chicago with all those dressed-up protesters just having a time and him not old enough yet to be there with them. He knows his cousin Dora is, though, and he'll sit here, hoping against hope she'll pop up battling with a policeman, maybe, or talking into the camera to explain what it all means to America, solemn as a little owl.

Clement will watch as long as the television people show their pictures, but I've about had my fill of this fashion show. In a few minutes, I'm going out to the garage to fire up that Thunderbird, the last remnant of my marriage to Gary Lee Imhoff, and drive down to see what's happening at the Nederland Club. They've got a big band night going on there, it says in the *Beaumont Enterprise*, and I do expect there might be an old boy or two at the event just dying to dance his blues away with Nola Mae.

I'm going to let Dora save the nation in Chicago and stop the war in Vietnam, while her mama worries about her and my little red-eyed boy Clement has impure thoughts about his politically involved cousin.

Me, I'm taking off to dance.

Clement

She's sitting here fidgeting, and I know what that means. I ought to, I know the signs, having had to study them and learn to predict what's coming next since before I can remember.

In a minute or two, Mama's going to lean over, slap me on the knee like a basketball coach does when he's fixing to put somebody in the game, and then she'll say something like, "Well, I need me an airing, and I believe it would do me good to get outside and move around a little. Don't you stay up so late watching some old picture show that you'll be too tired in the morning to pay attention in school and learn something."

"All right," I'll say, or maybe I won't say anything but grunt. Used to, when I was too little to have better sense, I'd cry and argue and carry on and try to find a way to talk her out of leaving me there by myself in the house or apartment or the room or whatever it was we were staying in at the time.

If I'm feeling like it, when she says that to me, I might cross her up and say, "Be careful, Mama. But be sure to have a good time." But it's not likely that I'll feel like sounding like somebody's daddy giving them directions. Playing that used to entertain me a little bit, but not any more, really.

So when I grunt back at her or say "all right," Mama'll slap me again on the knee and say, "Cover up good if you're cold. Anything goes wrong you know how to use a phone, don't you?"

I'll stick my thumb to my ear and my little finger to my mouth and make jabbering motions with my lips, and she'll laugh big and get on out of here.

Looking for some fun, I guess you could call it, since that's about all Mama ever named as a reason she was clearing out of a place the times I'd try to delay her by asking for an explanation. Just looking for some fun.

One of the old boys she was with once, I believe his name was Henry or Hank or something with an H sound at the front of it and he did stay around for several days, I remember, though he was never one of the permanent ones, he was sitting in a big brown leather chair one night, jiggling one foot up and down enough to make the floor feel like it was moving. He said a thing to me that led me to say something back which proved to be useful to me ever since.

I was watching television, of course, a cartoon of Felix the Cat, one of my all-time favorites then and even now when I can find it to watch. It's not on much any more except really early in the morning, the little it is, always before six o'clock.

Hank or Henry or H, whatever his name was, he was sitting in his big leather chair, leg pumping up and down, floor vibrating, and Felix was in a situation with the old crazy professor who's always inventing some gadget that'll let him take over the world, maybe even the whole universe if he can get it working just right.

H looked over at me, where I was sitting in my favorite position back then, directly in front of the TV set on the floor, so close I could see the little dots that make up the picture. I liked the fact that it was out of focus at that range, almost not able to fool you at all into thinking it was a real image. Everything was dots and lines, and the characters were cartoons, and they moved in little jerks, when they moved at all, not anything like the way people really move, smooth and gradual and full of shadows and planes and roundness with other sides to them you can't see ever, no matter how much you might walk around them to study what they really were, if they'd let you do that. But they won't, because they're able to look back at you. Felix and his kind take no notice at all.

Anyway, H looked at me there in front of the tube, from his vantage point in the chair covered with leather, a skin hide that had come off some animal, a cow I guess, that probably didn't want to give it up, and he said, "Well, Buster, you like your cartoons, huh?"

I nodded, not saying anything, figuring that would shut him up, and then in addition to jiggling his foot up and down, H began rattling the change in his pocket. I looked over at him when I heard that, knowing full well what power coins had, and H reached on down deeper into his pocket and pulled out a handful of nickels and quarters and dimes and pennies, when he saw me look over at him.

"Here, Buster," he said, "how about letting me finance your cartoon watching. Suppose they were to ask you to pour some money into that slot there on the back of the TV set or else they'd shut it off and stop broadcasting. You wouldn't want that to happen, would you?"

That was a silly thing to say to me, I knew, but it was a step up from what most of Mama's boyfriends, or male companions as she liked to call them, would say when they were trying to be polite and take notice of me, maybe score a few points and impress her or cause me to act like they existed in the same universe where I was sitting. Usually, what they'd say was something like how old are you or what grade are in or do you like baseball or football or basketball or you name the sport. Swimming, race cars, horses running, tennis, on and on.

I wouldn't answer those kind of questions, just look at whoever'd asked me until he broke eye contact and then I'd turn back to the television dots and lines. But when H talked about a slot for coins on the set and held out a handful of change, I thought it worth a word or two back to him.

"No," I said, "I wouldn't like that, if there was a slot for money on the TV set. But there's not."

"What if one opens up some day?" H said. "You want to be ready, don't you?"

"I guess so," I said and held out both hands for him to drop the money on me, and he did, and I turned back to see what was happening between Felix and the mad professor.

It was a shield he had come up with this time, the professor, one that was portable enough to move around wherever he needed to keep sunlight from hitting the earth at any point.

"Oh, no," Felix was saying, "that will be bad for the plants and animals. Without the light from the sun, they won't be able to grow."

"Yes, Felix," said the professor in that strange voice he has, sounding both low and high at the same time and coming out of him without his lips moving, originating in his nose I imagined at the time, believing that meant something about the kind of man the professor was, evil and twisted. I've learned better since. It's just cheaper not to show his lips move. Like everything else, it's just money running it.

"Wherever the sunshield casts its shadow, all life will cease," the professor said and then laughed his mad scientist cackle through his nose.

"Yep," H said, "you're set up now, Buster, aren't you? If that slot opens up and they start charging for your cartoons, you can pay your bill like a man."

I wanted to hear what Felix was saying back to the professor, and I particularly needed to see what Felix the Cat would pull from his bag of tricks to put the sunshield out of business, so I didn't say anything in response to H. I couldn't ignore that he was there, though, since I could feel the weight of the money he had given me in my hands, which had started to sweat a little from the metal of the coins, and since H had started jiggling his foot up and down again, harder and faster this time, enough so that I was afraid I'd start losing control of my money from the vibration H had set up in the floor.

And then he changed the subject, turning to what was really on his mind, as I'd already learned grown people would eventually do when they got tired of trying to talk to someone my age and category.

"Your mama takes her time getting ready, I've noticed," H said, foot pumping up and down as Felix sorted through the collection of antidotes and disabling devices in his famous bag of tricks, seeking just the right one for the job at hand, saving the Earth's plants and animals from an evil shadow.

"Yes sir, she is making herself pretty, but she has got a lot to work with, and that takes time and effort and lot of choosing from this, that, and the other thing," H said.

Felix had about found what he was after, and I was leaning into the collection of dots on the screen to see just what my favorite cat was selecting, and it was a Felix cartoon I hadn't seen before and the professor was being particularly evil and gloating, and the fool waiting on my mother would not stop shaking the house with his jiggling foot and he had something else he wanted to say that would require me to answer him back. I was as nervous as Felix had been when he first reached for his bag of tricks, hoping there was something inside to help him get the job done, and then H spoke again.

"Your mama," he said, "Nola Mae, she is a real doll."

"Yeah," I said, the answer I needed to shut H up and stop his jiggling foot popping into my head just as Felix pulled out an instant sunshield vaporizer from the bag of tricks. "Mama is a doll, all right. A crocodile."

That did the job. The professor's sunshield wavered once and melted, H said not a word back, and his foot stopped jiggling like it'd been cut off, and Mama walked into the room in a cloud of perfume and lipstick and hairspray smell.

Felix smiled his big cat smile, I smiled mine, the professor said oh no, and H said look who's here and it's sure been worth the wait.

I had a double handful of quarters and nickels and dimes, and I knew I'd learned something I could use. If I said the right thing at the right time, my words would shut people up. Thanks to old H, jiggle-footed and big-mouthed as he was, for teaching me that.

"What in the world are you grinning at, Clement?" my mother says on the sofa beside me. "You think it's funny to see somebody get the pure dee Hell knocked out of them with a billy club?"

"I was thinking about something else," I say, "not about what's happening on TV."

"What?" Mama says, "Dora? I've not seen hide nor hair of her, and didn't expect to, of course."

"No," I say. "I was thinking about Felix the cat and his bag of tricks."

"I'm going out for a while," she says, and slaps me on the knee. "Lock the door. I've got my key."

"Have fun, Mama," I say. "Don't let all this Democratic convention stuff prey on your mind. Try to think about something else, something pleasant and uplifting for a change."

By the time I get that out, wasted on her, my mother is out of the door, it's swinging shut behind her, and I'm here by myself watching all these electronic dots working together to bring a picture into being. I have to do my part to help, because if I don't focus and let my brain fool itself into believing that all these impressions floating and banging into my cranium add up to something, nothing will mean a damn.

It's tough work and a heavy responsibility, organizing all this data into a statement, but I've always been up to it so far in my life here in the nerve center of southeast Texas, and I'm not figuring to fall down on the job and let things slide. Not just yet.

I've got to do my part to give shape to reality, just like Felix the Cat's been doing for years, and I will continue to perform my duty of slapping the right names on all the things around me and calling them what they really are.

Clement, for example. I was always the only kid around named that label in each and every school I found myself in, no matter where located or how big or small, in whatever town in whichever state my mother set us down in.

Clement, what does it mean? How can it be me? Would I be the same person if I were called Johnny or Bobby or Frank-Frank the Boy Baboon?

I used to say the name Clement, the word Clement, over and over to myself until it became just a sound, until it became nothing more than the noise the tires make when they roll along the highway, bumping over the dividers one after the other as regular as a clock ticking. Cle-ment, Cle-ment, Cle-ment, Cle-ment.

Doing that was the only escape I had from the sound they used to name me, and there was a comfort in that which had to satisfy me since that was all there was in supply, until that day I saw in a newspaper my name with another syllable attached to it. And that syllable was *in*, and I knew what that little word could do and what it meant since I had already by then been told by my mother what it did to the word *valid* which I had discovered attached to it on a ticket I'd found for admission to Six Flags Over Texas.

"No," she told me. "When it says *in* in front of the word, like it says on this ticket, *invalid*, it means it's no good."

"Why make a ticket to Six Flags Over Texas if it's not good?" I asked her. "Why do they lie about it? What's wrong with people like that?"

"It's to advertise," she told me. "It's to make you want to go."

"I already want to go," I said. "Stupid invalid people, they don't need to make me want to go."

And that was the bad use of the little word *in* to cancel out with one sound what had been offered with another, but when I saw *in* in front of my name Clement, I found it could work for me, too, as well as against my best interests.

"I am *in*Clement," I told myself, not needing ever again to say the name itself over and over until it became just sound. Now I could cancel out all that word Clement meant about me and where I was and where I lived and what people thought when they said that name by one simple trick, so clever even Felix the Cat would admire it. Say *in* first, and Clement was turned inside out. Clement with *in* was not Clement, but the reverse, the anti-Clement, all that was not what that name meant alone.

So I had found a way to handle the sound of my name and the way people used it to put a straight pin through me and stick me up on a piece of plywood like Gerald Dartez did with his science project in the sixth grade that time in Old Lady Manning's room. Gerald had caught him a bunch of bugs—roaches, mainly, and grasshoppers and a bee or two and and a dirt dauber and the main one, a big orange butterfly—and he had stuck pins through each one of them and wrote underneath on a little piece of paper the name of what he put on display for his science project.

The pins were all stuck at different angles, I remember, and they weren't all the same size or color, either, and one of them was not even a straight pin, but a safety pin bent to make the point stick out and not fit back in the part made to receive it. There was no safety left in that pin. And Gerald Dartez, being the boy he was, hadn't worried about getting the lines of roaches and grasshoppers and wasps and bees arranged in straight rows, either.

His science project was right beside mine, of course, because of the alphabet, which has never been my friend, and everytime I would go to that end of the room to give my project another inspection, I'd have to see Gerald's, too. I was proud of what I had made for Mrs.

Manning's science project assignment, a crystal radio, even though it didn't work because the antenna wasn't long enough or made of the right wire for the purpose, so I spent a lot of time at that end of the room trying to focus on what I had made and fiddling with it to coax some sound out of the earphones.

But each time I wandered down there, trying to give the impression to anyone watching me that I was just happening to pass that way with no intent of posing beside my crystal radio—Peggy Whisnant, Janelle Watts, Jannis Hooks, and a couple of others that never gave me a passing look, ordinarily—I couldn't stop my eyes from going to Gerald Dartez's production on the sheet of plywood. He had put a name for it in capital letters across the top, done by Gerald's hand, so the letters were all different sizes and shapes, too, and what they said his science project was was this: Insects of the World.

That in itself was wrong, I knew and was deeply bothered by, since this was Southeast Texas, not the world at all, and in fact a long way away from the world, wherever that was located. But the thing that bothered me most was the centerpiece of Gerald Dartez's display, the orange butterfly, a Monarch I learned later when I got to the eighth grade, and the fact that Gerald had chosen that one to fix to the piece of plywood with the straightened-out safety pin.

There it was, out of position in reference to the cockroaches on each side of it, stuck through its middle with a safety pin and labeled below with a scrap of paper on which Gerald Dartez had written "A Big Moth." It was the wrong name for the wrong insect with the wrong pin stuck through its belly in the wrong end of Old Lady Manning's sixth-grade classroom in the wrong part of Texas, not in any part of the real world I read about in books and saw on TV.

And it was next to my crystal radio with its antenna so wrong it couldn't pick up a peep of static much less music from a radio station in Houston.

I have never forgotten that label and the way I tried to fix it with a Scripto pencil, nor the way Mrs. Manning grabbed hold of the collar of my shirt and drug me away from Gerald Dartez's display as I was writing the little word *in* right after "Big" and before "Moth" on the scrap of paper Gerald was using to name the poor orange butterfly.

You can use words to handle the sound of names and take away the labels ignorant people put on things, but you better not let them catch you doing it. I learned that.

Keep it inside your own head when you're doing that, and no one can be the wiser, but if you leave something lying out there visible to them, they will take great offense and not allow you to rearrange that in a way calculated to let you live with it.

Seeing is difficult. How do I handle the way I look to anybody that decides to let their eye rest on me even for a second or two? That is the question I haven't answered yet, and the problem a change in sound won't do a thing to take care of. You can control what's inside your head, but not what's outside for folks to see.

I have been hearing comments all my life from people about my coloring, all the way back to the point when I first became able to figure out what those sounds coming out of the mouths of grown-ups meant.

"Cute," those ladies would say to my mother. "Your little boy must have his daddy's complexion," they'd say. "He sure doesn't have your pale skin and blue eyes, does he?"

"My, my," one of them might say, grabbing me by the chin and leveraging my head up from whatever I was inspecting at the time so as to look at my eyes, ruffling my hair back and forth to see the skin of my scalp better, twisting my face to the side to obtain an angled shot at my profile. "He is different looking from you, Nola Mae, Clement is, isn't he?"

"Yes, he is," my mother would say right back, ready always with an answer to any question that might come up about any subject. Nola Mae always had the goods on everything, and still does, and forever will, and she has spent untold hours trying to instruct me in how to pattern my response to the pokes and prods and pushes people are always making at you, as they labor away at figuring how to get you fixed in exactly the right place on that display sheet of plywood. They have the safety pin ready, too, all straightened out and bent for the job, and they are dying to slam it home.

"Clement," Nola Mae would say, "looks just like his great-great grandmother. All that dark hair and deep brown eyes and that olive complexion, that's a carbon copy of the way she looked. I wish I still had the picture of the whole Holt family to show you. It was taken sometime right after they arrived in Texas after the Civil War. The husband's name was Amos Holt, and Clement's great-great grandmother was Carolina Cameron Holt, and that picture of her looks like somebody has dressed Clement up in a woman's clothes and stuck a wig of long black hair on his head. My grandmother had that picture the last time I saw it."

"You don't say?" the woman with the straightened-out safety pin would say. "Holt was the family name?"

"Yes," Nola Mae would answer, her eyes gone all dreamy as she spoke, "the Holts of Virginia. Very FFV, you know. That means first families of Virginia, but I expect I don't have to tell you that, do I?"

"Well, no, I reckon not."

"Yes, after the war ended, Amos Holt just left Virginia and the plantation, and of course all his property and slaves had been taken by the Union army, and he just said hang it all and came to Texas where he felt like he could draw a full breath again. That's the family story handed down through the generations, and we just cherish it."

"Where is that picture you mentioned?" the lady would say, trying one last time to get Nola Mae still enough to get the pin aimed true and certain. "I'd love to see it."

"I would give anything to see it myself," Nola Mae would chunk right back at her. "It vanished somewhere in the family's moves, I do believe. But I used to study it, my cousin Dicia and I would, and I've got it by heart, and the resemblance between Carolina Cameron Holt and my handsome little boy is just remarkable."

My mother has lived a remarkable life, too, when I think what word to come up to describe it. *Legendary* would be another one. But *mobile* would be the best word of all.

My last name is Dohlan, that's what alphabetically put my crystal radio display up beside Gerald Dartez's exhibition of the insects of the world back in the sixth grade, but when I look at myself in the mirror, I know that the strongest thing my last name has got going for it is legality. Nola Mae was married at the time when I was born to a man named Gordon Dohlan, a real estate developer she's told me he was, in Galveston, and I've seen my birth certificate to prove it. Texas says it's true.

I've never seen him, naturally, the owner of the father's name on the birth certificate, but I've seen all the other ones Nola Mae has entered into arrangements with since, and I have seen a picture of my dear old Dad. He's standing by my mother with his arm around her—all her men she's standing by in pictures have her hugged up to them—he's wearing a white sport coat, she's all fixed up, too, and behind them is a big old Buick in which they're about to be going somewhere. He's grinning and squinting in the sunlight of the day the picture was taken, and Gordon Dohlan's as sandy haired and light-complected and blue-eyed as Nola Mae herself.

But family resemblance is funny, and blood is strong, and I am told and given to believe that the coloring of a great-great grandmother had the power to skip ahead all those generations and zap me with the skin and eyes and hair of what somebody not in the know would call that of a native of Old Mexico.

I believe that and so would Felix the Cat, since he's seen what that crazy old cartoon professor can do with the right kind of new invention.

Maybe it was a darkening ray that hit me, or could be it was a melanin projector the professor cranked up, another word I've come to know and study and appreciate. Melanin, that is, a word which would be a pretty name for a girl.

But if I keep moving and don't hold still long enough for somebody to get that straightened-out safety pin aimed at my thorax, they won't be able to get me nailed to the plywood with the right name, that one printed in crooked letters, below me and my fellow cockroaches. Not just yet.

What could it be, that name? *Villareal, Franco, Sotamos, Verde, Felix*? Whatever the true word to call me might turn out to be, just don't let it be *Dartez*.

Dora

This Ford Fairlane station wagon must have spent its entire existence on the Gulf Coast, judging by the way those two huge holes are rusted through the floorboards just behind the back seat. All the way from Chicago, fumes from the exhaust pipe, which is bound to be cracked and worn out, too, have been blowing up through the rust holes into the back seat every time our speed drops below some magic number. I think it's just over fifty-five miles an hour or a little lower, because I've been watching the speedometer all the way through Illinois and Tennessee and Mississippi and across Louisiana and keeping count.

It's given me something to do, and I'm grateful for that, every time Hilda Woodell's head slumps to the side where she's sitting in the seat ahead of me and I get the chance to see the dashboard. The more Hilda nods off to sleep the more I'm able to see the tip of the red needle nudge the numbers one way or the other as we pound along the highways and roads.

Above fifty-five, the station wagon is able to outrun its exhaust fumes and I'm free to draw a breath without inhaling the smell of burning gasoline and hot oil and scorched rubber. Below that point, all that stuff seeps into the car, including the carbon monoxide, but that's not detectable by smell, so I can't tell how close I am to death by chemical poisoning as I'm riding home.

I know it's having a semi-lethal effect, though, since my head had been throbbing for hundreds of miles, and particularly by the way John Charles Storey keeps saying the same thing over and over again, the same words in the same order he started up in South Chicago and has maintained off and on ever since, and here we are coming up on the Sabine River in a few miles.

"Dump the Hump," John Charles is saying, sounding drugged and turning his head toward me as though he's actually trying to carry on a conversation, though his eyes are shut while he's mouthing what he considers a witty political statement. He claims that he was the one to come up with that phrase, and that when he said it the first time, there in Grant Park at three in the morning, everybody around him recognized it for the stroke of genius it was and took it up immediately.

Oh, everybody was saying it, over and over, but it certainly didn't mark a signal breakthrough in human understanding when the first one to think of it gave it voice. Dump the Hump, John Charles says again. Dump the Hump.

"Look," I explained to him somewhere back in Illinois well before the carbon monoxide began killing off so many of John Charles's brain cells, "that is no big deal, saying that, no matter who first thought of it and no matter how many people have picked up on it since. It rhymes, John Charles, it rhymes, and that's the easiest thing in the world to think of, a repetition of the same sound of two syllables with only the initial phoneme changed."

"This is not English class, Dora," John Charles said, triumph just bugling in the tone of his voice, "This is not poetry. This is life."

And he thought he'd said something when he said that, so pleased with himself and puffed up with the notion that he'd had an insight that he congratulated and rewarded himself by trying to put a hand on my breast.

Dump the Hump, indeed. Bullshit. So for the last six hundred miles, I don't know, maybe more—I lost count along the way of the numbers on the odometer that Hilda keeps blocking from my view with her head and that bandana—I have had to fight off John Charles Storey, so proud of himself and determined to be revolutionary and involved he has to keep trying to paw at one of my breasts, then at the other.

Does he think that when I stop him from squeezing one that I'm simply prohibiting that part of my chest in preference to another, and that the one I'm currently not defending is therefore fair game for a try on that side?

"Sure, John Charles," I feel like saying, "This one on the left is the cold one, but my right tit is burning up with lust for a nice hard pinch and a good rubbing up and down."

I haven't said that, and won't, because John Charles would believe it, literally, and not because he'd be pretending to believe it and therefore jollying me along for a quick squeeze in appreciation of a witty response from him.

There is no irony in John Charles Storey, not a smidgen, and there is, in fact, no irony in this entire station wagon full of Lamar College students. Or, for that matter, in that entire mess in Chicago, Illinois, where I spent three days looking for something. Not irony, exactly, but something.

I don't know what I expected to find in Chicago in any kind of specific way, but I certainly thought it wouldn't be just more of the same mindset that continually drives me mad in Texas.

For one thing, I was looking forward so much to experiencing tentativeness in the people I'd meet in Chicago, some measure of uncertainty, for God's sake. I wanted to see people groping toward understanding, taking small steps in the service of a large movement, being dissatisfied with their limitations, being humble as they worked their way along, eager to test and be proven wrong in their assumptions, ready to grow stronger from their failures, not automatically retreating behind their defenses and throwing up instant barricades against any idea not already their own at birth. I wanted to hear people say why.

When I tried to express some of my disappointment and frustration with encountering the same old fearfulness and infuriating confidence in Chicago I'd grown up with in Texas to John Charles Storey, supposedly the leading revolutionary at Lamar, and I used the term "movement" when I did, he said, "Do you mean like a bowel movement, Dora?"

And then, he laughed like a fucking hyena, throwing his head back so far his beads rattled and I could see the roof of his mouth. "Is that your fiery rhetoric now?" I said to him. "Where's the rest of it? All that talk at the rallies in Beaumont and during that week in Houston, the things you said about the dispossessed and the powerless when they let you have the mike in Hermann Park? What about when you said those things about solidarity on the status of women? What about all that, John Charles?"

"Women," he said, and then he delivered that line he'd ripped off from reading something, though he would have claimed to be original with him, if anybody had asked. "Women," he said. "Let them eat cock."

With that, he has touched me for the last time, though he doesn't know it yet. Let him learn it at home in Texas, where it'll sink in better. Let him get it by heart.

Hilda has woken up again, and lifted her head enough for me to see past it to the speedometer in this old Ford, and it's about to click off the twenty-five hundredth mile I've ridden in it during the last five days. If someone had asked me when I left Pine Island Bayou what change would have taken place in me by the time that number of miles had clicked off, I'd have been able to talk for half an hour about what I expected.

But now, seeing the signs for the bridge over the Sabine River coming at me, I feel like the whole experience has accomplished nothing more than what happens when you pick up an hour glass and turn it upside down. The grains pour through, a few at the time, gathering in the part of the glass holder that's closest to the earth where gravity lives, just sucking away continually, and when they've all collected together again in the bottom, you're supposed to know that an event has taken place and it took a measured amount of time for it to happen. But the hourglass and the grains of sand in it are not a bit different and show no sign of being changed by the experience, and if you turn that little device for measurement over, it'll do the same thing it did before, backwards this time, but it doesn't know that and it doesn't care.

It is as satisfied one way as it is the other, and what comes down goes up, and one direction is the same as the other. It's just sand, after all, closed up in a bottle, and whoever says different is a fool.

Here comes the bridge, and the Sabine River, and when the last highway dividers bump against our wheels to show we're across the bridge, we'll be back in Texas again, and the other states we've come through will all be behind us.

It never happened, the whole thing, and the sand is either up or down, and who can tell which way is which. Nothing's changed.

I won't tell mother that, because she's already told me that, and I will not let her have the satisfaction of knowing I know what she knows and what she has said is true is true.

It was incredible, I'll say to her, and indescribable, and moving, and enlightening, and consciousness-changing, and transcendent. It was, I'll tell her as I look directly into her eyes, an experience best described for me by one word.

Revolutionary.

Bump goes the last highway in Louisiana, dark water on my side of the car, unmoving and dull and hardly a river at all, and a bump means it's Texas as the bridge ends and the highway starts again.

Howdy, says Texas. Dora, you're home.

Dicia

She hit the door headed for the bed, and she slept for almost two days. She didn't want to talk, hardly saying a word to me, letting her possessions drop from her hands and off her shoulders and from around her neck, kicking her shoes off so hard one flew up and landed on that side table, the little one that GrandMaude kept by her bed up in the country, and tugging at her belt and buttons as though her clothes were smothering her.

I wasn't bothered by the way Dora entered the house, coming home from Chicago, though she wanted me to be, and I was glad to work at giving the appearance of being stricken by her attitude. But that was an act, a dramatic role I've spent long years in perfecting, and one I play with zest and assurance, dark-browed though the scene often demands me to be.

What I actually felt was relief so sharp and immediate that my breasts ached enough to make me want to lift my hands to them, and the little string I had been imagining as the support attached to the top of my head, the one holding me upright while Dora was gone, seemed suddenly as needless and weak as a spider web.

I wanted to fall to my knees and reach out to her as though she was three years old still and needed some comforting for a slight she'd just suffered outside at play. I wanted to shout thanks and hosanna the way Great-Aunt Abigail would have done. Instead, I asked my daughter if she was hungry and recited a list of what was available in the refrigerator for her to eat, and she said no and went to bed.

Now, the evening of the day after the one that saw her come home, Dora is seated at one end of the table, the place where her father always sat to take his meals, and I'm at the other, closer to the kitchen. If it were still Warren there where Dora's located, he'd be sitting at alert, or at least appearing to be, offering to get up to fetch and carry whatever anybody needed in the course of the meal underway. I would always beat him to it, and he'd let me, having made the point that he was attentive to the needs of others and willing to serve them, if somebody else didn't get there first.

When I think that, a thing I never said to him all our time together, I don't mean that Warren was consciously trying to mislead or that he wouldn't have gone for the forgotten bowl or the pitcher of iced tea or some more napkins or a serving spoon or whatever was in short supply at the time. No, he would have done it. And there was a time early on in our marriage that I let him be useful and attentive and praiseworthy.

Finally, I learned to settle for praiseworthy, though that was easy to arrange and took only a word or two or a big smile or a pat on my husband's shoulder when I went by him on the way to get done what had to be, whatever it was he would have left something out of, or not completed, or forgot what he was after in the first place and brought back more bread, say, when the basket on the table was filled with it and he'd gone after the salt. But he meant well, I guess, though I hate to realize I'm thinking that, since that's the phrase I heard all the women in the family use about their men when I was growing up.

I used to promise myself I'd never settle for a man I had to forgive for being who and what he was by claiming that at least he had good intentions. I'd have one who never worried about what he was going to do or what needed doing. The will and the act would be one for him, and he'd move ahead as steadily as GrandMaude did making biscuits or telling the fieldhands where and what and how to tackle the day each time the sun rose or straightening out Great-Uncle Lewis when somebody had sneaked enough whiskey to him to get him drunk and crazy and rearing and him a blind man.

My husband would be in charge, but easy with that fact, not having to be assured and reassured about his doing or lack of doing. He'd love me fully, and know I loved him, and he'd not have to question whether I really returned his feelings or not. He would think about a matter one time, come to a conclusion about it, and move on to the next thing in line, ready to sort it out and be done with that one.

Would he take me for granted, this husband I imagined and deserved? No, naturally not. He'd think about the way I might take things, but he wouldn't agonize over matters that might prove to be troubling. He'd be too certain of me and himself for that, and he'd be confident enough never to worry unduly. He wouldn't worry at all, in fact. That was the point.

So then I married Warren Binswanger, a tall man with straight shoulders and light blue eyes and look of settled confidence, and I hoped our children would have eyes exactly like his and a demeanor to match. But we had only one, Dora, and hazel brown seems stronger than blue somehow, though I'd never use that language to explain eye color around Dora, revealing as it is of a lack of education, and her eyes are about the color of mine and of my father Richard's and of GrandMaude's.

On the surface, Dora appears confident and assured and ready, God knows, but behind all that is something else as tangled and dark and submerged as the things that live in the creeks and rivers and bayous in our home country by the Sabine. Not necessarily ominous or threatening or perverse, but hidden so deeply you only catch a flash of them the rare times that they come up for an airing.

They are quick, and they are knowing, and they learn by instinct the arts of disguise and submergence, and the best way to live with them is to pretend ignorance as much as you can. Don't notice what they're doing, and you see them at it.

Clement arrived to eat supper with us first before his mother, at least two hours before the time I told Nola Mae for them to come over, and he did that, hoping to be able to see Dora for as long a period of time as he can. He's sitting at the table now, watching every move his cousin makes, each bite she lifts to her mouth, the way she tears off small pieces of bread before she eats them, the sips of water she takes from her glass—she asked for water, not iced tea like Nola Mae and me, and Clement followed Dora's suit religiously—and he maintains his observation of Dora as discreetly as he can make himself do it, only occasionally giving himself away by staring too long before he remembers and drops his eyes to his own plate and table ware.

Nola Mae is doing her usual good and efficient job of feeding herself, tucking into what she likes and pushing away the portion of whatever it is she's not attracted by. Tonight it's eggplant, a vegetable Dora has taken to because she likes the deep color, as purple as a bad bruise, and one I know she'd eat at least some of if I cooked it. It's different enough to attract.

Nola Mae's not watching Clement, nor me, and only now and then glancing at Dora, but not for the same reason Clement is, because he adores her in the way a loyal subject regards his sovereign queen, and he must observe her to show that. No, Nola Mae is different. She gives Dora an appraising look now and then because it's habit, a practice begun in youth and perfected over a lifetime. She is born to the manner, and the manner comes from her need and compulsion to judge all women she finds in her company on any occasion as to the quality of their appearance and presence. Do they make the grade?

In her prime, it took Nola Mae only a few seconds always to conclude that the other females in any given location were far out of reach of providing her reason for another look. She was in first place, ahead of the pack, leading the field, and she could relax and enjoy herself.

That habit has been hard to break for my blonde, blue-eyed cousin with that profile, even now with both of us touching fifty, and she can't refrain from reflexively going through the motions, here in my dining room with the only man present an eighteen-year old boy and he her son, and the only other woman in the race, other than me and I don't count, disqualified by age, Nola Mae's cousin, thirty years younger than she.

But she does it, gives the foe, the competition, a hard eye without even knowing she's doing it. Who's ahead, who's gaining, who's on a pace to win?

I can't tell Dora that later, not even to try to share a laugh over it, because she'd be disgusted by the thought and convinced more than ever that her mother is going soft in the head. Don't mention that game, she'd tell me. Women these days, Mother, don't play it, if they have any respect for themselves or for men, either. That's a sport designed to create losers, and even to acknowledge its existence is to give it a status it doesn't deserve. I won't hear of it, my daughter would finish her statement by saying, and she'd nod and close her eyes for an instant, and as she did her eyelashes would reveal themselves to be so long and luscious and darkly beautiful they'd break a man's heart.

"Don't you like the eggplant?" I say to Nola Mae. "Have I cooked it too long and made it into a mush?"

"Is that what this is?" she says. "I've seen them in the produce section, but I've never even picked one up." She pokes with the tines of her fork at the smidgen she's put on her plate, wrinkling her nose a little as she does. Nola Mae's done that too many times over the years, measured against her own scale, since I can detect a spray of fine wrinkles answer that movement. She can't tell that, so it's all right, and I'll keep that observation to myself along with the others I've saved up.

"Why egg? It sure doesn't look like one with this awful color it's got."

"Maybe it's a spoiled one," Clement says, looking at Dora to see if she'll think he's being witty.

"It has wonderful taste," Dora says, not amused. "On the edge of being bitter, with a nice tang to it.'

"I've never seen an egg with seeds in it," Nola Mae says, "and I sure don't put anything in my mouth if I know it's bitter."

"The seeds are nutritious," Dora answers in a kind tone. "Full of vitamins."

Clement lifts a forkful of the offending eggplant to his mouth, solidarity with his cousin written all over his face, and begins to chew away. I know the skin will give him trouble—I should have removed that—but he's making a statement, and taste and texture don't stand a chance of daunting him in his mission. I'll see if I can break some new ground in the conversation.

"I can imagine what Great-Aunt Abigail would say if she heard you say you don't like to put anything bitter in your mouth, Nola Mae," I announce. "Can't you?"

"I can't think of the exact scripture," Nola Mae says, taking the opportunity to move her eggplant portion even farther away from the rice piled up beside it. She has always liked rice and anything that can be done with it. "But I know my grandmother would've found something in the Bible to come back at me with."

"How about this?" I say. "I can't quote it right, and I don't know where it's found in the Bible, but somewhere it says it's not what a man puts in his mouth that defiles him, but what issues forth."

"You got it," Nola Mae says and laughs. "Something like that I heard from grandmother a thousand times."

"Or a woman," Dora says.

"A woman?" Nola Mae says. "What do you mean, sweetheart, when you say that?"

"I mean you could just as correctly say a woman as a man in that statement Mother just quoted. What issues from a woman's mouth would also fit."

"It sounds to me like an excuse somebody would offer for taking a drink of whiskey or beer," Clement says. This from her younger cousin Dora likes and gives him an approving look, going even so far as to add a smile to it.

"Or maybe it's good advice to a man about not judging other people and making critical remarks about them," I say, thinking even before I get halfway through the statement that now I've done it, proven the truth of what I'm saying by making the same mistake the words warn against. I have that talent.

The only sound for a space is the clink of forks on plates, and then Nola Mae saves me from having to hear just what Dora will come back with as reprimand, thought-through and well-couched.

"She didn't want me ever to take the first drink of alcohol, grandmother didn't, and the idea of drinking to be social and civilized was never a thing she could ever imagine or abide," Nola Mae states.

Putting down her utensils and looking at me in a way calculated to give her coming announcement a proper platform, Nola Mae speaks again.

"You know why that was, Dicia?" she says. "Why my grandmother and your grandmother were always so deadset against drinking alcohol the way they were?"

"Because they were Baptists?"

"That, yeah," Nola Mae admits, "I guess. But the real reason was because of one person. And you know who. Great-Uncle Lewis."

I am thinking how I want to put what I want to say back to her, when Dora sets down her waterglass with a clunk a little louder than necessary and says something strange, just the single word *again*, and I wonder why she's chosen that to say and what she means by it. Then she saves me the trouble of trying to understand by going on.

"Again," she says, looking straight ahead down the table at a spot some space above my head almost where the eyes of a man would be if one would be standing behind me, a tall one because Dora's head is tilted back a little as though she's meeting the man's eyes straight on. If there were a man, that is, instead of just the idea of one.

"Every time in this family when some topic happens to get touched on, just happens I'm saying, not that it's ever intended to have been brought up, somebody always turns it into the life history of somebody else among the Holts and the Camerons and the Blackstocks and the rest of the bunch. It always has to end up being about a person, one of us, man or woman."

"Topic?" Nola Mae says. "Topic, what's that? What does that mean?"

"There you go," Dora says. "I stand vindicated and proven right."

"Whiskey," Nola Mae says, "was the ruin of Great-Uncle Lewis. There's no way to argue about topics when the talk turns to whiskey and Great-Uncle Lewis Holt. It blinded him, didn't it, Dicia?"

Nola Mae has turned now to look at me, not beseechingly exactly, but with an expression plainly meant to seek some support.

"Not directly," I say. "Drinking alcohol didn't cause Lewis to go blind in and of itself. But it put him in the situation that did that, certainly."

"That's what I mean," Nola Mae says. "There's your topic you're looking for, sugar. How alcohol did what it did to Lewis Holt all those years ago."

"And that makes it real," Dora says, still looking at the invisible man standing behind my chair, her eyes fastened on his and her expression bland as egg custard except for just the corners of her lips.

They're tight. "The fact that it involves somebody named Holt, is that what you're saying? That's the topic?"

"Well," Nola Mae says. "I've traveled here, and I've traveled there, and I've lived away from home for years at a time, but I've never not been a part of this family, if that's what you're saying. As far off as Pennsylvania, I remember waking up one morning after having to be with a bunch of terrible people in Philadelphia all the night and the day before, and I just said to myself, thank you, God, I'm who I am and I'm from where I'm from."

"I don't have to say a word to make my point, do I, Nola Mae?" Dora says. "You put it so much more eloquently than I could."

"Dora," I say. "Would you like some more eggplant casserole?"

"No," Dora says directly to her completely receptive partner over my shoulder, "I've had my fill of eggplant and Bible verses and family stories."

"I heard that one before," Clement says, "from Mama. The story about old Great-Uncle Lewis in the knife fight."

"Don't worry if you missed some details of that one along the way," Dora says. "You'll get plenty more chances to fill them all in and commit them to memory in years to come."

"I seem to detect," Nola Mae says in a tone of fine precision, "that you think your family has been a burden to you somehow. Am I right, Dora? Is that what's depressing you and making you feel so bad?"

"I don't feel bad," Dora says, finally taking her eyes off the spot of empty air about two feet above my head, "and I'm certainly not depressed, at least in any clinical sense. On the contrary, I feel wonderful, I feel liberated, I feel more aware of who I am and where I am and what causes me to be that than I ever have before in my life."

Nola Mae is preparing herself for a pronouncement, I can tell, shifting in her chair and leaning forward toward the one she's about to speak to. If there were a man present now other than her son, she'd be toying with the top button of her blouse with her left hand, caressing her necklace or pendant if she were wearing one, doing whatever it takes to cause attention to shift from her face to her bustline and then back again. Nola Mae has always known how to get her audience ready to receive a message, at least the male portion of it.

"Chicago," Dora is going on, "was a revelation to me. I found the world in Chicago, but most of all I found myself there, too."

Nola Mae has already opened her mouth to speak and is poised to deliver what she has to say, but she pauses at what Dora has just announced, physically pulling back as though she's been surprised by seeing something unexpected in a drawer she's just opened to remove some tried and true ornament she plans to affix to her dress. It's just the piece she knows will fit and complement what she's wearing, but she's discovered something strange in its place. It's nothing scary, exactly, but it's different from what she's anticipated, and it just won't do. It's not really ugly, but it lacks taste.

"That's where you found yourself?" Nola Mae says. "Well, Dora, what in the world did you expect? That's where you were, Chicago, and where else do you find yourself but where you are? If you're not where you are, then where are you? That doesn't make sense, what you say you're so proud about, sugar, does it?"

And then Nola Mae turns to direct her attention to me, a look of bewilderment touched with triumph on her face. She believes she's put this dark-haired, attractive young woman in her place, cousin to her though she might be, and she wants me to confirm the fact, mother to the young woman who's said something so outlandish though I might be.

Dora has looked away from the spot above my head which has been so convenient to her up until now and is staring directly at me, waiting her own confirmation from me. I'm afraid to look at Clement. He probably has me in his sights, too.

"You see what I mean, Mother?" Dora says. "Are you beginning to comprehend the dimensions of what I'm working my way through and out of?"

"Dimensions," Nola Mae says, "topics, Chicago. All I know is that I've always known where I am all my life, if I ever wanted to think about stuff like that. But I've never had to, and I'm glad, glad, glad I haven't. Here I am, sitting where I'm sitting in Pine Island Bayou."

"I know that's true for you, Nola Mae," Dora says, my daughter dropping her voice into the level I've noticed her choose when dealing with store clerks and gas attendants, a tone supposedly calculated to recognize the humanity of someone serving a physical need of hers at the moment, I suppose. But it's also one that makes me think whenever I hear her use it that I probably didn't spank her enough as a child.

"I know that feeling you cling to gives you comfort," Dora goes on, "and I would not deny you, nor anyone, whatever measure of assurance you require and derive, Nola Mae, from such habits of thought. But I cannot and will not take that route."

Pausing, Dora looks from me to Nola Mae and then back at me again. "And on her best days, neither will Mother," she says. "Will you?"

"It wasn't really a knife fight Great-Uncle Lewis was in, Clement," I say, "that night he got stabbed in the head and lost his eyesight. I know you've been told that by your mother, and probably me, and by lots of other folks in the family who pass along stories to whoever will listen to them."

"It wasn't?" Clement says. "What was he doing then? Was he in a car wreck or something?"

"No," I say, "he wasn't. Great-Uncle Lewis was running out of a whorehouse in Beaumont trying to get away from a pimp after him with a knife. I don't know why the pimp was after him, but I'm sure he had a good reason for it. Lewis ran the wrong direction, it turned out. The pimp was waiting at the bottom of the stairs, according to what the police said, and Great-Uncle Lewis Holt found himself that night on Crockett Street in Beaumont with a knife stuck in his temple and all the lights out for good."

All of them are looking straight at me now, Nola Mae shaking her head back and forth with her lips pursed, Dora with her mouth open and her eyes popped wide, and Clement with a look of comfort and joy lighting up his face.

"I wish you all would help me eat up this eggplant casserole," I say to the ones of my family gathered there, "I expect it's not worth eating stone cold, and I don't want to have to get every last little bite of it down all by myself."

1990

★

Lake Annette

Kay-Phuong

He has white hair growing out of his ears, and he is so short that when he hugs me I can see this big clump of bristles not two inches from my face. They look exactly like the ones in the shaving brush Dad left in the bathroom back when he moved out of the house for good, black at the root, then gray, then white.

I keep it in my little box in my room, the one with hyacinths painted on it, and now and then I take it out to stick it up to my nose to smell. I used to do that all the time, but not so much anymore, since it's lost most of the scent of soap Dad used to slather on his face and then shave off. Still, though, I like the way it tickles my nose when I brush the tips of the bristles back and forth across my face. I do that when I need to, less and less now.

I hold my breath, though, when the little man runs and grabs me the very instant Mom and Gram and I get out of the car here in the middle of these woods. I just kind of suck in a supply of air as soon as I see what he is about to do, hoping I have taken in enough to last me while he's in smelling range and that I won't have to exhale and inhale in the danger zone following him around. I can almost see it in the air, the smell, just saying old, old, old as it comes at me. Besides, who knows when he had his last shower? Days? Weeks?

His clothes are just awful, though I can tell that, like the rest of them milling around here among all these old tombstones, he thinks he's all dressed up. He's wearing a suit coat and a pair of trousers that seem to match, if you don't bother to look close. But I always do, and the coat and pants just don't quite link up, which is the worst thing that can happen in putting an outfit together.

The reason for that is obvious. It looks like you're trying to match, but don't know how or don't have a good enough eye to recognize when you're not quite there. Not quite there is so much worse than not being there at all. Contrast is contrast, and that's OK, and can be, if it's done right, stunning absolutely, if it shows you know what you're doing, and you're doing what you know.

But if what you intend is not what you get, oh my, oh my, what a sickness.

Another thing I catch as this little old gray-haired man reaches out with his arms all spread wide to grab me is his tie and the way it's knotted against the collar. The knot, much too clumpy, and the tie, much too short as it swings back and forth when he comes at me in this sort of stumbling run oldsters use.

I didn't see it immediately, there being way too much to take in the short time between his spotting us getting out of the car and his arriving right up in my face, but looking at his shirt now as he stands some distance away, holding on to somebody else—thank you, thank you—it's got some busy pattern that simply clashes with the tie and his mismatched coat and trousers.

You would think that by accident some single part of an outfit would complement or coordinate with some other part of it, planned or not. It must take some kind of talent not to let that just happen. Like that thing Mom is always saying, a method to the madness, or something like that she's read somewhere.

But the worst thing about the first greeting I get up here in this old cemetery in the middle of the woods is not the little old man's clothes. Also, it is not the way I know he must smell, though I've been able to avoid getting more than a whiff of him, and it is not even the big clump of white bristly old hairs sticking out of his ears. None of that. Hardly. No. It is what he says after he grabs me and crunches me in against him so close I can feel his body on mine from my neck down to my knees.

It is like being hugged by a bunch of brittle sticks, tied together with string, the way I feel when he has me in his clutches, completely inside my space the way he pushes and grabs at me, but I just grit my teeth and hold my breath and smile. Then, finally, he steps back, looks up into my face through these glasses with enormous heavy rims, which make his eyes look the size of an owl's, and says, "Well, look who's here with Dicia and her little girl Dora."

I ease back a step farther, still smiling like I mean it, and Mom steps in.

"This is cousin Felder, Kay-Phuong," she says, putting a hand on the old man's shoulder and sort of applying a little pressure to turn him away from where he is standing directly in front of me. Mom is good at stuff like that, but I hate it when she tries to use it on me. "Cousin Felder is Gram's cousin, so that makes him your cousin, too."

"Really," I say, or something meaningless like that, I don't remember, and then old cousin Felder twists away from Mom's hand on his old suit-coat covered shoulder and turns his head to one side to get a better angle to look at me, I guess. And then he says this, the worst thing I've had to endure at the funeral in East Texas up until now, but there's a lot of time left, naturally. It's hardly even started.

"Honey," the old man Mom calls cousin Felder says, "What is your name again? And just exactly what are you anyhow?"

"I'm a girl," I blurt out. "What are you? A wood gnome?"

Mom immediately begins putting up a wall of words, as she is always doing and thinks she does so well, and I guess does, really, if you aren't the one she's building the wall around, and I head for the car toward Gram, a good excuse to put some distance between me and this old relative. I know that by the time Mom gets through with old cousin Felder he'll know a lot more than he bargains for about everything pertaining to me and why I look so weird to a woods dweller like him.

Gram hears what he says to me, since as old as she is, over seventy for God's sake, nothing ever gets by her or escapes her notice, and she begins telling me that her old cousin doesn't mean anything evil by what he says, and he's a lot older than her, even, anyway and doesn't get around much, and blah blah blah.

"Wood gnome," she says finally, holding back a laugh I can tell by the expression on her face, her lips turned down at the corner and her eyes moving back and forth a little faster than ordinary. "Where does that come from, Kay-Phuong? Where'd you hear that?"

"I read books, Gram," I say. "You know that. Lord of the Rings."

"I know you used to," she says. "Do you still read, even at sixteen?"

"Not as much as when I was a child," I say. "I don't have the spare time any more to do that."

"You will again later, Kay-Phuong," Gram says, "Once you get past this phase, you'll find all kinds of time on your hands. I guarantee it, sweetheart."

She thinks, she wishes, but I give her a big smile and say something agreeable to make her think I believe her, but I know different. I used to read about life and the things people do when they're living it, but now I'm doing that on my own at last, and I don't intend ever to stop being in the middle of that business myself. I will not falter, I will bear down, and I will never let myself make the mistakes my mother and Gram have. I will live every minute to the fullest. I swear.

Most of the crowd now is clumped up together in one spot under a big tree, jabbering away at each other, though a few of them are wandering around in twos and threes looking at first one tombstone and then another. Some of the old ladies are giving me a close look, not even bothering to disguise it or having enough presence to know how to bother about not being completely obvious when you're looking somebody over, and it's giving me a creepy feeling to the center of attention from people like them. If there were some regular people here, it would be easy to ignore all these senior citizens, but regulars are few and far between in these woods.

Any minute now one or the other of the old ladies will get it together enough to split off from her grouping and come lurching toward me, arms all spread open to fold me inside and clouds of medicine smell and toilet water billowing up around her. I won't wait for that to happen, thank you, just now, and staying close to Gram certainly won't help me, either, her being an old folks magnet. Instead, I'll wander down that little path that leads out of all these tombstones into the woods, the one with the sign saying *Spring* on it. I know that's not really a verb meaning to hop up in the air, but something to do with water, though I'd like to do just that. Levitate and hang above this whole crowd until old cousin Nola Mae's funeral is over and done with and I can get back to Houston.

Dicia

She looks as delicate as a flower, though one that never blossomed in East Texas, certainly, with that perfectly straight black hair that frames her face like the setting for a pearl completely free of any flaw.

If she were dressed right, you could set her down today in Saigon or Ho Chi Minh City or whatever it's called now, and she'd look as though she fully belonged, except for her eyes. They're a shade of green, and that's not her mother's, nor mine or GrandMaude's, and they're certainly not David Nguyen's, of course. His are so dark the iris and pupil seem to be the same shade of black unless you see them in full sunlight, and then you can tell the difference.

She's taller than her father and mother already, at just sixteen, and I know that not because I've seen David in years but because standing side by side with Dora he was a hair shorter than she. That bothered him, though not Dora, I'm certain, since she's always thought she wants everything to be a bit against the grain, including a woman's choice of mate, much less his height.

She was hoping I'd object or look shocked, at least, when she brought David Nguyen home from California as her husband to meet me.

"Mother," Dora said, coming through the door first to maximize the shock value she anticipated as part of the freight of the first encounter between her husband and his mother-in-law, "Here's the man who's meant for me, David Nguyen." And then she spelled his name for me, including the David part, though I didn't rise to the bait, paying close attention instead to what she was saying as though I needed and appreciated the instruction and the spelling lesson.

"Welcome, David," I said and hugged him, as new mothers-in-law are supposed to do, "Welcome to Texas and to Pine Island Bayou," and then noting the red and green and yellow jacket he was wearing, I tried to make a joke. "And you're in Joseph's coat of many colors, I'm pleased to see."

"Pardon me?" he said. "Joseph's coat?"

"Mother means what you're wearing, Love," Dora said. "She has never missed a chance to make a Biblical reference in her life."

"I'm Christian," Dora's new husband said, smiling and bobbing his head. "My parents were Christian, even back in Vietnam. Roman Catholic. The French influence, you know."

"That's nice," I said. "Louisiana is not fifty miles from here."

"Pardon?" he said again.

"Mother means the French," Dora translated for him. I could tell she was still waiting for me to respond inappropriately to something said, but I didn't want to do that yet, though I knew I would have to eventually, not wanting to deny my daughter at least something of what she wanted and needed at my first meeting her Vietnamese husband.

"The Acadians," Dora went on, "the ones displaced from Canada by the British in the eighteenth century. Dropped down into the swamps to starve after a war."

"But they sure haven't done that," I said, figuring I'd plunge ahead and provide Dora the motherly misstep she was counting on and get that part of the act over with, "The Cajuns have their own way of cooking, that's really true. It's a little spicy for some people, including me at times. I don't like the way that cayenne pepper sauce leaves a burning sensation on the tongue. Do you, David?"

"Mother," Dora said, her voice lifting a little despite herself in appreciation of the lame statement I'd made to her new husband. "The cuisine of David's culture depends heavily on condiments and spices. That's where the variety comes from. It's heavenly."

I only saw him twice more, Dora's husband from Vietnam with his doctorate in economics and his habit of standing just as tall as he possibly could beside his bride from Texas—his stance is that in every picture I've seen of them together—that and his beaming pride in the woman he's married. The second time was when Dora brought Kay-Phuong home from California a few months after she was born, David in attendance, to show her off and shock the family and all her friends from high school and Lamar. He was already sagging by then, David was, looking as though he'd lost at least two inches in height, no matter how tall he tried to hold himself.

A man will do that when he begins to sense his wife doesn't love him in the way he needs, and that's a contradiction I've come to notice as truth. A man wants most the kind of regard from his woman that will allow him to forget about having to acknowledge or even realize it. He needs it of a quality that allows him to forget it. And that is true whether he's from Pine Island Bayou, Texas, or Nam Loc, Vietnam. It comes with a territory that's non-geographical in kind. That country is the country of the male.

When the woman loves him in the way he needs, he is not required by nature to know that, and he certainly doesn't want to have to. The whole world is there outside him, bigger than any felt satisfaction residing within and located in the place where the woman's regard beholds him. What's outside invites a man's notice and satisfies his requirement. He looks there, because he's inclined to and he can.

It's only when that regard from the woman begins to wane in strength and direction that a man must acknowledge it. And then at that point, it's not to appreciate love, but to whisper goodbye to it.

So David Nguyen was there in that place the second time I saw him, in a state of recognition that what he didn't know he had was fleeting even as he was coming to know it was there. His new baby was with him in the world, a girl child with his hair and coloring and manner of expression as she gazed on all those fawning over her, except for the color of her eyes, and what that color said about who she was. David's American wife from Texas stood beside him, taller somehow than simple measurement would have shown, herself a doctor too, now, with her daughter in her arms belonging to her fully, in the way a child can belong only to its mother, and David was discovering himself shrinking in that process of being forced to know what he dreaded and shunned.

The third and last time I saw my son-in-law he was alone in my living room, sitting on a straightback chair rather than one of the overstuffed ones, choosing that one as though in acceptance of punishment and penance, leaning forward with his head in his hands as he shed copious tears. The amount of them amazed me, though David carefully caught them one and all in a series of handkerchiefs he pulled from his pockets. Only one or two escaped to splash on the coffee table he leaned over, and I pretended not to notice as he delicately wiped them away, as neat as a cat.

Dora had left him, taking Kay-Phuong with her, and David had come to me hoping I might have some influence on my daughter's behavior and direction, as though I would acknowledge the fact if I did.

I assured him I couldn't affect her and never had such power from the time Dora was able to know she was a creature separate from me, and I offered him my sympathy and understanding and even some share of sorrow as well, as he sat in my small living room all those thousands of miles from the airport in California he had departed on his journey to Texas.

"I thought," he said through his tears, his voice as clear and dispassionate as though he weren't fixed in the core of loss and sorrow, as though the tears were a thing apart from himself, merely testimony of a condition and not the condition itself. "I thought that perhaps you as Dora's mother could have some influence on her decisions and might provide true and wise counsel to her."

"No," I said, "I'm sorry, David, but I can't. It does not work that way between us and never did. What little I've been able to do to direct my daughter in the way she lives her life has always had to come from cunning and schemes. And now she's way beyond anything I can do to fool her. Dora is scheme-proof."

"Oh, doleful time," he announced, my Vietnamese son-in-law revealing before me the only instance of what I could tell was an utterly foreign turn of phrase and sense of identity, "oh, sad passage."

That comment from David Nguyen did not sound American, and it was assuredly not Texan. I've never seen him since that day, but I'll never forget that judgment he made in my house and the manner in which he proclaimed it.

LaVonne Rush is coming through the gravestones toward me, not quite sure I'm who she thinks I've got to be, but the closer she gets the more the light kindles in her eyes, and she's about to be able to say my name, coming up with it as though she's found a trinket in a drawer she's been rummaging through for no particular reason. She's touched a thing her hand remembers now, though it's not transferred the full knowledge of what the thing may happen to be to the place in her brain that lets her say its name and know she still owns it.

"Dicia," she says in full triumph, her voice bugling across the grave markers. "Dicia Holt."

"Hello to you, LaVonne," I say, "I'm Dicia, all right. It's me, but my last name's not Holt. It never has been, you know."

"Girl," LaVonne says, "It doesn't matter what your last name may happen to be. You're a Holt. Look at the expression on your face and those eyes. They just snap at you."

I move forward to let her hug me, and it's like sinking into a feather pillow when she does, except for the way the brooch LaVonne Rush is wearing digs into my collarbone where the flesh is so thin. I turn a little to the side to adjust, but she wrestles me back around to where she wants me. She is a powerful woman.

"Are you still living down there in Jefferson County?" she says. "How do you folks on that old Gulf Coast stand the mosquitos?"

"They spray chemicals for them every night during the season," I say. "The city does, and it keeps them down pretty well."

"It's a sad occasion on which to have to see you, though, isn't it?" LaVonne says. "But I'm so glad to be able to lay eyes on you again. Poor Nola Mae, she had a really rough time of it, that girl did."

"She enjoyed her life, and she lived it," I say. "Nola Mae did that. Always, no matter what came, or what didn't."

"She was always so pretty," LaVonne says.

"Yes," I say. "Nola Mae was beautiful, and that she particularly enjoyed, too."

Clement

I wish my mother could be here at her funeral. She would have loved it, though I certainly wouldn't be able to call her that if she were here to preside. I mean Mother, or Mom, or Mama, or Mommy, or any of those labels sons and daughters generally get to slap on the female component of their parenting unit.

No, no, she'd say, as she always did when I slipped up in a soft-hearted or soft-headed moment and called her something other than Nola Mae, you mustn't use that kind of language around me. You know that. Somebody might hear you and think I'm an old woman, and you wouldn't want them to believe that, would you? You wouldn't want somebody to think that I'm not your pal but some old lady who tells you what to do and how to act? That's not the way it is between you and me, is it now, Clement, my little man? I'm Nola Mae, and you're Clement, and we live together and help each other out and have good old times, don't we? I don't tell you what to do, and you sure don't want me telling you how to behave.

Yes, I do, I used to tell her before I gained enough sense to know when to let things alone I couldn't change. Yes, I do, NM—she finally allowed me to call her that instead of Nola Mae, at least when she was in what passed for her as a maternal moment—I do want you to tell me how to act and what to do.

I know why, Nola Mae would say right back to me, you can't fool me with that kind of statement. You want me to tell you how to act, Clement, just so when I do you can take just the opposite direction from the one I'm telling you. You just want to be told how to act, so you can act different and show me you're your own man. I'm just saving us both the trouble of going through all that rigmarole. Get Nola Mae a cigarette out of a new pack, Clement, so it'll be fresh. Be reasonable.

She never made it easy to pick a fight that would be interesting enough to continue. She knew deflection, Nola Mae did, as well as she knew how to mix a Manhattan or whip up a bowl of great guacamole, causing me to spend way too many hours of my youth strategizing new and more effective campaigns of opposition.

It is a burden upon a male child seeking confrontation with the female component of that parental unit, particularly when the male side keeps shifting personnel and identities, to have to struggle against a mother who refuses to admit she even occupies the role, much less recognizes a responsibility to defend its prerogatives and perquisites.

The only time I ever really got NM to assume spontaneously any semblance of a maternal stance came after the two of us had visited cousin Dicia and her girl Dora, a cousin in her own right to NM and me, daughter though she was to Dicia. All that cousin business, forced on me so early and so often, gave me a knowledge and familiarity with kinship systems profound enough to stun a PhD anthropologist. But I learned to swim around in it like a feeding shark, following blood trails and picking up wounded stragglers for snacks as casually as though I'd drawn the family tree myself. I could compete head to head with an eighty-year-old aunt, if called upon.

We were back home after our visit with Dicia and Dora, home being an apartment in Beaumont, I vaguely remember, somewhere just off Calder Avenue in a changing part of town, NM being between men at the time with the rent well-overdue along with the rest of the bills as well, and I was in a state of mind I couldn't have named at the time. It was deep longing with no defined object, I came to know later, well after that knowledge could do me no good personally but certainly could and did work to the financial benefit of a therapist. When you are able to fasten the right name to what you remember as a sense of lack earlier experienced, that is supposed to be a comfort and a healing event in the present moment. Right. Empires are built on that faith and belief, and homage in the form of money is laid on its altar every day that rolls.

We were back from visiting our two cousins, old and young, big and little, mother and daughter, and I had already headed for the sofa and cranked up the TV to catch the last few minutes of Bozo the Clown who generally ended his show with another rerun of a Little Rascals short. I had seen them all, already, all at least of the ones our Bozo in Beaumont had in his vault, but I needed to watch something after the visit to Dicia and Dora, I didn't care what, I just needed the electronic bath, and the more familiar it might happen to be the better for me, given the way I was feeling.

NM had lingered outside the building for a few minutes, doing what I didn't know and didn't want to think about—catching some air as the sun set above the refinery skyline behind the apartment, smoking a cigarette, watching the cars go by, stretching herself like a cat, something beneficial to her—and I had found a box of Count Chockula cereal with some left in the bottom to scrape up as I waited for Spanky and Alfalfa and Buckwheat and Darla to start up their story again.

Bozo made his announcement, the Little Rascals reel began to unwind one more time, and it was one in which Spanky's mother was making him watch his baby sister sleep while she left the house on an errand. The baby would not take her nap, and Spanky was wanted outside to play baseball with his pals. As I watched Spanky try one way after another to drive his sister into sleep, I methodically crammed handfuls of Count Chockula into my mouth and found myself beginning to weep, tears and spit and snot mixing with the stale chocolate-tasting munge filling my cheeks and coating my lips and tongue.

It wouldn't go down, that growing wad in my mouth, but I kept plugging away and trying to swallow and get the job done, just as Spanky was doing, as one of his tricks after another failed to lure his baby sister into unconsciousness. By the time Nola Mae came pushing through the screen door into the living room, I was covered from nose to chest with the chewed-up mass of brown I couldn't get down my gullet, Spanky was in despair about his failure to get his sister to sleep as he listened to the happy cries of his friends outside the house, and I was crying so hard and so loudly people driving by on Camellia Street could have heard me if their car windows were rolled down.

"Clement," my mother said, coming toward me with her hands lifted before her face as though she was trying to ward off a light so bright it burned her eyes, "What are you doing? Are you sick?"

"No, NM," I said, "She won't go to sleep, no matter what Spanky does, and I don't want to be me anymore. I don't want to be this boy. I don't want to be Clement."

"Don't want to be Clement?" NM said, grabbing me up off the sofa and pulling me into her face and chest so close and tight that the chewed-up Count Chockula was smeared all over the light-colored blouse she'd chosen to wear for our visit to Dicia's house, "What can you mean not want to be Clement?"

And then it came to me that the worst thing I could say to NM had something to do with Spanky's inability to carry out the task assigned him by his mother, and I had to shield NM from having to hear about that, to be forced to confront the truth that the little sister would not take her nap, would not be tricked into doing it, could not be controlled, and would stay awake to laugh and giggle and defy her brother as he struggled to carry out the job he'd been given.

"Don't look at the TV," I said, "Don't look at the TV, NM. This is all it is. This is all. This is everything right here. It's all."

"What's all?" NM said, "What's all it is, my baby?"

And hearing her say that, hearing my mother call me that, let me know what to say to save us both from what was happening to Spanky McFarland.

"I want to be a girl," I said, through the mass of Count Chockula still in my mouth. "I want to be Dora."

I have no further memory of the episode beyond that, none at all. It was as though Spanky may have failed to convince his baby sister to take her nap, but he succeeded with me. I went to sleep. NM never mentioned to me what happened that day, I never spoke to her about it, and I had no further need to shield my mother from knowledge of Spanky's plight by saying I wanted to be my girl cousin. I had said it. But NM was my mother at that moment, she said she was, and I felt that she was through the mess of Count Chockula smeared between us, and I used that memory whenever I have needed it in all the years since, NM calling me her child, Spanky fuming on the screen at his giggling little sister, and my ideal cousin Dora existing somewhere above the refinery skyline, by herself, assured and separate, and in a free float above us all.

Her coffin, or as my mother would call it if she were here to judge and approve, her casket, is being pulled out of the rear of the hearse, sliding on rollers as quiet as grease, and it is a good one, natural dark walnut with a close regular grain, and it is a statement.

That is why Nola Mae would call it a casket rather than a coffin.

"The words you use to name a thing are a statement about the nature of the thing itself, Clement," she would tell me in reaction against the language I had learned to use to downplay the importance of the cheap and shoddy goods that defined my days when I lived as a child with my mother.

"Don't call the piece of furniture you keep your clothes in a chest of drawers. It's a chifferobe, and that's such a nicer way of naming it, don't you understand? You will, little man, you will. Don't say Chevrolet, say Impala. Don't say knife and fork, say place setting. You get what I'm telling you, Clement?"

"No," I'd say, "Give me the knife and fork. I want to go sit outside in the Chevrolet and eat my chest of drawers."

"People have put their minds to it and thought hard to come up with nice words to mean different things, Clement," she'd answer. "And you should respect their insights and labors. Respect is a good word, insight is good, labor is so much nicer than work."

It is top of the line, though, I admit, Nola Mae's casket. I made sure of that, and it's heavy enough to give the old fellows lifting it out of the funeral cortege—let's name the death wagon that, instead of hearse—reason to take deep breaths while their faces turn red with the effort.

It's heavy because it's itself, made of what it is, not because of what it's holding, the mortal remains of Nola Mae, she of the many last names. It's heavy and solid and real, because it's dark walnut, dense and thick and close-grained, not because of the empty shell within it, the little tatters of flesh and bone left after all the living is over with and done.

Only one of them has showed up here at the burial in the woods, only one of all those providers of surnames for my mother—at one point I had arranged all their labels in sequence to make up a catchy little jingle to entertain myself at odd moments—and he's not one of the ones that stayed around the longest, either. He didn't have one of the biggest cars, as I recall, either, nor did he take us to live with him in a place more interesting than the Gulf Coast of Texas. It was Tomball, over by Houston, where he worked in an insurance office, I believe it was, so his investment in Nola Mae, by all accepted measures, was a smaller one than most of the others had made.

But he tried to make it last, hoped it would pay off in the long run if commitment and faith would serve, yet I can't come up with his name even though he's spotted me and is starting in my direction, his hand held out as though he's stretching for a lifeline to save him from deep and treacherous waters.

He's changed, in appearance and affect, they always did in the course of their sentences with Nola Mae, and I never really looked at any of them often or hard enough to be able to pick them out of a crowd. I was proud of that fact, and I worked diligently always not to allow any more information about any one of them seep in and settle into my brain than was unavoidable. It's more of a task than it looks to do that, to keep the doors of perception closed, when a grown man married to your mother, or not married as the case might have been, tries to make a connection with you as he struggles to impress the mother of a weird kid with his wholesome suitability for male role model-hood. Sealing that out was a fulltime job.

This one approaching, though, stepping lightly as he comes through the gravestones as if trying not to spook a shy creature set to bolt at the slightest notice, is becoming more familiar the closer he gets. And now I remember his first name, and that's because I was able to link it handily those months in Tomball, Texas, with the way he looked. He had thick hair then, a mixed hue of dark and lighter brown, and when he needed a haircut it rose up like the manes of lions on TV, the real ones in documentaries and the cartoon beasts as well, and lions were called Leo, and his name was Leon.

"Leon," I say, before he can speak first as I grab his front paw to give it a manly shake, "It's good to see you again after all these years."

"Clement," he says, "Clement, you certainly have grown up since the last time I laid eyes on you."

"Back in Tomball," I say, "but I can't name the year."

"Actually, it was after Tomball back when your mom and I were married and living there. I came by a little apartment where y'all were living in Houston several years later. Remember, you opened the door and talked to me for a few minutes. Nola Mae wasn't home, so I never got to see her then. Or since."

"Sure," I say to Leon, who has lost most of his mane, only a fringe of it remaining and that gray. "I remember now." But I don't. I must have been able to close off all penetration of sense data that day, and I feel a small prickle of pride realizing that. I learned concentration early in my travels with NM, and that has served me well.

"But I can't believe," Leon says, still not letting go my hand, though I've been giving him the muscle-language sign I'm ready to drop the paw for as long as he's been talking. "I can't believe she's gone," he says, beginning to blubber and giving an excellent imitation of Bert Lahr at the gates of Oz, unintended and unconscious and therefore so much the better and more successful at capturing Bert in his cowardly suit.

I hate to see an actor know what's he's doing, particularly when what he's doing works. They can never contain it, when that happens, and I always wish I had an instant way to inject a massive narcotic dose directly into their spinal columns at the moment they realize they're being artful. But I never have that capability. Oh, if I didn't know what I know, I'd know precisely what I need to know. And then I could forget it.

"She was always so lively," Leon is saying. "Nola Mae just…she just…well, when she was there with you, she was right there with you. There wasn't a doubt about it."

"You're right, Leon," I say. "There was no ignoring NM, no matter what you might try to do."

"NM?" he says.

"My mother," I say. "Nola Mae, it's what I called her at times."

"She never wanted you to call her mama, did she? I remember that. She said she thought it made her sound old. Old, ha. Nola Mae old, can you picture that?"

"No," I say. "She was always the same age, all her life."

"And that was young, always," Leon says. "Wasn't it?"

"It was the same," I say. "Always."

"She never even wanted me to introduce her to folks as my wife," Leon says, beginning to look depressively leonine again, "But it wasn't because she didn't like me. She said that, and I believed her, and I believe that today. She wouldn't have lied to me about that."

"She liked you fine, Leon," I say, stepping back a bit as he totters a little toward me on his hindquarters. "NM liked everybody, especially the men she married."

"Yes, she did. Bless her heart," Leon says, lifting his gaze toward the sky and the trees behind me, his eyelids closed. "She was so pretty. I just loved to study her face."

"Well, yeah," I say. "*Study* is the right word for it."

"Are they going to open the coffin and let folks see her?" Leon says. "You know, one last time to be able to say goodbye?"

"They've already done that back at the funeral home, Leon," I tell him. "There at the service or viewing or whatever it's called. So I expect not. The lady preacher will talk, and that'll be it. Maybe some singing."

"Oh, no," Leon says, lion-faced again as his jowls drop and the pouches beneath his eyes seem literally to wax fuller as I watch them. I want to look away to the side or up at the treeline against the sky, but I've always been a great admirer of special effects, and these are remarkable. If only Bert Lahr had had Leon's makeup man and computer enhancement director he'd have gotten the Oscar, for sure. But back then was a simpler time, more real and therefore less convincing. Lie, as I always tell an actor, lie like you mean it. There's nothing so true in this world.

"I thought I'd be able to get me one last look at Nola Mae before they put her in the ground forever," Leon says, moving both hands randomly as though he's forgotten the bit of business he's supposed to do with the tuft of hair at the end of his tail. Either he's not being well directed, or he's so caught up in creating his moment he's come again to believe it's real and has not saved back the part of the mind that lets you do what you have to do to add the finishing detail that convinces. Leon, Leon, get hold of yourself. This is not life, it's a show, and it never is, and it always is.

"Look," I hear myself saying—what? Have I allowed it to happen? Yes, I have. I've become audience, and I believe, I believe, I do, I do, I do—"Leon, I'll see what I can do to get the guy running things to let you have a last peep at NM."

"Oh, can you, Clement?" he says, looking at me with the fullest expression of appreciation, gratitude, and connection ever given me by one of Nola Mae's husbands, even the one in oil who took me up for a plane ride in his own Cessna aircraft in his last days with her and offered to send me to college, all expenses paid if I'd just get my mother to let him stay around for a little while longer while they "worked things out."

"Could you do that for me? Would you try, please?" Leon's saying.

"Consider it done, Leon," I tell him, looking around me for the head man who's wearing a tux, I swear, spotting him over at the little tent they've put over the mound of dirt from the hole they've dug to put her in, "I have influence with some people here who're well-connected with this event."

"Oh, thank you," Leon says, now utterly absorbed in character. If there were a tail and it had a tuft, it would now be tickling his nose and catching each tear he shed, and the action would look as natural as Brando brushing the tips of his fingers across his cheek as he considers what to tell Michael Corleone to do about the Turk. And with Leon, as with Brando, that edge would be there. You would know he was acting, and that would make it mean and mean fully the way nothing else in life ever does.

"I just saw it by accident in the paper, and I came all this way," Leon is saying, "and I'll be able to know I've seen her again to say goodbye. My little girl, my sweet little girl."

"One thing you should know, Leon," I say. "Nola Mae would not want you to see her the way she is now. She wouldn't want people—no, she wouldn't want people who knew her, particularly the men she married—to look at her when she's not here anymore. When she's dead, I mean, Leon. The way that looks."

"I don't care what it did to her," Leon says, face swelling as though the venom from all the bees in some huge hive had been injected into his lymph system and was in control, "Death couldn't take everything away from her. She's still there, Clement, something of her is bound to be. Still, still, always."

"Leon," I say, "I'm afraid you're right, do all I can not to believe it. You wait here. Don't move from your spot. I'll go talk to the director."

Dora

Kay-Phuong has wandered off into the woods—alone, I hope—mother is surrounded by a bevy of old ladies wearing print dresses containing enough material to make a main sail, my famous cousin has been intently conversing with a little old fat man for fifteen minutes—you'd think Clement was making a pitch to a producer judging by the way he's focused on the little fellow, though by the looks of the man he makes a living as a WalMart greeter—and I'm standing here in this almost muddy—sticky, certainly—cemetery, watching this menagerie of old folks totter about looking for just that special tombstone to marvel at and moon over.

I feel like a minor character in a lesser novel of Dickens. I've got the funny name explaining my essence, I'm uncomfortably out of place where everyone else is perfectly at home, their knowing all the moves and the things to say and not to say without having to think about it, I'm dressed in an outfit I wear so seldom that I'm horribly conscious of it, and I can't leave until I've said my lines and fulfilled my function, one-dimensional though it may be.

They also serve who only stand and wait, as the man said, and he offered that as a comfort, unbelievably, but that's what he thought he was providing. Poor poet, to think we wouldn't twist it later in any of the ways needful to us, one and all. What would he care, though? He had God's ear. He thought.

The air is nice, though, for this time of year, and the sweat on the brows of the little old ladies has yet to burst through all that talcum powder and foundation. I wonder what Clement is thinking about the material real and imagined these folks represent and are carrying around with them? The make-up, the clothes on top and the clothes beneath, the new shoes and the polish on the old ones, the eyeglasses and the hearing aids, the hairspray and even, for God's sake, some ladies' hats, the ties and the suits on the old boys along for the ride, many fewer in number than the women, and most of all, the place, the location, the plot of earth with a new hole dug in it, the stones engraved with the ethnically similar names, and the one name that pops up in every direction I look. Holt, Holt, Holt.

I'm not a Holt, and Mother is not a Holt, and Clement is not, and Kay-Phuong is most assuredly not a Holt, and the woman at the heart of it all, the reason all these people drove here from all points of the compass surrounding the cemetery, as though they're being called together by some sub-species chemical signal announcing a compelling need to gather, Cousin Nola Mae herself, the one admittedly and verifiably dead among all these folks who don't realize they're moving around in the same condition, she is, was, and forevermore will be, definitely not a Holt.

Yet my mother Dicia feels the tug, acknowledges the Holtness within her, though she wouldn't admit that or argue with me about it, and in fact during my growing up with her never allowed me even a partial discussion of what that family allegiance was or what it did to her and me and all of us obeying that unconscious connection. When I began to acquire the language and the vocabulary to probe at it, she became increasingly silent whenever I would broach the subject. The less able I was to speak, the more open she always was to listening to what broken and partial discourse I offered. As I grew linguistic, she fell silent.

"Why," I remember saying once to her, "Why do we have anything to do with Cousin Nola Mae? She's not like you in any way, Mother. Why does she come here to our house? Why do we go to see her? And why is she always living in a different house when we do? Why doesn't she stay in one house like you and I do? Why does Clement act so weird all the time? Why does he follow me around every time I see him?"

"Too many whys," my mother said. "You have more whys than any other girl in this part of Texas. Where do they all come from, all these whys, Dora?"

"You're changing the subject," I said to her. "I know what you're doing, mother, and you can't fool me anymore by doing that."

She was cooking, I remember, what I can't recall, and she was letting me watch, not that she could have stopped me. She always thought I'd want to help, be seized by some primordial female urge to pick up a ladle and stir something in a pot, but I never was, ever, instinctively wary, I suppose, of the seductions that might lie down that road. I just wanted to watch, always. I enjoyed that part, and still do, the preparation of the food for cooking, the cutting and chopping and peeling and opening up that must occur before the actual submission to fire takes place. That satisfies me now, and it did then, and mother could think what she wanted about the basis for my interest. I knew what worked for me, and I knew that early.

"I'm not trying to change the subject," Mother said. "I'm just pointing out what everybody knows is true about you, Dora. You have to always ask why, and you're never satisfied with the answer you get once you get it."

She said that playfully, and her tone was pleasant, so I was not offended. Put on guard a bit, I suppose, but there's nothing wrong with assuming that stance, a realization I came to young and one which has served me well over the years each time I sense opposition or obstinacy. It's taken me a while to learn to disguise that sign of defensiveness, I admit, and I have continually to work at being one who by indirections finds directions out.

I am an ongoing work in progress, it's true, but there is great comfort in not being fixed and set and like all these names in the graveyard around carved in stone. When they can do that, set down your vital statistics with certainty and faith in their validity for all time, you may as well crawl into the earth and pull up the blanket.

"I ask you why, Mother," I said as I watched the knife in her hand chop away at something, its edge a lighter and brighter shade than the rest of its metal—I remember liking that, for some reason, feeling reassured as I watched the steady up and down motion of the tool—"I ask why because I want to know. I want to understand."

"All right," she said, "fair enough. Here's why we go to see Nola Mae and Clement and why we ask them to come see us and why we like to know how they're doing and why we're glad when they're well and happy. They're part of our family, and we always know that, and they'll always be that."

"Clement is never happy," I said. "He's never smiling when we see him, and he's always scrunched up in a little bitty space on the sofa or in a chair watching TV when we walk in the door."

"He's still your cousin," Mother said, transferring chopped and cut and sliced parts of whatever it was she was working on to a pot, "no matter what he's doing or what his posture may happen to be. You say he's never smiling, Dora. What does he do every time he sees you come into a room where he is?"

"He jumps up and comes toward me," I said, "and then he goes everywhere I do the whole time we're there."

"What else does he do?"

"He gives me a big goofy grin."

"He smiles at you," mother said, "because he likes you, and because you're his cousin. That's what he does."

So that was one of the cooking lessons I had from my mother, and along with many others of its nature, it provided me with what I needed to know about the obsession with family ties hounding this group of people I happened to share biological sameness with. Possesses, present tense. Shall possess, future tense. Shall have possessed, future tense perfected. Tense, all of it tense.

So when Kay-Phuong demanded to know why I was dragging her, along with me and her Gram, away from civilization as she comprehends and loves it, all the way up into East Texas to attend the funeral of an old woman named Nola Mae, whom she had seen maybe once, twice tops, I discovered myself saying, chillingly, the same thing my mother had told me repeatedly all those years ago in Pine Island Bayou.

"She's your cousin, Kay-Phuong," I said as she sat primly before me on a hassock in the den, one foot jiggling up and down in impatience and misapprehension, "Nola Mae is your cousin, and she's my cousin, and she's Gram's cousin, and we're obliged to recognize that by going to Lake Annette to her funeral."

"We're not going to Lake Annette," Kay-Phuong said. "Be accurate, Mother. Lake Annette's a place where you can have fun, if you like to water ski, and if you work at enjoying yourself. I've been there, and I've seen people do it. We're not going there. We're going to some little creepy cemetery off in the woods somewhere near Lake Annette, but not nearly near enough to matter."

"Touché," I said. "True enough. Let me go at it from a different angle, though I won't retreat from the assertion that Nola Mae's being cousin to us both is central to our purpose in going to her funeral. We're honoring the connection, and it is proper and fitting and meet that we do so."

"Meet?"

"Meet," I repeated. "That word, like most, can mean more than one thing. In this case, I intend it to mean appropriate. Approximately, that is."

"It means what I think it means," Kay-Phuong said, triumph in her tone. "You know that. Just because you say it means that doesn't mean you determine how I'm going to understand or interpret it."

"Understand this, girl," I said, losing it and therefore letting her win, a sixteen-year-old deconstructionist, "you're coming with me and Gram to that damn funeral."

And then my daughter was perfectly willing to yield with no further argument, having made her opponent lose her temper and the debate and be reduced to the status of a mother exercising brute will and power. Kay-Phuong had now become victim and therefore blameless in the surrender, and she was ready and content to go along for the ride, captive to unreason and oppression. She flounced off to her room to pick out a proper outfit for the expedition, not able to resist beginning to hum a tune under her breath before she was even all the way out the door to the hall, happily justified.

I knew she wanted to meet Clement, at any rate, though she would never have admitted it to me. She had it both ways now, and I recognized that and she knew that I did and knew that I knew she knew it. I had to give her credit, and I wouldn't have been surprised if she had turned a cartwheel as she left me in her wake, a mental one, Kay-Phuong not given to verifiable demonstrations of triumph, but there she was, fully realized and poised in emotional balance. Forced by her mother to do something conventional and stupid, while simultaneously headed for a meeting with a movie director from Hollywood, and he her cousin, no less.

Kay-Phuong was in for an orgy of conflicting emotional mood swings, and she was ready for the experience. She'd be able to record pages and pages of deep-seated feeling in her journal, and she had enough material coming to fuel hours of conversation with her two best friends. She always has claimed at least two of those, one as a spare, I suppose, if the first one were to fall short in some way. So Michele and Heather were in for some rich sessions once Kay-Phuong's journey into the interior of East Texas was complete and she returned to civilization to reveal all.

Clement hasn't talked to me yet, except for a brief hello when I alighted from the car and began to help mother get out. I had parked near a fire ant mound, not noticing where I was until I had the door open and had walked around to the passenger side to open hers. I saw the mound, looking like an eruption of wet sawdust against the green around it, just as mother set both feet next to it, and I was certain the ants would be swarming all over her shoes before I'd be able to get her out of harm's way.

"Don't worry, Dicia," Clement said, "they've had a man out here spraying all these fire ant beds, starting yesterday. He's done them all, three or four times each."

"Hello, Clement," Mother said. "Are they all dead, then?"

"Oh, no," he said, taking one of her arms as I held the other, "you can't kill fire ants that easily. But you can discourage them for a while.

They've all retreated away from the poison he put here on the ground, and they've gone far below to bide their time. They'll be back."

"Revenge of the Fire Ants," I said, and Clement leaned forward around mother to give me an air kiss. He didn't learn that little courtesy on the Texas Gulf Coast, I warrant, and he's perfected his technique.

"Hello, Dora," he said, having obviously heard such cute and witty remarks as mine somewhere before. "I like the title. High concept. Wonderful to see you. It's been years, hasn't it?"

After that, he was called off by one of the funeral home guys to make some arrangement decision, mother was swarmed not by fire ants but by decked-out ladies native to the area, and I was left to watch Kay-Phuong smolder contentedly beside me, not yet introduced to her famous cousin and letting me know that by a loud silence.

And now she's wandered off into the woods, but I will not follow to call after her as long as I can restrain myself from doing it, and Clement is headed this way, his face still betraying a little of the semi-autistic expression he cultivated as a child, not blank but focused supremely elsewhere.

I say to him the words you say to a relative whose mother has just died, and he replies in the formula language true to his roots—Clement always knew what you were supposed to say and how you were supposed to say it, but he played against the burden of the song, desperate to maintain something of himself apart from the overwhelming demands of the context in which we all had our ground and being—and if I didn't know him so well I'd be convinced he was actually a good and dutiful son speaking directly and simply from the heart.

"Nola Mae was not like the rest of them, was she?" I say. "They didn't know what to make of her, precisely, and she kept them off-balance always, the whole bunch."

"That's what appeared to be true, all right," Clement says. "So yes and no I have to say to that question, Dora."

Up close, he looks different from the boy he used to be, at least in the externals—the expensive suit, the eye glasses, the tie, the haircut, the footwear he's sporting, which doesn't appear that different to me from what a man might buy in a department store in Houston but is, probably, and is likely cut of leather from the softest and finest grained animal hides in all of Portugal. I'm glad I'm not able to tell that, though. That is one of the distinctions about material goods I'm pleased I'm not equipped to make. An earned and blessed ignorance all my own.

"Yes and no?" I say.

"NM was at heart exactly like the rest of the women in her generation in this part of the world," Clement says, "but it wasn't until I got away from living with her that I came to understand that. After I got the right distance from her, I began to know my mother. Sort of. Some, maybe."

"She was glamorous for East Texas, though, don't you think? Everybody believed that. I know I did. God, cousin Nola Mae. Those eyes. That pale unflawed skin. All those men around her."

"I hated her then. At least, I tried to. I really worked at building up a loathing for her."

"Everybody hates her mother, or his mother," I say. "You mustn't let that bother you, Clement. It's perfectly understandable and normal."

"Oh, I don't, now. And I really didn't then, try like a bastard though I did. Nola Mae made me what I was as a child by all those situations she dragged me through."

"But then you got away and made yourself the person you became and are now, right? Reaction formation. Spite and willfulness and defiance."

"I tried to believe that for a long time, Dora. I'm my own freak, I'd tell myself, and I dedicated myself to achieving that, and believing all my mother and her relationships amounted to was a springboard which let me bounce higher than I ever could have without it."

"Nice outfit," I tell my cousin, "especially the shoes."

"They are?" he says. "Thanks. I'll tell my buyer. Name's Ito. He's good, he informs me regularly, and everybody swears by him. Nola Mae would've loved him. And he'd have been crazy about her."

"But you aren't your own freak, you're implying," I say, withdrawing from my comment on the shoes which didn't work at all as I intended. "You didn't spring completely free out of your mother's force field, as I did."

"As you did, I won't argue," Clement says, giving me a look I remember, one he used to turn on me when I tried as a child to say something cheering to my little boy cousin at moments I felt sorry for him, or sympathetic, or superior—identical emotions, one and the same, though I didn't realize that fact at the time.

"No," Clement goes on, "I gave up finally trying to deny it and accepted that the truth I thought I had learned to live by on my own really came from Nola Mae."

"Tell me," I say. "Don't hold back now and make me guess. What truth?"

There's a little old lady hovering just within range, about to put out a hand to touch my arm and stop all this tete a tete between me and

Clement, so I deliberately give her a cold eye and a shift to one side so I can't see her. It works. I can hear her shoes crunch and slip in the sandy soil as she moves off, in a huff, I hope.

"What are you talking about, Clement?" I say. "What truth did you realize about you and your mother?"

"Not about me, not at first," he says. "About Nola Mae, I mean. She taught me to appreciate a good performance and to recognize it is a performance when I see it. That's the first and truest lesson she set for me to study and learn. And the last one she taught me is how not to praise to excess the actor performing."

"To excess?"

"To excess," Clement repeats. "Don't make them conscious of the control or lack of control they have. You have got to learn how to lie, to know you're lying, and then forget it. And that's the truest thing of all I've learned, and I got it by heart at my dear old mother's knee. The forgetting part, in particular."

"Did Nola Mae know she taught you that?" I say. "Did you ever tell her?"

"No, she didn't know it, and if she had, she wouldn't have able to set the lesson for me in the first place. Her genius was not located in making choices and setting directions. What she did best she did by instinct, and that's why she was the best performer I've ever seen or ever will see. All I've ever been able to do is aspire to copy some of what NM played out in her flesh and blood, no more conscious of doing it than you are about what your liver's up to at any given moment. And what NM just did, I have to think about every minute."

"Genius, you say. You think your mother had genius?"

"She did," Clement says, "she did. The same way that lake full of water over there does. Or the inscriptions on all these old gravestones. They just sit there and mean stuff without knowing it, and all us smart people think we can figure it out if we try hard enough. But we can't."

"Many a flower is born to blush unseen," I say, "and waste its sweetness on the desert air."

"Oh, that's right," my cousin Clement says, "You do literature, don't you, Dora? Words, words, words."

"You bastard," I tell him. "You little shit."

"Forever and always," he says. "Yours truly."

Something is happening around the casket with Nola Mae inside it, beneath the tent squatting over the hole they've dug close to one of the big cedars, and I watch the crowd beginning to shuffle toward the focus of the day, the reason and excuse for our being here.

"It's started, Clement," I say. "We should go on to the graveside. The service for your mother has begun."

"The service for my mother began a long time ago," Clement says. "It's continuing, Dora. It's still going on, and I wish it would stop."

Kay-Phuong is back, coming toward me now with her grandmother holding her arm, and I'm relieved to see her, though I will deny her the satisfaction of showing her that. She can't win everything all the time, and I've got to show my daughter that, not all at once, since the whole truth revealed will dazzle her eyes. Bits and pieces of it will have to serve, an insight here and a realization there, a glimpse of what's beneath the surface of a thing, a single thought that touches the mind for an instant and then flees never to be consciously recalled again.

But I can hope a fragment detaches itself now and then for her, becomes caught in an eddy long enough to register for use later, as need demands, before it rejoins the steady flow downstream.

Clement is embracing my mother, and talking to Kay-Phuong, and now she's met her famous cousin, and I didn't have to be the one who introduced them.

Near the grave where they'll put Nola Mae, some women begin to sing in unison a hymn I've heard before many times, but not lately, and there's something different about the sound of the words they're singing together, not the words themselves, but the accents of the women. What they sing is not in their language. They're all brown, they're people of color, they're Native American I can tell as we walk closer to them, standing in a semi-circle with their faces lifted toward the treetops at the same angle, their eyes shut against the light. Who are these women? Why are they singing a song for my cousin Nola Mae?

Nola Mae is in her casket, and she is Clement's mother. Dicia is mine.

The Reverend Dr. Vanessa Millard

Brothers and Sisters, loved ones and relatives, dear son, all of us here as children of God, we gather today in this place of beauty and remembrance to testify to the passing of the earthly body of Nola Mae.

At this point in the service of Christian burial, it is customary to read the full name of the person whose soul has been called home to God's heavenly mansion, and to provide the dates and locations marking the time in this world spent and the locations lived by the departed.

I will not choose the usual in the case of Nola Mae, I will not speak of her in terms that are ordinary. For Nola Mae was not an ordinary woman, and the resources of language are meager and bare when applied to her.

Had she a name? Was she born into this life at a particular time and in a specific location? Indeed, yes. Nola Mae was of a time and a locale, and all who knew her thank the Creator for those facts of the circumstances of her life.

She was identified by many names in her time among us, and these were separate and these were different. But one thing had they all in common, and that was love. That was admiration. That was appreciation. That was gratitude for her presence and the blessings of being able to know her.

Those who knew Nola Mae were touched forever by her, and none who received that blessing are ever to forget it, to find it fade into the mists of memory, no matter how long the road behind them, no matter how narrow and brief the path lying before them yet untrodden.

It is not my way, nor the way of any preacher of the Gospel, the good news of Christ's life, death, resurrection, and promise, to allow the earthly facts of a departed one's existence to intrude on the central reason for our consideration of his or her passing.

Yet with Nola Mae, I am compelled to acknowledge more fully some details of her life lived with us than is usual.

I see smiles upon the faces of many of you, and I celebrate that fact and accept those smiles as recognition and approval of the different road I take here today in my message.

There are friends before me, touched by remembrance. There is a cousin here, there is one there. And this being East Texas, this being Blue Water Chapel cemetery where the family in which Nola Mae was a member commits its departed to the earth—this being true, I say, there are cousins all over the place today.

Thank you for that laughter. I join you in it, and Nola Mae would, too, were she still with us in body.

I see a son before me, and with you, and with his mother always, and her with him until and after he, too, passes through the Gates of Eternity into the pleasant and lasting fields beyond.

Clement, beloved son, Dicia, dear cousin, and all the other children and brothers and sisters and nephews and nieces—and all those loving cousins whom you acknowledge so sweetly and truly in humor and affection—these come to testify to the fullness and completeness of the life lived by Nola Mae.

Her name is known by you through her life, and it is known most truly and fully by God as she comes before Him.

I would read now the words of Paul, in his message to the Corinthians, and I admit to you I chose these particular passages of scripture with some fear and trepidation. I say that not to judge the truth or validity of any word from the book given us by our Heavenly Father as guide and testament, but because of the interpretation some students of that book now present of the Apostle Paul.

Nola Mae spoke to me at the time she knew her sojourn on earth was near an end, and she asked me specifically to include these passages from Paul's injunctions to the Corinthians in the conduct of her funeral service. I cannot resist reporting that conversation with her.

"Read from First Corinthians," Nola Mae told me. "I want you to speak these words from the first chapter." And then she pointed them out to me, and I was stopped at her choice.

"Why these, Nola Mae?" I asked. "Surely you've learned through our study together of the New Testament that Paul has earned the reputation of not being friendly to women, of seeing us as lesser vessels, of demoting the female to a mere servant status."

"Vanessa," she said, for she called me that, not Doctor Millard, and assuredly not Reverend—I join you again in that laughter and what it says about dear Nola Mae—"Vanessa," she said, "Just read these words to the folks at my funeral. Paul says in them much more than he knows he's saying. Remember, Vanessa, Paul was a man, but he couldn't help that."

Thank you, again, and now that we have that out of our systems, we may listen in reverence to the scriptures which Nola Mae chose so carefully for us to hear.

Paul says, "But God hath chosen the foolish things of the world to confound the wise; and God hath chosen the weak things of the world to confound the things which are mighty; and base things of the world, and things which are despised, that God has chosen, yea, and things which are not, to bring to nought things that are; that no flesh should glory in His presence."

These are the words which Nola Mae would have us ponder.

Look behind you now, please. All please turn and look toward the broad water of Lake Annette spreading there, coming so near this burying place, one of the oldest cemeteries in this part of Texas, this chapel place and the graveyard for those families who founded and built it and who lived here.

Where we stand is where Nola Mae's ancestor Amos Holt first preached the Gospel many years ago. And when he did, there was no Lake Annette, there was no water visible but for the tiny spring still bubbling behind that hill.

Since then, the Sabine River has been dammed, and Lake Annette has been created for all the benefits which a great body of water will bring to people who must have it. That land was flooded years ago, and to our eyes, it no longer exists. That time is past. It is all a blank.

Yet beneath the pleasant and copious waters of Lake Annette, home sites yet exist, the stumps of mighty trees are hidden, roads and paths still trace their lengths.

And from the mighty dam which holds the Sabine River in check to maintain Lake Annette and all it offers still flows the stream which is the river. It still meets the Gulf and empties itself into the deep, and it will as long as there is left to us a world of earth.

Nola Mae will be buried today in body, her soul will reside with God for eternity, and as long as we who knew and loved her remain in this life she is here, too, and the Sabine River flows.

Let us pray.

Clement

That's what I'm talking about.

2003

★

Sabine Pass

Native Son Returns to Make Movie

Civil War Revisited
by
Spencer Guidry-Diem

Of the *Port Arthur News*

We caught up with Clement Dohlan in the condo leased for him by Warner Brothers in Beaumont late one afternoon last week. He answered our knock on his door himself and welcomed us inside for a conversation which lasted for almost an hour.

Dressed in jeans, sandals, and a T shirt sporting the likeness of cartoon character Felix the Cat, Clement Dohlan hardly looked the part of one of Hollywood's most artistically admired motion picture directors (*TumbleUp, Tell Her What She Wants, Clean Full of Holes*, among his best known, and, the critically acclaimed and Oscar-winning *Darl*, his masterpiece to date).

Dohlan was alone in the beauti-fully appointed condominium, apart from his cook Maria Sanchez at work in the kitchen, and he was open and welcoming to our questions. Over a table of iced coffee, fruit juices, and the best guacamole this reporter has tasted in the Golden Triangle, we discussed Clement Dohlan's current project, a film set at Sabine Pass and focused on the proudest moment in that community's history, the successful Confederate military defense in 1863 against a Union invasion force.

Our transcript of that exchange follows:

News Reporter Guidry-Diem: Welcome home, Mr. Dohlan. Are you excited to be back?

Clement Dohlan: Thanks. Yes, I'm always stimulated when I come back to Jefferson County, sometimes so much I have to lie down for a nap to recuperate.

Guidry-Diem: What strikes you most when you come back to the Golden Triangle and Port Arthur in particular?

Dohlan: The atmosphere, I suppose, the smell of petroleum and chemicals in the air. Each time I get off the plane, I take a deep breath, feel that bite, and say "I'm home."

Guidry-Diem: Do you visit often?

Dohlan: It seems that way at times. Like I've never been away.

Guidry-Diem: When were you here last?

Dohlan: Three or four years ago. Seems like yesterday. It always does.

Guidry-Diem: That's great. Do you have family still here?

Dohlan: Some cousins still living, but most of the family's dead and gone now. My elderly cousin Dicia lives in Nederland now, and I've always been close to her.

Guidry-Diem: She is the mother of Kay-Phuong, isn't she? (To remind our readers, Kay-Phuong is widely regarded as one of today's top super models).

Dohlan: Actually, she's Kay-Phuong's grandmother, my cousin Dicia is. Kay-Phuong's mother is Dora, an English professor at Rice University.

Guidry-Diem: In Houston? I didn't know that.

Dohlan: Yes, Dora is my cousin, too, and a lifelong friend.

Guidry-Diem: I can tell you're really involved with your family. But to cut to the chase, so to speak, you're here to work on a big project, a film about the Battle of Sabine Pass. Why that subject?

Dohlan: The Civil War has always interested me. The idea of a nation turning against itself, breaking up into parts trying to wipe each other out, brothers killing brothers, states fighting states, Illinois going for Alabama, a family at its own throat—that makes for some fascinating material, don't you think? I always have.

Guidry-Diem: Oh, yes, I do. Could you go on?

Dohlan: You read about the battles, you know, you watch the Ken Burns thing on PBS, you see Ted Turner spending millions to re-create scenes of bloodletting—why would he do that?—I've looked at all this, and I've come up with a notion about why it was all so savage and nasty. So robustly bloody, the whole thing. So horrible and inevitable in our history.

Guidry-Diem: And that is?

Dohlan: It's a weak little insight, but most of them are, and what gives any realization its importance is not its subtlety, any way. What makes an idea powerful is not its merit, but how intensely you believe it. And I've come to believe this one.

Guidry-Diem: I'm not clear what you're saying, Mr. Dohlan. What is the idea?

Dohlan: Oh, the idea, for what it is, is simple and paltry enough. Civil wars are so bloody and the participants are so ready to charge into cannons and bombs and such and risk certain death for only one reason. They figure they may have a chance to kill a member of the family. If they're lucky enough. And they'll never have to answer for it. No consequences.

Guidry-Diem: What an insight.

Dohlan: Yeah, isn't it?

Guidry-Diem: So who are the stars to be in this epic and when does shooting begin?

Dohlan: I can't provide names now. We're in negotiation, but I hope to start production in a couple of months.

Guidry-Diem: So you're here just scouting things out?

Dohlan: That, and writing, and getting a feel for what took place in 1863 at Sabine Pass.

Guidry-Diem: That was really a major battle, then, in the Civil War?

Dohlan: Oh, no. It was minor, it was meaningless. If it hadn't happened, nothing would have ended up any different. Not a thing. That's why I'm fascinated by it. How hollow it was in itself. The story here is the back-story. It always is. Not the thing itself, but what it comes out of. What made it happen.

Guidry-Diem: Fascinating. You're a Thomas Jefferson High graduate, right?

Dohlan: No, I went to Thomas Jefferson part of one year, that's all. Just a few months, a fragment.

Guidry-Diem: Fragments are important to you, then, Mr. Dohlan? Is that right?

Dohlan: Always. Pick up a broken-off piece, try to stick it to another one. See if it fits. Make things go together, if I can. Let the audience do the real work of seeing how it all belongs in one story.

Guidry-Diem: Now, two big questions to end things up. First, do you keep your Oscar for *Darl* on display? On the mantelpiece, maybe? And second, any chance Kay-Phuong will be in your new movie?

Dohlan: I keep the Oscar in a vault in the middle of Beverly Hills. And, as to Kay-Phuong, she's been in a couple of pictures already. None of mine, though. This one, I don't know, and I've never had a chance to work with my cousin. She'll visit with us, I expect, though.

Guidry-Diem: Thank you, Clement Dohlan. We're all eager to see what the new movie will be like. We're expecting the best, as always, from one of the Golden Triangle's favorite sons.

Dohlan: Yes. Well, that's a good way to be, I guess. Expectant.

Dicia

He always wanted to hear a new story. From the time he was old enough and able to understand what was said to him, Clement would come through our door asking to be provided with a string of words making up something that had a beginning and an end.

He wouldn't let me get away with simply describing the way something looked or the way it worked or what use it might have, if put to it properly.

I remember once when Nola Mae left him with me and Dora while she went off somewhere for two or three days with some man or another, not one of the ones she married, as I recall, or even one she stayed with for any length of time. It was important to her to be with him at the time, though, probably because of where he was taking her—Galveston Island, maybe, or New Orleans, somewhere with lots of colored lights and loud music and a lot of motion going on, enough to make you think something exciting was about to happen if you waited around and kept watching close—whatever it was and whoever the man was, it was convincing enough to Nola Mae to leave Clement with me and not look back.

He was young, smaller than most children his age, tiny enough to draw attention because of his size, probably because he was a boy. No one remarks on how small a little girl may happen to be, except to praise her for it. But a boy undersized for his age is a different case. People mention it in his presence, not caring that he hears, or at least they used to in those days—I don't know what they say now about such matters, and I'm glad I don't—and they mentioned it in tones which implied the small boy was blameworthy for not being as big as he ought to be. It reflected a failure of will on the boy's part, a letting down somehow.

Boys don't get over that, totally, even when they become grown men and achieve a stature and presence comparable to other males.

Clement now at his age, over fifty it has to be, still moves like a smaller man, careful and conscious in his gestures and posture, as though he's still trying to take advantage of every inch of height and every pound of weight rightfully belonging to him. I don't mean that he puffs himself up or lifts weights like so many do, but he stands straight, doesn't slump in chairs when he sits, or throw his feet out to the side as walks—and he carries himself as he does in accordance with old habit, not current choice.

He learned to position himself consciously in the world a long time ago, and it became custom and habit so he doesn't have to think to do it any longer. I expect people who don't know him from before believe otherwise, though, and he's gained that advantage without having to dwell on it. It's compensation for beginning with a disadvantage, I suppose, but now it's shaken down and belongs to him the way his eye color and complexion do, noticeable by others, but not by him any longer.

Nola Mae had left Clement with me that day, closed the door to my little house in Pine Island Bayou behind her, and she was in her own mind to where she was going before she had even got into the car with the man taking her there. Clement was dressed better than usual—his wardrobe was always divided into two distinctly different categories by Nola Mae, with one being rag tag hand-me-downs given by other boys' mothers who happened to know Nola Mae and recognized her son could use what others had outgrown or lost interest in, and the other bunch being overly ornate little outfits, price no object, that had caught Nola Mae's fancy when she was in the mood to dress Clement up like a miniature manikin in a store window and happened at the moment to have the funds to do it.

That day he fell somewhere in between in what he was wearing, clothes neither scruffy and worn down nor those of a child fashion plate out of a 1930s picture show. Clement was looking about himself with interest, revealing no signs of suffering from feelings of upset or distress or abandonment at his mother's absence, and I remember being relieved at that, not having to deal with a weeping child finding himself in a strange place. But as soon as I realized the experience was not likely to prove difficult to survive for me and Dora, I immediately began to feel in myself the emotions I dreaded to recognize in Clement.

It was as though the feelings were floating around somewhere in the air of the living room, feelings appropriate to what a normal boy of five years or so should be experiencing in the situation of being pushed through the door of a relatively unfamiliar place by his mother, told to be good and to mind, and seeing before him a woman he recognized, admittedly, but spent little time around, and across the room an older girl with her head buried with determination in a book, not about to look back at him.

I felt abandoned. I felt lost and uncertain, and I felt that nobody who really knew me was anywhere around.

"Dora," I said, sweeping Clement up in my arms and squeezing him so hard against me that I felt a dull ache in my breasts "Isn't it nice that your cousin Clement's going to be staying with us for a few days? Let's say hello to him and tell him how glad we are he's here."

Dora finished the sentence she was reading, or maybe it was an entire short paragraph, before she slowly lifted her gaze toward me and Clement clutched up and standing together across from her on the other side of the coffee table, and then she deigned to speak from her few-years-older vantage point.

"Hello, Clement," she said. "Can you read yet? I can read a whole book."

"No," he said, drawing away a little from my grasp, politely, in order to get perspective for a better look about him. I eased up immediately, though I didn't want to. I still felt like holding him against me much more tightly than he wanted to allow. "I can't read words yet, but I can do all my letters."

"Don't say the alphabet out loud," Dora said. "You don't have to show me."

"Oh, yes, Clement has to say the alphabet to us, Dora," I said, giving her a look which caused her to put her book down and sit up straight on the sofa. "I want to hear him, and so do you, don't you, Dora?"

"Yes," my daughter said. "I guess I do."

"Guess, nothing," I said. "We are dying to hear our cousin Clement say his letters."

"All right," Clement said. "And then I want to talk about that," pointing toward a ceramic bird on a side table, a blue jay I think I remember. Yes, it was a blue jay. It comes back to me.

So after the last part, the xyz, Clement asked to be set down, and he pointed again toward the ceramic figure, moving toward it but stopping short, just out of range, and spoke.

"Tell me about it," he said.

"All right," I said. "Dora can help me tell you. It's a bird, it's big, it's blue, and it flies from tree to tree, making loud noises."

"It's part of the crow family," Dora said. "The blue jay is. That's in a book."

"Yes," I said. "It is. And the blue jay eats corn and berries and nuts, and it drinks water out of puddles and ponds and creeks."

"What then?" Clement said in a small voice. "What else?"

"That's all I know," I said. "That's the blue jay pretty much. Right, Dora?"

"Yes," she said and began to sneak a look at her book, at the place on it where she'd kept a finger fastened. "That's all there is about the blue jay."

"No," Clement said, his voice even lower, and as I realized he was beginning to cry, he choked out some more words. "Tell me about that blue jay there. What happened to him? What did he do? What? What?"

"Oh, that one, that particular one," I said. "You mean him. He has had some real adventures, that blue jay has."

And I made up a story, not a very good one, but it sufficed, since Clement listened, as the tears dried on his face and as Dora stared at us from across the coffee table, her book forgotten as I rambled on about a blue jay, not even a real one, but one made of glass.

He would have a story, always, about whatever seized his attention, in that case a ceramic blue jay, in others a cat or dog he might notice, or somebody in the family who struck his fancy, and the older he got, the more he began to make up his own stories.

"Clement lies all the time," Dora would complain to me after he and Nola Mae had made a visit or we had gone to wherever they were living at the time. "I can never tell whether something he tells me really happened or not. I'll listen to something he says about a kitten or a chicken or a man who lives close to him or a new friend his mother has, and the minute I start wanting to know more about what Clement's saying, he'll let me know it's not really true."

"Does that bother you so much?" I'd say. "The little stories he makes up?"

"Yes," Dora would say. "Why don't you tell him not to do that? Why does he want to make everything different from what it is? Why not find out what's really true and then talk about that?"

"Have you asked him that?" I'd say.

"Of course, but he makes up a different answer every time I ask him. He never says the same thing twice in the same way. And I don't like that. I want something to be what it is and stay that way and not keep getting mixed up with new stuff that's not even true."

"Don't you think Clement wants that, too?"

"No, he doesn't. He likes every thing to be whatever he wants it to be, and he'll change anything he says to something different from what he said it was the first time he talked about it. Nothing stays the same. It's very annoying."

"Annoying? Where'd you get that nice big word annoying?"

"It's in all the books, Mother. I see it in every thing I read now, and I like that word. Annoying is good."

"I thought you didn't like things that are annoying," I said. "Like the stories Clement tells you."

"I like the word," Dora said. "I don't like what it's talking about. They aren't the same thing."

"So a word is not what it means?"

"A word is a word," Dora would tell me, speaking with the tips of her fingers to her lips as she looked thoughtfully into the distance. "It is not what it's talking about."

"Oh, I'll be sure to tell Clement that the next time I see him, what you believe about words."

"It's not what I believe," Dora would explain patiently. "It's what's true."

The umbrella is a big one, well stuck down into the sand, and it casts a good shade, but it does interfere with the little breeze that always blows in off the Gulf if you stay near enough to the waterline. It never reaches very far from where the waves splash up and die, and retreat and come back over and over, though, the wind doesn't.

I wonder why that's true, and if it's true about beaches everywhere in the world, even the ones in Canada and Norway and all those frozen places, the wind coming in only so far and then stopping as though it's hit a wall which won't let it go any farther from where the ocean ends.

I'm not talking about storms at sea, and certainly not hurricanes, since the wind from those reaches hundreds of miles inland when it wants to. I mean to refer to just an ordinary day down by the water at the beach, McFadden Beach farther on west a few miles, or just here at Sabine Pass, south of Port Arthur where the river comes into Sabine Lake and then into the Gulf of Mexico.

It's probably so hot in Texas most of the time that the air off the water gets discouraged, eaten up by having to run into all that heat coming off the land, having the life and motion sucked out of it the way the heat from the radiants in a heater will drive you back from getting too close to it, even on a winter day when a blue norther has blown in.

But if you don't get back too far from the line in the sand where the waves end up, you'll always get a little breeze, even in July and August on the Gulf Coast, and Clement knows that and has taken advantage of it for me by putting the umbrella here where he has, not too far away from the water to catch the motion of the air.

He's standing closer to the line where the waves come in to die on the sand than where I am in my folding chair under the umbrella, close enough that the breeze is rippling the cloth of his yellow shirt as it blows, lifting the hair sticking out from beneath his baseball cap, making it look as though Clement's having to lean into the wind to keep his balance. That's an illusion. The wind off the Gulf isn't that strong today, and the reason Clement is leaning forward, I can tell, is so he can see more clearly down the beach to the point where the river loses itself and is no longer the Sabine, but just a part of the Gulf of Mexico.

I can see an odd thing, though, when I'm looking through my sunglasses, and what I see vanishes when I take them off. With the shade, I can see the stream of the Sabine River extending out into the waters of the Gulf as far as my eyesight reaches, making it appear that the Sabine is still there intact even without the boundaries of land which shape it before it leaves Texas behind. The Sabine is still a river, still itself held together by its own will and motion. The Gulf waters which are receiving the river are not making it vanish into being just a part of them, at least as far as I can tell from where I'm looking. Instead, the Sabine River is causing the Gulf to form new banks for it, just as the red clay and the sandy loam and the gravel beds back on land in Texas are what stay still and never move and watch the river flow by forever.

The Gulf water is bluish green, and the Sabine River moving through it is darker and definite and dense, and it makes its way not in a straight line but with curves and different widths and directions, just as though it's taking its own course as it's always chosen to do back in the country behind it, the Texas it's left except for the part it still carries with it. The Sabine remembers it is a river, and that sustains it through the new deep waters that are now.

I can take off my glasses, and I can no longer see the Sabine shoulder its way into and through the Gulf heading for the horizon. I put them back on, and I decide I'll keep them there. I like the view.

"You can't really see any part of the old fortifications," Clement says, turned toward me now, his words reaching me easily as the breeze carries them, though we're a distance apart that wouldn't allow me to hear him if the air were dead and locked up in a room with walls and ceiling containing us somewhere. "Not any more," he says. "It's been too long."

"No," I say, but I'm speaking into the wind, and I know Clement can't hear and understand me in the way I can him. He knows what I'm saying, though. He's always been one able to operate on small bits of information, picking up signs and signals from what's around him that most people wouldn't give enough attention to be of any use to them, but sufficient to him.

"The fort would have been built of logs and earth, wouldn't it? And the first couple of hurricanes that came along must have gotten rid of all that sign a long time ago." I'm proud to have said that. I'm holding up my end, old as I am.

"Not a bit of indication left of where Dick Dowling and that bunch threw up breastworks," Clement is saying, now come close to where I'm sitting under my umbrella for both of us to speak in normal voices, "The winds and the waves and the tides and time have taken care of all that, haven't they, Dicia?"

"That's what I was thinking," I say. "The very thing."

"But you can tell where it would have had to be," Clement says, turning to look back at the point where the Sabine takes its first step into the deep to make its own way now, no land to help shape it. He makes a gesture with his right hand, sweeping his arm out with his palm cupped as though he's moving a handful of air to a spot somehow more advantageous for his purpose. The hair on each side of his head peeping out from the baseball cap is gray now for the most part, only a little of the black which used to color all of it still visible. Nola Mae's little boy, my little cousin, is a middle-aged man in his fifties, full of responsibility and weight and authority, but one thing's the same. He's in the middle of a story, and that's where he always lives.

"They would have built it on the land side of the bar, don't you see, because the ships coming in would have to slow down so much to pick their way over it, and that would have given the defenders their best opportunity to draw good beads and make the cannon shots count."

"That's not the same bar," I say, "and it would have looked some different back then."

"Not the same one, Dicia," he says, looking at me again, his eyes not yet dancing but on the verge of that. "You're right, but it's close enough to give me what I need to work with. I can take care of that."

"You think you can make it be like it was?" I say. "Take it back to the way it used to be?"

"Oh, no, Dicia," Clement says. "I can't do that. I won't even try to do that. I'll make it better than it was. I'll fix it so that people seeing it now will have an advantage over the ones that were there in 1863."

"How can it be better for us now than it was for them then? They were in it, they were part of the real thing, what really happened. How can you do better than that?"

"Yes, that's the point, exactly," Clement says. His eyes are dancing now for a surety, and he's beginning to make those little gestures of indecision that always appeared when he was a boy telling somebody something he thought they needed to hear. It worked like this, with

Clement, at those times, and it did in the past, and it still does, and knowing that it does satisfies me in the way looking at the Sabine River still being itself as it works its way into the deep water where all rivers empty and come together and lose themselves does.

Go far enough out, get enough distance between yourself and where you came from and what you did and the paths you took to be who you are, and a fading starts. The difference in colors is no longer apparent, and the energy of the movement is slowed and gone, one thing is the same as another, and no better or worse than any part of what's around it, and the Gulf is the Gulf itself, not a collection of all the rivers and streams that have fed into it.

Before that end finally comes, though, lines and paths and direction and shapes and hues and differences can still be traced, and that's what makes my kinsman Clement's eyes dance and his movements start and stop and hesitate and be unpredictable. A truth is there, and he's moving around it, trying to find a way to the heart of it, and he never will, because there is no final way ever to the heart of a truth, as there is no separating of the waters of the Sabine from those of any other river or of the Gulf itself.

The trying is all, and that has to do. And it does. For as far as I can see with my proper glasses, I can still trace in the Gulf the shape the Sabine has in its leaving that goes on forever.

"Jean LaFitte built slave pens back up the river about thirty miles from here," Clement is saying. "People don't know about that. Not enough of them at least. And you know what else, Dicia?"

"No, Clement," I say. "Tell me."

"At the end of the Civil War, when word got down this far that the South had quit and it was all over, and slavery was no more in the whole country anywhere, there was a boatload of Africans in chains working its way up the Sabine."

"There was slave trade still going on in Texas," I say, "during the war itself?"

"Yes, there was, Dicia. And those slaves on that boat, over two hundred of them, were put off on Pelican Island in leg chains and manacles and abandoned with no food or water."

"Why?"

"The captain or owner or whoever it was just jettisoned useless cargo, I imagine, as he saw it, worth nothing anymore, and he left for the Caribbean before the Union troops got here."

"What happened to the slaves on the island?"

"They all died, starved to death, and people were still finding bones and slave chains on Pelican Island fifty years afterwards."

"Hard to believe, though I'm sure you know it happened. I have never heard of that before."

"Isn't that a story, Dicia?" Clement says. "And no one's told it yet."

"But you learned about it," I say. "So people do know it, some do at least."

"They know the facts," Clement says, "but they don't know what happened. No one's told that yet. There's always too much to tell, to tell it all. Always. You can never tell it all."

And now Clement is looking out at the Gulf, at the deep water where the Sabine is making its path, as I am, and I wonder if he's noticing the same thing I do about the shape of the river still holding with no banks to guide it, but I won't say anything about what I'm seeing there to him. He will see what he needs to see, as I do, and he has to choose that himself.

Dora

I should have done anthropology, not literature. What's not satisfying emotionally about verbal works of art is the question that immediately comes to mind when I critique my career choice. And the answer needs no stating, though I do provide it to myself. Nothing, nothing's not satisfying emotionally about the experience of a poem, a story, a construct made of words.

That's not the point, though, and standing here in the heat watching my cousin and my mother move closer and closer as they talk, he bent over her in her seat in the folding chair, both of them becoming so animated, even her at age eighty-five, as they trade words back and forth, I know precisely what's the source for all their intensity and concentration. They're talking about some collection of data which in their minds is falling into a shape with point and interconnections. It's a story, and they love stories, and the two of them are as happy as either ever gets, brought together in their marveling at something taking form as they talk it into being.

And here Clement Dohlan—God, who would have thought it ever possible those years ago with his being raised by Nola Mae—here he is back on the Gulf Coast, an Oscar-winning motion picture director working up a project, and he's emotionally converged with an old lady from East Texas at the same level of focus and appreciation and wonder at the thing they're constructing in language.

So that's literature, and that's the power of the story, and that's what sucked me in and led to my professional and emotional life's being led the way it has, but I can be proud of the fact that I knew it was happening, at least. I wasn't blind.

I also wasn't a dumb little female awed enough by Sylvia Plath or Virginia Woolf to let myself fall into literature like a sorority girl from Dallas giving it up, wide-eyed and wet-thighed, to some lout because of his good eyes and deep chest. I was seduced by words, all right, but I saw it coming.

I knew what I was doing, and it was easy, and I was good at it, and I could use it to take me somewhere. I told myself all that, and all that's been true, I proved it and more's the pity, as my mother would say.

The pluses accruing from the choices I made are obvious, and I don't need to list those to myself, except maybe sometimes at three in the morning when I can't sleep and I'm alone in the bed and Kay-Phuong has called and reminded me of something or some things I'd prefer to keep locked in the attic, thank you very much. Then I go over them, the trophies, and I realize the merit and value of rosary beads to a believer, though I can't and don't believe belief itself myself, naturally, but I list them. I do.

Anthropology is about fictions, too, but what would have been attractive about it to me as a discipline and a habit of mind and an approach to determining the real and the false and their interactions would have been precisely that it was seductive in the way literature used to be to me. All those stories, all that pleasure as the mind moves through the experience of a narrative, all that suspended anticipation, all that delay of the orgasm of relief and resolution to come.

It's a lie, the notion of closure, but that's why mother has always loved stories, and why Clement's obsession and ability to concentrate like an autistic child has made him the rich and recognized man he is now.

And Kay-Phuong, my own daughter, so beautiful in her Asian features and carriage, yet so tall and green-eyed that no one can not notice her and marvel—she herself is a living story, and doesn't realize it, and would deny it. And she is as infected by a lust for the fictive as the rest of the family we're all locked into.

We have all been brought up to believe that events conspire, that they head toward something conclusive, that there's a reason out there somewhere waiting for us to realize it, and that when we do, particularly the women of this bunch, that when we do happen upon that reason and know it for the truth that it is, we'll be able to reconcile all we had to go through to get there. The suffering, the groping in the dark, the plugging along day by day with no sense of accumulation or direction—all this will be suddenly, marvelously, blazingly, transparent and realizable as pattern. All will be gratulant, rightly understood.

That's the lie that festers at the core of what all the women of this family have used to keep them going, one particle at a time, one tiny step after another, taken in the dark with no goal in sight but that of doing it over again. And again and again.

And that for us has had to be the bread eaten in darkness to sustain enough strength for persistence. We endured, oh yes, we endured all right, I did, and my mother and her mother, as little as I know about her, and Great-Aunt Abigail, and the rest, all the way back to the ur-woman of the family, stepping into Texas to found this part of the line of descent.

So that's why I should have done anthropology with its limited and slim dependence on connection and modest resolution, rather than literature that leads to everything and therefore to nothing. To experience all of anything is to lose the capacity to comprehend, to chisel out a part commensurate to one's ability to envelope and analyze, to hunt down some portion of reality and to corner it, consume it, and make it part of oneself.

One scene, one exchange, serves perfectly as emblem of the consequences of the intellectual choice I made, or was forced by my nature and my nurture to make, dependent on how much will I allowed myself to claim and confess along the way.

It was at a dinner party soon after I'd begun my appointment at Rice, and David and I were still together as man and wife, though in name only by then, Kay-Phuong hardly more than a toddler, providing by her existence what stasis there still was in her parents' relationship, though uncomprehending of that fact, and therefore an ironic comment. Had it been a few years later and had David and I still been together, Kay-Phuong may have understood the situation and her function in it, but it would not have mattered to her then and she would not have cared. She has always been timely and of the moment careful, my successful little girl, from her first cool appraisal of the way the world works to her coming to know how to maneuver so adroitly in it.

Several couples from the Rice Department of English and a single or two were in someone's backyard in University Heights, drinking wine and slapping the mosquitoes citronella candles wouldn't stop, and the session had reached the part of the night where people had begun talking about their parents. Some there were drunk, some were drunker, and some were drunkest of all.

"So, Dora," Roxanne Hasty-Sharp said after a brief silence into which we all had fallen to allow someone's drunken wife to weep publicly about an unsatisfactory relationship with her father, "you've never said a word that I can recall about your family. You're from Texas, right? So I know you've got to have one."

Roxanne Hasty-Sharp drew a laugh at that, even from the weeper, and was much emboldened thereby. Roxanne's character matched neither of her hyphenated surnames—women of a certain type were still doing that, then, with names, to show independence and spunk, I guess it was—but she was neither hasty, nor sharp. Slow and dull, perhaps, but I didn't say that in retort, since it would have been too easy.

"You're actually from the Gulf Coast, aren't you?" she went on, shifting her great haunches in her lawn chair. "Beaumont, right?"

"Yes, near there, actually," I said, and then popped into my head the words appropriate to the moment and to the actors in it.

"I left Beaumont and Lamar to go to San Francisco, like Janis Joplin did, thinking I'd find the freaks I needed at UCal Berkeley. But like her, I came back. Make your own freak, where you are, girl, I told myself, starting with you. You'll know when you've succeeded in achieving freakdom because there are so many conventional tubs in Houston to measure your crazed vessel against."

I was proud of what I'd said to Roxanne Hasty-Sharp, and it registered with all who heard and understood me, but I suppose you had to be there. I told that story to Clement once, in great and glittering detail, but all he did was ask me to repeat it twice, claiming he must have missed something.

"I thought she asked you about your family," he said. "This Roxanne hyphen person. And that you were saying something about that to put her in her place. But no, huh?"

"Family is easy, Clement," I said. "I'm an expert on kinship patterns, and so are you. That's nothing. What's important and what counts is what you do and how you live a life despite family."

"True enough," he said. "You have to learn that, and once you know it, you have to forget it. So?"

Mother is gesturing at me now, from across the beach, her hand so thin and white it looks like the feathers spread at the tips of a gull's wing, and Clement is looking in my direction, trying to smile, though he's never been any good at that, not even at faking it. Clement has always loved me, his own cousin. He can't hide that fact, even now.

Clement has forever believed and clung to his own stories—that's his problem—even the ones he's taken from other sources, real and imagined. I've never been guilty of something like that myself, and I never will be.

The walk across the sand is hot, and there's no breeze blowing, none at all, not a breath of air, but here I am, still doing what I'm supposed to do and going where I'm called.

Kay-Phuong

They're all gathered in a clump around that huge beach umbrella which Clement brought in to shade Gram from the Texas sun. It must have its own history, that umbrella, like almost everything Clement owns, or locates, or has trucked in, or flown in, or boated in, if that's the right word for what's done to have some bit of business delivered by water to a location.

That particular bit, that portable shadow, was probably used by Clement's people to keep the sun beams from causing Gwyneth Paltrow to crinkle her eyes too much between takes on the Isle of Skye or on Queen Charlotte Island or Aruba or on a lot in Burbank somewhere.

He'd be able to tell me exactly where it was last unfurled and for whose benefit and for how long a time if I asked him. But I won't do that, because it would kick him into telling a story, and I'm not that up for a dose of narration just about now.

Worse than that, since I can always find the means to endure someone telling me their tale, just the particular one they think exactly right for me to hear from them at that special moment—I can nod, smile, look puzzled, express concern, demonstrate interest, register surprise and delight at a clever turn in the progress of the words they're offering, do enough non-verbals to get me by and slide me right through it—worse than experiencing an apt illustration of the point at hand, if Clement were to sketch one for me, would be what it might provide Mom the excuse to do. Put a question to me. Raise an issue. Seek a response. Investigate more fully some aspect arising. Query me on that topic. Ask me stuff. And some more stuff.

Time was I could hold my silence at such, widen my eyes a hair, refocus slightly to one side or the other, tilt the chin, and walk off into the sunset.

No longer. I'm almost thirty now, and I'm moving into the area of being answerable. And answerable not only to people who want something from me—on a shoot, maybe, or backstage before I hit the runway, in some one's office somewhere with lawyers and agents stalking around or hovering over pieces of paper and documents and contracts, on telephones, for God's sake, or cells—but answerable again to members of my own family.

I never thought it would come back to that again, not after I'd worked my way out of that snarl of connections at age eighteen when I was finally seen by somebody in Houston that mattered, who had the ability to see me for what I was and what I had and the power to make that seeing mean something, and mean something in places that matter. Not Houston. Not Texas. Not here.

New York. Paris. Milan. Rome. L.A.

And you think that once truly seen, always seen. When the real beholder beholds, you are beheld for all time and forever. And the shutter has opened, and found and fixed the image, and that image is there now and will be and cannot be blurred and will not be lost, ever.

But now as I can feel myself slip into becoming answerable, I wonder about a couple of things in particular, among a lot of other things not in particular at all, but general, general, general all over the place, and these are, number one—when the thing beheld in perfection begins to fade, when that image starts to dim and blur at the edges, does the beholder fade, too?

I'm afraid I think so. I'm afraid I do. I'm afraid the eye of the beholder loses luster at the same rate that the light leaks out and leaches away from the thing beheld, and that is the scariest thing of all to realize and contemplate. That is the roach wing at the center of the chocolate truffle.

Because if you have faith in the truth and power and rightness of the eye which picks you out from all the rest and declares you worthy, then it has to follow that when the slippage begins and you know it has, then what the recognition gave you in the first place, when you knew in every bone and hair and cell that it was happening and you were real, you were what you hoped and suspected you might be—this recognition was wrong. It was a mistake. You misjudged.

Your trust was misplaced, and the beholder which certified you as you really couldn't do that at all to begin with.

So what they told you and what you believed was true because they swore to it and you could tell they meant it, that was as flawed as every damned thing else in the world.

So you become answerable again, just as you were when you were only building up to it and weren't there yet. You have to acknowledge questions again, you have to pay attention to them, and you have to figure ways to respond to them so they'll leave you alone again for a while. But it's only for a while, at the very best, and you know that now, and you have to learn to live with knowing it.

That's number one, the first one of the couple of things I now have to worry about, want to or not, choice of time or place not my own.

The second one follows, close on the heels of the first, and it is the tiny twisted twin of the first, the malformed sister which didn't die at birth though it should have, and it is identical, not fraternal, though no one can tell that but you.

It is a hard question, like diamond, one my mother would love to hold up in the light to view from every angle and examine in every detail, and it has to do with slippage and the way it operates.

Why doesn't it happen at a steady rate? That is the big "huh, what's happened and when exactly did it do it?" It comes after you ask the first one, the one about the value of faith in the beholder, and it comes as sure as those waves flopping in on this ugly beach where the sand is not white and pure but brown and speckled and full of oil and chemical clot and spill.

Slippage comes in fits and starts, and it cannot be measured in the way you can be sure about gauging the amount of water moving in a river flow by a set point in a given time.

You cannot predict when a slippage will occur or how far it will move before something catches and stops it for a time or how long an individual amount of slip will take and how far it will go before the next pause in its career.

I'd rather it went all at once, just a great sluice coming and lasting hard and fast until all it had to give was gone.

Then there could be one question, and you could answer it with one word, and it would be over and done and finished, and one scream would use up all the sound there was, and everything would be quiet forever. No more little questions, no more having to pay attention, no more compulsion to offer answers to each one in its own time and hope that would be the last one.

But in the meantime, and it is mean and it is time, the waves flop in and slink back to get ready for the next go at it, and the sun stands in the sky like a stone fixed and burning down, except for the circle of shadow that Clement has arranged to protect Gram from the worst of it.

And they're all here at Sabine Pass waiting for me, and they have questions to put, and I am answerable now, and I'll walk over to my family and take queries and pay attention and offer responses to each of them in turn, one by one by one.

Clement

I always want to have them talk to me, no matter what they're saying or how many times I've heard it before, whatever it happens to be. At times, it's all I can do to keep from rushing up to Dicia after not having been with her for a length of time, seizing her by her frail little shoulders, not even bothering to say hello, how are you, how have you been, isn't it hot and my God the humidity, and demanding she begin to narrate.

Tell about Great-Uncle Lewis in the whorehouse on Crockett Street, Dicia, I want to beg. Then, do the one about Joleen Bobo and the crepe myrtle, a wagonload of it with both pink and purple blossoms on the same branch and Abigail riding on top. And finish up this session, please, by telling about the truck from the lumber company pulling up to the house and stopping and the driver not getting out for too long a time, too too long a time, and GrandMaude knowing what that meant and falling to the porch but not being able to pass out and not know what was happening, try as hard as she could to do it.

And don't leave anything out, I want to say, looking deep into her eyes, clouded as they are with years, put it all in the story, every whisper. Everything that happened, every detail, and whatever you do, don't hurry to tell it and don't slide over a single word without giving it all the voice it deserves and ought to get.

Once she asked me, cousin Dicia did, when I was not more than ten or twelve years old, sitting in her little house in Pine Island Bayou, why I wanted to hear the same things told me over and over again and told me in the same way I'd first been told them.

"Don't you ever get tired of hearing me go over these same old stories again, Clement?" she said. "Don't you get bored by them, honey? Don't you think you finally will have heard them just that one time too many?"

I couldn't answer her then, to her satisfaction or to mine, though I tried, I remember, tried until I grew frustrated to the point of tears, finally leaving her there in the house and running outside to climb a china-berry tree in the backyard and sit as high up in it as I dared until it got too late in the day to be able to see how to get down without breaking my neck. Dicia had to bring a ladder she pulled from beneath the house, prop it against the treetrunk, and climb up it to coax me down, rung by rung by rung.

I thought about her question for years, not able to come up with an answer that would let me stop worrying about why I couldn't understand that compulsion in myself to hear the same tales told again and again, and with relish and anticipation and gratitude for the experience, far beyond all normal reason. And then one day in Greece, sitting in a little café drinking wine with a crowd of people, I found an answer, maybe not necessarily the true and right one, but right enough to serve.

It came to me as I sat holding an old coin in my hand, turning it over and over, feeling the stamp of design on each side of it, rubbing my fingertips against the coin again and again, and deriving as much pleasure each time I did that as I had done before and as I knew I would as long as I chose to turn it in my hand from one side to the other and back again.

I have carried the coin since then. The surface of it feels the same to my fingers each time I touch any feature of its design, and I know that design, and I have known it, and I will continue to know it as long as I touch it. But when I pick up the coin for a session of that tactile knowing of it, it is cool to the touch at first, and it's not me, it's metal, and the weight and the feel tell me that. But as I handle the coin as I've done so many times before, the design its maker gave it grows warm in my fingers, and the temperature of the metal becomes exactly the temperature of me, my body, my physical self, and I am joined to the metal and its design, and it's joined to me as much as something not me can become me. And that is why I handle the coin without tiring of it, and that is why I want the same stories told me with no change, no alteration, no improvement.

I want the same coin and the same design given it, and I want the story, and I will have it and we will be joined, one, part of each other. I turn them in my mind, and they warm to the touch, the stories do, and they and I are joined again, one and the same, fresh and new and old and known, of one piece again.

I can see Dicia looking beyond me now, her face lifted in the shade of the umbrella as she watches someone, whose footsteps I can hear crunching in the sand, come toward us. Her shadow comes before she does and falls on the material of the umbrella, and it is a perfect outline of a perfect profile, an accidental cameo flawless for the instant it takes my sight to register it, and then it's gone, lengthened and distorted by the angle of light striking at an oblique, as true in its shape now as it was the instant before, distorted though it is.

"Kay-Phuong," I say, "possessor of the most beautiful and perfect profile of all this family's women."

"Don't try to make me feel bad, Clement," my cousin says. "I can do that much better on my own than you're capable of causing."

"What do you mean, sweetheart?" says Dicia, putting out her hand toward Kay-Phuong. "What do you have to be upset about this afternoon on the beach? Does the heat bother you?"

"I meant what I said, Kay-Phuong," I announce to all three women, each of them looking in a different direction, Dicia directly at Kay-Phuong's face, searching for her eyes, Kay-Phuong focused on the edge of the umbrella where it stops being umbrella and leaves off being anything at all, and Dora, mother of this perfect design and physical presence, fixing her gaze on something in the big water of the Gulf. Probably nothing in particular, just the nothing of the width and depth there in such abundance, a simple brooding upon the brooding of an expanse of water.

"You really are a culmination of all the women, and the men, too—I won't deny them a part—of all our family in Texas, all the ones behind you."

"Everybody in the whole world is that, Clement," Kay-Phuong says, and Dora now looks at her daughter, interested and a little surprised and proud that Kay-Phuong has given voice to an insight. A little epiphany here at Sabine Pass, and Dora has always been relentless in trying to turn one of those up, wherever she can find it, believer that she is in understanding.

"Each human being," Kay-Phuong goes on, "is the result of everybody that's gone before them in the whatever-you-call-it, their gene pool, right?"

She's a little proud of having said something like that herself, my beautiful Asian slash Texan slash cousin slash gene sharer, and she wants to expand a little on the micro-truth she's spoken.

"Well, sure," I say, working to keep the tone light and ongoing, "everything is all connected, what comes before and what is and what's going to come. But to make it interesting or mean anything, you've got to break it into segments and pretend they stand alone and complete in themselves."

"How does that work?" Dicia says, just before Dora speaks up. I can tell Dora had a modification or a clarification or an amendment to add to what I said, and I'm glad Dicia has beaten her to the punch. Dora subsides in silence, but she'll be back. Just wait and see. "Can you explain that, Clement?"

"I think what I mean, Dicia," I say, "is that we've got to pretend we believe a story, in this case the one of the Holts coming to Texas to live and work and fall in love and marry and divorce and flourish and decline and die, that the story had a beginning, a place to start, and an end, say where we all are today, here where the Sabine River ends up in the Gulf of Mexico and is no more. Then when we think about all that's happened, it can become interesting."

"Interesting?" says Kay-Phuong, now looking directly at me. "What's interesting?"

"Nothing's interesting in itself, I admit, Kay-Phuong. But if we let ourselves fool ourselves like we really always want to do, we can make things play along, hook up to each other, and seem to mean something. That's what we want, really, and we shouldn't deny ourselves that. It's the only real pleasure there is."

"The Sabine River doesn't actually end here at Sabine Pass," Dicia says. "It keeps on going, and if you look at the water from just the right angle through the right glasses for seeing it, you can tell that's true."

"There you go," I say. "Dicia gets it."

"But if I take them off," Dicia says, "my own shades, and look for the river still going on out in the Gulf, I can't see it anymore. Then it appears that the Sabine River really does just end. It's no more."

"That's an illusion, Mother," Dora says, getting a classification stated, finally, to bring us all back to an accurate contemplation of the true. "It's optical. The eyes are deceived by the polarization, and they pass that deception on to the brain."

"Which one is the deception?" I say. "Can you tell me that? Can you be sure?"

"The unaided perception is the true one," Dora says. "Always, Clement."

"Dora's got it, too," I say. "Some of it, anyway. Now's your turn, Kay-Phuong. What do you think?"

"I think it's hot," Kay-Phuong says. "And I think if you set a Civil War production here on this dirty old oily beach, Clement, it will not make its nut. No way."

"Where would you film the story, Kay-Phuong?" I say. "A story about people in a family at war with each other, trying their best to kill off all the kinfolks they can as fast and as well as they can do it?"

“Somewhere scenic,” Kay-Phuong says, sweeping her gaze from one end of the stretch of sand visible to us to the other. “Somewhere people would think would be a great place to go have a good time. Somewhere fun. Somewhere pretty.”

“Kay-Phuong gets it, too,” I say, looking from one of my cousins to the other until I’ve seen them all in turn, each woman in my family here at Sabine Pass, where the river empties itself out of East Texas finally into the sea. “She gets it, and now so do we all.”

“It’s hot,” Kay-Phuong says. “It’s so hot. Let’s go home.”

Carolina Cameron Holt
1867

I knew I had to get away from the water, the way it laps and purrs and pulls at what all it touches. That is what I cannot stand to think of now, the steady tugging water makes at all that bounds it. Come, the river sings, come, let loose of all that holds and keeps you. Be in my flow, slide away, slide away, be with me forever.

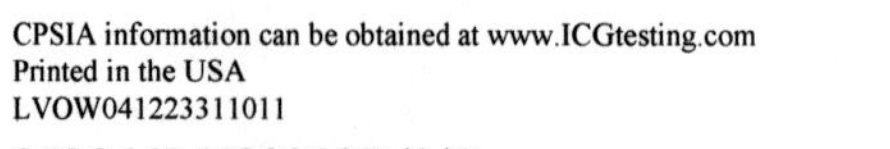
CPSIA information can be obtained at www.ICGtesting.com
Printed in the USA
LVOW041223311011

252844LV00003B/8/P